TRAGIC DESIRES

A Novel

A.M. Hargrove

Cover Design by Sarah Hansen at Okay Creations
Photo by Scott Hoover Photography
Cover Model Emmanuel Delcour
Formatting by Inkstain Interior Book Designing

TRAGIC DESIRES

A Novel

Prologue

8 months ago

GEMINI
Nick Was Right

FOR WEEKS THE drowning rains had kept me from doing what I love best, but today, the sun is bright, the sky as blue as a summer's day. Unusually warm for November, this means today is all about the mountain bike, the trails, and me.

Boulder, Colorado, offers plenty of places to choose from, but I decide on a combination of linked loop trails. They're all technically difficult, but I'm an expert—the tougher, the better. My roommate and boyfriend, Nick, gives me hell as I get dressed.

"Gemini, you know I hate it when you go off by yourself like this. It's not safe."

"We've been over this a dozen times. I'll be fine. No one will hurt me out there."

"I'm not worried about that and you know it, damn it. What if you fall?"

I laugh at him. "Nick, I always fall. It comes with the sport."

He sighs. "Yeah, and even the best riders get injured." Then he shakes his head and stomps off. He's pissed at me, but I *have* to do this. I've been penned up for weeks and I need the feel of the open space and the wind on my cheeks.

I follow him to our bedroom and lay my hand on his arm. "Hey, I'll be back before you know it." I kiss his cheek and leave.

A part of me knows he's right ... a big part. But I shove that thought away and feel the energy build as I think about what the day holds for me.

WHEN I REACH the parking lot, I can barely contain my excitement. I unload my bike, gear up, clip into my pedals, and I'm off. It's crazy how giddy I feel, but it's such an adrenaline rush for me to ride. Nothing deters me from this sport ... not the sweat, grime, mud, nothing. I'm not afraid of the steep descents or the sharp inclines. My body handles the jarring jumps as I move over fallen trees, rocks, and roots. Most of the time, my face is fixed into a permanent smile during these excursions. I was born to do this. My bike and I become one as we move over the rough terrain.

The trail I'm on is a single track, and brush and vines snag my clothing, but I couldn't care less. I'm in heaven. As I round the curve, to my left is the wall of a cliff and to my right, a fifty-foot drop. In the center of the path is a huge root, so I veer right and ride over a large rock embedded into the soil. There's plenty of clearance so I'm not concerned ... except that large, stable rock isn't so stable after all. Weeks and weeks of rain must've washed away the earth beneath it.

Everything happens so fast, I don't have time to think, to unclip and bail off my bike, or to do anything but go down as my bike descends. In a flash, I'm free-falling down the side of a cliff. A thicket of trees and shrubs rips me off my bike, tearing my clothes, slicing into my flesh, but it doesn't stop me. I continue to fall until my body slams into solid ground. Bones crunch and agony slashes through me as the wind gushes out of my lungs. The final jolt is when my head strikes the earth. The resounding boom echoes in my ears, and the horrific pain drowns out everything else.

My arms automatically reach for my head, but only one will move. There's no thought as to why the other one can't; I only want the pain in my skull to cease. When my hand hits my helmet, I find it's broken into three pieces, the strap still attached beneath my chin. Then the dizziness rolls over me and I become confused. When I try to sit up, a wave of intense nausea passes over me and the pain intensifies. It's impossible to inhale so I lie still for a second, hoping it will pass.

The next thing I know, I'm looking at thousands of stars twinkling at me. *Twinkle, twinkle, little star.* It takes a couple minutes for me to figure out that I'm lying in mud. What the hell is going on? Where am I? My head. Oh dear God! What did I do to my head? It's piercing, pounding, and throbbing all at once. My hands reach up to hold it and a searing pain runs through my left arm. I scream. But only for a second because it makes the torture in my ribs that much more excruciating.

What happened to me? My entire body suffers unbearably. I can't remember anything!

Where the hell am I? It's so cold out here, I know I need to move. Rolling to my side, I force myself to my feet. Dizziness threatens to bring me down, but I know if I stay here, I'll die. I'm shivering. I need to get out before severe hypothermia sets in.

Pushing through the thick forest brush proves nearly impossible. At times I'm barely aware of what I'm doing but I force one foot in front of the other. Night turns to day and then night again. I press on but am close to giving up at daybreak. In the distance, a tent glows, reflective of the sunrise, but I'm sure I'm hallucinating. As I get closer, the tent looks so real, but I know it's my imagination playing a cruel trick. This is the end of the line. My feet carry me to right outside the tent and my legs crumple.

VOICES SURROUND ME. My body is jostled around and it's terribly painful. When I try to lift my head, I can't because it's strapped down.

"What's happening? Who are you?"

A strange voice answers, "Search and rescue. We're getting you out of here."

Where the hell is here? What happened? I'm so confused. I grit my teeth because all this motion hurts like hell and makes me so dizzy. We've come to a stop and they push me into the back of a vehicle. More bouncing around. A man sits next to me and explains we're on a forest road and it won't take long until we hit the main road where an ambulance is waiting.

"Thank you." I don't know what else to say. I can't remember a damn thing and I'm totally freaked.

The ambulance is there as promised, and they move me to a gurney. When they do, I scream.

One of them says, "Get a line started STAT."

Someone tries to lift my arm and I squeal again. Everything hurts.

"Try her other arm."

They move to my other arm and I guess it's fine because I'm in and out of what's happening here. Then one of them asks, "Miss, are you allergic to anything?"

"No," I mumble.

"We're going to give you something for pain."

Thank heavens for that. As soon as I feel the effects, I drift.

SOMEONE IS TALKING to me. "Miss, we're at the hospital in Boulder."

When I try to lift my head, I notice they have it strapped again. They wheel me inside and the lights are so bright, I can barely stand them. Everything is a blur because of the pain medication. I wake up again and I'm in a bed in a room. Nick is sitting in the chair.

"Nick? What's going on?"

"You don't remember?"

"No."

He proceeds to explain.

"I'm sorry. I should've listened to you," I say.

"Forget about that. I'm just glad you're going to be fine."

"What's the verdict?"

"Severe dehydration, broken arm, several broken ribs, broken collarbone, lacerations, contusions, and a severe concussion," Nick explains. "You'll be here for a few more days."

I lift the sheet and see the cast on my broken arm. Then I try to remember what happened, but there's nothing other than leaving the house and riding for a little while.

"Why can't I remember anything?"

"The doctor said it may come back. It has to do with your head injury."

"Head injury?" I start to panic, thinking about all those poor people who suffer for years in the aftermath.

"Well, yeah. Concussions are brain bruises, so they're head injuries."

"Right."

Nick looks at me. It's odd because it's not like he's chastising me, but there's something else ... something different.

"I was going crazy, Gemini. I was so worried about you, I called the police."

"Thank you. For caring."

He stands and faces the small window. He's always been a quiet, gentle sort, but now I feel like he wants to yell.

"Nick, I understand that you're angry with me."

"No! You understand nothing about any of this!"

"Okay, maybe I don't. I already apologized. I don't know what else there is for me to say."

He inhales ... like he's been underwater forever. "There's really nothing else for you to say. Just promise me you won't do that again."

"I promise."

He walks over to me, kisses my forehead, and says, "I've got to get to work. I've missed a few days as is. I'll see you tonight."

"Okay. Thanks, Nick."

THINGS BETWEEN US aren't the same. Nick and I can't seem to get back on track. I can't put my finger on it, but since I've been released from the hospital, he's edgy and nervous. And I'm walking on eggshells, afraid I'll piss him off. He's always been so sweet and kind, but this new Nick is different.

Two weeks pass, and one night I wake up in severe pain. I'm experiencing the worst headache of my life and I can't even remember going to bed. Nick rushes me back to the hospital and they do another CT scan, MRI, and an MRA to rule out a blood clot. All the tests are normal and I'm diagnosed with post-concussion syndrome. The headaches hit arbitrarily and indiscriminately. They come with no warning and bulldoze me like a damn tank.

Post-concussion syndrome. I'd heard news reports about professional athletes who dealt with it, but I never gave it much thought before this. It sends my life straight to fucking hell. I begin waking every morning feeling like someone is taking an axe and splitting my skull into two. The neurologists prescribe all sorts of medicine, but nothing helps. The migraines are relentless, crippling me for days. Noise and light are unbearable. I'm moody, depressed, not at all the same girl I was before the accident.

When Nick eventually leaves for good, I can't blame him. I don't even like myself anymore.

Every specialist I visit tells me the same thing. This syndrome can last, in rare instances, for years. They tell me I need to find my headache triggers. I'm meticulous about keeping a diary, but nothing adds up. For months, I record everything I eat and drink, the weather, my mood, and try to piece together the mystery. But there is no rhyme or reason. The migraines are random things, hell-bent on destroying me.

That's when I turn to drinking ... a lot. Riding my bike is out of the question. My prior fearlessness is gone. Now I'm frightened of everything. What if I'm riding and one of these headaches hit? What will I do? What if I'm out shopping and one starts up? Or, God forbid, what if I'm driving? I can't function when they attack. I have to curl up in a ball and lie as still as possible until they pass. Sometimes it takes hours, and sometimes days before they go away.

My drinking gives way to other things. At first it's only weed, which seems to help. But then I want to escape from everything, so I start Xanax. And then I move to Lortab and Oxy. I mix all of the above, trying to forget the pain. Every day I look at the calendar and wonder how much more I can endure. Gone are my dreams of becoming a marketing specialist for mountain bike manufacturers. Gone is the girl who'd won so many mountain bike races. Gone is the strong, fearless girl I once was. In her place stands a scared, lonely drug seeker. If it weren't for the money I'd inherited when my mom died, I'm not sure where I'd be ... most likely living on the streets.

And that's why I decide to leave Colorado and move back to

Texas. I know I need to be closer to my roots. I grew up in San Angelo. I know I can't go back there, but Austin seems to be calling me. I find myself packing my things and loading the trailer that will take me home. Secondary to the migraines, it's a long ride. They force me to stop often and I don't dare drive with one. But I finally make it and settle in to living back in Texas.

Austin is a hip town, filled with restaurants, clubs, and eclectic shops. It's on the edge of the Texas hill country where the landscape changes from rolling terrain to rugged hills. It's quite beautiful and very different from San Angelo, where the land stretches far and wide, with barely a rise in the road. Austin has a couple of lakes if boating is your thing, and it's the live music capital of the world boasting festivals and concerts galore. It's a great place to hang because it offers something for everyone.

Unfortunately, I'm not able to partake in any of that fun. Living in Austin hasn't exactly brought any of that excitement into my life, though I'm not sure I would call this *life*. More like existing.

Chapter 1

Drexel
Eyes Like Onyx

THE BLARING RING of my phone wakes me. I'm pissed. I rarely sleep this deep and the one night I do ...

"This had better be damn important, Huff, to wake my ass up in the middle of the night."

"I wouldn't be calling if it wasn't."

"Shoot."

"You've had three messages from a Colton Knight. Says he's with the FBI and needs to talk with you. Says it's urgent. And the dude sounded like it was more than urgent. I didn't bother you with the first two, but when the last one came in, he sounded right upset."

I groan. Colt's a close friend from my former military days. "Yeah, I know him all right. He's a good guy. I'll take care of it. Thanks, Huff."

"Sorry I bothered you, boss."

"No worries, man. Talk later."

Troy Huffington was a great employee. He wasn't one of

those pains in the ass who asked me for permission on every tiny detail. But I wish he'd called me sooner on Colt. This must be important. Then again, how would Huff have known that?

I quickly press Colt's number and he answers on the first ring.

"Agent Knight."

"Colt? Drexel Wolfe. I hear you've been trying to reach me."

"Damn. Took you long enough."

"Sorry, dude. I was sleeping. Like any self-respecting citizen would be doing at 3 a.m."

"Shit. Since when have you been self-respecting?"

"Ever since I got away from your ass, that's when." I chuckle.

"Yeah, right. Listen, I need you. We have a situation. In Austin, Texas. Are you familiar with Austin at all?"

"A little. Why?"

"Ever hear of Dirty Sixth?"

I laugh. "You gotta be kidding me." Dirty Sixth is a section of East Sixth Street that is similar to Bourbon Street in New Orleans, but on a much smaller scale. It's open only to pedestrians on weekends and other special events and is the location for many clubs and bars where partygoers hang out.

"Not at all," Colt says.

It's not hard to miss the seriousness in his voice. "Okay, you got my attention. What's up?"

"We've had a string of young women who've gone missing from the bars on Dirty Sixth. Random disappearances. We think it may be human trafficking."

"No shit?"

"No shit. No trace of them. We're up to thirteen now. And we're afraid if we don't put someone in there, it's gonna get worse. I've got two sets of feet in now, but I need another. My problem is that I'm shorthanded. I need bodies on the outside watching the area so I want to know if you'll go in wired and start checking things out."

"Yeah, I can do that. How much time do you need?"

"At least a week, maybe two."

After a quick calendar check on my phone, I say, "Yeah, I can clear off a few things. When do you need me?"

"Yesterday."

"Got it. Tell me when and where."

Colt provides the necessary details.

"Not to worry, man. I'll be in position tomorrow night."

After we end the call, I text my pilot. Then I try to go back to sleep.

MY PLANE LANDS at two thirty and a car meets me on the tarmac. The 103° heat of Austin slams into me like a freight train, after coming from Denver, where the weather was in the low eighties. I throw my gear in the back of the SUV and punch the hotel address into the GPS. Soon, I'm on the expressway, on my way to meet Colton and his men. He's waiting for me in the lobby when I arrive.

"Hot enough for you? This is like Vegas," I complain.

"Tell me about it. I've got men stationed on rooftops wearing Kevlar at night. It's like the Iraqi desert in full battle gear. You luck out. You'll be inside with the AC."

"Good to know," I say, feeling sorry for those poor guys who get the rooftop duty.

"Come on. Get checked in and then we'll go up and I'll brief you."

When we walk into the suite, six heads turn my way. I know two of the guys—Hugh Phillips and Dylan McElroy. Colt introduces me to four more, tosses me a bottled water and we start in on what's been happening.

Dylan hands me a packet and I pull out photos of the young

women who've disappeared. All young and beautiful, their lives ahead of them. Gone without a trace. As I glance over each page, I'm as baffled as these guys are. There isn't anything we can sink our teeth into. Every one of these victims vanished into thin air.

"No witnesses?" I ask.

Colt shakes his head. "Not a single one."

"What about roommates?"

"Half of them didn't have roommates. None of them had boyfriends."

"Well, shit. That rules out the number-one suspect," I say.

Colton adds, "That would've been ruled out anyway. Why would one guy take all these women? If he had relationships with one, why go after all?"

I have to ask this, even though I hate to. "Serial killer?"

"Possibility, but no bodies," Hugh answers this time.

I rake my hand through my hair. I normally keep it cut short, but I haven't had time for a trim in a long time, so it's longer than usual. "All of these are happening on Dirty Sixth?"

Heads bob up and down.

"Did any of these girls have friends they were out with or were they out alone?"

"They all came alone. They usually met friends out, but they never came in with anyone," Steven says.

"So you're telling me that all these girls were targeted. The perp knew exactly who he was going to meet and he also knew if these girls would be alone. They would be easy to overtake."

"Exactly. He, or they, have been watching these girls and have been very careful about who they're taking," Colton says.

I shoot him a look. "Explain."

"Every one of these girls either lived alone, or had roommates that were gone for an extended length of time ... like, all summer. Their jobs were the type where they worked from home and didn't report in anywhere. They had minimal contact with their families so if they went missing, no one would know for a few days. It was orchestrated down to the greatest detail."

I shake my head. "They're pros."

"No fucking shit." Dylan stands and stretches. "Here's the thing. We've been casing the clubs now, but we don't know how or who to watch."

Colton looks at me. "And this is where you come in, Drex."

"Go on."

Colt points to a map of the Dirty Sixth area. "I want you stationed in the bars here. Keep a lookout for anything that might seem suspicious. We've got six men and that's it. I need two guys on rooftops checking streets from that vantage point. And I need one man inside relaying information back and forth. I also need a man in a vehicle standing by in case we need an extraction, because we don't have a clue who we're dealing with. That only leaves three ... you and two others to case the inside of the clubs down there." When Colton finishes, I realize we have more than our share of work cut out for us.

"How many clubs?" I ask.

Everyone laughs. "A shit ton," Dylan says as he runs his hand up and down the map, indicating the number of bars on Sixth Street. And he's right. There are many.

"Great. Just great. Okay, so are there any that the abductions have been centered around?"

"We're not even close to a hundred percent on that, but we think it might be these six clubs," Marshall adds.

"Well, at least that's something. Damn. This is bad. I can't remember working on anything that was so lacking in information."

"Don't remind us, Drex. But our focus is on those six right now. And the sad thing is we may be off base here." Colt stands. "Okay, guys, let's take a break. We'll meet back here around six thirty for some eats, and then afterward, we'll gear up and head out for the night. Drex, if you can stay, I'd like a few minutes."

Everyone heads out. When the door closes behind the last guy, Colt looks at me and says, "I've got a very bad feeling about this."

I try to read him. Colton and I go way back ... to our days in Iraq. We both served as Black Ops. We'd been stationed in the Middle East in the Special Forces when we were both culled and subsequently trained in that highly secretive group ... not that we truly had a choice. Well, I suppose we did, but back then, neither of us would've thought about refusing such an honor. The end result had turned out much better for Colt than for me. I'm thankful to be alive, but the price I paid was steep.

"Don't just say that and then go quiet on me. Spill it, Colt."

"I don't know, man. There's something here, but I can't put my finger on it. Human trafficking, yeah, I think we may have hit on that. It's the perfect profile. Young, unattached female. But the zero clue thing. Usually there is at least one to go on. But not here. Which leads me to believe someone big is behind this."

"Big, as in government?"

Colton pinches the bridge of his nose. "Naw, not government ... at least not ours. More likely corporate. I'm thinking overseas. Once these girls are gone, their pictures are plastered everywhere ... Internet, newspapers, TV, you name it. And we have zero hits. So that has to mean they've been moved out of the country. In the two or three days between their disappearance and when someone notices they're gone, they're already out of here."

"Mexico?"

"I don't think so. Unless they're using the same route that the Mexicans are using to come into the US, the patrols are so heavy right now, I doubt they could make it through. It would have to be by air or sea."

"And you don't think this is a serial killer. And that they're not dead already?"

He shakes his head. "I don't. There's nothing here that points to that. Then again, there's nothing here that says it isn't, either. My gut is telling me no, though."

"So, Colt, what are the local guys doing?"

"Everything we ask them to. They're as baffled as we are, which is why they called us. But, like us, they don't have a whole lot of manpower to spare. And a lot of their undercover guys are in narcotics and don't want their covers blown working on this. That's why we need you."

I nod. "You got me. I can't stay forever, but I've cleared the next two weeks."

"Thanks, man. You're the sharpest guy I know. If anyone can help, it's you."

His words strike a deep chord and it's one I don't want associated with me. "Hey, don't put that on me. I may not find a damn thing."

"I know. But I had to at least give you a shot. If you don't see anything, I don't know where we'll go next."

I stand to leave when Colt stops me. "Hey, Drex. I just want you to know that I'm happy for you. Happy that your business took off so well. If anyone deserves it, it's you."

We exchange a hard look and I nod. Unspoken words pass between us, words neither of us will ever say because of all the bitterness they would expose. But we both know the truth of things, and that's all that matters. We'll be brothers until they shovel the dirt onto our coffins.

THE CLUB'S CROWD swells as I gaze across the room. My seat at the bar is angled to give me a bird's eye view. The bartender picks up my glass and I nod, indicating my desire for a refill. I'm drinking Jack and Coke, light on the Jack. It's not my usual drink of choice, but I need the caffeine. The crowd mix is about fifty-fifty, so I keep checking the sea of people, looking for anything out of order. So far, nothing indicates trouble.

There's a dark-haired girl, in the right age range, alone. She's weaving her way through the crowd, heading toward me. A break in the line at the bar allows her to inch through. She scoots next to me and leans in to get the bartender's attention. He knows why I'm here. We've prearranged all of this with the owner, so I signal him with my head. She fits the profile.

"Can I buy you a drink?" I give her a quick glance as I divide my concentration between her and the crowd.

She inspects me and shakes her head. "No, thanks. I got this."

"Ah, you must be with someone, then. Maybe your boyfriend?"

She doesn't answer, but shrugs instead.

"Okay, my loss, his gain. Lucky guy."

She turns then and looks me straight on. Eyes like onyx, so dark, they're nearly black. In fact, it's close to impossible to distinguish her pupils from her irises. Fuck. Me. Dead. They're the most exotic things I've ever seen. Large, almond-shaped, fringed in thick obsidian lashes, I'm drawn into their startling depths. With great difficulty, I force my gaze away from them and move it down to her mouth. Damn if I don't want to suck my breath in because her lips have that kiss-me, lick-me, bite-me look written all over them. And I would pay for that mouth to be wrapped around my dick right now.

Shit! Get your head straight, man!

My mind buzzes as it tries to figure out if she's Hispanic, Italian, Asian ... Her olive skin and black hair are dead giveaways for any of those, but one thing is certain: she possesses the purest form of beauty I've ever seen. She's so damn perfect; it almost hurts to look at her. My lewd thoughts skyrocket as I continue to gape like an idiot. My dick wreaks havoc in my jeans, taking every coherent thought right out of my brain and sending it straight to my fucking balls.

Without a word, she turns back toward the bar and waits for the bartender. Clearly, she wants nothing to do with me, which is tragic in way too many respects. For once, it doesn't seem right that I land in a place where such hot beauty exists ... but I force those thoughts out of my head as quickly as they appear. Now I start to hope like hell she isn't a target because the thought of anyone laying a hand on her makes my gut seize.

The bartender hands her a beer, and she's gone. It's time for me to get my mind off my dick and back in the game.

As I scrutinize her, I notice she's alone. She switches from beer to shots of clear liquor, which I presume to be tequila. She's not wasting any time getting hammered.

My ear piece crackles. "Eagle One to Lone Wolf. You copy?"

"Loud and clear."

"Anything happening?"

"Nothing. Copy."

"Stay sharp. Out."

As far as I can tell, Onyx Eyes is the only female who's alone right now. It's time to start cruising the place. I motion to the bartender to let him know I'll be on the move. Slowly, I make my way from one end of the room to the other. There's a live band playing, so I weave around the perimeter, keeping Onyx Eyes in my sight, but also trying to scan the room for any other lone females.

My alarm bells start to ring when I see two guys approach her, but she acts like she knows them. They share some brief words and then she pulls cash out of her pocket and passes it to one as he hands her something. I've just witnessed a drug deal. What the hell is she doing? She doesn't fit the profile of a typical user. Then again, looks can be deceiving. A couple more minutes pass after the two dudes leave and she tosses back whatever's in her hand and takes a swallow of her drink. Then she walks to the bar and orders another shot. I snag some photos of her with my phone.

"Lone Wolf to Eagle One, you copy?"

"Eagle One. Come in, Lone Wolf."

"I may have a potential target. Copy?"

"Roger that, Lone Wolf. Details?"

"I just witnessed a drug deal and target is alone."

"Copy, Lone Wolf. Stay on target."

"Roger that."

The rest of the night is spent tailing Onyx Eyes, but nothing else happens. After the club closes down and we make sure the streets are empty, we head back to the hotel to debrief. No one has anything extraordinary to report, other than my incident.

"It may be that she's just a recreational drug user," Colt says.

"True, but my fears are that if she is, that puts an even bigger bullseye on her back. Easy pickins' and all."

"Okay, let's see what we have."

I send the pictures I took of her with my phone to Colt's computer and he puts them up on the screen for everyone to see. "Take a good look and keep her photo with you. I'll shoot this to you all. If you see her anywhere, tail her. We also need to find out who she is. Dylan, run a search on her. Let's see what we can find."

It's four in the morning when we finish and head to our rooms. My sleep is disturbed by a dark-haired goddess with eyes as dark as the midnight sky and my dick that's way too hard for comfort.

Chapter 2

GEMINI
The Axe Man Cometh

MY APARTMENT IS only a few blocks from Sixth Street, the place in Austin where all the nightlife is. It's convenient for me, as I am now quite the barfly. How nice. I never thought things would turn to this, but my desire for alcohol and drugs has to be fed and the clubs have connected me with the right people to do just that. My days are filled with sleeping off the effects of my evening rituals, dealing with a crucifying migraine, or usually both. If the pain subsides enough, that's when I make my way to the clubs.

This particular evening, I get out of the shower and look at the face that stares back at me in the mirror. Gone are the sparkly, laughing eyes. My hair that used to be so shiny is on its way to dull and lifeless. My lips are chewed and I wonder how they got that way; I can't remember doing that to them. The question that keeps firing through my brain is how much longer can I go on like this? This isn't life; it's just some sort of sad imitation. Oftentimes I think it would be so much easier to just take too many pills and not wake up in the morning. I've had them in my hand too, ready to swallow. But then a voice comes to me and changes my mind. That really isn't the answer, and I know it.

I pull on jeans, a black T-shirt, and finally my boots. I detangle my wet hair with my fingers and shake my head. That's it for styling—honestly, I don't give a shit how it looks. It's clean and that's enough for me. I put on some face cream and some lip gloss, to help heal my gnawed lips. Jewelry's a thing of the past. It holds no appeal anymore. And I take one final look in the mirror and realize how strung-out I look. I decide maybe a bit of makeup would be helpful after all. I add a touch of blush to my cheeks, some eyeliner, and that's it. Shoving money, one credit card, ID, and my phone in my pocket, I head out the door.

By the time I get to Red Skies, the band is playing and the place is crowded. My connection will be here around eleven, so I get a drink and cruise, checking things out. Some dude wants to buy me a drink, but I give him my best stink eye, though I'm not sure I even have an adequate one anymore.

The edginess that claims me eases when I see who I'm looking for. We make our transaction and as soon as they hit the road, I throw back the Xanax and down it with my drink. Now it's time for a shot of tequila to speed things up a bit. I need some relief and that's just the thing to do it. Soon, I feel that sweet calm seeping into my muscles, invading my bones as it inches along. My jangled-up nerves are soothed; scrambled thoughts are realigned. The numbing effect takes over and I'm breathing easier. The muscles in my neck gripping me like claws finally release and I can feel the tiniest hint of a smile. It doesn't last because I know this is only temporary. The monster that has invaded my body will return all too soon, taking my pleasure away with it.

As the band plays, I head to the dance floor and join the

others as they move to the beat. I'm enjoying myself but all too soon, it's closing time, so I make my way home. When I arrive, I know the morning will bring pain, and lots of it. I make sure the curtains are drawn as tightly as possible, not allowing even a slit of light through. Then I put an extra pillow next to me so if I wake up and my head is splitting open, I can put the pillow over it. The last thing I think of before drifting off is my mom and how much I miss her. I wish she were here to help me. She would find a way to get rid of my pain. I know she would.

THE AXE MAN is back and I'm his victim. I beg him to decapitate me and get it over with, but he ignores me again. I roll off my bed and under it, writhing in pain. This room can't be dark enough. After a few moments, I know I need to get my pills so I rock to my knees and struggle to the bathroom. Fumbling around, I locate them and pray they work. I'm shaking so badly, the water I attempt to drink pours everywhere except into my mouth. I pull off my shirt because now it's soaked and I crawl back under my bed.

In the distance, I hear a girl moaning. Deep in my mind, I recognize the voice but I never put two and two together that the girl is me. I want to injure myself somewhere else on my body, just so that I can forget how bad my head hurts for a moment. My mouth has a metallic taste, so I know I've bitten my tongue, cheek, or lip, but I don't feel it. Right now, I would bargain with the devil to stop this pain. It's relentless.

I crawl back to the bathroom and take another pill. Ice. I need some ice to put on my head, but I don't know if I can make it to the freezer. Knowing I must try, I set off for the kitchen. It takes me a few minutes because I have to stop several times before I get there. Finding a Ziploc is nearly impossible—my brain isn't functioning properly right now. Getting ice into this bag is like climbing Mt. Everest. More cubes land on the floor than inside the bag. Whoever thought such a simple task could be so difficult and painful? When I finally succeed, I don't have the strength to do anything but stay on the kitchen floor, holding the baggie to my head.

Crying only makes the pain worse, but my brain won't listen to me. It seems that crying and migraines go hand in hand, one bringing the other. The pain never gets better, but I become drowsy enough that I doze off.

"Gemini, where are you?" Her voice is always tinged with worry when she doesn't immediately see me.

"I'm here, Mom. Don't be such a worrywart."

"You know I can't help it. Don't leave my side when we're out."

"But I was only ..."

"Gemini, I don't want any back talk."

"Yes, ma'am."

I can't understand why she gets so out of sorts when she doesn't have her eye on me for a second.

"Mom?"

"Yes, honey?"

"Can I go to camp this summer?"

"Gemini, we've talked about this before."

"But all the other kids are going. I'm the only one who doesn't and I really want to."

"I know you do. But you know how I feel about it."

"I swear I won't get hurt."

"Gemini, you know what my answer is."

"Okay."

Images flash through my mind and now I'm celebrating my sixteenth birthday. I'm hoping for a car, but I doubt I'll get one.

"Happy birthday, sweetie!"

"Thanks, Mom!"

She's carrying a perfectly decorated cake with sixteen glowing candles. And then she sings me the traditional Happy Birthday song. When she finishes, she squeezes me so hard I think I'm going to crack in half.

"Gemini, I love you so much."

"I love you too, Mom. Is it chocolate?"

"You're going to have to cut it to find out," she teases.

When I do, I think about the other kids I know and the birthdays I overhear them talk about. How they have parties and do special things. But it's always just been my mom and me. No other family or friends.

"Hey, Mom ... How come we don't have any relatives or friends? I mean, I know you said my dad died before I was born and that your parents died when you were young. But didn't you have any cousins or anything?" It suddenly hits me how odd it is that we're so isolated.

My mom's usually tanned face suddenly pales. Her head slants away from me so now I don't have a clear view of her face. "No, sweetie, I never had any cousins." Her voice is choked.

"I'm sorry, Mom." I go to her and hug her. "I didn't mean to hurt you by that."

"It's okay, Gemini. You can ask me anything you want. It was just an unexpected question." She hugs me back. Then she leans away and asks, "Hey, you want to open your present?"

"Well, yeah!"

She turns around and hands me a tiny gift bag. It surprises me because I was expecting something larger, such as a box filled with clothes. Now, I think she must have gotten me jewelry. I grin.

When I open the bag, all I see is tissue paper. I pull it out until I find the gift. A car key.

"Oh my God. You didn't?"

She smiles. "I did. But before you go and see it, you have to swear to me you'll take the most care driving it that you've ever taken in your life. I mean it, Gemini."

My smile is so huge, I'm sure my mom can count every tooth in my head. Now it's my turn to squeeze her to smithereens.

"Gemini, I can't breathe," she squeaks. Then she grabs my hand and pulls me into our garage, where she apparently hid the car yesterday. It's a white Ford Escape and I'm in love with it.

"Do you want to take it for a drive?"

"Can I just ride in it first?" I'm too excited to drive right now.

My mom laughs so hard, tears form in the corners of her eyes. She's as happy as I am. We jump in and take my new baby for a spin. I play with the radio and the air conditioning and windshield wipers, just so I'll know how to work them.

When we pull into our driveway, my mom turns, a serious look on her face, like she's about to say something epic. But then she says, "Gemini, promise me you'll be careful. Please don't take any unnecessary risks." And then she says something very strange ... something that sticks with me for a long, long time. "And always watch your back, you know, your rearview mirror. If you think you're being followed, do not come home. Drive straight to the police station. Okay?"

"Yes, ma'am."

When I wake up, the ice has melted; I never zipped the bag, so I'm soaked. My migraine has eased a bit, enough for me to get back to my bedroom. I refill the bag and close it tightly before I go back to bed. Most people would say that I shouldn't drink or take drugs. And that if I didn't, maybe my headaches wouldn't be so bad. If only that were the case. But it's not. They're just as excruciating without the alcohol and drugs. In fact, they're worse because I get no reprieve at all.

As I lie here, I think about my dreams. It's been a while since

I've had any about my mom. It's probably because I miss her so damn much. Whoever said that time eases the loss of a loved one was a big fat fucking liar. The grief I feel now is just as overwhelming as it was when she died five years ago. Sometimes, like right now, it's worse.

Glancing at the nightstand clock, I see it's close to six in the evening. Time to get a shower and eat something. I've been out of it all day and my plans are to hit the clubs again tonight. Before that, though, I need groceries. Mother Hubbard's cupboard is bare. Going out in the daytime isn't an option. It's too bright and my headaches spike.

I shower, dress, and head out. It doesn't take me long to grab what I need, so I'm home in no time. My neighbors must think I'm a recluse because in all the months I've been here, I haven't met a single one of them. During my periods of gravest pain, I've wondered if they can hear me crying out. They never knock so I guess they can't. I'm glad for that—I couldn't answer the door anyway.

After I make a sandwich and eat, I dress and head back out to Dirty Sixth. I know I'll be able to score another Xanax from my connection at Red Skies. If they're not there, they'll be at the Hairy Hound, or one of the other clubs on Sixth Street. My mood lightens as I get closer to my destination. It pains me to think how much further away from my dreams of becoming a marketing expert I get each day. Before too long, it will only be a memory from the distant past.

Chapter 3

DREXEL
Birds of Prey

THE TEAMS ARE positioned in the same places as we were last night, with one exception. Dylan is in Red Skies with me. After our debriefing, we decided to tail Onyx Eyes to see if we would have any hits. There's something odd about her, though, and it has my wheels spinning. When we ran an ID check on her using the photos I took last night, we only came up with a blank slate. There weren't any matches in the system. That doesn't necessarily mean anything yet but I have Huff looking into it. I'm sure we'll hear something from him by tomorrow morning.

Tonight I'm sitting at the bar in the back and Dylan's in the front. I don't want her to think I'm following her if she comes in. Before I even spot her, I notice the two guys she bought her shit from last night. They're in my sights too—this may be part of their plan.

"Lone Wolf to Delta Mad Dog. Do you copy?"

"Copy, Lone Wolf."

"We've got Candy Men on premises. Brown shirt, skull and

crossbones and a Linkin Park baseball hat and then plain navy T-shirt, shaved head, spider tat on neck."

"Copy that. Candy Men in sight."

I sit back and watch the scenery. Girls dance with girls and guys break into the scene. Things are pretty calm. The Candy Men make the rounds, selling their stuff, and then I see her. She's weaving her way through the throng, headed right toward me. I don't want to be recognized, so I pull my cap down lower and look to the back of the room.

"Lone Wolf to Delta Mad Dog. Onyx Eyes is on premises. Grey Metallica T-shirt, jean shorts, cowboy boots, long black hair. Headed to the back. You copy?"

"Copy that. Got her in my sight."

She's drinking a bottled beer tonight and takes a sip as she approaches her sources. They make their exchange and she downs whatever it is she just scored. Then she scans the crowd and continues toward me. I don't notice anything suspicious until a few minutes later when I see two guys approach her. One stands on either side and they start talking to her. She shakes her head a few times and they leave. Everything seems okay as I watch her move to the dance floor. Whatever she took is hitting her now because I'm close enough to see her movements change. The question nags me as to why she feels the need to take drugs, but I push it away.

The rule I always follow is to not get involved with the subjects in my cases. If I can just convince my dick of that, I'll be in great shape. Right now, it's not cooperating. One look at Onyx Eyes in those damn jean shorts and Mr. Cocky is all fired up.

"Delta Mad Dog, you watching all of this?"

"Copy, Lone Wolf. Eyes on them."

"Copy."

She's still dancing when I see those two dudes approach her again. They act like they want to dance with her. The expression on her face tells me everything I need to know, but I stay put. No interference until necessary is the plan and right now, they're just two guys hitting on an attractive girl. She shakes them off and heads back to the bar I'm sitting at. She leans her back against it as she scans the crowd. I'm wondering if she's uneasy or just taking a break. And here they come again.

Now I try to take a listen to what they're saying, but the noise of the band makes it impossible. One of those little bastards puts his hand on her arm, and then she raises her voice. "I told you I'm not interested. Leave me the hell alone." She tries to tug her arm away but his hand clamps tighter.

It's time to step in. My hand closes around his wrist, the one he has on her arm, and I apply the perfect amount of pressure. When his nostrils flare, I say, "The lady says she's not interested." I have them both by a couple of inches and I'm sure by at least twenty pounds each. One has long, stringy blond hair and a beard; the other has a shaved head.

They both check me out and then stringy blond hair says, "Mind your own damn business."

"I am. You just made it my business when the lady said she wasn't interested. Now let her go before this gets ugly."

The bartender leans over and asks, "There a problem here?"

"Not if they let the lady loose."

"Guys, do I need to call security?" The bartender drums his hands on the bar.

"No, we're cool here." Stringy blond dude lets go and I release his arm. They walk away.

Once they're out of earshot, she says, "Hey, thanks." Her speech is slurred.

"No problem." Even in her drugged state, she's hot as fuck and Mr. Cocky is acting happy now. Goddamn, I need to rein this shit in fast.

She nods and turns away.

When she's moved off, I say, "Delta Mad Dog, are you bird watching?"

"Affirmative, Lone Wolf."

"Copy."

Not much later, I watch as she hits the dance floor again. She picks up the beat, drops her head back, and closes her eyes. She loses herself in the sound and for a moment, she almost looks like she's enjoying herself. The pained expression I've noticed her wearing most of the time disappears. All too soon, the song is over and that look on her face returns. I know that look. I know it well. I've worn it way too many times myself. Lost in a memory, I reflect back for a moment on things I don't need to be thinking about. Shaking my head, I look around and realize she's gone.

Damn it, what the hell am I doing?

"Delta Mad Dog, do you have sight on Onyx?"

"Affirmative. She's moving to the back of the room."

"Copy that."

I scan the back of the room and head in that direction. I don't catch a glimpse of her anywhere but I also don't want to be too obvious. My senses are on high alert.

My mike crackles then and I hear Dylan say, "Lone Wolf, two birds have flown the coop. You copy?"

"Copy. I'm on the move."

Now my pretense is over. My steps have purpose to them and they take me to the women's restroom. Not bothering to knock, I push open the door to a group of surprised faces, none of which belong to Onyx Eyes. All the stalls are closed, so I crouch down, inspecting the shoes, looking for those telltale cowboy boots.

"Hey, what do you think you're doin' in here?" one of the women asks.

I don't answer but I survey the place, looking for any escape route. There are no windows so the door is the only way in or out. They must've taken her out the back.

"Delta Mad Dog. Back alley."

"Copy that."

Sure enough, I bust through the back door, and they have her as she twists and struggles to get away. She never would've succeeded without my intervention, because right as I open the door, I see one of them inject something into her neck. By the time I get to them, she's limp as a rag.

"Let her go. Now."

They eye me for a second and take off running. I want to give chase, but my first concern is the girl. By the time Dylan arrives, I'm tending to Onyx Eyes.

"Shit. Good thing you called that, Drex."

"Seriously. They hit her with something, though, right as I opened the door. On top of what she already took, she'll probably be out for a while. We'd better let Colt know."

"Right. What happened to them?"

'They took off."

"Damn!"

"Eagle One, Lone Wolf here. I have target. Do you copy?"

"Copy, Lone Wolf. What's your position?"

"Alley behind Red Skies. The two birds drugged her and took off when I intercepted them."

"Shit. Sending someone over now for pick up."

"Copy, Eagle One."

Dylan grabs her wrist, feeling for a pulse when our radios crackle again. It's Colt.

"Lone Wolf and Delta Mad Dog, Eagle One here. Abandon operation. I repeat. Abandon operation. You've got six, I repeat, six birds of prey surrounding you, of unknown ID. Get out of there!"

"Lone Wolf here and that's a negative. Target is down. Unconscious. Cannot abandon."

"Drex, get the fuck out of there."

"I said no!"

Then I turn to Dylan and say, "Leave. Now. I'll take care of her. Just tell them to try to pick me up somewhere." He gives me a hard look. "It'll be easier for me if I only have her and myself to worry about. Now go." He nods and disappears.

Whoever is closing in wants this girl, and something inside me is willing to go beyond the norm to help her. Yes, I've been trained for this. But there's something else about her that begs to be saved. Call it intuition. Or call it my dick. Whatever. My arm coils around her waist and I toss her over my shoulder. She only weighs about one fifteen, if my guess is accurate.

"Eagle One, direct me the hell out of here."

"You've got one block in any direction before you're in contact so don't use any streets. Back alleys and between buildings are your only options now."

"Copy. Lead the way."

And he does. I follow his directions and run as hard as I can, avoiding main streets, until he tells me I'm clear. Then he instructs me where to go for my pickup. When I get there, one of the guys is waiting in a black Tahoe. I toss my target in first and then hop in behind her as he speeds away, taking us back to our hotel.

"FUCK YOU, COLT! I was *not* going to leave her there. And since when would you have done something like that? The Colton I remember would *never* have done that!"

"Careful, Drex, you're treading on very thin ice here."

"You think I care? What? You gonna fire me?"

His lips thin and he rolls his shoulders. "Fuck!"

"My thoughts exactly," I say.

"We have a huge issue."

Of all the things for him to say right now, that wasn't one I expected. "Really?" I laugh. "Understatement of the year, Colt."

"No, you don't get it, Drex. Thing is, we can't ID her. None of our databanks have a goddamn thing on her."

"What the hell are you saying?"

"Just that. She comes up as an empty sheet of nothing. She doesn't exist. No name to go with the photo."

Reaching into my pocket, I toss him the driver's license I pulled from her pocket. "See if this helps."

Colt checks it out for a second and nods. "Yeah, this should do it. But I still have a bad feeling about this."

"Why do you keep saying that?"

"Because I'm going with my gut, man."

The air in the room just got a little thicker. "I need to check on her. I don't have any idea how long she'll be out or what they gave her. I have a feeling it was propofol or ketamine. She'll probably be out for a while. You know, enough time for them to have gotten her out of the country. Did you ID those guys?"

"Nope. We're still trying to figure out who the hell the condors were."

"You have photos?" I ask.

"Yeah, and video. And it's not good."

"What's that supposed to mean? Nothing in these cases is ever good."

"Listen, Drex, those first guys you chased off didn't have anything to do with the birds of prey. I want you to look at something." He brings up the video and I watch everything go down. Six men wearing masks swarm the alley and right after, two cars pull up. They start talking, very animatedly too.

"No sound?" I ask, but I already know what that answer will be.

"That would've been impossible unless the back of the club was wired."

"I know. But still. Can you close in on the cars?"

"Yeah, and we got a partial on one tag. But so far, nothing."

"Those aren't any of ours, right?" I had to ask.

"None that I know of. And look at their equipment. None of it speaks government issue."

"Don't be so damn naïve, Colt. You remember how we operated. They have AK-47s. We carried those too."

"You're not thinking ..."

"All I'm saying is don't rule anything out. If it walks like a duck and quacks like a duck, it doesn't always have to be a duck."

"I got it." He's frustrated. "Why would a hit team be after her? And why not just take her out with a sniper?"

"Dude, you've been institutionalized too long. They don't want her dead, fool. They want *her* ... or rather somebody else does."

"Then the real question is, why?"

"That's what we need to find out. I'm gonna grab some sleep. She's down for the count. I'll cuff her to the bed in case she wakes up, but I need to crash so I'm fresh when things heat up with her."

"You've got her then, yeah?"

"Yep. And thanks for bailing my ass out of there."

"Well, I should be kicking your ass."

"No, there's something going on with her. We'll find out what it is." As soon as the words leave my mouth, I hope they're correct. Because some big bad guys are after Onyx Eyes and I'm curious as hell to find out why.

Chapter 4

GEMINI
Shoot Me

THE FIRST THING I notice is that my mouth is like a desert. When I try to roll over, my arm prevents me from doing so. The room is so bright, I scream. The skull-splitter is back. A pillow! I need a pillow to block the light. My hand reaches for one, but it comes up empty. My right wrist is latched to the bed by something, but I don't dare open my eyes to see what. Oh God, what is happening?

"What's the matter?" a deep voice asks, but I can barely breathe, much less answer him. My hand covers the left side of my face, trying to block the light as I cry out in pain. Whoever is in the room pulls my hand away and then I'm faced with my worst nightmare—blaring sun in my eyes.

"No, no, no, no, no ..." I repeat.

A hand grasps mine and squeezes it so tightly that pain shoots up my arm. Ironically, I'm relieved for a bit because it takes my mind off the axe man ... but only for a moment. The torturer, in his usual way, swings his blade at me again with all his might and forces me to focus back on him. He leaves me with no choice. I'm convulsing now. My brain erupts in flashes of brilliant fireworks and I have to find a way to tell this person to shut the damn curtains, but I'm not sure I can.

My jaws are clenched so I do my best. "Curtains ... c-c-close."

"What?" He growls as he clamps down on my hand again. I'm sure the bones will snap.

By now, water is gushing down my cheeks and I want to die. "Sh-shut c-c-c-curtains!" The words burst forth in a scream and suddenly the room darkens. It helps but my pain is too far down the path of agony. I writhe, and the only thing I want to do is to curl up under the bed. But I can't because my wrist is tethered. I am a prisoner.

"Tell me what's wrong," the mystery voice demands.

The words penetrate and under other circumstances, I might laugh. But I can't now because the only thing that's possible for me to do is roll from side to side.

"Shoot me," I mutter. Death would be a welcome sweetness ... the absence of pain.

Maybe he's planning on doing that anyway. If I ask him, perhaps he'll get it over with quickly. My thoughts are so scrambled, though, I'm not sure if I even said those words out loud.

He lets out a short laugh. "You want me to shoot you?" Even though my mind is distorted with pain, I can see he's not going to help me. "That's a good one."

"Please."

"Why?"

Why does he have to ask so many damn questions? Can't he see I'm not fucking coherent? "Pain."

"What hurts?"

My finger points to the great offender. "Migraine." My voice is barely a whisper now. But only a little bit of time passes before I feel a cool cloth across my forehead. Again I want to laugh, knowing it won't help. But just a bit later I feel something else, and I recognize the cold of a cloth wrapped in ice across my forehead. My hand latches onto it like it's gold and I move it over my left eye, the same one the axe man is hacking into.

"Need meds." I lick my lips, or try to anyway.

"Where are they?"

"Home."

"What do you need?"

My mouth is so dry, it's difficult to talk. My tongue works around the inside trying to stir up some saliva. "Maxalt. Tramadol. Lortab."

"Not sure I can help you with those."

The pain comes in waves and it's on the increase again. My breathing is erratic and if I don't get something in me, I'll go insane. The only thing I know to do is to make something else hurt worse than my head. So I jerk my wrist against whatever it is hooking me to the bed.

"Stop it. You'll hurt yourself."

My mind processes that he's angry with me. I don't care. That's the idea, I want to say. But I'm at the point where I can't speak again. The only thing I focus on is making something else hurt worse than my skull. But I don't succeed because he grabs and holds my arm before I can do any real damage. My loose hand fists his shirt and I try to pull him to me, but I'm so weak with pain, I fail. How can I make him understand how badly I hurt?

He must understand that I need to tell him something because he leans close to me. "Do something ... anything," I groan in his ear. "If I can't get my pills, I want to die. Please."

"Christ. What the hell is wrong with you?" he asks. Then he pushes me away. This is the mother of all migraines. They've been bad before, but I've always been able to medicate. I won't make it if I can't get something in me.

His fingers touch my neck and he says, "Damn, your heart rate is through the roof." He gets up and I assume he makes a phone call because I can hear him talking to someone.

Rolling to my side I try to look where he's gone. I see a handgun on the small table about five feet from me. If I can get to it, I can end all of this. Right here and now. The pain will be gone forever. I don't think twice before I try to sit up and reach for it. There's one problem: I'm so wobbly, weak, and dizzy that my equilibrium is sketchy. Standing will be a huge issue. But I go for it. Jackpot. As my fingers wrap around the beautiful, cold metal, I pick it up. But I'm so shaky, it may be a problem for me to fire it. I'm still going to try.

I turn it toward me and take aim and as I squeeze, he yells, "Noooo!"

Nothing happens. I squeeze harder, but by that time, he slams my hand against the headboard and knocks the gun away. It skids across the bed and thumps to the floor, shattering my last hope for relief. That slight bit of work has zapped me so I collapse on the bed, thinking how my big chance at ending my pain has slipped through my fingers because I was too weak to pull the gun's trigger. How pathetic is that? I can't even kill myself.

"What the hell are you doing?" he asks. He grabs me by the neck and forces me to look at him.

"You don't understand," I whisper as I reach for my head again with my free hand. "I can't do this ... anymore." And the writhing takes over.

My mom... somehow, thoughts of her soothe me. I try to focus on when I was young and we'd do fun things together. Once she took me to the county fair and we rode the merry-go-round. Afterward she bought me cotton candy. And she laughed at me because I had sticky stuff everywhere. When she grabbed my hand to hold it, we stuck together like glue. She told me how she didn't have to worry about losing me ever again, since we were permanently attached. For a while, I believed her. That is until we got to the car.

But as quickly as that memory fades, the pain rips into me again. My body jerks off the bed and I crash against the headboard, feeling pain sear my arm. I'm momentarily grateful for it, but it doesn't last nearly long enough. The pain in my head overrides it and it's all I can feel again.

The door opens and closes and men are talking, but I can't hear what they're saying through my agony. I'm caught in the vise of it and I can't concentrate. Maybe they're discussing what to do with me. Maybe they'll kill me. I wish they'd be quick about it.

Then I hear, "Fuck. Colt, we have to do something here. She's in so much pain, she tried to shoot herself."

"Let me see what I can do, Drex."

"Well, make it fast. You have the names of her medications. Have one of the guys slip into her place and get them."

"Drex, you know ..."

"Goddammit, then I'll do it. I'll take responsibility. Have you gotten that rusty?"

Their words don't make sense to me other than one of them wants to help me. That's more than anyone's done in a while. Well, that's not really fair. People *have* tried to help. My case just seems resistant to treatment, they say.

"Get one of your men in here on watch. I need to pull up the data on her apartment."

And then it's quiet for a bit. The jackhammer pounds away, the axe man still splitting my skull. I lie still on the bed, my hand gripping my head, my heart praying for relief.

Chapter 5

DREXEL
Aali Imaam

NEVER IN MY life have I seen someone suffer like that from a headache. Torture, yes. But not a damn headache. What the hell happened to her? After I make a thorough check of her apartment complex using Colt's computer, I figure out the best way in and out. Since I have her keys, getting in won't be a problem. My worry is that the place is being watched, and I don't want to alert them to my presence.

"I need a long-haired blond wig. A hat and some sunglasses. Get me some ratty jeans and some boots with three-inch lifts in them. And I want a tattoo on my arm of a scorpion."

Colt shakes his head. "Anything else?"

"Yeah, fake teeth. Big ones that are brownish-yellow. Something someone would remember if asked. Oh, and a bushy mustache."

"You got it. Give me thirty."

I didn't think any of it would be a problem, other than the teeth. But they use the new dental impressions now and can make them in no time at all. And I won't need the kind I can eat with, only the kind for show.

About a half hour later, the guys return with the disguise. It takes the tattoo dude about ten minutes too long to get the scorpion on my arm, but when he does, it's big, red, and perfect. Anyone would remember it if they saw it.

"How long will this stay on?"

"You can wash it off when you get back."

When I'm decked out, I check myself in the mirror. I swear if my mother saw me, she wouldn't recognize me.

"See you in an hour. If you don't hear from me in two, send in the posse."

"Wolfe, be careful."

"Always am, Colt."

I DRIVE AROUND her building a few times before I park. Sure enough, her place is being watched. One car with two men inside. As I make a phone call, I video and photograph the car so the guys back at the hotel can see them. I get in and out without a problem. Apparently my getup works because no one stops me, but when I'm driving back to the hotel, I pick up a tail. It's a different car than the one at the apartment. They must've had her place bugged.

I call Colt. "Hey, I'm being tailed."

"No surprise there. What do you want?"

"A freight train. Can you get me one?"

Colt laughs. "Doubtful. I can detain them for a bit, though."

"Better than a freight train. Why didn't I think of that?"

"Um, because I'm so fucking creative."

"Oh, right, smart-ass. Where do you want me to go?"

"For a joyride. I need a few ... maybe five. And then head over to I-35 south. Can you do that?"

"Got it." I make all kinds of turns and eventually head to I-35 where the blue lights pull my tail over. I drive back to the hotel.

When I get to the room, Onyx Eyes—or Gemini, based on her ID—is still a wreck.

She sees me and shakes her head.

"It's only me. It's a disguise," I say as I pull off the hat and wig and spit out the nasty teeth. I fill a glass with water and take her some pills.

She grabs my hand, greedily takes what's in it and guzzles the water, spilling the rest all over herself. "I need another Lortab," she says as she wipes the water off her lips.

"Give it a chance to work."

She shakes her head and without hesitation says, "I'm a drug abuser. One's not enough."

Well, what do you know. I hand her another one and she downs it with more water and falls back on the bed.

"Do you want water?"

She shakes her head no. Eventually, her breathing evens out and she falls asleep. The drugs must be doing their job. That lets me breathe a bit easier, but I still wonder what the devil makes her head hurt so fiercely.

The skin on my arm is raw when I finish scrubbing clean the scorpion. In my former profession, having any kind of permanent identifying marks was considered dangerous, so I never got any ink. But recently I've entertained the idea. The scorpion looked great, but if I ever did anything, I would put it on my chest.

When I'm satisfied the ink is gone, I peel off my grubby clothes and jump in the shower. I'm drenched from the July Austin heat and wearing that wig was no picnic. The cool water feels great as it washes away the sweat.

Since all my clothes are in the other room, I wrap a towel around my waist. She's still asleep, so I take my time getting dressed. This gives me a chance to think about what I saw in her apartment, which was a whole lot of nothing. A couch, a chair, one coffee table, a bed, and a nightstand. No pictures on the walls, no photographs, no dining table and chairs, very little to indicate she had much of a life at all. No wonder she'd been targeted by the traffickers, but why was she living like this? When I searched her closet, I did find a few items of clothing, not anything like most girls her age would have, but there was a broken-up bike helmet. It must have some significance or it wouldn't have been there. And why is her background so blank?

My phone rings. Colt.

"What's up?"

"Those guys who were tailing you are Afghani."

"What?"

"We think they're attached to one of the suspected terror cells here in the southwest."

"Christ. Who the fuck is this girl?"

"That's what we want to know. Her ID shows her as Gemini Sheridan, right? And we have a last known addy in Boulder, Colorado. She graduated from CU Boulder last year. But here's where it gets sticky. She has a dummy Social Security number. Her permanent address is listed as San Angelo, Texas. When we checked it out, apparently that house was ransacked two days ago. The local police have been trying to find her since then."

"What the hell is going on, Colt?"

"Whatever it is has nothing to do with human trafficking. We just stumbled onto this thing by accident. She may be part of Aali Imaam."

"You're kidding. As in Aali Imaam, the terrorist group? And you think there is a local cell here trying to bring her in?"

"We don't know. But somebody wants her and is going to extremes to get her. Think about it. Her info isn't solid. No one seems to know her. She has no known living relatives. Her creds don't add up. The only thing of note we could find was that she was in some kind of biking accident last fall and sustained a head injury."

"The headaches."

"Most likely."

"Boulder PD just told us they found a body yesterday—it was her former boyfriend. Shot, execution style. Back of the head. They found him in a ditch on the side of a country road."

"Shit. This is deep, Colt. CIA or Homeland Security deep."

"I'm getting ready to make that call."

"Wait."

"Why?"

Something doesn't add up here. And when I smell a rat, I'm usually right. "A hunch. That's all. Let me talk with her when she wakes up."

"Drex, I need to get back to the issue at hand here, man. I've got girls disappearing."

"Think about it. Those dudes know we're onto them. They'll lie low for a while. But something's rotten in the woodpile where she's concerned. What if her life's at stake here? With all due respect, I can't, in good conscience, leave her when I don't have all the facts."

"Drex ..."

"I know what you're thinking and I'm no longer Black Ops. Things are different now. *I'm* different. I'll send two other guys from my company down to help in my place."

"Dude, sometimes that heart of yours gets you in way too deep."

"Not true. I was trained to save lives, when possible. That's what I'm trying to do. My heart fucked me up one time and I won't let it do that again."

If he were standing in front of me, he would be giving me one of his trademark looks. "You have forty eight hours. That's it.

Give me something or I'm shutting you down."

"Thanks, man." I make the call to get two more men down here to give Colt a hand.

SHE STIRS. THERE'S nothing I want more than for her to wake the hell up so I can find out what's going on. Is she a terrorist? What is her involvement, if any? How aggressive should I get with her? The fact that she's beautiful weighs heavy on me, but I'm going to have to pull my mind out of the sex gutter and stay focused on the main task here. The camera I've set up is running so everything she says and does will be recorded for later analysis.

One thing is certain—that headache wasn't an act. She was in major pain. No one can put on like that, the way her body contorted and the look on her face.

My chair is next to the bed so when she awakens, she looks directly at me. I hand her some water and another pill. If she's an addict, she'll take it without any questions. If she's not, she won't want it. She's shaking and wolfish as she grabs it, so I have my answer.

"Are you hungry?"

Her eyes narrow a tiny bit and she nods.

"Can you eat?"

Again, she nods. I dial room service and order a couple of sandwiches and fries. After the order is placed, I lean back in the chair, cross my arms, and begin.

"Who are you?"

"I might ask the same of you," she says. Her voice is hoarse which leads me to believe she needs hydration.

"You might, but then you're not the one in charge here. Drink." I hand her another glass of water.

My observational skills are at work. She guzzles the water, then rolls to her side and pulls her knees to her chest. I want to see her face because every human emotion is expressed there. Yes, you can detect emotions from body language, but the face shows everything. "Gemini Sheridan."

"I know that. What I don't know is who you work for. Roll on your back and look at me when I speak to you."

She does as I ask. "I'm unemployed. My migraines have knocked me out of having any kind of job."

She must think I'm all sorts of stupid. I sneer, but before I can say anything else, she asks, "What happened? How did I end up here? And where am I? Why do you have me handcuffed? What do you want from me? Are you going to kill me? I remember you. You're the guy from the bar, aren't you?" She rubs her eyes with her free hand, and for a moment, the innocence written all over her face makes me almost fall for it.

She sits up and scrutinizes me. And once again, I find myself beginning to get pulled in. Fuck. Me.

Knowing that I can't afford to lose myself to those kinds of thoughts, I say, "Damn, you're really good. Anything else?"

Her face screws up in confusion. If her dark eyes weren't so damn difficult to read, I might be able to cut through the bullshit a lot quicker. If the light's not just so, it's impossible to distinguish pupil from iris. That puts me at a huge disadvantage because I can't tell if she's lying.

"Good?"

"Come on, Gemini. You know damn well that diversion tactic's not going to work."

"Huh?"

"Just tell me who you work for. Are you a courier? Or are you in deeper?"

"You're not making any sense. I told you I don't have a job. I was disabled from a mountain biking accident and now I suffer from severe post-concussion syndrome. You saw me in the glorious throes of a migraine. Did I look like someone who can hold down a job? I won't even drive a car, for Pete's sake."

She rubs her temples and forehead. I take a good hard look at her and wonder if she could possibly be telling the truth. How could she perform in any capacity if one of those headaches hit?

"Okay, so how often do you get these headaches?"

"Every single day."

"And they can't be controlled?"

If looks could kill, the one she gives me would shrivel me on the spot. She huffs out a breath and says, "I'm treatment resistant. Why the hell do you think I'm a drug seeker?"

"Is that why I saw you buying at Red Skies?"

"Jeez, have you been spying on me? Are you here to arrest me?"

"No, I haven't been spying on you. I just happened to see you score your stuff. And no, I'm not here to arrest you for that, either."

"Then what do you want with me?"

"You were drugged and two guys tried to abduct you. I prevented that, but in doing so, something else was set into motion. Seems someone is after you and we thought you might be able to help us find out who that is."

We are interrupted by a knock on the door. When I look out the peephole, I see it's room service.

"Not a peep out of you or I shoot the delivery guy. Understand?"

She gapes at me and nods. I go back to the door, sign for the food, and take the tray. I put the food close to her on the bed. As we eat, I ask her to tell me about herself.

"Would you have really shot him?"

"Just make a sound during the next delivery and you'll find out."

She looks at me and then says, "I could always scream."

"You could, but you see, the rooms all around us are occupied by my men, so it won't do you a bit of good. Besides, if you get too annoying, a strip of duct tape can take care of that. It's your choice. You can comply or make it difficult on yourself. It's really that simple."

Her nostrils flare, and then I can see her concede.

"So, tell me about yourself, Gemini."

She goes through the basics. I want to know when she moved to Austin.

"A few months ago. I had my wreck last fall. I went out on a Saturday for a late morning ride. It turned out to be pretty sucky, actually. I crashed and then lost my memory and wandered around in the woods for a couple of days. I don't remember much about it at all. Apparently I found some backpackers and crashed their campsite. They called for help and I was rescued."

"You were alone?" What was she thinking going out alone?

"Yeah. I ended up with some broken bones and such but it's the head that really messed me up. It's fucked up my life. It drove away my boyfriend too."

"Um, this boyfriend, Nick Lowry?"

"How do you know Nick?" She stops eating and her full attention swings to me.

"We've been trying to find out everything we can about you."

"Why? That's pretty creepy."

How can I tell her what we know and have her remain calm? There isn't any good way, I decide. "I know it sounds creepy, but you have to understand it from our perspective. Here we are, trying to investigate why women are disappearing from Dirty Sixth—we think we have a lead when suddenly our case does a one eighty and you enter the picture. You're unconscious, I have a group of men chasing me, and it's obvious it's you they want. So yeah, we needed to find out everything we could about you. That's how we know about Nick."

"So what about Nick?"

Her hand clenches her napkin and it's only inches from mine, so I reach over and pick it up. "I'm sorry to tell you, Gemini, but Nick is gone."

"What do you mean? Where did he go?"

"He was killed."

"What? Killed? Oh my God! None of this makes any sense. What happened?"

"I'm so sorry." Then I tell her what we know. I also tell her about her house in San Angelo.

Her head is lowered and she doesn't say anything for a while. Then I notice it's because she's crying. Not the loud, obnoxious sobbing, but the silent, valiant type that I wouldn't have even noticed if it hadn't been for her shaking shoulders. She must've loved this Nick guy.

Handing her some tissues, I ask, "When did you last talk to Nick?"

She shakes her head and shrugs. I'm not sure if she can't remember or just doesn't want to talk about it. I give her a moment, because eventually there will be questions.

She finally comes around and says, "The last time I spoke to him was when he left. He couldn't deal with the way I'd changed. Who is doing this and why?"

The muscles in my neck are tense. I roll my head, trying to ease the tightness. "I don't know. That's what I hope you can help me with. Tell me about your family."

She wipes her nose and tears. "I don't have any. My mom died in a car accident when I was eighteen and I never knew my dad."

"Do you at least know his name? Maybe we can find him."

"No. My mom never told me his name."

That raises a red flag. In this day of full disclosure, the fact that her mom withheld that kind of information is a shock.

"And you never checked your birth certificate or wondered about that?"

Her lids drift shut, and I think she's trying to shut me out. "My mom told me not to worry about him because she had more than enough love to go around. I heard that story forever so I never questioned her. I always assumed he died and that she loved him too much to want to talk about him."

"That's not good enough for me, but we'll let that slide for now." I hear her suck in her breath, but I don't give a damn. I need to figure out her attachment to Aali Imaam, and if this is the way to flush it out, so be it. "So about last night. You were drugged by two men who we suspect are involved in human trafficking. We had Red Skies staked out and those two guys who wouldn't leave you alone were the ones we think might be the culprits. When you disappeared out the back, I went out just in time to see them drug you. But as we were waiting for our team to arrive, my leader informed us that a different group of men were closing in. So I picked you up and ran. That's how you ended up here. But what we wanna know is why those guys were after you."

She stares at me. When she speaks, her voice is so quiet, I have to lean in to hear her. "Why didn't you leave me there? Maybe they would've killed me."

"Maybe. Maybe not. We don't know what they would've done to you because we don't know why they want you. Do you know why, Gemini?"

"No, but maybe they would've put me out of my misery." Her voice is raw and bitter.

"You wouldn't say that for long." I see that she's earnest in her comment. She doesn't care if she dies. "Because if these people get you and don't want you dead, your worst nightmare would begin. They'd bring new meaning to the word pain for you."

TWO DAYS AND she doesn't stray from the same story. Her headaches are brutal. They debilitate her and she's absolutely dysfunctional when one hits. One thing is solid, and that is her story has been consistent.

"You know, this might be easier on you if you just tell us what you know."

"Might be easier on you too. You must be super dense because I've told you already that I don't know anything. I don't even know who you are or where I am. So if you think I'm gonna magically have this epiphany and get infused with all this information, then we're gonna be here a long time."

We've watched her on the video and see nothing to indicate that she might be anything other than Gemini Sheridan.

"Well, we could always withhold your medication."

Panic flashes over her. "Oh God, please don't. Or if you do, just kill me instead. I don't know what you want with me. Rape must not be what you're after or you would've done that already. If you were going to kill me, I think you would've done that too. Either way, go ahead and get it over with already. I'll beg if you want me to. If you want the sex, just go on ahead and take it. But please, don't withhold my drugs."

Later that night, I run through everything she's said and I have to believe her. I've never had a detainee that behaved like she does. Most beg to stay alive. Most will say they'd do anything to remain alive. Not her. She truly acts like she doesn't care about dying. And from witnessing what she goes through, I can certainly understand why.

And her reaction to my remark about withholding meds clenches my gut. She had that trapped look that made me feel like a shit. I realize there's no way in hell I would ever do that to her.

I call Colt. "I'm pulling out. I need to go to San Angelo."

"Are you sure about this?"

"She doesn't know anything, or at least my gut tells me that."

Colts groans. "Drex, my gut tells me you're getting in too deep. Let me make the call."

"No. If you do, I'm afraid something terrible will happen to her. That's what my gut tells *me*. Trust me on this, Colt."

"Your call. You're the one with the connections."

"Thanks. And good luck on finding your perps."

Chapter 6

GEMINI
Tall, Dark, and Mysterious

How can Nick be dead? How is that even possible? What did he do to deserve this?

Tall, dark, and mysterious is back and sitting next to the bed. He's finally unhooked the handcuff. He was nice enough to get me some clothes and allow me to shower, though he most likely did it for selfish reasons. I was reeking up a storm. My mind reels with questions and I can't just sit back and not know the answers.

"How did Nick die?" That question burns a hole through me. Nick, sweet, gentle Nick, who would never be unkind to anyone. Dead.

The man looks down as if he doesn't want to answer me.

"Please, you have to tell me. I need to know."

His answer sickens me. "He was shot in the back of the head."

It's so shocking, I gasp. The first thing I think about is whether he knew it was coming or if it took him by surprise. Did he suffer first? So I ask him that.

When his head slowly slices up and down one time, it's almost more than I can bear. My body crumples onto the bed. It's a good thing I wasn't standing or I would've face planted. Then something else hits me. How does this man know all of this? And who is he? Is he going to do the same to me? All those weird things my mom used to say rush back to me at once.

"Gemini, be careful around others, especially men. They'll always tell you things just to get something from you. Never trust a boy. He'll only break your heart and take your money."

At the time, I didn't know we had any money—I thought she was being melodramatic. What I thought she was trying to tell me was not to let them get in my pants. But now ... holy hell, I'm not sure about anything anymore.

Lifting my head, I look up at him suspiciously. "How do you know all of this? Are you ever going to tell me who you are?"

He shrugs. "My name is Drexel Wolfe and I'm a private investigator. I was hired by the FBI to look into the disappearance of young women from the Dirty Sixth Street clubs. We've suspected human trafficking but then as I told you, things shifted since we ran into you."

"Why a private investigator?"

His elbows rest on the chair arms, his fingers joined in a perfect steeple. He examines me before he answers. "Good question. The field agent in charge called me in on this because he needed an extra pair of feet on the ground."

"Show me your ID." I try to mask my fear with anger.

He smirks and then reaches into his pocket and pulls out what I'm asking for. He shows me his ID, a temporary FBI ID, and his business card that reads *DWInvestigations*. Like all this is supposed to comfort me. It doesn't. At all.

"Pretty smart to ask for that."

My head lists to the right and in the snarkiest tone I can muster, I say, "I'm not stupid, although it may appear that way.

And just so you know, if I weren't in such a bad way with these blasted headaches, I would be doing everything in my power to get away from you. The only reason I haven't is because I know it's hopeless. You got that?"

The tears elbow their way past my lids again as thoughts of Nick move into focus. The last weeks we spent together were awful. I would lose my temper and yell at him for no reason, other than the stupid fact that my head was splintering. He would try to soothe my tattered nerves, but I was so distraught I wouldn't let him. That proverbial cycle continued until one day, he simply looked at me with regret and sorrow and then told me he couldn't deal with it anymore. With slumped shoulders, he walked away and I never saw him after that.

Now he's dead, a bullet in his head, which truly should've been in mine. Where's the justice in that?

Lord, I have to stop thinking about him. If I don't, these thoughts will drive me to the brink of insanity. How the hell did all this happen? My head falls onto my arms crossed over my raised knees.

Then his voice startles me. I'd almost forgotten he was here.

"Gemini, we have a big mystery to solve and I need your help."

"I need some Lortabs."

He fetches me some from the bathroom. I take them without a word.

"How many doctors have you seen for this condition?"

"Enough. Not that you would give a damn. None of them helped. I've given up on doctors."

"You didn't see the right one."

Who the hell is this guy? "Thanks, Einstein. Do you have any idea what I've been through?"

"Matter of fact, I do. When I was in Afghanistan and Iraq, I knew a lot of guys who were victims of IEDs. They suffered from severe concussions and headaches, hearing loss, that sort of thing. But right now, we need to figure out why those men went to your mom's house."

"It's *my* house. I inherited it from her when she died."

"Okay, your house. So why would they go there?"

"Hell if I know. I haven't been there in two years. I just have someone take care of the thing."

Now he turns brusque. "Tell me everything you know."

"I already have," I snap as we glare at each other. My temper is short secondary to pain.

His eyes are beautiful. Not blue and not gray, they're fanned with thick, dark lashes. His lids have a way of drifting to the half-closed position, giving him a very sexual look. I'm not quite sure if he's trying to achieve this or if it's a natural thing for him. Whatever the case, it's ridiculously hot. Why the hell I would notice this now baffles me. This dude is holding me prisoner. He's probably trying to trance me into developing a bad case of Stockholm syndrome. That's all I need. My fingers pinch the bridge of my nose.

"Stay with me, Gemini." His voice is stern and he's losing patience.

"Can I lie down while you talk to me?"

"Yes."

Why must he always be so brusque? "Um, what did you say your name was again?"

"Drexel," he says. "You need to understand something. I need solid information from you *now* or your case is going to be turned over to Homeland Security or the CIA or both. Then I'm not sure what will happen."

Something in his voice stirs me. Moving the ice bag aside, I sit up and lean on my elbow. "What's that supposed to mean?"

"Somebody wants you, Gemini, and whoever they are, they sent a number of men to get you. Here's the tricky part: when I went to your apartment, it was being watched. And when I left, I was tailed. Our men intercepted the tail and we suspect them as being part of the terrorist group known as Aali Imaam."

What is he saying? That terrorists want me? Why would they want *me*? How do they even know me?

"Wait a minute. You're talking about the same terrorists that destroyed the World Trade Center? Why do they want me?"

"That's what we want to know ... what we keep asking ourselves. They're tailing you for a reason. Either you know them or you have something they want. They've taken out your boyfriend and now your house in San Angelo has been worked over. What are they after? My FBI buddies are over your shit and ready to hand you to the CIA or Homeland Security and let them fight over you because this is out of their jurisdiction and frankly, it's out of mine, too. So Gemini, I'm at the end of my rope here trying to figure out your game. Are you ready to go to Langley or Colorado Springs? Because that's where you're gonna end up if you don't start giving me answers. What's it gonna be? Are you gonna dig up something for me? Or are you just gonna lie here and keep on whining about your dead boyfriend and your fucking headaches?"

He's successfully scared the crap out of me. Even though my head throbs, I sit up.

"Go to hell!" How dare he make light of what happened to Nick and how can he be so unfeeling about it and my headaches? But then, what if he's right and those guys want me dead? For the first time, I take a long look at Drexel. I should be frightened of him, but I'm not. Drexel Wolfe is hard. Everything about him screams it. His clipped, precise actions tell me he doesn't mess around with crap or take it from anyone. He's tall, muscular, and looks as though he could kick serious ass. But he hasn't laid a finger on me since I've been here. So I start to vomit information.

"My mom was very overprotective. To the point of

ridiculous. I always wanted to do everything the other kids did, like go to camp, stuff like that. But I never got to go. She was worried I'd get hurt. Or so she said. Maybe she knew something. Or maybe it's my dad. But I'm screwed all the way to Sunday on that. I don't even know his name."

He thrums his fingers on the table. "Did your mom have any friends?"

"None that I know of. She never hung around other women."

He mumbles something.

"What did you say?" I ask.

Shaking his head, he says, "She's the typical profile of someone in the WPP."

"What's that?"

"Witness Protection Program. Changed ID, no friends, stays clear of everything. Maintains a low profile and completely flies under the radar. That's your mom."

What the hell is he talking about? That idea is so preposterous. I'd be more inclined to believe him if he told me she was the Tooth Fairy. "No. My mom wouldn't be anything like that."

"We're going to San Angelo." Just like that, he drops the bomb. He moves about the room, throwing things in a duffle.

"What do you mean?"

He turns and his eyes drill into mine. "How can I be any plainer? I need to check out your house. We need to go in the dead of night. When no one would suspect or see us."

He taps his phone and a few minutes later, he's chatting with someone named Huff.

"I need the Lady Belle in San Angelo." Silence. "How long?" Silence. "Huff, that won't work." Silence, except for the drumming of his fingers on the table. Then his hand plows through his dark brown hair. If he's not careful, he's going to yank it out by the roots. "Can't do that. I don't want any rental records." Now he stands and paces. "Then do that. Two stops should do you. You're about a thousand plus miles away. Flight time of maybe six and a half hours. Bring someone. Your choice. You'll need help. And then you'll have to catch a flight home, unless you want to hang with me. Get there as soon as you can. We'll be heading out shortly and I'll be in touch in case we need an extraction somewhere else. Thanks, man."

"What's the Lady Belle?" I have a strong feeling I'm not going to like this.

"It's a helicopter."

"And why would you need that?"

"For a getaway. Do you not get what I'm telling you? Terrorists want you. I'm pretty fucking sure they want to take you or possibly even kill you. And they don't play nice. Now get your stuff, because we're heading to San Angelo."

"I don't have any stuff, remember?"

"Right. Hang tight for a minute. I need to talk with the team leader. I'll be back in a moment." He leaves and I think about everything. And then my mom's words crash into me again. I don't know him from the man on the moon. For all I know, *he* could be the terrorist, acting like the agent. I haven't seen this team leader or anyone else. And he expects me to trust him. The only thing I trust right now are my mom's words and myself. I decide it's time for Gemini to skedaddle.

I quickly search for my apartment key and find it on the bathroom counter, along with my medicine. I grab them and anything else I think will help. I spy my wallet with credit cards and ID, my cell phone, and a bit of cash. I snag those too. Then I bust through the door and hit the hall at the closest I can get to a sprint.

The elevator isn't my best option, so I head for the stairs and trip down them as fast as my Lortab-addled legs will carry me. My chest burns as my heart pounds. It's obvious my lack of exercise coupled with my excessive reliance on drugs these last few months have taken their toll.

At last the end is in sight. When I shove the first floor door open, I run right into the concrete wall of Drexel.

"Going somewhere?"

My lungs are in such need of oxygen, I can't answer. And this is from running *down* the stairs. So what does the bastard do? He spins me around and marches me right back up all those damn steps. After about three flights, he gives up and throws me over his shoulder like a sack of potatoes. He must be in damn great shape because he runs the remaining stairs in twos. I'm breathing hard just watching.

We get back to his room and he slings me across the bed. He's pissed. He paces in front of the bed, fists clenched, and it's like he's at war with himself.

His breathing slows. That's when he rips into me.

"What the fuck are you doing? I'm risking *my* ass, trying to save *yours*, and you take off on me? What the hell do you call that? Huh? Tell me something, Gemini, because I'm about to blow a damn gasket here."

My eyes dart between him and the door and he sees it. "Oh, so that's how it is? Do you even know what those motherfuckers will do to you if they catch you? Do you even know how they will torture you to get answers? Answers you claim not to have? At least if you had some, they'd get what they wanted and would shoot you. But not this way. They'll keep you alive, just to try again and again. You say you wanna die? Believe me, this is not the way to go. And trust me on this. I've experienced it firsthand, Gemini. It's beyond your worst nightmare."

"How do I know I can trust you?" My body shakes with fear.

He laughs and it's ugly sounding. "The way I see it, you don't have a goddamn choice."

Chapter 7

DREXEL
Alone

THE DUMBASS TRIED to leave. After everything I've just explained to her, she walks. Well, runs is more like it. And she says she wonders if I'm the terrorist. I throw all my IDs on the bed and tell her to inspect them closely.

"None of them are fake." I call Colt. "Can you come here for a sec? I have a situation."

"On my way," Colt says.

Gemini is still lying on the bed watching me when Colt knocks on the door. I let him in and introduce him to Gemini.

"Will you verify what's been going on here? She's having some trust issues and we need to get the hell out of here. We're losing precious time."

Colt pulls out his FBI ID and hands it to her. Then he tells her who I am. After she thoroughly checks it over, she nods and thanks him.

"Satisfied now?" I can barely control my snide attitude. The whole thing is ridiculous. I'm trying to save her ass and she's acting like I'm the perp.

"Yes, thank you," she says. Colt nods and before he leaves, I ask him how the other two men are working out. He assures me all is well and wishes me luck on this jigsaw puzzle I'm trying to piece together.

Then I turn and give Gemini the most brutal look I can muster. I've interrogated all sorts of nasty guys for years and can make even the most seasoned criminal cringe. She takes it without flinching. Begrudgingly, I admit to myself, I'm impressed. She's shown a lot of moxie, especially considering her condition.

"Let's go."

We head down to the parking garage below the hotel. As soon as we turn the corner to go to the car, she makes another break. This time I let her go. It's her life and she can do what she wants with it. Who am I to stop her?

My mind screams at me to follow her. She won't last ten minutes with those guys. But damn it, I can't keep trying to convince her if she doesn't want my help. And I don't need this complication. I head back upstairs and as I unlock the door to the room she's been in, I begin to think about her out there alone. She's not thinking clearly and she's been through a lot these past two days. Suddenly, I find myself turning around and breaking into a run for my car.

When I get back to the parking garage, I have a fucking mental debate on the merits of saving her ass. Why the hell should I care? Because she doesn't know what she's getting herself into, that's why. What if she really is one of them? Come on, you fucktard, you know damn well by the looks on her face she isn't. And that face of hers ... those damn eyes, and that mouth. If I never see them again, I know they'll haunt me forever, not knowing what happened to her. Mother-fuckery.

Inside my SUV, my hands slam against the steering wheel.

Now I have to figure out where she went. I hope to hell she doesn't try to use a credit card because that will bring everybody and their brother down on her. My best guess on finding her is either the Dirty Sixth or her apartment. I pray she didn't choose her apartment. It's dusk now, so I drive the route and keep checking for her. No luck. When I get close to the club area, I park and wait for it to get dark. It's much better for me to work at night, unnoticed. The moment that happens, I start to hoof it toward her apartment. My heart pounds in fear—I'm afraid something has happened to her and I'm surprised that I even care. Now I'm questioning my judgment on being out here alone, looking for her.

I cut through backstreets and yards of nearby homes. When I arrive at her building, I find a strategic place where I can watch for a few moments. It's not long before I see movement in her window. Damn it! I check the status of the street and notice that the tails are gone, but that means nothing. Others were most likely assigned and are now inside, holding her hostage. A head count is what I really need to see how I can outmaneuver them.

There are two ways in and out of her place—the front door and a sliding glass door on a small balcony off her bedroom. I decide to get on the roof and drop down onto the balcony. I'm pretty much naked out here without backup. I'm not wearing any Kevlar and this is probably the stupidest thing I've ever done. There's not enough time for me to make a call to Colt and wait on him to send anyone, so I move on ahead.

I kick myself for being so unprepared, but I check my firearms and my two knives. I'll head for the tree on the left side of her building. It'll give me good access to the roof. Once I'm up there, I'm careful to tread lightly. One can never tell how sturdy the roofs are in these places and I don't want to trigger an alarm of any kind. It doesn't take long before I'm in position to drop onto her balcony. I need to make sure I'm as quiet as possible.

When I drop down, I crouch. I want to remain unseen by anyone inside this apartment, plus I don't want to raise alarms for any passersby. I peek in her slider and don't see or hear a thing. When I try the door, it's locked. Picking the lock is child's play and when I hear that click, I let myself in. That's when I hear their voices—they're speaking Pashto, a prominent language of Afghanistan.

Then one of them says to her in English, "Tell me what you know."

"I don't know anything," she says. I hear a crack and she cries out. They hit her. The slimy fucking bastard just smacked her. My blood boils. That's my signal to move. I'm fluent in Pashto so I know they plan to get her out of Austin. They're only waiting for instructions. There are three distinct voices so taking them down shouldn't be a problem, depending on how effective they are at fighting. In my experience, they're better with weapons than hand-to-hand combat.

They talk about their leader and what he wants—it's some kind of list. One among them argues with the other. One wants to use harsher means with Gemini, but the other is afraid because their leader wants her alive.

"If you do not tell us what you know, you will not live to see another sunrise," one says.

"Fine. Kill me. I don't care."

That comment sets off a huge argument, which gives me my break to get in there.

I speak to them in Pashto. "Good evening, gentlemen. Nice of you to drop by and pay us a visit. Unfortunately, the next time, you need to wait until you're invited." And then I break loose. It doesn't take long for me to disable them, and I take great pleasure in it. Two are unconscious, but I leave the third awake so I can have a little chat with him.

In his native tongue, I ask, "Who is your leader?"

"I don't know what you mean."

"Oh, come. You know very well what I mean. Tell me everything you know and this will go a lot easier on you. You know, no waterboarding at a black site ... that kind of thing."

"Your government does not allow that anymore."

"Wanna bet? Don't answer the question and you'll have a chance to find out." I pick up my phone and dial Colt. I speak to him in Pashto so our new friend understands he's in big trouble. "Hey, buddy, I have a group from Aali Imaam over at Gemini's right now. Come on down and make your big arrest."

"We were only told to get the girl. I don't know anything else," the terrorist whines.

"Right. Well, maybe you'll remember this ... never, ever hit a woman, fuckface." I plow my fist into his nose, grab Gemini, and get the hell out of there. I don't want her anywhere near this joint when the feds show up.

She's over my shoulder, again, as I run through yards and alleys until I get to my car and toss her inside. This is looking more and more like it's becoming a routine with her.

I don't stop for anything until we're on the highway. After a few minutes, I spot a place where I can pull over.

Reaching across the console, my hand curls around the neckline of her shirt and I pull her close to my face, nose to nose. I'm so furious with her, I grit my teeth and say, "Do you think this is all for shits and giggles? Because let me be very clear. It's not. They play for fucking keeps. But mostly they kill. Without im-fucking-punity. What about 'they're after you' did you not understand? Because I'm about done with your shit. I'm asking myself right now, why the hell I even care. But then I *knew* you'd be in trouble. I just *knew* it. And I knew they'd take you. My fucking conscience wouldn't let that sit with me. So now you're risking *my* life too. And I don't have time for this shit. Are we clear?" I release her shirt and push her away.

"Yes. All clear. I'm sorry. I don't know what I was thinking. That you were lying to me, I guess. Why else did you handcuff me?"

It takes several deep breaths for me to calm down. "When someone's name is associated with the most lethal group of terrorists in the world, that's how we operate. That's what I was trained to do. Does 9/11 ring even the tiniest bell with you? I'm sorry if you didn't like my methods, but until we confirmed you were who you said you were, we had to assume you were one of them. Got that?"

"Yes, sir." Her voice is laced with sarcasm.

She has the damn audacity to smart off to me. I feel myself turning into a raging maniac. "Don't you *dare* be a fucking asshat. Not after what I just went through to get your ass out of there." I rifle through the center console and toss her tissues for her bloodied nose. "Here." Then I throw her a baseball cap. "Put this on. Pull it down low over your eyes. And try to get your hair up in a bun or something. Your damn hair and eyes attract way too much fucking attention. We may have to shave it or cut and bleach it blond." That's the last thing I want her to do. A bleached blond only draws more attention, but I want to shock her. I know it's harsh, but I'm trying to pay her back. It doesn't work.

"Can you pull this duct tape off my wrists?"

"Not until I know you'll behave." That elicits a good loud huff.

"You didn't tell me you spoke Arabic," she says.

"Oh, and I'm supposed to tell you everything about me? That's not how this works. And it wasn't Arabic. It was Pashto, the native language of the Afghanis. They also speak Dari or Farsi and I'm fluent in those as well. I speak Arabic too."

"Whoa. Where did you learn all that?"

I glance at her for a second and find her staring at me. "I was in the Special Forces, stationed in the Middle East. Give me your hands." I jerk the tape off her wrists. She bends down and pulls the stuff off her ankles.

"You have any scissors in here? And more tissues?"

"I think there might be some in the console. Should be more tissues in there too. And don't try to stab me with the scissors." I point to the storage console between us. She finds the tissues and wipes her nose. It's still bleeding from their blows.

"Funny."

"Funny is the last damn thing I'm trying to be, after all the shit you've pulled. How can I trust you now?"

"Oh, that's a good one, coming from someone who's held me captive for the last two days."

"I only did what I had to in order to figure you out. And I still haven't got that part done. You're a real fucking mystery."

She shrugs. "Well, we're even then, because so are you. And you expect me to trust you when there are men out there who maybe want to kill me."

It's hard to argue with that. "Is your nose broken?" She's still holding a tissue against it.

"I don't know. It hurts a little."

Suddenly, she pulls her hair in front of her and cuts a chunk off.

"What the fuck are you doing?" I'm shocked.

"You said to cut my hair, so I'm following orders."

Jesus Christ! "But you can't even see in here."

"I can see well enough. Besides, what does it matter?"

Oh God. Her hair is magnificent and I don't want her to cut any more off.

"Stop! Don't cut any more. If it's too short, you can't change your appearance like you can when it's long." She's hacked off about four inches.

She gives me an odd look and nods. "I'm sure it's all crooked now."

"We can even it up later." She is so nonchalant about the

whole thing, I can't help but ask. "Why the hell did you go and do that?"

She huffs, "Because you said ..."

"I know what I said, but most women would balk at the mere suggestion of cutting their hair and here you go, chopping it off without a clue as to what it'll look like."

She blows out her breath and is back to massaging her head. "You're going to have to stop talking out of both sides of your mouth."

That comment grabs my full attention and then she screams, "Watch out!" I've let my attention wander away from the road.

"Fuck!" I slam on the brakes. She's addled me. I need to get a damn grip here. Now I'm rubbing *my* temples.

"You need to pay attention to your driving." Her admonishment almost makes me laugh. A smile tugs the corner of my mouth.

"You need to quit distracting me!"

Her gasp makes my smile widen a bit more. "What's that supposed to mean?"

"Exactly what it was intended to. And I'm not talking out of both sides of my mouth."

"Yes, you are."

"No, I'm not. I was just trying to piss you off."

Out of the corner of my eye, I see her mouth open and close several times.

"Why would you do that?" she finally asks. She dabs at her nose again.

"Why the hell do you think?"

"You're not one of those people who has to get even all the time, are you? Or has to one-up the other person? I hate those kinds of people."

Damn! She has me figured out. "I'm sorry for being an ass. I *was* retaliating and that was wrong. The comment about cutting your hair was intended to rile you up. I never thought you'd actually do it."

Her eyes bore into me. Not the most comfortable feeling in the world. It's a good thing I'm driving as it gives me an excuse not to have to look at her. I feel guilty as hell, like I just broke my mom's favorite lamp. How does she do this to me?

Then I'm surprised to hear her say, "I'm sorry too. For running. That was really stupid. I freaked out. It won't happen again. And thanks for saving me from those guys. You've done way more than you should already, so I owe you. I can pay you and I will. We can go to a bank and I'll withdraw however much money you need. I have money, so that's not a problem."

My head snaps up. "Okay, now that's something you should've told me about. Where did all this money come from? And, by the way, you don't have any money for the time being. If you make any transactions, it'll trigger the watch they have on you. Gemini, you're being tracked. You can't use any of those things right now. Clear?"

She nods.

"So, tell me about the money. Where did it come from?"

"I don't know. Here's the weird thing. I grew up in a small house and my whole life, we lived very frugally. I always thought we were poor. When my mom died, this attorney contacts me and unloads her will on me. He informs me how much money is in her estate and it's millions. Honestly, I can't tell you off the top of my head where all the accounts are. I keep everything in a safe deposit box. And this broker handles the investments and stuff. But yeah, I never would've known the way I grew up."

My wheels are spinning. Now I'm wondering if her mom had ties to the underworld or maybe a drug cartel. "Did your mom ever have clandestine meetings with anyone?"

"None that I'm aware of."

"Any strange people ever show up at your house? Were there

any times where she would send you to your room to get you away from any strangers?"

"No! I promise I would remember that. We talked about her not having boyfriends. I used to tell her I wanted her to find a daddy for me. And her face would always look so sad that I stopped saying those kinds of things. My mom was beautiful. Even when most kids thought their parents were nerds, I never did. My mom was the most beautiful woman I'd ever seen. And the older I got, I always wondered why she never dated. She kept to herself. You'll see when we get to the house. I have lots of pictures of her."

Nodding, I say, "This sounds more like she was in the Witness Protection Program, then. Keeping to herself. Was she suspicious of anyone?"

"Maybe. I just always thought she was too protective. But thinking back, she could've been suspicious."

"Think about things she told you. Clues to what she might've been hiding."

After a few quiet moments, Gemini says, "I don't think there's anything. I'll keep thinking, but the only things she would tell me were to be very wary of men."

"Bingo. Go on."

"Just things like not to trust any men. That they were only after one thing. I just thought she was talking about sex."

"Anything else?"

"Yeah. She told me to keep to crowds. And never walk alone. Like I said, I just thought it was basic safety stuff that all moms told their daughters."

"Makes sense."

"Once, when I was pretty young, I came home from school with one of those beanie dolls. They were the thing back then. She went psycho on me ... kept wanting to know where I got it. It was some kid's birthday and she gave all the girls one and the boys got something else. Anyway, my mom went bat-shit crazy on me and I remember crying. She scared me so much."

"Okay, that's completely irrational behavior. She had some deep secret she was hiding and we need to get to the bottom of it. Can you think of anywhere she would hide something? Did your mom work?"

She's rubbing her hands together now, as if cold. Without thinking, I put my hand over hers, and what feels like electricity shoots up my arm. What the hell was that? Her movements still, and then she surprises me by latching onto my hand.

"I'm really scared, Drexel."

Her voice is so soft. I give her hand an encouraging squeeze and say, "Don't be. I've been in way worse shit than this."

"Tell me?"

Great. I fucking opened the door on this one. This isn't something I want or need to discuss. It's nothing but bitter memories all the way around, but I have to tell her something to ease her mind.

"I told you I was in the Special Forces. Afghanistan. Iraq. We were sent in to do a lot of dirty work. Infiltrate terror cells. Find and destroy them after we got what we needed. They operate like well-oiled machines, with far-reaching tentacles. We would gather intel in ways you don't want to know about. Once, we were hiking out of a zone that we'd been watching for weeks. We found ourselves outnumbered and surrounded. Bastards are deceptive. They act like farmers, moving from one village to the next, but beneath their tattered clothing, they're armed to the teeth. Sometimes strapped with explosives. It's hard to see because they wear *payraan tumbaan*, loose-fitting pants and tunics, so they can hide just about anything underneath. You can't trust anything you see out there and your nerves are constantly on edge. Luck was on our side that day when another team came to our rescue. They were in range when they got our call. Otherwise, I wouldn't be here today."

"How long were you there?"

"Too long and not long enough."

"I don't understand."

"I know. You can't." I won't say anymore because there's just too damned much.

"Were you ever scared?"

"Every day. But you learn to live with it. You learn to control it. If you don't, it controls you and you die." Her hand squeezes mine, as if to offer a bit of comfort. Oddly, it does.

"I guess I need to grow some nads, then, huh?"

The humor in her question hits me and I laugh. "Yeah. I guess we all do."

"Oh, I'd say you already have some."

Hmm. I'm not sure how to take that comment. It falls somewhere between her thinking I'm tough or I'm hot. Or maybe I'm overthinking things ... or imagining what I want her to think. She's certainly gotten under my skin. Or maybe I should say she's gotten to my dick, because that's a damn fact. That's unusual because even though I can be a softie when it comes to helping people, getting involved with the opposite sex is *not* something I *ever* do on the job.

But when I look at her, it's not just my dick that reacts. My whole body wants her. On me, around me, I want her every-fucking-where. She's unlike anything I could conjure in my wildest fantasies. But she's a total fucked-up piece of work. And that's the last thing I need. And Aali Imaam is after her. Doesn't that make for the perfect girlfriend? What the hell am I thinking? Girlfriend? Where the hell did that come from?

"Is everything okay over there?" she asks.

"Yeah, why?"

"Because you're squeezing the crap out of my hand."

"Shit. Sorry." I let go.

"That's not what I wanted. I just wanted you to ease up a bit. I like it when you hold my hand."

"Well, don't get too used to it. We have a job to do." That was harsh. I rub my face and try to figure out what the hell I'm doing here.

"Okay. It was just ..." She stops.

"What?"

"Nothing."

We're both quiet for a while. I look over and she has her head back, eyes closed. Maybe she's sleeping. She'll need it. We have a long night ahead of us.

WE PULL INTO San Angelo around nine o'clock. She directs me to her house. It's a small bungalow in a quiet neighborhood. Since I want to make sure there aren't any people watching, I drive around the block. She's hunched down on the floor so no one can see her. There aren't any other cars on the street, but I won't take chances.

"Give me the neighborhood layout. Are there any alleys?"

"No. There's a street behind ours and then a school. There's a park two blocks to the east and a church two blocks to the west."

"Is your backyard fenced in?"

"No."

"What about your neighbors' yards?"

"They weren't when I lived here, but they might be now."

"Let's find a place with Wi-Fi and check out Google Earth. It's updated fairly frequently but may not give us the most recent images. We can look and see anyway. It's the best we have right now. I should've called my office. I'm usually much better than this." Jesus, if I keep fucking up, I'm going to end up losing everything, including her.

It doesn't take long to locate a coffee shop and luckily, none of her neighbors have fences, so that cements my plans.

"We'll park in the church lot. Then we'll go in on foot and enter through the back. Have you ever worn night-vision goggles?" I ask.

"Sure. I wear them all the time."

"Okay, smart-ass."

"Seriously? Drexel, where in the world would I wear night-vision goggles?"

"I don't know. Hunting?"

She shakes her head. "Yeah, my mom and I used to hunt big game in our backyard when I was a kid. Lions and tigers. Once I even shot a wildebeest."

"Okay, enough. You'll be wearing them tonight. No lights allowed. Got that?"

"Yes, SIR!"

"Cut the crap, Gemini."

"I'm not your subordinate."

"You are tonight. You'll do as I say. Understand?" She salutes me. I say, "You're not doing it correctly."

"God, you're such a douche."

Then I laugh. Really hard. Soon after, she joins in. She has such a beautiful smile and I want to get lost in it. Well, that and in her pants. But I know we have to get this job done.

Her next question throws me for a loop. "Do you do that thing with your eyes on purpose?"

"What thing?" I'm puzzled.

"The way you look at me with your eyes half closed."

"I don't know what you mean." I honestly haven't the slightest idea.

Her cheeks pink. They look amazing. It's the first time I've seen any color in them. She bows her head so I prod her. "Tell me, Gemini."

Her voice is a whisper. "Your eyes. Sometimes when you look

at me. They're ... um ... well, they're sexy."

She takes me by surprise and I don't know what to say.

"I guess I shouldn't have said that."

Her voice pulls me out of my stupidity. "No, I'm flattered." There are all sorts of things I'd like to say to her, but this isn't the time for this conversation. Maybe later. "Shall we?" I ask as I extend my hand.

We drive to the church and park in the most obscure spot we can find. Then I put on my backpack, loaded with my necessary gear. I also hand her a set of night-vision goggles, help her into them, and give her a quick course on how they work. After I put mine on, we set off on foot, through the neighborhood. "Remember, once inside, no talking. Only write on the pad I gave you. The house may be bugged. Look for what's not obvious ... and grab whatever you think may help us. It can be even the smallest thing. If you think it's important, take it. Anything that will give us clues to what your mom may have been involved in. And if you have any letters she wrote you, I want you to grab those too."

"Got it."

The yard is overgrown and the back door is boarded shut. We'll have to get inside another way, a window perhaps. Careful not to make any noise, I check all the windows in the back. I eventually locate one that isn't locked. The window is broken so it's easy to open. After I push her through, I go in behind.

The place is a mess. Drawers emptied, pictures torn off the wall, cushions slashed, closets emptied. It's been destroyed.

I motion to her to come toward me. Then I write to her, "Grab everything." She nods in understanding.

Gemini walks off to another room so I tag along. She enters what I presume to be her bedroom and goes to the closet where she pulls out a shoebox. I empty the contents into my backpack.

The answers are in this house. I know they are. My gut shouts at me. Think, Drex. Where would you hide something this important?

I quickly scan the floor. It's carpeted. I pull a utility knife from my backpack and slice into the carpeting. Gemini looks at me and I shake my head. What I need to know is what's beneath this carpet. When I lift it up, I find old linoleum. So I move to the next room. I find the same thing in all the rooms.

Grabbing my notepad, I write, "Attic?"

She leads me to a door with a narrow set of stairs. I head up and find myself in the attic. There's no way her mother would leave anything important out in the open. If she were indeed in the Witness Protection Program, she would've hidden this type of information safely away. I head to the rafters to check if there are any enclosed spaces up here. Nothing.

Once I'm back downstairs, I check the closets, looking for false walls, but I come up with nothing again. Frustration mounts. There's a fireplace in the living room. I write another note. "Ever use this?"

Gemini nods yes. That blows that possibility.

"Basement?" I write.

I follow her down some steps. The room's been redone, which mean here's my best chance. The first place I check is the walls. All the pictures have been pulled off so I don't have to bother with that. The more I think about it, the more I realize that it will be somewhere so obscure that I may have to settle for the fact that we won't find it.

I write Gemini another note. "Any walls patched?"

She smiles and motions for me to follow her. We get to the laundry room and she points to a wall covered with shelves.

I help her remove the shelves. Behind them is a two-by-two-foot square in the sheetrock that doesn't quite match the rest of the wall. But it extends to the floor where the molding doesn't match, either. I dig in my pack and find my multi-purpose tool. I pry the wood away from the wall and behind it is a space devoid of sheetrock. Instead I find a metal box wedged inside. I pull it out and motion to Gemini to head for the stairs. We need to get out of here.

We head in the direction of the church, but my instincts proved correct. I hear cars on the street of the otherwise quiet neighborhood.

"Run, and keep to the shadows. Follow me." She has trouble keeping up so I do the usual and toss her over my shoulder. Yep, this is getting old.

We make it back to the car, and I don't waste any time getting us away from there. Something tipped them off and I'm sure it was the noise of us ripping the molding off the wall. We have a couple of hours before the Lady Belle arrives, so I head out of town to our designated meeting point.

"You know, you're going to have to get in better shape," I tell her.

She inhales and it sounds like she's just sucked all the oxygen out of the car. "You can kiss my ass. I used to be in great shape until these skull-smashers ruined my life, so before you make any more comments about the crappy shape I'm in, you can shove them all right the hell up your tight ass."

"Well, I guess you told me, didn't you?"

"Yeah. So why don't you shut up for a change?"

"A bit touchy, aren't you?"

I see it coming at me, but I don't expect the strength behind it. She nails me with a good old-fashioned punch, connecting with my right deltoid. She has a knuckle popped out so it digs into my muscle. Stings a bit.

"Damn, girl. That hurt."

"Good. Now stop saying such stupid things. I don't do well with stupid."

Rubbing my arm, I say, "Duly noted."

"Where are we going?"

I want to laugh, but I know it'll piss her off. "To a friend's. He lives about twenty miles out of town. That's where the Lady Belle will pick us up."

I grab the phone and call Jeff Stone. It rings a couple of times before he answers.

"So what's your ETA?" he says in his Texan drawl, and then laughs.

"Just leaving San Angelo now," I explain and tell him we're closing in on his place.

"Just ring me when you're a couple of minutes out and I'll open the gate," Jeff says.

"Thanks, man."

"Do you know everyone?" Gemini asks.

Shaking my head, I say, "No, but when you're in the military, you get connected."

"I'll say. Do you think those guys were the terrorists?"

"Either that or CIA."

"Why do you think the CIA wants me?"

"Because the terrorists do. They think you know something if the terrorists want you. Besides, now that we have this box, there may be something in here that they really do want."

She shifts in her seat and looks at me. "Why all of a sudden? Why not try to get me before now?"

I pause to think for a minute and then it hits me. "Your accident. You said you were missing for a couple of days, right?"

"Well, yeah."

"Did your boyfriend file a missing person's report?"

"Yeah."

"Then your picture was plastered all over the news. That's why. These people have been hunting down your mom for a long time. Let me ask you something—do you resemble her?"

"Maybe a little. She was dark haired but had intense blue

eyes. She was really pretty. I'm not even close to what she looked like. Where's that backpack? I'll show you a picture. I have tons."

"It's behind my seat, but my guess is you're a dead ringer for her. And that's how they found you."

She fumbles through the pack. When she pulls out some photos, she shows me a picture, and I take a quick look. "You're a mirror image. No wonder they're after you now."

The rest of the ride is silent. I ring Jeff when we're a few minutes out and the gates are open when we arrive. We drive down the half-mile road to his house. He's on the porch, waiting for us.

"Hey, bro. Thanks for doin' this."

"No worries." We man-hug.

"Jeff, this is Gemini." They shake hands and he invites us in. He offers us drinks but we both decline, asking only for water.

"So, what brings you out to my country? I know it must be more than an ice pack. You look like you got into a bit of a tussle."

"Long story. And yeah, she needs an ice pack."

"Dude, when have you ever had a *short* story?"

It's the damn truth. "You're right. But this one is complicated and you're way better off not knowing, if that's okay with you."

"I got you. So what time is your ride?"

I glance at my watch. "Should be here in a couple hours. Huff's supposed to call when he's an hour out. And you're sure it's okay for my helo to land here?"

"Yeah, I've got that huge open field out back."

"I remember. That's why I thought of you. Jeff, would you mind if we had a little privacy? We need to review some stuff."

"Not at all. Give me a second and I'll bring you the ice." He shows us into a small den and closes the door as he leaves. A couple minutes later, he's back with ice and is gone again.

Gemini looks at me. "Isn't that a little rude?"

"Naw, he's fine. He knows how I operate."

She shrugs and doesn't say anything. I open my backpack and pull out the locked metal box. I rifle through my pack looking for my lock-pick tool and set to work. I hand the opened box to Gemini. It did, after all, belong to her mother.

She holds onto it. Then she runs her fingers across the top and stares at it for a second. "I'm scared of what this thing holds, Drexel. What if I don't want to know what it tells me? What if I just want to be Gemini Sheridan from San Angelo and stay that way forever?"

Placing my hands on her shoulders, I say, "No matter what's in this damn box, you *are* Gemini Sheridan from San Angelo. You'll always be that girl. That's how you were raised and that's how you'll live the rest of your life. What's in that box will only tell you why evil people want to kill you. It won't change who you are in here," I point to her head, "or in here." I point to her heart.

She nods and hugs the box to her chest. "Well then, Drexel Wolfe, we might as well get this over with, huh?"

Chapter 8

GEMINI
Rachel Miller

THERE ARE MANY defining moments in one's life, but only a few that impact it so much that you'll remember them forever. This will be one of those. When I open this box, I know that if I live to be a hundred, I'll remember every single thing about this.

My hands shake as I unlatch and lift the lid. Inside are envelopes, stuffed thick with papers. Some are letters addressed to a Rachel Miller in New York City. I open them, one at a time, and as I read, I hand them over to Drexel. The chess pieces begin to move into place and I am delegated the most difficult and crucial player: the pawn.

Rachel Miller, whom I can only assume at this time is my mother, was put into the witness protection program after doing something for the CIA. The letters I'm reading have nothing to do with that, but they're letters to Rachel from her family in Connecticut. Apparently I have, or did have at one time, relatives in Connecticut. Grandparents, perhaps even aunts, uncles, and cousins living on the East Coast. They talk about her modeling career in New York and things such as that. Then there is an obituary, citing her terrible drowning on the Jersey shore. There were no witnesses and no one knows what happened, only that her body washed ashore after being reported missing for over a week. She was identified by dental records. That was the end of Rachel Miller.

I feel such a profound sense of sadness for this woman who had to give up the life she knew in order to save herself. Even her family thinks she died. But where do I play into all of this?

"Are you okay?" Drexel's voice interrupts my thoughts.

"I guess so. This is all so unreal. Why would she do all this? What did she know?"

"I'm hoping we'll find out as we dig deeper. How's your head?"

"It's good right now. I usually do pretty well at night."

"No pain meds?"

"No. I want a clear head for this."

He nods and I continue to rummage through the papers. I find an old birth certificate in the name of Rachel Marie Miller. And then I find something else deeply disturbing. I jump to my feet, dropping the metal box, spilling its contents. The piece of paper floats to the carpet in slow motion, like a feather in the wind. I stand unable to speak or move.

"What is it? What did you find?" Drexel is holding my arm, but the most he can get out of me is a shake of my head. Back and forth it moves, like a metronome. He snaps his fingers in front of my face and I see them; I'm simply too shocked to say anything. Can that possibly be me? Was that me at one point? Is that why she was no longer Rachel Miller?

Drexel looks to the floor to search for what I saw. When he spies it, he picks it up as I watch him, still in slow motion. He moves to me and his voice is stretched and garbled. Why does he sound so weird? When my legs start to crumple, my brain figures it out, but it's too late and my lights go out.

THERE'S SOMETHING NICE and cool on my head. I touch it. A bag of ice. There's a large, warm hand on mine, and my thoughts pinball until they begin to make sense.

My lids flutter open and his face comes into focus.

"Hey. You okay there?" he asks.

"I think so." I move to sit up but he gently pushes me back.

"Not so fast, Gemini. You fainted on me. Let's take it easy for a minute."

He's right, so I nod. What happened? And then it hits me. Holy shit. My real name.

"Drexel! Did you see that birth certificate?" My words are frantic.

"Yeah."

"That's me! It has to be. That's my birthdate. What was that name again?"

He hands it to me and I take a long look at it. It's from the state of New York. I was born in New York City. My real name is Amira Assaf. *Holy fuck!*

"Holy shit. My father. That's the connection. It has to be with that kind of name. Amira Assaf. But why didn't she name him on the birth certificate?"

"Maybe she didn't want him to know."

"Then why give me an Arabic name?"

"Good question. So he must've known, but didn't want to be named."

"Or maybe he thought he was."

The questions are so numerous now, I can't think straight. I take my time sitting up. "All these years you think you're this one person. And then you find out you're not who you think you are."

He doesn't speak. Is there anything he can say?

"My mom was the least likely person to be involved in something like this. She must've been a terrorist too." The thought of that makes me want to scream at her, and then cry. Why would she do such a thing?

"Maybe she just knew him and she wasn't a terrorist. You're leaping to conclusions now. Don't do that until you have all the facts."

"Maybe she was a turncoat," I say as I grab more papers. Now I find things addressed to Michelle Sheridan, and a letter entitled, "Project Gemini." Finally, my hands land on another envelope with my name written across it in my mom's handwriting. Part of me wants to rip it open right then and the other part is petrified to find what it reveals. All of my information is contained in here. The rest of the box holds nothing but meaningless papers. At the very bottom is another small envelope with my name on it. I open it; inside is a key. I want to tear my hair out.

"Gemini, that letter may tell you everything. And the other may be a key to a safe deposit box. You said you had one, right?"

"Yeah, I do."

"It could be for the same bank."

"But you said I couldn't go there without raising flags."

"True, but let's see if Colt can do anything on his end."

Drexel calls Colt and they have a conversation while my mind churns with this information about my mother. What happened to you, Mom, that you did all this? Suddenly, a thought shoots through me. My mom was smart ... smart enough to keep us alive all those years. She wouldn't have put those boxes in the same bank. No way. And besides, even if Colt helps, as soon as they access my account, the CIA will be notified.

"Drexel, no." He looks at me and I tell him to end the call. When he does, I explain all of this to him.

"We were just discussing that."

"Is Colt trustworthy?" I have to know this.

"Yeah. I can't say the same for the rest of his men, but he is."

"Can't his calls be traced?"

"What are you getting at?"

"If the CIA is looking for me, wouldn't they be tapping into his stuff?"

"He didn't tell them he had you."

"What about the other men?" I know I'm paranoid, but I can't help it. "And this Jeff guy. It all seems too easy."

Drexel looks at me squarely. "I can understand why you'd say that. And yeah, it does seem easy. But it came at a steep price a few years ago." He stops and looks like he's muddling through some things in his mind. He finally says, "Jeff, Colt and I served together on a task force in the Middle East. I trust them with my life. Therefore, you can trust them as well. Do you follow me here?"

"Yeah, I do." If it was good enough for him, it was good enough for me.

"So, now we're back to square one in trying to figure out what this key unlocks. Did your mom have any favorite places she liked to visit? Vacation spots? Things of that nature?"

"Yeah, we'd go to Panama City, Florida, a lot. She always wanted to be where there were crowds."

"Anything closer?"

"San Antonio and Austin. She loved the River Walk in San Antonio. Even though it was touristy, she liked that kind of thing. I used to think she was nuts, but now I guess she felt like she could melt into the crowds and feel safe. She also liked going to the zoo in Austin. And UT football games."

"All big, crowded events. Try to think if she would've left you clues anywhere too. Was there anywhere in particular you would stop when you'd visit those places?"

I scoot my butt to the edge of the sofa and drop my head into my hands. He's there, right in front of me, asking me if I'm okay.

"That's a question I'm not sure I can answer."

"I meant physically."

"I'm sick, Drex."

He gives me a lopsided smile.

"What?"

"Only my close friends call me that."

"Sorry. I ran out of energy to say your whole name."

"I wasn't chastising you. I was letting you know it's okay for you to call me that."

"I'm afraid to read that letter. I don't know if I want to know what it says."

He takes my hands and says, "I can read it for you. And then if it's bad, I'll let you know. You need to know what's in it, Gemini."

He's right. Why does he always have to be right? "You would do that for me?"

"Yeah. Finding out what's in there is paramount to your safety."

I fumble through the pile of papers and hand him the letter. He gently opens the envelope and I watch his face as he reads it. He gives nothing away. Then he lifts his head and asks, "Are you ready?"

"You tell me because I don't know." My hands are clenched together and he pries them apart.

"Gemini, knowledge is your best defense. One thing is clear. Your mother loved you more than anything."

"Read it to me," I say.

My dear sweet Gemini,

If you're reading this, it means I'm no longer living and for that I can only say I'm sorry because there are so many things I wanted to tell you myself. You were so young and there was so much to say. I had intended to tell you everything when you turned twenty-one. But since that day never came for me, I wrote it all down here so you would learn the truth from me, and not the lies that I'm sure others are trying to convince you are true.

Let me start at the beginning. By now you've learned a few things about yourself, namely that your birth name is Amira Assaf. When I was eighteen, I moved to New York City to pursue a career in modeling. It wasn't as easy as I was led to believe. The money wasn't there so I was forced to earn it through other means. I know you will think terrible things of me, and I suppose I don't blame you, but I did what I had to do to survive. Perhaps I should hang my head in shame, but I won't. I'm not proud of what I did, but the past is the past, and it cannot be changed.

Through my modeling, I was introduced to a man who told me he would see that I would be given a means to earn a lot of money. He became my pimp, if you will, and I became a high-paid call girl. That's how I met your father, Hakeem Assaf. Hakeem was a Middle Eastern oil tycoon who spent a great deal of time in New York. After seeing him for several months, he asked that I give up my life as a call girl and become his mistress. I agreed because I was in love with him. He set me up in a lavish apartment and I lived a grand lifestyle. He treated me with the greatest respect and kindness and showered me with gifts.

Then one day, to my surprise, I learned I was pregnant with you. At first I feared telling Hakeem because I knew he and I could never be married. But I knew I had no choice. When I finally told him the truth, he was ecstatic. I'd never seen him so filled with joy.

The day you came into this world was the happiest day of my life. Hakeem chose your name because Amira means princess, and he said you would always be his darling princess. He was the most attentive father I've ever seen and when he held you, he was filled with so much love for you. You look a lot like him, though he said you are exactly like me. You have his eyes. As you grew older, I would see so much of him in you.

When you were two years old, we were in the park one sunny afternoon when a woman struck up a conversation. She told me what a beautiful child you were. After she left, I noticed a note in your stroller. It said there were people who had information about Hakeem and asked me to meet them at a coffee shop.

I was confused, but curious at the same time. I knew the coffee shop and deemed it to be safe, so I went. Sitting at a booth were two men in dark suits. They saw me enter and asked me to take a seat. What they told me turned my world upside down.

They said Hakeem was funneling his money into a large terrorist organization ... one that had been responsible for a recent bombing at the World Trade Center. It was the one in 1993. At first I refused to believe them. I ran out in tears. But the CIA pursued me, feeding me more and more information until I couldn't deny it anymore. The man I'd loved for more than four years was a killer.

The CIA told me I couldn't leave him. I knew they were right. He would never let me leave because I had you. They said they could help. All I had to do was get them information. A list of contacts. So I did. The CIA taught me how to find what I was looking for. I even transferred his financial records.

But one day I found a file. I copied it and then deleted it off his computer. Even the CIA didn't know I did that. Maybe I was wrong to do it, I don't know, but I wanted some kind of insurance for you. They promised me protection in the witness protection program, but I wanted more than that. I wanted something for the future in case anything ever came up.

They held up their end by faking my death, changing our names, and relocating us to Texas. And so we began a new life. Now you know why I was so overprotective of everything you did. I was frightened to death that one day Hakeem's associates would find us and kill me or even you. They took your father into custody and as far as I know, he remains in prison somewhere. I asked not to be told, because the truth is that even though he did terrible things, I still loved him. And I hated myself for what I'd done. I know it was the right thing to do, but I wish I could've talked to him about it and asked him why he killed so many innocent people.

There were so many days I simply went through the motions, but the only thing that made it worthwhile was you. I would gaze at you while you slept and know that I did the right thing. Deep in my heart, I knew there were children whose parents I might have saved, simply by removing Hakeem's money from the hands of the terrorists.

If you're wondering about the money left to you upon my death, it came from Hakeem and his oil funds. He set that money up for you when you were born; the CIA and I prearranged that it be transferred to you when you turned eighteen or upon my death. It was not dirty money.

I am so sorry that everything I've left for you has been so secretive, but it's all for good reason. There is a very important file that you must find Gemini. It contains information that I won't disclose in this letter, but trust no one. This is very important. Your life may be in danger over this. I've gone to great lengths to make it difficult to find, but when you do, I hope you understand everything.

In closing, you will make up your own mind in the end about the choices I made in life. I understand that. But remember one thing: I loved you with everything I had in me, Gemini.

With undying love,
Mom

By the time he finishes reading, I'm weeping. Her life was filled with such profound sadness it's hard for me to believe I never suspected it. Drex kneels in front of me and hands me a tissue to wipe my tears away.

"Her life was so sad."

"No, it wasn't. You filled it with great joy."

Shaking my head, I say, "Not really. She sacrificed her happiness."

"Maybe so. But you would do the same. If you found out someone you loved were a terrorist, you wouldn't want hundreds to die because of that person. She knew that she did the right thing. The sad part is that she was killed before she could tell you face to face. She deserved to have at least that much."

"It all makes sense now. She always told me I would know when I met the man I loved because love would rule all. She must've loved him a great deal."

My heart is so tangled up over this letter, I can't decide if I'm relieved he read it. The truth has now been revealed and I'm no longer in the dark about who my father was.

"Do you think he's still alive?" I ask.

"Who? Your father?"

"Yeah."

"We can check."

"And I guess the other thing we're searching for now is the file she took off his computer that she didn't give to the CIA."

Drex is holding my hand, sliding his thumb across the top of it. It's distracting. "Yeah. I wonder what it is."

"Just another list."

"No. That's not it. It's something much greater than that."

Oh, Mom! What the hell did you do? Why didn't you just take what they told you to get and be done with it? Why did you do all this?

"What are you thinking?"

I roll my head, my muscles screaming at me. "I'm pissed off at my mom."

"For this letter?"

"Nah. For taking that extra information. If she'd left it alone, she'd probably still be alive."

"No doubt you're right." He stands and grabs my hands. "Come on, let's get out of here for a little bit."

We leave the den and Jeff is there, wanting to know if we need anything. Drex asks him if he'd mind going over the papers from the box to see if we missed anything.

"Don't mind at all."

"We're hunting for clues and I'm not saying anything else. I want you to have an open mind on this." Jeff nods. "We're going for a walk. We'll be back in about thirty."

Drex walks me through the house. We go out the back door and head down a gravel path about thirty yards. I hear water and we reach a patio area with a lit fountain. The stars are out. It's a nice quiet night.

"My head's exploding."

"You need something for pain?"

"No, I need some answers on what my mom hid."

"Listen, Gemini, there's always that chance you may never get them."

That's a discomforting thought. I can't stand it. My breath leaves me in a rush. "I'm not prepared for or willing to accept that."

"We need to straighten out your hair," he says as he grabs a handful and lets it slide through his fingers. That intimate gesture catches me off guard. I don't know what to say.

"That was random."

"It was meant as a distraction."

One thing that *is* distracting is his mouth. He has beautiful lips and when he smiles, one corner lifts slightly higher. Dark brown hair, almost black, falls across his forehead, and he wears it completely messy. It looks like he just rolled out of bed and I have an urge to slide my hands through it. He's tall, well over six feet. But he's as hard as a brick wall. When I ran into him at the hotel, he was solid muscle. I could almost count his six-pack under his shirt. But his eyes are his hottest feature. Smoke in the center but blue on the periphery. And in the middle of his iris, they merge together. I guess you might say the total package of Drexel is very distracting.

"What's going through that mind of yours, Onyx?"

"Onyx?"

"That's what I called you before I knew your name. Your eyes ... they're like onyx. Dark as night but like gemstones."

Don't ask me why I did it, but I close the distance between us and wrap my hands in his shirt. Before I take the time to think, my lips press on his. My fear that he'll push me away dissolves when he hitches me up against him and wraps one arm around my waist. The other one grabs my hair and winds it around his hand. He kisses me back. The kiss intensifies as he takes over and demands more from me with his lips and tongue. I'm butter in his hands, and I melt like I've never done before. This man knows his way around a girl's mouth. He nips at my lips, the effect of which I'm sure he can feel as my heart pounds against his chest. My hands leave his shirt and make their way to his neck, my fingers buried in his hair. I can't ever remember getting this much out of a kiss. How is this possible?

He stops but leans his forehead against mine. We're panting like two dogs in a heat wave. I want to check if my tongue is hanging out of my mouth.

"That was certainly unexpected." His voice is low and sexy.

Now I feel shy. "I ... I guess I should apologize."

"I wouldn't dare do that if I were you." Did he just scold me?

My lower lip is between my teeth, but I feel myself grin. "Okay. I won't. And I'm not the least bit sorry, either."

Now he laughs. "Good, because I'm glad you kissed me. I've wanted to kiss you since I saw you the first night in the bar."

"You have?"

"I have. I've wanted to do much more than kiss."

"Tell me."

"Dirty things. All kinds of dirty things I shouldn't be talking about."

Oh, hell! I'm grinning again and want to kiss him some more, but footsteps crunch on the gravel. We break apart just as Jeff comes into view.

"I take it you're Amira Assaf?" Jeff asks.

"Yeah," I say.

"From what I can gather, your mother entered the WPP when you were two or three years old. And you were too young to remember your life before then. This key," he holds it up, "is the real key to what you need to know. The why of it all. Whatever file she took was important enough for her to go to these extremes. She was wise not to keep whatever it unlocks in the same place as these documents. So my guess is that's it's close so she could access it whenever she needed. Maybe within a few hours, no farther."

Drex asks, "What kind of box do you think it is?"

"Not sure. It may not be a box at all. This certainly isn't a safe deposit box key or anything similar. It looks to me like an ordinary lock, maybe a padlock or ..." An odd look crosses his face and he smiles. "My best guess is that it's a key to a storage unit somewhere."

"That's it. But the million-dollar question is, where?" Drex paces. Seems when he thinks really hard, he gets energized and can't stand or sit still. "Gemini, you went to Austin and San Antonio a lot, right?"

"Yeah."

"Any other cities close to here? Think. She would've wanted

somewhere that she could've gotten to and from within a day. Maybe even while you were in school."

"No, only those two," I answer.

"Then it has to be in either of those two cities," Jeff says. "That's the most logical."

"So how do we find it?"

The men look at each other and shrug. Drex says, "It'll have to be a process of elimination. Gemini, I want you to focus on things you did in those two cities and things she would say to you."

"Okay, this is a long shot, but for whatever reason, she used to love to walk around the downtown area of Austin. Even Sixth Street. All the cafes and things. And then we'd window shop. She'd also take me down South Congress too. That's one of the reasons I moved to Austin. It brought back memories of a happier time."

Drex says, "Anything similar with San Antonio?"

"Only the River Walk area. But now that I think about it, we really went to Austin a lot more than San Antonio."

"Then that's where you need to focus first," Jeff says.

That thought worries me to no end.

"It's going to be risky," Drexel says. "That's where they're all looking for her right now. So we'll need a wig and some different clothes to disguise her."

"Can you spend the night here?"

After he takes a deep breath, Drex asks, "Is it safe to keep the helo here over night?"

"Yeah, that won't be a problem. We're twenty miles out of town. Farmers crop dust all the time. No one will think twice about that."

"What about my men? Do you mind if they stay?"

"Not at all. You know I have the two small guest houses and three bedrooms in the main house, so I have plenty of room."

"Thanks, man."

"No worries. You hungry? Can I get you some food?"

My stomach must've heard the question because it answered before I had the chance.

Jeff laughs and says, "Follow me."

We head inside and he leads us into the kitchen where he pulls out sandwich fixings from the refrigerator.

"Would you like an adult beverage. Beer, wine?"

"Please," I say.

"Help yourself to whatever you find in the fridge. And if you need anything else, just hunt it down."

Drex and I make up sandwiches and sit down at the island to eat. My last bite finished, I ask, "I could really use a shower. Do you think Jeff would mind?"

"Would I mind what?" Jeff asks as he walks back into the room.

"I need a shower and was wondering if ..."

"Right this way."

I follow him upstairs and into a bedroom where there's a light turned on. Then he shows me to the bathroom.

"This is a Jack-and-Jill bath, so Drex will be sharing it with you. His room is on the other side. Unless you want to share one. That's your business, not mine, so I'll leave it up to you. Anyway, you'll find plenty of towels in the cabinet. Help yourself to whatever you need. Make yourself at home. I don't have much as far as women's clothes go, but I'll leave a pair of sweats and a T-shirt on the bed for you."

This man is a godsend. I place my hand on his arm and thank him. "This is so kind of you. You can't know how much I appreciate this."

He nods and leaves the room as I head for the shower. My excitement soars at the thought of scrubbing off the day's grime. My muscles quickly relax under the hot water. When I'm done, Drex is standing outside the bathroom, holding sweats and a T-shirt for me.

He surprises me and I can't help the gasp that escapes.

"I didn't mean to scare you. I'm sorry. I was just going to leave these for you."

"Thank you." It's an awkward moment, one that I wish I could smooth over. Instead, I grin. What I'd really like to do is kiss him again, but I don't want to be that bold twice.

"How's your nose?" he asks.

"Good."

"Good? It looks like it's sore. You have two black eyes and bruises on your jaw from where they hit you. I wouldn't exactly call that good."

"It's way better than a migraine," I say.

His gaze scours me and my body heats. "I'd better go before I do something we'll both regret," he murmurs.

"I don't think there's anything you could do that I would regret." Where is this assertiveness coming from? I've never acted like this before.

We exchange scorching looks and I freeze as a fire sparks within. He walks up to me, puts his hands on either side of my face, and slowly kisses me. He groans into my mouth and everything that was on my mind before this fades away and is replaced by all that is Drexel.

Chapter 9

Drexel
Bad Idea

THIS IS NOT good. I know better than to start this, but something pulls at me from down deep and for once in my life, I'm not in control of my actions. Oh, I suppose I could stop. But that's the last damn thing I want to do. Her long hair is nothing but wet tangles hanging down her back. Her gorgeous black fuck-me eyes stare straight into mine and I want to tumble head first into them and never crawl out. And don't even get me started on her mouth. When her tongue flicks across her lower lip, there's no doubt I have to taste her again. Oh, fuck me now. *Please.*

She's in my arms and her mouth is on mine before I can think twice. There's no hesitation, either. It's me, her, and nothing but the skimpy scrap of cloth between us. And that's where I have to draw the line. I don't want to. God, I don't want to. I'd like nothing more than to jerk that towel away from her and see what lies beneath, but I refrain. It would be wrong on all kinds of levels, but God help me, it's all I can think of right now.

And then she lets the damn thing go to put her arms around my neck so I know that with one tiny movement, it would fall at our feet. Give me some damn strength because I sure as fuck need it.

My cock is nearly busting through my jeans and I'm kissing her with a ferocity I need to tame. But it's impossible because her passion matches mine. It's like I'm back in high school again, hormones raging, making out with my latest girl. But this is way more intense than anything I've ever experienced. Unfortunately, my need for oxygen necessitates that I break off the kiss. When I do, I rub my cheek against hers and move my lips close to her ear.

"Goddamn, Onyx. I need a minute here." My breath comes in rough bursts. Her fingers tighten in my hair and I feel her tug, so I lean back to look at her. "Everything okay with you?" I want to make sure she's good with this.

"More than okay, I'd say." Then her hand moves to my cheek in a tender caress, her thumb tracing my brow. She looks as though she wants to say something but isn't sure if she should. Then that same thumb travels to my lips and she traces my lower one until I capture it with my teeth and give it a gentle bite. She studies me intently and finally says, "I've never been kissed like that before."

"Like what?"

She shakes her head a little. I'm not sure if that means she doesn't know or if it means something else.

Then she lets out a tiny laugh and says, "I don't know. I guess so thoroughly. Or maybe so passionately." And then she kisses me and we're at it again. And I know that I want this girl. I want inside of her. I want her on top of me and underneath me. But I won't take her. I can't. At least not here or now. My dick is not happy about this, but too bad. I can't let her go just yet, so I hold her even tighter and move my hand into her wet hair as I cup the back of her head. I imagine what it would feel like to sink my fingers into the cheeks of her sweet ass.

Our tongues twist and play as we discover all the hidden secrets of each other's mouths until we're both breathless once again. Of all the women I've ever been with, she has the power to brand me with just her soft touch and her mouth. Oh dear God, that mouth of hers. I know it will be the only thing I can think of for days on end ... how those lips would feel wrapped around my dick and her tongue working me over. That, and how I want to be inside her.

When we break, I say, "Don't move, Onyx, or you'll be naked." Why do I have to be such a fucking gentleman now?

Her sigh is so damn sexy, I want that towel to fall away, just so I can glimpse her. "Thanks for reminding me." Her voice is breathy and my damn pants grow tighter, if that's possible.

"Gemini, I wish I could photograph you right now because I've never seen a more beautiful sight."

At first she gapes and then lets out a hearty laugh. "I'm a mess! My hair is lopsided. I didn't brush it. I have bruises all over my face. I must look awful."

"No, you don't. Awful doesn't exist when it comes to you. You look sexy as fuck, bruises and all." I take her hand and put it on me. "See what I mean?"

She stills and our eyes meet. "I ... I think you're sexy too." Her voice is so husky, my dick jerks when she speaks.

"I think you need to get dressed because if you don't, I may stop acting the gentleman."

Her face falls. Was that disappointment? I hope so because I don't want her to get dressed. I want her naked as hell.

My arms tighten around her for a second and then I kiss the top of her head, right before I lift her chin. "My men should be here any second."

"Oh! I forgot all about that."

I take her hand and put it on her towel. “Hold on to this unless you want me to see you naked.”

“I don’t mind if you see me naked. I’d love to be naked with you, Drex.”

Damn, my guts jumble. “Onyx, I can’t think of anything more I’d rather be than naked with you.” I cup her cheek and give her a quick kiss. “But I think we need to get our asses downstairs.”

“Right.”

“I’ll meet you down there. I’m going to take a shower.” And I don’t tell her it’s going to be an ice cold one. I have a raging boner that needs taming.

She gives me a funny look and I nod. So she knows after all. I head into the bathroom and when I’m finished, Gemini is waiting on me.

“I didn’t want to go down without you since I don’t know them.”

“Shy, are you?” I ask.

“In certain situations.”

She’s trembling and I notice goosebumps on her arms. “Hey, no need to be nervous. You’ll really like Huff. He’s a great guy. And so is Blake.”

“I’m not nervous, Drex.”

“Then ...”

“Drugs.”

“You need something?”

“I want to get off them,” she tells me.

“But your headaches. What will you do?”

“I haven’t figured that part out yet.”

Turning to face her, I put my hands on her shoulders. “You need them for the pain. I’ll be honest with you. I’ve never seen anyone in agony like you were. I don’t want to see you like that again.”

“You will. In the morning.”

That's something I don't want to hear. "We're gonna get this thing figured out, Gemini." I take her hand and we go downstairs.

Huff and Blake Strickland, another of my employees, sit at the island with Jeff. They rise when Gemini and I enter. I make the introductions and fill them in on what's going on. As we discuss the situation, they agree that Austin is the place to be.

"So, for tomorrow, one of you will need to get the Lady Belle refueled," I say.

"We took care of that before we landed here," Huff says. "Took a side trip into the airport in San Angelo."

"Great thinking. Then I'll need one of you with me and one of you to drive the car back."

Blake volunteers to drive.

"On the way back to our hotel, Blake, I'll need for you to get Gemini a wig. Short hair, light brown, big sunglasses, and some baggy clothes. Maybe a bohemian dress or something. Can either of you do fake tattoos?"

Jeff says, "I can. I have some here. What are you thinking?"

"Something visible, maybe on her neck or forearm. I want it to be identifiable so that if they see her, they automatically discount her."

"Yeah, I can take care of that. No problem."

"Great. Then we'll leave tomorrow morning." I look at Gemini and see she's not doing too well. We share a look and she shakes her head. Then I think about her headaches and the morning hours. "Gemini, if you have a migraine in the morning, we'll delay departure until it's gone. Okay?" She nods.

When I explain her headache situation, they agree that would be the best plan. Then Huff makes hotel reservations for us near the University of Texas. It's so hectic there, it'll be ideal for us to be coming and going. One more glance at Gemini tells me I need to get her upstairs.

"Jeff, I need a glass and then we're going to catch some sleep.

I think Gemini's feeling a headache coming on."

"Sure thing," he says.

Once we're upstairs, I ask again if she needs pain meds and she tells me no. "Gemini, it's not a good idea to cold turkey this stuff. Tapering is what you need to do. You can end up in lots of pain and right now, the last thing you need to deal with is the complexity of withdrawal. I'm not saying you shouldn't do it, but I don't think now is the right time."

She chews her lip and crosses her arms over her belly, hugging herself.

"What are you feeling, babe?"

"I'm nauseated and my stomach is cramping. And I'm freezing."

"Are you going to be sick?"

"I don't know."

She needs a pill. At least one. So I go and get one, along with some water. When I get back to her, she's sitting on the edge of the bed, rocking back and forth.

"Here. Take one."

She downs it. Then I tell her to stand so I can pull back the covers. She gets into bed and I get in behind her. Her shivers are so fierce, the bed shakes. My arms find their way around her and I pull her against me, leaving no space between us.

"Drex, can you lie on me?"

"Is that what you need?"

"Y-y-yeah."

Her body shivers so badly, every part of her is in a massive shakedown. I lie on top of her, but since I'm so much larger than she is, I don't want to crush her. I support most of my upper body weight on my elbows.

"N-n-no. Lie on me."

It worries me that she won't be able to breathe, so I say as much. But she burrows into me like a small animal searching for warmth. After a bit, her trembling evens out and her breathing eases.

"Better?" I want to make sure she has enough space to breathe.

"Mmm. Thanks. I think the pill is kicking in too."

Raising myself to my elbows, I look at her and say, "Gemini, you can't fucking do that anymore. I get that you want off those things. But, I need you centered. I need your mind to work alongside mine. I can't solve this thing and help you if you're not lucid or physically capable of helping me. Understand?"

She scrunches up her face. "I'm sorry. I thought I was doing the right thing."

My heart contracts with the sincerity of her words. She wants to be off the drugs and I don't blame her. "You've changed."

"What do you mean?"

"Just a little bit ago, you wanted to shoot yourself. Now you want to get off your meds." I shake my head.

"You act like that's a bad thing. And I'll want to shoot myself again, when another one hits. It's not that I have a death wish ... it's just that the pain gets so bad, I think sometimes that's the only thing that will get it to stop. If these would go away, I would never think that. I didn't use to be this way."

The look on her face twists my guts. I slide my hand in her tangled hair. "Well, it's not a bad thing to want to get off those meds. We'll get you through this. I'll help you. I promise."

She puts her hand on mine. "I want to believe you; I really do. But I don't think there is any help for this. They've tried everything, Drex."

"You've never seen my friend, Brady. The neurologist. I know he can help you. Brady Griffith is a genius. He's helped more people with post-concussion syndrome than you can imagine. He works with military guys that have been victims of IEDs. I'm going to figure out how to get him here."

The doubt lingers in her eyes, but that's a promise I make to myself.

"You can't be charging off and trying to do these things for me. Don't you have a business to run and a life somewhere else? You need to get back to all of that. But I want you to know how much I appreciate everything you're doing for me."

There's something about this girl that nudges my heart. She's different than the others I've known. She's probably the one who needs me the most, but the one who asks the least of me. I find that so unusual.

"Gemini, I want to help you."

"I know, and I don't know why. But you didn't answer my question. You have a business to run, right?"

"Yes, I do." And before I can say another word, she jumps in.

"Then you need to get back to wherever it is you live. I can take care of myself and get all this figured out. It's not fair to put you in danger. You don't need to risk yourself for me."

"I live in Denver. And I was a soldier, and that's what soldiers do. I'm used to it."

"But it's not right, you doing this."

"Why not? If I don't help you, you won't make it out of here alive. I'm telling you, Gemini, these guys don't play nice. They will tear you down until you beg for death. And I can't let them do that. This is what I was trained for and it wouldn't be right to know that I could've stopped that from happening. This is my choice, so stop worrying about it."

She has a way of pinning me with one look. It's very disconcerting, like she can see into my soul.

"Why, Drex? Why me?"

And that's a very good question. One I'm not sure I can answer. "When you were drugged that night, I knew if I left you there, something terrible would happen to you. Colt gave the order to abandon the operation, but I couldn't leave you. So here we are. I believe everything happens for a reason, good or bad. Maybe we'll both figure it out one day."

"I don't want to be the one responsible for you getting hurt or for messing up your job."

She doesn't know anything about my job or business. I suppose I should tell her.

"You can't mess up my job. The company's mine."

"But don't you have to run it?"

She hasn't a clue about the size and scope of DWInvestigations. "The headquarters are in Denver. I started it up right after I left the military and used my contacts to network. It catapulted me into a whole other bracket and I hit it big. I have a crew of awesome employees and they take damn good care of things. Initially, the business took off so fast I was spread too thin and working nonstop. So a friend recommended this guy to help manage things and he's the one who guided me into making the right business decisions. Part of the reason why I was so good was that I had the right connections with certain people and could get things done where other PI firms couldn't. We do high-profile cases ... kidnappings, cyberespionage, corporate espionage, stuff like that. So don't worry about disrupting my business. It's in good hands."

She frames my face with her hands and whispers, "But that still doesn't guarantee you won't get hurt and I won't take a chance with that."

"Well, I guess we'll have to promise each other *we* won't get hurt." Her closeness is more than I can take and before she can say another word, my lips crash onto hers. They are simply too tempting to ignore. With that sweet body of hers beneath mine, I know I'll have to cut this short. So I end the kiss, even though that's the last thing I want to do.

Rolling off her, I ask, "How are you feeling now? Chills gone?"

"Yeah," she says.

"Good. I'm going back down to talk with the guys for a bit and let you get some sleep." I know she's disappointed, but it's the right thing to do. If I stay, things will happen ... things with consequences ... things I'm not prepared to deal with.

"Thanks for warming me up."

What she doesn't know is that I'd like to do way more than just warm her up. Instead, I paste on a smile and get up.

"Sleep well, Onyx. You know where to find me if you need me."

WHEN I REJOIN the men, I tell Huff I want to get Brady here and why. He assures me that shouldn't be a problem.

"Where do you want him? Here?"

I think for a moment. "Not Austin. That's too much. Where can we fly him, Jeff?"

"San Angelo. Midland/Odessa."

"How long can we stay here?"

Jeff laughs. "You gonna pay me room and board?"

"If you want."

"Indefinitely. And that's without the fees."

My face must be all sorts of serious because Huff says, "Dayum, boss, you're gonna give yourself a tension headache if you don't ease up."

He's right. My head feels like a band is tightening around it. "I want Gemini to see Brady. She suffers from severe migraines due to post-concussion syndrome. I think he can help her."

"Shit. That sucks. Well, if anyone can help her, it's Brady," Jeff says.

"My exact thoughts. So Huff, let's see if we can get him here ASAP. I want her to see him before we do anything else. She can't travel during the day. Hell, she can't do anything during the day. The daylight kills her. I've never seen anything like it."

"Boss, are you, er, involved with her?"

Our eyes meet and without hesitation I answer, "That's not any of your business." But that's all I say, because I'm not sure what the hell one would call things between us.

"Our plans are on hold until Brady sees Gemini. Now, I want to go through her things again and see if there's anything we missed."

I grab the box and we go to work dissecting it again. I'm troubled by the fact that her mother didn't leave any clues to the file she took from her lover's computer.

"Why wouldn't she leave Gemini any clues? It doesn't make sense."

Jeff stops what he's doing and says, "She did leave clues. We're just not finding them. She was smart, Drex. She did it this way on purpose. If she hadn't, Gemini and she would never have survived for as long as they did. As good as the WPP is, you and I both know they have holes as big as Texas. Let's find the key we're looking for. And not the metal kind ... the one that will lead us to what this one opens." When he finishes speaking, he's holding up the small key Gemini found in the envelope.

We fumble through the papers and as we do, I break things down in my head. This isn't the smart way to do this.

"Stop. Everyone each take a document. I want each of us to read it as though it has something encrypted in it."

Huff asks, "Like what? Got an example?"

"Not really. I just have a gut feeling that each of these things holds a clue. Why else would they be in here? Why wouldn't she have destroyed them? They don't really tell us anything, do they?"

"He's right," Jeff says. "Let's look at these one by one. Pay particular attention to dates and numbers."

It takes us more than three hours to find a pattern, but eventually one emerges. And it's Jeff who finds it. "Drex, do you know when Gemini was born?"

"Not off the top of my head, but isn't her birth certificate in there?"

He digs through the box and finds it. A smile spreads across his face. "I think I may have something here."

My curiosity is all consuming. "What is it?"

"Huff, Blake, what are the dates on the documents you checked?"

They thumb through their papers and say, "June."

Blake says, "Years ranging from 1993 to 1994."

"Mine are the same," Huff says.

"So Gemini was born in June '91, correct?"

I nod. "June fifteenth."

"Then all these documents are from that month and then when she was two to three years old. What I'm thinking is that the clues must center around her birthdate of six and fifteen. Or maybe zero, six, fifteen and maybe the year too. What I'm not sure of is if it leads us to an address. But it's a starting point."

"How so?" Blake asks.

Now it's my turn to smile. "She was very clever, this Michelle Sheridan. Or Rachel Miller. By using Gemini's birthdate, we can cross-reference all the storage facilities in the Austin area for addresses that contain those numbers. Jeff, where's your laptop?"

"On it," he says. Upon returning, he searches storage units in the Austin area, looking for any with addresses comprised of the numbers six, fifteen, and possibly parts of either 1991, 1993, or 1994. After just a few, he hits on one, ironically located on none other than Sixth Street.

"Jesus. That has to be it—1615 W. Sixth Street. You've got to be kidding me." I rub my face as I think about everything and what we can possibly find inside that unit.

"Okay, Drex, now we need a plan to get in there. You know

the unit number will be similar, right?" Jeff asks.

"Yeah. I'll get Gemini to call and say it was in her mother's name. I'm sure Michelle Sheridan left something in the lease giving Gemini access, in case of her demise." I think about Gemini's reaction when she hears this. "Hey, I need some shut-eye. Let's pick this up first thing in the morning."

Sleep is most likely the last thing I'll be able to do. I'm troubled over what in the hell Michelle Sheridan could possibly have hidden. Whatever it is was dangerous enough to have gotten her killed and to have her leave such cryptic clues. I'm also wondering when the CIA is going to be banging on Jeff's door. I've no doubt they'll find us ... either they will or Aali Imaam. And then there's Colt and his op to worry about. I need to check in with him to see if he has any more leads and to find out if the guys I sent are doing their jobs. Finally, there's this thing bursting between Gemini and me. I could try to lie to myself, but what good would that do? Something big is happening because I never have these kinds of feelings about a woman and if I do, I can usually shove them aside and move forward. But not with her. She's in my head and other places too. I absolutely need to keep my shit straight here.

Chapter 10

GEMINI
No Going Back

IT'S LATE, MAYBE four in the morning, when I wake. I'd hoped the axe man wouldn't visit, but he's returned, axe swinging away. For a moment, I'm disoriented. Then it comes back to me: I'm at Jeff's. I need my meds. How in the world did I ever think I could get off these things? I guess I felt so good around Drex that it gave me false hope of living a normal life. I move to stand and the blinding pain is so fierce, I hit the floor and moan.

Shit! Moving is nearly impossible, but I know I must if I'm to get any reprieve. I push to my hands and knees and inch my way to the bathroom. Now I'm faced with another dilemma. I don't even know where the Lortab is. Drex has put it somewhere. Maybe if I kneel I can find it with my hands. But that doesn't work because I can't reach. As I try to stand up, I end up face-planting on the tile, smacking my cheekbone in the process.

I'm so dazed I don't hear him speaking until he turns on the light, and then I scream.

"Oh hell. I'm sorry." The light switches off and he picks me up and puts me in bed. Then I feel his hand on the back of my neck as he supports me and hands me my pills with water. I make a mess of things because my hands are shaking so badly and I can barely swallow.

"Don't move. Just stay still. I'll be right back." I'm not sure what's going on and I dare not check to find out. He soon returns with an ice pack and cool cloth. But I'm in such a bad way, I can't lie still.

"What can I do, Gemini? Just tell me and I'll do it."

There's an urgency in his voice. But why? This is the same thing that happens every day. I wish I could answer him, calm him down, but I can only writhe in pain. His hand is on my back, but I hurt so much I don't want him to touch me. I pull my knees to my chin and ball up. Why must these headaches come on so damn strong and hurt so damn bad?

His hand is in mine and I'm squeezing it. I have to be hurting him, but he doesn't say a thing. He lets me squeeze away. Weirdly enough, this action soothes me. The pain crests and I feel the wave slacken, thank God. My breathing slows and I release his hand.

"Better?"

"Only just."

He lets out his breath, as if he's been holding it.

"Jesus, Gemini. We've got to get you some help."

I nod.

He brushes my hair back and when his hand touches my cheek, I wince. "What's wrong?"

"I fell. In the bathroom."

"Let me see." He angles my face toward the moonlight streaming in through the window and says, "You've got yourself quite a knot there. It'll match the other bruises you already have. I need to get you another ice bag."

I clutch the new ice-filled bag to my cheek and the other to my head. If the axe man weren't visiting, I would laugh at the picture I must make. The bed moves as he gets in and the covers are pulled over us both. He must've decided to sleep the rest of the night with me, which is fine. I don't want to be alone.

"Thank you, Drex." My voice is thick with the effects of the pain meds. "It seems my debts to you keep mounting."

"You're welcome. And they're not debts."

"Then what are they?"

"They're things friends do for each other."

"So is that what we are? Friends?"

"Mmm. I would hope so."

It was my hope we would be much more than friends, but I'll settle for that right now. "It's nice to have a friend. You're my first real friend, you know."

"You can't mean that."

"But I do." The Lortab has made me loose lipped.

"Tell me, how is it that I'm your first friend?"

"When I was young, my mom discouraged friends. Or maybe that's not the right word. She never *encouraged* friendships with anyone. I wasn't allowed to spend the night anywhere and after I said no a few too many times, people stopping asking. And of course, I was never allowed to have overnight guests. Now I know why, but back then, I always thought she was just being mean. And now that I think about it, she always made me fade into the background. None of my clothes were cute or stylish. My hair was always cut in some drab style and I was never allowed to wear makeup." The thought that she never wanted me to stand out or for others to admire me stings. Though I know why she did it, the idea that she let me grapple through my adolescent years without any way to become my own person gouges my heart.

Drex doesn't seem to be able to keep his hands off me. He touches my face, my arms, shoulders, everywhere. I find that I don't want him to stop. "Don't let it do this to you."

"Do what?" How does he know what I'm thinking all the time?

"Upset you. You've gone all tense on me. I can see your frown, even in the moonlight, Gemini. She was only trying to protect you."

"Maybe, or maybe she was working with them. Who knows?"

"She wasn't working with them. She was running from them and was doing everything she could to keep you safe. The letter and box with its cryptic messages are proof. Tell me what happened when you went to college and why you didn't have any friends there," he says. He's great at getting my mind off this.

"I think by that time, I didn't know how to make friends. I went through my whole life without learning how. By the time I hit college, I was lost in the sea of students. So I kept to myself. I was so awkward and uncomfortable. And the dorm ... gah, that first semester I wanted to crawl in a hole every day. My social skills in a group setting pretty much suck so I would huddle in my bunk most of the time, avoiding my suite mates. They thought I was on drugs because I acted so sketchy around them. But I honestly didn't know what to say to them.

"Then I met Nick at the end of second semester. But I never felt like we were friends. We went from acquaintances to dating to being in love and living together. Or at least I thought we were in love. I had feelings for him, but not *those* kind ... the right kind. And then it all exploded after my injury. The stress of it. And now he's dead because of me."

Drex's voice is soft. "Onyx. You can't beat yourself up for that. You didn't know. Couldn't know. It wasn't your fault."

"No, maybe not directly, but it the end, it *was* my fault."

"Stop. Don't do this to yourself." He takes my hand and kisses it. "Let's get some sleep."

Insomnia chokes me as thoughts of my mother and what

she's done eat at me. All this talk with Drex has driven home how methodical she's been over the years. I never thought of my mother as calculating, but was I ever wrong. You always hear how children are the result of the environment in which they were raised, and it makes me wonder what the long-term effects will be of what she's done over the years.

MORNING COMES WAY too soon, and so does the blinding light. Drex has the curtains drawn, but they're not the blackout kind like I have at home. I need to take another pill, so I move to get out of bed and notice I'm not in my room—I'm in his. He must've carried me to his bed last night. I find myself grinning at the thought.

"What has you smiling like that?"

He's awake and watching me. I decide to tell the truth. "You."

He squints and says, "Me? Why me?"

"Just because."

"That's it? Just because?"

"Yep." I give him a sneaky grin. But I know I need my meds, so I carefully make my way to the bathroom. I hear him say, "On the right side by the mirror."

"Thanks." I down a pill with some water and head back to bed.

When I get settled in, he says, "We really do need to get your hair evened out."

"That bad, huh?"

"Let's just say it's not something you'd see coming out of a salon."

That comment strikes me as funny. Drex doesn't seem like the salon type. "And you would know that how?"

"I'm only assuming, you know."

"Ah, I see. Think you can go back to sleep?"

He raises his brows and says, "Gemini, I'm in bed with an extremely sexy woman. How can you even ask me that?"

Holy shit! My eyes wander to his chest—how did I not notice that he's shirtless? What's wrong with me? Have I suddenly gone blind? The man is perfect. Before I can think about it, my hand reaches out and touches him. I don't dare look at his face because I know one look from him will melt me on the spot or give me an indication that this isn't appropriate, and I don't need him to tell me that. I *know* it's not appropriate. Hell, it's not appropriate for me to be in his bed, either, but here I am, and damn if I'm not going to enjoy every minute of it.

My fingers trace the curves and slopes of his rigid muscles, down to his tiered abs. He doesn't have a six-pack; he has an exquisitely sculpted set of matching eights that lead me to that sexy V. I know where that V leads, but I can't go there because his boxers are in the way and I'm not brazen enough to slip past the elastic waistband.

But before my thoughts take me any further, his hand traps mine.

"Gemini, what do you think you're doing?"

My voice is lost, trapped in thickness. *Desire.* I'm shocked to find I want this man. Lust unfurls in my belly and it's bad enough that I swear I can taste it. My tongue moistens my lips as my mouth has suddenly become as dry as the Sahara.

"Aren't you going to answer me?"

His voice is deep, yet soft, and sends a current racing through me. Even though it's only his hand touching me, I feel him all over my skin.

"Um, I ..." I find I have no words.

"Gemini, look at me."

Oh God. I know if I do, I'll be lost. I am so screwed.

"Gemini?"

My head tips upward and I'm nailed by his heated stare. He's giving me the half-closed, sexy look.

"You can't touch me like that and not expect repercussions."

What does he mean by that?

"You don't think I'm going to let you do that and not retaliate, do you? All I've been doing since you walked into my life is fantasizing about fucking you and here you are, running your fingers across me. Do you think you can get away with teasing me like that?" I don't have to wait long because as soon as he finishes his sentence, he's on me like a cat on prey.

His kiss is pure heat and fire and it ignites one inside me. Our breath mingles as we consume each other with our tongues. His hands set my body aflame. Our actions are frenzied, crazed, and a part of my mind screams for control. But then I cut it off because for once, I don't want or need control. I only want this to be about the moment.

He must've read my mind because he stops for a second and asks, "Do you want me to stop? Tell me now."

"No! Please, don't!" I pull him back to me.

"I don't want this to be difficult for us afterward. Think about it before we go any further."

"I don't care about anything right now but this." And that's the damn truth. Maybe it will be difficult after, but if so, I'll deal with it then.

"I know, but are you prepared to handle the aftermath?"

"Yes! I want you, Drex. Do you want me?" I'm suddenly barraged with doubt.

"Look at me. Touch me. Feel what you do to me. Do you even have to ask?"

His lips are parted and those damn eyes draw me in. But when my gaze drifts down to his boxers, I find my answer. My hand reaches for him, and when I feel how hard he is, I know there's no stopping us now. We both know it. I sit up and pull my shirt off and watch him as he studies me. The rise and fall of his chest quickens, matching mine. I hold my breath as his hand extends because I know what he's going to do and I'm not sure I'll be able to stand it. When his thumb slides across and pinches my nipple, it feels as though a million sparks ignite in my belly and radiate outward. My back arches as I push myself closer to him and sigh. I drop my head back and let the sensations take over.

My sigh turns into a moan when I feel his lips, and then his tongue take over and lick me. But when he turns it to aggressive sucking, my arms find his neck and I jerk him toward me. There is nothing gentle between us. It's rough, hard and the most erotic sensation I've ever experienced.

His hands push me until I'm flat on my back and he resumes his delicious torture of my breasts. First one, then the other, until I'm twisting beneath him and he can barely maintain his hold on me. His mouth travels south and hits my ribs where he scrapes his teeth and gently bites me. But when he moves to the softer flesh next to my hip bones, I'm once again a writhing mass, as pleasurable sensations zing through me.

My borrowed sweats are tugged off and I feel the cool air graze my scorched skin. His fingers dig into the muscles of my thighs as he spreads my legs. "Tell me what you want."

I'm speechless. I've never told anyone this before. The truth is, I've only ever been with one man, and that's Nick. What do I say?

"I want you to keep doing what you're doing." My voice sounds breathy.

"Is that all?"

"No." I decide to be bold. "I want you to put your mouth on me."

"Here?" he asks and kisses my thigh. And then bites it.

Now he's teasing me and I don't want to be teased. "No."

"How about here?"

He kisses me right above my pubic bone.

"No!" I say in frustration.

"Then tell me exactly where you want my mouth. And Gemini, I want you to be *very* specific."

Holy shit! I can't say that! Instead, I point. "Right there."

I can hear the laughter in his voice now. "Uh-huh, you need to *tell* me, not show me."

So I blurt out, "On my hoo-hah."

"Your what?"

"You know." I can't resist. I have to look at him—he's got the goofiest grin on his face. "Please don't make me say it. Pretty please?" My hands cover my face as it burns. This is so embarrassing.

He's not going for this. He grabs my hands and pulls them back down so I'm forced to look at him. Then he takes his lower lip between his teeth and says, "Only for today will I grant you a pass. But after this, no more." His hands cup my ass cheeks as his mouth drops down. My hands find themselves in his hair, as I get lost in the way his tongue works me over. He pushes my thighs apart and up and I'm completely exposed for him to do as he pleases. And boy, does he please.

When he adds his fingers to his tongue play, I'm quite sure I nearly rip his hair out by the roots. My orgasm is so forceful, I can't stop the noise that erupts from me. I clamp my hand over my mouth, shocked that I'm so loud. But by then, he's crawling up my body, kissing me along the way, until he gets to my mouth. "I take it you and your hoo-hah enjoyed that."

"Fuck, yeah," I breathe.

He shakes his head. Then he gets up and I'm so disappointed because I want to lie there and have him hold me. But then he's back, holding a condom between his teeth.

"For you," he says, smiling.

"For me? I think it may be for you too."

"Yeah, I think you're right. Will you do the honors?"

Hmm. I've never done this before. Shall I tell him? I think I need to in case I don't get it on right.

"Only if you tell me whether I'm putting it on correctly," I murmur.

"Well, that tells me a lot."

"I'm sure it does."

"Your first time?"

I'm not sure if he's asking me if I'm a *virgin* virgin or a condom-putter-onner virgin.

"First time?"

"For putting on a condom."

"Yeah. I've never put one on a man before."

"So ... does that mean you've put them on women before?"

My mouth drops open as he chuckles.

"Well, then, I'll be happy to be your teacher. It's the least I can do."

"It is if you want to have sex with me."

"Touché."

I open the packet and he tells me what to do. I love the feel of him in my hand. "Mmm. This is nice."

His voice is strained when he replies, "Yeah, it is."

He pinches the little bubble at the end and looks at me afterward. He's serious again and his gaze is pure heat.

"You're nothing short of beautiful, Gemini. And you taste so perfect. But when you came, it was fucking sexy as hell to watch. That's something I want to see, hear and feel again and again."

He's let loose a regiment of butterflies in my stomach and I want to crawl all over this man.

"Then what are you waiting for?"

"For you to tell me what your pleasure is. Top or bottom. Front or back."

Front or back. I hope he doesn't mean *that* kind of back. "Er, your choice," I say.

"Uh-huh. You decide this time."

"Bottom."

"I get the feeling my lady doesn't like to be in control."

While that's an interesting observation, it's one I don't care to analyze right now. "Hey, can we get back to the moment here?"

"Not only does she relinquish control, she's impatient." And as soon as those words leave his mouth, he plunges into me, filling me until I can't possibly take any more. I cry out, then sigh as he pulls out and repeats the motion over and over. I pick up his rhythm, my hands gripping his hips to pull him back to me every time. Then he hooks his leg around mine and we roll to our sides where he pulls my leg up and over his hip as he continues to move in and out of me. My body feels like liquid fire is pouring though my veins. This is not easy, it's fierce ... intense. Exactly like Drex. Just like I imagined it would be. He's all power, dominance, and control. Just like he is in everything else. And I find it so exciting that I want him to always be like this.

"Onyx, kiss me. Let me taste your sweet mouth."

I couldn't refuse that request if I tried. But why would I want to? He's so much more than sexy. His dark hair is messy and he has several days' scruff. His bedroom eyes are almost more than I can take, but his mouth, as he runs his tongue across first his upper and then his lower lip, makes me want to taste every bit of him. My mouth clumsily hits his—we're both moving so fast and hard—but when I latch on, I suck his lip. I'm not gentle, either. He returns my actions and it follows the pace of our lovemaking. Our breathing is ragged and we're both near climax as our bodies pound against each other's.

Then his hand slips between us and he rubs circles on my clit and says, "I want to watch you orgasm again, Gemini. Do it for me so I can come too. I want to feel you come on my dick. I need it, babe." His words are husky and demanding as he breathes them into me.

"Ah, yessss." He sends my body straight into the spasm land of orgasms and he is right there chasing me. Sweat rolls off us and I love it.

Then he flips me on my back while he's still inside and hovers as he stares at me, right before he dives down for a mouthwatering kiss. This one is slow, sensuous, sweet. He kisses every part of my face—eyelids, brows, cheeks, nose, and chin.

While one hand holds the top of my head, the other caresses the nape of my neck. "Wow. You're beyond awesome, Gemini."

"I think you are too. That was quite the thing, wasn't it?"

"Quite."

I rub the rough of his cheek with the back of my hand.

"Did I scratch you too much with this?"

"No. I like it. Especially when you …" I shut up before saying it.

"When I what?"

"Nothing." Now I'm mortified.

"Gemini, we've just had one amazing fuck, and that was after I went down on you. It's not like we're twelve. Tell me." He grabs my hands in one of his and pulls them over my head, trapping them.

"I'm not used to speaking about this stuff."

"So? Tell me. I'm going to make you get used to it, you know."

"Okay. I like the scruffy part on you when you go down on me. It's very, um, arousing." I have to look away because this is too awkward.

"Really?" He's surprised by this. The fingers of his free hand thread into my hair and he forces my head to face his. His forehead rubs mine and our eyes meet. "So it's nice, then?"

"Yeah. It feels really good because it rubs me in the right spots."

"Okay. The scruff shall remain." He moves to the side and

rubs his scruff against my nipple. Oh lord, it feels so rough but so good. I groan. He does it again and again all over my girls. This guy knows exactly what he's doing.

"Yeah, I think you really do like my scruff. I see all sorts of possibilities here."

That makes me smile. "Drex, what we just did was really great for me. I mean totally, you know?"

"Can I ask you something?"

"Anything," I say.

"When you were involved with Nick, didn't you ever discuss this kind of stuff?"

Whoa. I was not expecting that. "Um, no."

"So, you didn't talk about what turned you on and what you needed?"

"No," I squeak.

"How did you know?"

"I guess we both assumed. I don't know. Sex with him was just okay. But it was never like what we just experienced. Can we not talk about this?"

"Sure. But I'm warning you now. We *will* talk about this stuff. A lot. Sex has to feel good. All the time. And when it doesn't, you have to tell me. I'll certainly tell you. Sometimes I like it hard and rough. If it's too much for you, you have to tell me. I want it to feel great for you."

"I will."

"And sometimes I like to talk during sex ... dirty talk. And I'll want you to talk back to me. I need to know if you're into what we're doing. It's damn easy for you to tell when I'm into it. Like just a few minutes ago."

I smirk. "So you're saying you're into me?"

"Not anymore," he says as he pulls out, laughing. But the levity disappears and he's again serious. "I don't ever get involved in my cases, Gemini. This is the only exception I've ever made."

"I'm sorry. I didn't mean to ..."

"I didn't tell you that for you to apologize. I wanted you to know that this kind of thing is not the norm for me."

"But I'm not one of your cases."

"What do you mean?"

"I never hired you, remember?"

"True. But I'm taking you on nonetheless."

"Okay. Well, then, since you don't sleep with your clients, are you saying you're not a manwhore?"

"I didn't say that. I just said ..."

"Oh, so you admit to being a manwhore?"

I don't give him a chance to say anything else before I smack him with a pillow. And then it hits me. "What time is it?"

He looks at his watch. "Eight thirty-three. Why?"

"I don't have a headache. At all. Nothing. I haven't gone without a morning headache since the accident."

He grants me a huge smile. "It must be me, Onyx."

For that comment, he gets another big whack with the pillow.

Chapter 11

DREXEL
More Trouble

GEMINI LOOKS AS though she wants to crawl under the bed. Dr. Brady Griffith has asked her everything under the sun, but now he's asking her about her sex life. She insisted that I stay with her for the examination, even though Brady and I both tried to talk her out of it. Now I think she regrets that decision.

"So, Gemini, are you sexually active?"

"Well ..."

Deciding to save the poor girl, I say, "Yes, Brady, as of this morning, she is. She and I are sleeping together."

He looks at me and nods. "Good."

Gemini's mouth opens.

Brady laughs. "Gemini, new data supports sex as an effective tool for reducing the incidence of migraine. Or rather, orgasm can. Did you notice any difference?"

So help me God, I tried to stop my laugh from escaping. I really did. But I couldn't. Gemini punches me in the shoulder. Hard. "Ouch!"

"Too bad, asshat. And yes, Dr. Griffith, it helped. A lot. This morning was the first time since the accident I didn't have a headache."

"Interesting," Brady mumbles.

Gemini fires a missile at me with one glance. The only thing I can do is shrug. But then a thought occurs to me.

"What about Nick?"

Her face turns shades of scarlet. And if I thought she looked pissed before, I'm really in for it now. I fucked up.

Her voice is icy as she says, "Nick and I weren't sexual after my accident."

Me and my big mouth want to dig a little deeper, not because I want to know for her headaches' sake, but because my ego is fucking nosy. And then I look at her lips that are tightened into two thin lines and decide to keep my stupid-ass mouth shut.

Brady clears his throat and says, "Okay, so can you give me a list of all the drugs they tried you on?"

"Maxalt, Lortab, tramadol, naproxen, and acetaminophen."

"No preventive? No oral contraceptives?"

Shaking her head, she says, "No. None of that. I did keep a diary."

"Idiots." Brady's pissed. "Did they try you on any other triptans?"

"I don't know what those are," Gemini says.

"It's your rescue treatment. Maxalt is a triptan, but there are several others. I'm wondering if any of the others would've worked better."

"Oh, they put me on Imitrex but it didn't work at all."

"Okay. Let's stick to what we have, then. But I want to put you on topiramate. It works as a preventive. But you have to titrate up slowly. Twenty-five milligrams a day for a week, then fifty, then seventy-five, then a hundred. That's the dose I want you on. So it'll take you a month to get there."

"Okay, every week I increase at twenty-five-milligram intervals."

"Then I want you on a birth control pill to get your hormones regulated. The week that you're normally on the placebo, I want you to take a very low dose of estrogen. That will help any breakthrough headaches. How much hydrocodone are you on?"

"What's that?"

"Lortab."

"The maximum. And I can't go without it." Gemini looks at her clenched hands, her hair covering her face. And this is where Brady shines.

He crouches down in front of her and takes her hands in his. "Listen to me, Gemini. Your medical care sucked. I'll be honest with you. You should've been on this other stuff from the beginning. Anyone who they say is treatment-resistant really isn't. There are ways to tweak everything to get you functioning again. I know. I do it with my patients all the time. You're tolerant to hydrocodone now ... you're not an addict. Got that? I want you to repeat that. Now. Say, 'I am not an addict.'"

Gemini smirks and says, "I am not an addict."

"Good. Now, what we're going to do is slowly decrease your dose. But I don't want to do that until we have your headaches controlled. How does all of this sound?"

She sighs and grins. "Good. Sounds good."

"And maybe you can tell the big guy here to keep it going in the bedroom. Knowing him, though, he'll probably need a lot of instructions from you."

Her jaw hits the floor.

"Don't be so shocked. Like I said earlier, there's a lot of evidence to support that. It has to do with endorphins. And if this doesn't work, we'll try other things. So, how do I need to write these prescriptions?"

"Now that may be a problem," I say. "Let me think for a sec."

I'm worried if the prescriptions are in her name, it'll trigger something in the database. "They can't be in her name. I can't tell you why, other than it's for her protection."

"Yeah, no worries. Just tell me what to do."

"We need to establish a false name, and that may take a while. Let me talk with Huff."

AS WE WALK into the kitchen, Jeff, Huff, and Blake are checking out the news. Apparently, something went down on Dirty Sixth the night before.

"Did they get the guys?" I ask.

"It looks like it. The police aren't releasing much. They're just saying there's a solid lead in the disappearances," Huff answers.

"Well, that's a relief for the people of Austin. Huff, make a call to our guys over there to see how things are going," I say. "And I need fake ID for Gemini ... the works. We need to get her some prescriptions."

"You got it, boss. I'll call the office and have them get on it," Huff says.

"And Brady needs a ride home."

"Copy that," Blake answers. "The jet is still standing at San Angelo."

"Hmm. Let's move that thing somewhere else," I say.

"Where to?"

"Jeff?"

"Midlands/Odessa isn't too far. Have it fly there and then you can get Brady there by helo."

As we're waiting, Jeff hears a beep. "What the hell!" He walks over to his security cameras and says, "Gentlemen, we have company." The monitors reveal two black SUVs outside his main gate. Then the buzzer sounds.

"What do you want me to do?" Jeff asks.

I stare at the screen. "Looks like feds, wouldn't you say, guys?" Heads nod all around. "Well, I've gotta tell them something."

The buzzer sounds again.

"Let's get out of here," I decide. I look at Jeff and say, "You can say we were outside so you didn't hear them buzzing. It's your property and you have the right to deny them a search. If they have a warrant, we haven't left anything behind anyway."

"Okay, go! Get out. Make sure you didn't leave anything upstairs."

Gemini and I sweep our rooms and grab everything, and then check the bathroom. We only had the one backpack between us so it only takes a few seconds. Then we grab all the stuff that was in the locked box and head out the back. Huff has the chopper running and we climb aboard and take off like lightning hit us. I mentally run through everything, checking off things I had with me to make sure nothing was left behind in the car, either. I'm positive I have it all.

"Fuck!" I slam my hand against the side of the aircraft. "How the fuck did they find us?"

"GPS," yells Huff over all the noise. "It's the only feasible answer."

"Yeah, but whose? Mine's secure like yours and Blake's and they wouldn't know Brady is here." Then a thought hits me. I turn to Gemini. "You wouldn't happen to have a cell phone on you, would you?"

"Yeah, but it's dead by now, I'm sure."

"Jesus, Drex. You need to stop thinking with your damn dick and get your shit together here," Huff yells. He's right.

"Give it to me." My voice is harsh as I extend my palm toward her.

She hands it over. I take out the SIM card and crush the damn thing. Then I demolish the phone while she watches.

"Hey!" she shouts.

"Fucking-hey-nothing!" I shout right back to her. "They've tracked every step we've made through that damn thing. And I'm the fuck job who didn't think about it. That's what I get for ..." I almost torch everything by saying something I'll regret. And she knows it. Her lips thin and her hard-as-nails eyes pin me down until I'm squirming. Me, the one who *never* squirms. She has the ability to do that to me? What. The. Fuck!

"For what, Drex? For fucking me?"

Oh motherfucking hell! "No! That's not what I was going to say, and this isn't the time or place for this discussion." I glance around. The men are trying their damnedest not to pay attention, but it's next to impossible. Poor Brady bears the brunt of it because he's in the back with us, facing us in our seats. We're in a damn helicopter the size of a small walk-in closet. There's nowhere to hide.

"I think this *is* the place. Right here. Right now. Just say it, Drex."

"My judgment was clouded, Gemini. That's what I was going to say. I should've destroyed your phone hours and hours ago. I was stupid and fucked up. That's how they followed us to San Angelo. To your house. And I'm a shit ton smarter than that. But not this time. Fuck!"

"Well, I'm the one who clouded your judgment. So it's my fault."

"Stop it. Right now. We got away. And now they won't figure out where we are."

"Oh, and in the meantime, we've messed up Jeff's life. All because of a little romp in the hay, right?"

We can't talk about this now. It's completely inappropriate. She's angry, I get that. But this is going to have to wait. I ignore her question.

"Blake, how long until we get to Midlands/Odessa?"

"Thirty."

I can feel her glare boring holes in my back, so I turn and say, "This discussion is shelved for now." She knows I mean business, but she's not happy about it. She gives me a nasty scowl. I'm not going for that, so I reach for her hand but she shrinks away. I go for her anyway. My hand finds hers and grasps it tightly. Then I pull her close so only she can hear me.

"If you think for one minute that I regret what we did, you're only fooling yourself. Being with you was singularly the best thing that I've ever experienced. Yeah, my judgment is clouded, but you'd cloud the judgment of a fucking saint." She stares at me, quiet. Her hand relaxes and she lets me hold it. I'm not sure if she's still angry, but I know there will be more words when it's just the two of us.

And so help me God, I have to restrain myself from kissing the hell out of her.

WE LAND IN Midlands/Odessa and the G-550, the company jet, awaits. I make a quick change of plans because I need my team around me for some strategizing.

"Change of plans. We're heading home." Gemini looks at me and frowns. "This is for the best," I tell her.

"I don't understand."

"My team is the best. I think if we leave a bit of time between us and Austin, we can get rid of some of the heat. Besides, I need to pull my team in and brainstorm. And then there's that little thing between you and me that needs discussing."

She nods. Her hair's a mess, still sexed-up from earlier. I want to grab and kiss her until her lips are swollen again, but I don't. Instead, I lead her to the jet and guide her to a seat. An attendant waits on us. The group settles for water only.

We're Denver-bound as soon as we're cleared for takeoff.

Gemini grabs my hand as the plane picks up speed.

"What is it?" I ask.

Her eyes dart around and then they're back on mine. "Did we screw up by sleeping together?"

"I wish there was an easy answer. In a way, yes. I'm missing things ... important things. You are a huge distraction. I've never done this before and it's not possible to separate myself from this case now. I can't look at it objectively. So I guess I may have fucked it up in that sense. Would I do it again? Yes. Because I've had you on my mind from the very minute I saw you. Is that a good thing? Guess that depends on who you ask."

"I'm in the way."

"Hell yes, you are. You've been in the way from the beginning. You're the very reason we're here. So I'd say you're not only in the way, you *are* the way."

"Maybe we should part ways. I don't want to mess up your business or get you hurt by your involvement in this."

"Oh, Onyx, if you think for one second that I'm letting you out of my sight again, you've lost your fucking mind. The last time I did that, you ended up in the hands of Aali Imaam—you still have the bruises to show for that. Those are brutal men with a complete disregard for human life. I know you've said you don't care about dying, but do you honestly feel that way now?"

She ducks her head for a moment. "No. I never really wanted to die. I only entertained the thought when I was hurting so badly."

"Okay, so listen to me. We know they want that file. That has to be what they're after. There's a good chance they'll kill you to get it, and I can't live with that. So you're stuck with me, babe, whether you like it or not. And I'm sorry this turn of events isn't quite what you imagined, but as they say, it is what it is. I think what we need to do is solve the damn puzzle of your life and get those bastards off your tail."

"But ..."

"It's not your choice anymore, Gemini. Besides, I'm a lot better at this than you are. Understand?"

She takes a deep breath and nods. "Okay. But I need you to promise me something."

"What's that?"

"If you get to the point where you want to get out of this circus, you tell me."

"Fair enough." What I fail to mention is that the chance of that happening is zilch.

The flight to Denver is only about an hour and a half. We land at Rocky Mountain Metropolitan Airport, which is much more convenient than dealing with the chaotic Denver International.

Denver is an oddity. When flying into the mile high city, as it's called, one would think they were in prairie country. But in the distance, the great Rocky Mountains can be seen, with their snow-capped jagged peaks. Their beauty is captivating and within thirty minutes on the interstate, you're gaining altitude and surrounded by incredible views. The city of Denver itself is just as amazing. It offers everything from university life to the big city atmosphere, with mild weather and most of the days being sunny.

When we deplane, two cars are waiting—one to take us to the office and the other to take Brady home. Right before we depart, Brady says, "Let me know what you want to do as far as Gemini's prescriptions go. I can make it work however."

"Yeah, I will. As soon as I have a name, I'll get it to you. And I owe you huge one, man."

"Oh, I'll send you a bill."

"No. I'm paying you in cash, remember?"

"Right." Then Brady turns to Gemini. "Drex knows how to reach me. Call me if you need me. Anytime—I mean that."

"Thank you, Dr. Griffith." They shake hands and we climb in

the back seat while Huff drives us to the office.

"Hey, Drex," Gemini says, "Is there somewhere I can grab some clothes?"

She's still wearing the oversized sweats from Jeff. "Yeah, I'll get Jill to work on that for you."

"Jill?"

"My admin at the office. She'll take care of it."

My phone rings and I see it's Jeff. Shit. I'm sure this won't be good news.

"Jeff, what happened?"

"The boys are pissed. I held them off but they got a warrant and searched. Of course there wasn't a damn thing here, which pissed them off even further. They said I was aiding and abetting a criminal. I asked them to which criminal they were referring and they wouldn't answer. Drex, you know when The CIA wants something, they're relentless. You need to watch your back. They're gonna start pulling in favors of all sorts and then you'll be screwed."

"Eh, I'm not worried. They don't know it's me. And now they don't know where Gemini is. We figured out how they found us and it was through her phone. I destroyed it somewhere over your ranch."

"Drex, I'm serious, man. You might need to talk with them and see why they want her. They'll be knocking on your door up there."

"It's not happening. If they figure out I have her, I'll have my people stall them. They'll try to butt in and I don't want them screwing things up."

He breathes into the phone. "I got you, man. Just let me know if there's anything else I can do."

"Will do. We'll be back down there to finish up."

"What do you mean? Aren't you in Austin?"

"Nope. We came home to figure out our best strategy. I

figured a few days wouldn't hurt."

"Not a bad idea," Jeff says. "Keep in touch."

"Will do."

Huff pulls in the office's underground garage. We pass through the layers of security and Gemini asks, "This is all yours? This entire building?"

"Yeah." At the elevators, the armed guard greets us and I enter the security code. Then we're on our way up to the executive level.

When the doors open, Sally welcomes us from her desk.

"Welcome back, Mr. Wolfe, Mr. Huffington, Mr. Strickland."

"Thanks, Sally." I keep moving, my hand on Gemini's back, guiding her along. When we get to the back offices, Jill stands.

"Mr. Wolfe. I didn't expect you today."

"I know. I need all heads in the conference room."

We move toward the double doors at the end of the hall. They slide open and I flip on the lights.

"Gemini, make yourself comfortable while we wait for everyone to get here."

She gapes at the room loaded with state-of-the-art everything, including surveillance equipment, computers, and telecommunications. She's finally going to see the full power and scope behind my company. Maybe now she'll understand exactly how much and how prepared I am to help her. When she sees my team at work, hopefully the questions she has about my abilities will be answered.

Chapter 12

GEMINI
Seriously?

THIS IS QUITE unexpected. When he said he owned the company, I sure as hell wasn't thinking this is what he meant. He owns the fucking building, with a Fort Knox-like secure underground garage. There's no telling what he has at the main entrance. Then we take the elevator to the *executive level,* where a very beautiful receptionist, Sally, sits in front of a frosted-glass partition. She's dressed in chic business attire with her hair and makeup artfully done. And here I am with my mane a mass of snarls that I haven't brushed since our morning sexcapade, wearing oversized sweats that I can barely keep on. Can it get any worse?

Oh, yes it can. We continue walking, his hand on my lower back steering me, and we eventually reach the inner sanctum, where Jill, greets us. Well, that's not exactly true. She greets all of *them*. She ignores me like I'm a dreaded virus. Just as Sally did. Who can blame them? I look like a street urchin. Or maybe even a crack whore, which isn't far from the truth. Gee, don't I have a lot to be proud of? Not only that, their boss is screwing me! Yabba Dabba Doo!

My head is already pounding. When Drex ushers me into his conference room, I don't know whether to be shocked or amazed. My guess is the FBI or Pentagon would be envious of this room. Good lord, who is this guy? I mean, really?

As I observe him, he fires up his toys. Soon, every wall is filled with images as his men file in, each carrying their own laptop. Drexel is so animated as he speaks, it's as if he's on an adrenaline high. That's when I get it, when it all sinks in. He thrives on this stuff. This is his life. It's not just a paycheck. It's the driving force and energy behind everything that he is. Here I sit, exhausted and whipped, but I look at him and see someone who's refreshed and renewed. It's like looking at a man who just stepped off the plane after returning home from a two-week vacation. The corners of my mouth turn up.

What captures my attention most is what everyone else is dialed into. It's all in his delivery. He has every one of those six men in the palm of his hand. They hang on his every word. And when he asks someone to do something, it's with clarity and authority, but with the knowledge that they understand why they're doing it. By the time he's made his points, even I'm ready to jump at his command. He is one badass boss.

When he finishes, everyone departs, but I still have the awestruck, goofy-assed expression plastered on my face. "You're really something," I tell him.

"What are you talking about?" The man is clueless.

"This." I sweep my arm in front of me. "It's your calling. I don't know if you ever wanted to do anything else, but it's good that all things led you here. You're a wonder to watch in action. You're so animated and engaged in this whole process, I couldn't stop watching you. Hell, I'd go to work for you right now."

Something darkens his gaze. "I don't know about all that."

"Well, I do. My great observational skills were at work."

"Come on."

"Where to, boss?"

He snorts. "I can't imagine you taking orders from anyone. Let's go home."

"Hey." I hold my gigantic pants away from my legs. "Clothes?"

"Right. Sorry."

We leave the conference room and head back toward Jill but we don't stop. Instead, we turn and head toward another door. Then I see his name, Drexel Wolfe, CEO, on the door. I follow him inside. His office is expansive and filled with sleek, modern furniture. The only things that soften the look are the beautiful Persian rugs scattered everywhere.

"Want a drink?"

"Do you have any water?"

"Well, yeah, but I was thinking of something a bit stronger."

"Water, please."

He hands me a bottle and my stomach growls. I'm starving.

"Shit. We haven't eaten all day. I'm sorry. I tend to forget about that." He looks humble all of a sudden.

"I pretty much forgot about it myself, until just now. I also need a pill." He reaches for his backpack, pulls the bottle out, and hands it to me.

Then he walks over to the phone on his large desk. "Yeah, Jill, we need some food. No. Yes." He looks at me and asks, "Pasta okay?"

I nod.

"The lobster ravioli, light on the sauce. Two salads. Dressing on the side. Bread with his olive oil mix. Tiramisu for two." Then he's listening to her speak. "Jill, did I ask you your opinion on my diet? No? Then that's what we want. Oh, and Gemini needs some clothes. What size? Hang on."

He looks at me.

"Size four maybe. I don't know really. Or a small. Or medium." He laughs.

"You don't shop much, do you?" he asks.

"No. I hate to shop."

"Jill, get her size four and small and medium for the shirts. And you only have to pick up a few things." He disconnects and rakes his eyes over me. I'm immediately conscious of how terrible I must look.

He saunters toward me and his hand is on my arm. The next thing I know, he's dragging me to the couch. "You're the strangest woman I've ever met."

"How so?" I'm curious.

"You hate to shop. That's just not possible for a woman."

"Apparently, you've met the wrong women. Shopping is boring. And not to change the subject, but do you think this plan of yours will work? You know, to find those people in Aali Imaam?"

"That's not my only goal. I also want to flush out why The Company wants you."

"Which company?"

"The Company. The CIA. By hunting down Aali Imaam, it'll trigger the alarm within the CIA and they'll send someone. It may be the men who showed up at Jeff's. I can't be certain, though. But somewhere along the way, we'll flush out whoever is after you ... or was after your mother and find out how deep their involvement is."

"This is pretty tricky."

"It may seem that way, but it's relatively basic. We know Aali Imaam wants you, because of the unknown file. I'm pretty sure The CIA knows what that file contains, but they won't say. So if we can dangle the carrot, so to speak, we can draw them out."

"How will we do that?"

He laughs. "Gemini, weren't you in the conference room a

little while ago?"

"Yeah."

"Didn't you listen?"

"Um, not really."

"You were staring at me the entire time. What were you doing?"

"Thinking about how damn hot you look and that you were made for this job. I didn't hear a word you said."

He rubs his forehead. "I don't know whether to laugh or strangle you."

I scrunch my face. "I'm pulling for the laughing bit."

"Christ, you're a handful."

His lids drift to the half-closed position again and my fingers grab hold of his shirt's neckline. There's one thing I want to do and it's to pull him close to me so I can kiss his lips. I am preempted when someone raps on his door.

"Great timing, huh?" he asks. In a booming voice, he says, "Yeah, come in."

It's Blake. "They're calling for you. It's the CIA. I put 'em off but they'll be ringing again."

"It's fine."

"Drex, think you should talk to them? They said it's urgent and threatened to pull all of our government contracts."

Drex lets out a boom of laughter. "Hell, Blake, they can't pay any of their bills as it is. Do you think I care about that? I don't give a shit. Besides, our livelihood does not rely on the government at all. If that were the case, this corporation would never have taken off. The only reason they do business with me is because I can get them answers when their bureaucratic agencies fail them. This'll only hurt *them*, not me, and they damn well know it. You know the major sum of our income comes from the private sector anyway."

"If you say so, boss."

"I do say so. Trust me. Their threats are laughable. I'll let them stew for a while. When I talk to them, it'll be on my terms."

Blake walks out and I'm left wondering about their exchange. "Exactly how much work do you do for the government?"

"Maybe twenty percent of what I actually do. But it's not twenty percent of the company's income. They suck at paying most of the time. And when they do, they don't want to pay what my services are worth."

"Why do you do it?"

He shrugs. "For country. I was a soldier and that motto never dies. Plus they gave me my start. Got me connected."

"So when you left the military, you started this business. When you told me about it, you didn't indicate it was this huge."

"I tried. It's a bit difficult to tell that to someone. I started out on a loan but I picked up some high-tech jobs. And then I had the help from my military connections. Things just expanded. I opened this business at the right time. Cyber hacking is a huge part of our business ... we find the hackers. We have select teams that work on that. I have teams that specialize in cyber espionage. So many corporations have their inventions and developments stolen before they even hit the market, some before they're patented, all because of cyber espionage. My firm helps catch those hackers. We also deal with bank theft via cyberspace. Banks have to deal with protecting their systems against hackers and getting compromised. It can be difficult to stay on top of it all, so we can send teams in to identify weaknesses and help develop stronger security. We work with software developers—our team helps them come up with programs that are more difficult to hack into. We're extremely broad in what we do. Mid-sized to huge corporations are our main clients and we charge a lot for our services."

I'm amazed. "Wow. I thought when you said you were a private investigator, you just spied on cheating husbands."

"Yeah, you and a million other people. And that's okay with me."

"But why? Don't you want the world to know what you do?"

"The world does know. At least the world as it pertains to me. We're the best at what we do and corporations beg us to take them on as clients. We have way more business than we can handle."

He makes a damn good point. "Wow. I concede."

"Hmm, I didn't know we were having a contest."

When he looks at me like that, my limbs hang off my body with no strength of their own. We're both silent, caught in each other's gazes, until we're interrupted by another knock.

"What is it?" His tone is not at all friendly.

"It's your dinner, sir."

"Shit," he mutters. "Come in."

The door swings open and in marches Miss-Everything-In-Its-Place-and-the-Epitome-of-Fashion. "Where shall I put this, Mr. Wolfe?" Her voice is husky.

She's eyeing him like she wants to lick him. And why the hell wouldn't she? He's lickable. Her head swings my way so I smile. Maybe it's just me being petty here. I'm uncomfortable looking a mess, and I haven't eaten all day. But I swear that woman gives me a bad vibe.

"Put it on the coffee table, Jill. And thanks."

Did she just flutter her eyelashes at him? Good lord, let's be a bit less obvious, Jill. She's definitely flirting with him.

"Oh, and Jill, you can head out now and shop for Ms. Sheridan. Call me if you get done early. I might have you swing by my place."

"My pleasure, sir," she purrs.

She sashays out, her hips about to knock her off her too-tall shoes. I couldn't sway my hips like that on a good day.

"Shall we dig in? Gemini? Hello, is anyone home?"

"Oh! Sorry. What did you say?"

"Wow, someone was a million miles away."

"Yeah, I suppose I was. Um, how long has Jill been working for you?"

"A little over a year."

"And she knows where you live?"

"Yeah, why?"

"Isn't that a bit unusual?"

He shrugs. "I don't think so. Why do you ask?"

"Because I've never known where any of my bosses lived."

He stares at me, rubbing his chin. "You're not jealous of her, are you?"

"No, of course not." I'm quick to answer but the truth is I'm jealous as hell.

"There's nothing between us."

To hell with this. "Have you slept with her?"

The expression on his face is priceless. His usual half-closed lids have popped open. In fact, if the situation were different, I would laugh because his eyes are nearly cartoon-like in their appearance. "Absolutely not. I would never sleep with an employee. I thought I made it clear to you that I don't get involved with my clients."

"True," I say, "but she's not your client."

"When I made that statement, I meant that to include my employees as well. That would be considered gross moral turpitude in my estimation."

I take a good hard look at him and determine he's telling the truth. "She wants to sleep with you. In a very bad way. We probably should've had this discussion before we slept together, but if you and I continue to have sex, I would ask that, um ..." and I run out of steam. I feel strange making demands on him because I have no right, but I have to say this. "This is weird since we don't really know each other, and I know I have no right to make this demand, but I don't sleep around, Drex. And I guess what I'm saying is I would prefer if you didn't either."

He gives me that raw, sexy look that causes goosebumps to erupt all over my skin. He stomps to the door and the lock clicks into place, then stalks back, his gaze so intense, it penetrates my skin. Every nerve ending comes to life. How he does it, I have no idea, but it's like his eyes weave a spell on me. They melt away everything except for the burgeoning heat that blossoms inside me. I want this man. I want his hands to touch me all over. Now.

When he's standing in front of me, he reaches down and fists my shirt, hauling me to my feet. Then his other arm wraps around me and presses my hips into his as his mouth possesses mine. But before he kisses me, he says, "There'll be no other partners for me as long as you do the same. But if you don't, there *will* be hell to pay. I. Don't. Share." He kisses me once. Hard. Controlling. And dominant. And then says, "Now, let's eat before our dinner gets cold."

He releases me and I drop, none too gently, back onto the couch, breathless. He certainly plays this game well. And he just taught me something: Drex Wolfe likes to be in control, not only in his business life, but where his women are concerned too. Damn is he ever territorial and he's just made that abundantly clear. The corners of my mouth lift as I discover that I quite like that quality in him. But how the hell does he expect me to eat after that?

I observe him as he pulls the food out. He's unwrapping everything, apparently unaffected by what just transpired. I, on the other hand, can't catch my breath. As he's working to get our dinner set up, he hands me a napkin and fork, but his hand lingers on mine, sending currents of heat up my arm and into my belly. Shit, how does he do that?

"Eat, Gemini. You haven't had anything all day. And with what I have in mind for you, you'll need some nourishment."

How does he expect me to eat after he says that? "Are you always this bossy?"

He pierces me with one of his looks. "Oh, Gemini, I think you have it all wrong. You're the one being bossy."

"Me?"

"Yes, you. Did you not just give me orders that I couldn't sleep with anyone but you? In fact, if I recall correctly, you all but insisted."

"Yeah, well, it's something any self-respecting woman would say."

"Did you hear me argue with you?" He runs his finger across my cheek. That's it. Now it's my turn.

My hand folds around his and I grasp his shirt with the other one and pull him to me. Right as my mouth is about to touch his, I say, "No, you didn't argue. Now quit teasing me." And I kiss him. But it's not a short one. It's long, delicious, wet, passionate. He ravages my mouth and I revel in it.

When we're breathless, he says, "You don't care about your dinner?"

"Do I look like I care?"

"It'll be cold."

"Ever hear of a microwave?"

"Sit up."

"I can't. You're lying on me."

He leans back and pulls me into a seated position. My shirt disappears in a whoosh and my bra follows. When he leans his head toward me, I stop him with my hand on his chest. "Oh no, you don't. I'm not sitting here like this while you get to play and I have to look at you in that damn shirt."

He laughs at me. "And you say I'm bossy."

"It's only fair."

"Point taken."

He strips off his shirt and I relish how his muscles ripple with his movements. My arms stretch out to touch them. He's everything a man should be ... hard yet smooth, solid and firm, yet velvety. My body fires everywhere and I can't sit still. He pushes me back down on the couch. "Lift up," he says, tapping my hips. I do as he asks and he slides my sweats off. I'm suddenly conscious of the fact I haven't showered since last night, so I freeze.

"What's wrong?"

"Nothing," I say as I sit up.

"Bullshit, Gemini. You're the worst liar. One minute you're panting after me and the next, you're like ice. What the hell?"

This is really uncomfortable. My face heats because of it, so I raise my hands to cover it.

"Tell me." He's demanding at first, but then he must see how awkward I feel, so he moves between my now very naked legs. Then his arms are around me and his mouth is next to my ear. "What is it, Onyx? You can tell me."

"I haven't had a shower since last night. I don't want you to do that."

"Do what?"

"Go down on me."

"Ah, I see. Well, then, come on."

He pulls me to my feet and I follow, naked, into the bathroom. Why didn't I realize there'd be a shower in here? He turns on the water and when the temperature is just right, we get in and he gives me a very thorough scrubbing. Everywhere. I'm slick with shower gel and suds, but it feels so good, I tell him never to stop as his fingers massage me until I'm calling out to him over and over.

"Drex. I need you."

"No can do, Onyx. No condoms in here."

Acute disappointment rushes through me. It's nearly painful. I slide my body down his with the intention of returning the favor he just bestowed on me, but his voice stops me.

"No, not now. As much as the thought of your luscious, wet mouth delights me, I want us to eat and go home so I can bury myself in you. I want to feel all of you on me, babe. You good with that?"

"Yeah, I'm good," I say as I rub my cheek against him. Then I let him pull me to my feet.

When he shampoos my hair, I know I've died and gone to heaven for the second time.

"Jeez, babe, you sound like you're coming again," he laughs.

"Oh God, this feels divine. Why doesn't it ever feel this good when you wash your own hair?"

"I've never thought about it."

When we're finally finished, he dries me off and wraps my hair in a towel. "Why, thank you. You do a fine job of this. Maybe you should think of changing professions." I wink at him.

He smacks me on the butt as we move into the other room.

"I'm sorry you don't have any other clothes here."

"That's okay. I'm wondering how I'm going to get a brush through my hair since there wasn't any conditioner."

"Here, let me." He takes the brush and starts to work through the tangles. And there are tons of them. "Tell me if I hurt you."

"Just do it because I know there is no other way."

When he's finally done, he says, "How about some dinner?"

We laugh as he carries the pasta containers to the microwave. When the food is again warm, we polish off our plates in record time.

"I'm still hungry. We'll stop for round two on the way home."

"Round two?"

"Yeah. That was just the appetizer."

I laugh. "I thought the shower was the appetizer."

His head turns. "Nope. That was the sex-etizer. We need nourishment if we're going to have any kind of strenuous bedroom activities. By the way, how's your head?"

When I stop to think about it, I marvel at the fact that it doesn't hurt. "Pretty good, I'd say. I took a pill when we got back here, remember?"

He gives me a cheeky grin. "True, but I plan on keeping things this way, Sheridan."

"You do, Wolfe?"

"You bet I do." He extends his hand. "Let's get out of here."

DAMN IF HE isn't serious. He hits a drive-through on the way home and picks up burgers and fries. Even though I protest and say I can't eat a bite, he insists. It only takes us a few minutes to get from the burger joint to his place. He lives in LoDo, or the Lower Downtown area. LoDo is the oldest and most historic section of Denver. It's a mixed-use neighborhood with trendy shops, night clubs and restaurants, but it's also the home of museums, art galleries, and Coor's Field.

"I've always loved this area," I say.

"It's very convenient for me to get to and from the office."

We pull up to a parking lot outside an old warehouse. He parks next to another black SUV. "What's with all the black SUVs?"

"Company cars. I keep several all over the place."

"But why that particular car?"

"It can carry a lot of men and equipment if the need arises."

"So, is this your place?"

"Yeah, come on in."

We enter through a huge wooden door with a high-tech security system. Once his code is entered, he waits and a voice tells him it's okay to unlock the door. Inside, we're in a foyer that opens all the way to the ceiling. It's bare with wooden beams and ductwork showing, giving it a dramatic yet warm effect. Off the hallway to the left appears to be an office. He leads me right and into a large living area that extends into a vast kitchen.

"This place is impressive." It's open to the ceiling again, huge windows affording a view of the cityscape. The walls are old brick and the same wooden beams run across the ceiling. The furniture is comfy and lived-in, not the sleek design of his office, but he still has the state-of-the-art electronics as well. There's a huge fireplace and along one wall hangs probably the largest flat screen TV available. I'm guessing that somewhere hidden amongst all this is an unrivaled sound system. One thing I notice is the absence of any personal touches, such as photos. It's all done very nicely, but there is nothing here that speaks of Drex's love for anything in particular.

"Thanks. I've been here a couple years now and I really love it."

"Cook much?" I'm checking out his professionally designed kitchen.

"Never. I use the microwave, but that's about it. The elegant kitchen is the interior designer's fault. She talked me into it. I would've been happy with a fridge, a warming plate, and a toaster."

The rest of the place is divided into bedrooms. A curved stairway in the back leads to the second floor—two bedrooms, two bathrooms. His bedroom and master bath, a huge space, sits on the main floor down the hall from his office.

"So, you enclosed the ceiling," I say as I look up. No wooden beams or warehouse features in here, other than the brick exterior walls.

"Yeah, it's way too noisy. Plus I added the bedrooms upstairs in that space."

"Oh. I didn't think of that. This is really something. And that bathroom."

"Again, that was the architect and interior designer. I would never have put in something so elaborate. I've never used that tub."

The jetted tub could hold four large people. "Never?" I find that hard to believe. I would think he would've wowed his female companions with its grandeur.

"Not ever."

"Not even your …"

"My what?"

"You know."

"No, I don't."

He's toying with me.

"Your friends with benefits?"

"Nope, don't have any."

"Fuck buddies?"

He laughs. "Don't have those, either."

"Girlfriends?"

"I didn't have one … until yesterday."

"But, we've only just met."

"Gemini, wasn't it you who said that if we were to continue sleeping together, that I wasn't allowed to sleep with anyone else?"

"Well, yeah."

"And didn't I tell you that I don't share? Ever?"

"Yeah."

"So if we're seeing and sleeping with each other exclusively, in my book, that pretty much constitutes us being together … as in dating. Now, that doesn't have to mean anything serious. It just means that we're with each other and won't fuck around. So you need to tell me how you want to do this because I'm a simple guy and right now, I'm getting mixed signals from you."

Wow. He cut through all the bullshit.

"You don't waste any time, do you?" I smile.

"Not when there's something I want. I usually go after it. And

I want you, Onyx." He spreads his arms wide.

His grin is too damn hard to resist and with his arms open as they are, I walk into them. "Well, I guess you could say you've got yourself a girlfriend, then."

A half second later, I'm naked and he has me against the wall. My hands are over my head and his knee is between my legs, hitting me just so. "Goddamn, babe, I didn't think I could ever wait for this. You've had me so jacked up since the office, I can't fucking think straight. I want in you. I want to feel you around me ... I want to feel how tight you are."

Oh, hell. He takes me from zero to sixty with just words.

"Tell me you want me, Gem. Tell me how. Tell me where."

"Right here, Drex. Up against this wall. Hard and fast."

He lets me go for a second and the cool air hits my hot skin. I hate to feel his absence. But soon he's back, holding a condom. He hands it to me and I tear it open with shaking hands. He groans as I roll it on him. God, how can something like putting a condom on someone feel so damn good? As my hand slides up and down his shaft, he makes that sound in the back of his throat that almost has me coming.

"Gem." He brushes my hand away and crushes his mouth on mine. I feel him spread my legs again as his hands move to my ass. Suddenly, he lifts and slides into me, all in one swift movement. I'm lost in the sensation of everything that's Drex. And it feels so fucking good.

"Ahhh, Gem." He's rough as he moves in and out of me. When I cry out, he stops and asks, "Are you okay? I don't want to hurt you."

"Don't stop. You're not hurting me. This is definitely not hurt. It's good. Or great. Yeah. Oh yeah. Right there, Drex."

"Tell me. Tell me how you feel."

"I love it when you fuck me, Drex."

"You like this?" And he thrusts into me, hard.

"Ah, yes! Like that."

Next thing I know, he's carrying me somewhere, and we end up in the kitchen. He puts me on the counter and I lean back and watch him. My legs are now over his shoulders and he's still moving in and out but his thumb moves to my sex and I'm getting ready to climax.

"Come for me, babe. I need to feel it. Now!"

His demands push me right where I want to be and then I hear his groans and know he's right there with me. When things calm down, I realize I've dug my nails into his arms. Blood seeps to the skin.

He hears me suck in my breath and follows my gaze. "Shit, babe, it was worth every damn drop."

Chapter 13

DREXEL
Twists

GEMINI SLEEPS AS I lie in bed, revisiting what we talked about last night. She's a quirky one, all right. She's asked to be in the thick of things and I don't blame her for that. I suppose if decisions were being made regarding my situation, I'd want to be involved too. She started talking about finding a place to live, but I had to put my foot down. She needs to be here for the time being, until all this is settled and I can determine she's safe. Yes, I can see her point about us not living together. But not right now. It's simply too risky.

The funniest thing was when Jill showed up with the shopping bags full of clothes. She only stayed a few minutes, but after she left, Gemini insisted that Jill looked at me like I was dessert.

"I would prefer if she weren't your admin. She makes me uncomfortable. Can she be moved?"

"To where?"

"To a different job, that's where. If we're going to be dating, I don't like the way she looks at you ... like she wants to ... never mind."

"Jesus, Gemini."

"It's true. I know I have no right to ask this of you, but I tell it like it is. There's something about her that gives me a bad feeling and it's probably because she wants you. In her bed."

Thinking over it, I guess she has a point. I've chosen to ignore it, but I know how Jill looks at me. I've never said anything because I've always known it would never amount to anything.

"What are you thinking about that has your brow so furrowed?"

Turning to Gemini, I tug her warm body on top of mine. I was so deep into my thoughts, I didn't notice she'd awakened. "Just that you're right."

"About what?" Her fingers find their way into my hair. She says she loves my hair and I laugh when I think about it. It's never been this long before.

"What you said about Jill. I'm going to transfer her to a different department. And then hire a new admin."

She grins. "You have to hire someone named Gertrude or Myrtle or Ethel."

I'm laughing before I know it. "What? I'll never find someone with names like those. I would think you rather have a Sam or a David."

"Well, there's a thought."

"Nix that. I was only joking." Hell will freeze over before I'd hire Sam or David so they can eye-fuck her. "But I'll never find a Gertrude or Ethel."

"Yes, you will. I want you to hire someone who'll take care of you. And bring you chicken soup to work or a casserole or something. And who'll make sure you have proper food to eat for dinner because you're working late."

When I brush the hair back from her face, one glance at her

tells me she's serious. All humor has been replaced with concern. Her sincerity touches a place I've never felt before. "You really want someone to cook for me?"

"Yes, I do."

Grabbing her hand, I kiss her palm and my throat tightens. "Okay. I'll look for those qualities in my next hire."

"Good. At least I'll know you'll be eating right. Then I won't have to worry."

That takes me by surprise. "You don't have to worry about that. I'm fine. I know what I'm doing."

"That's not all I worry about. I'm scared about these crazy people that are after me. These are terrorists for God's sake. And there's always that one possibility. For all the precautions my mom took, look what happened to her?"

"But I'm trained in this stuff. I know things your mom didn't or couldn't know. Remember how I told you that story when I was in the Special Forces? I was in the most dangerous place in the world at the time. But look, I'm here now. And that night I rescued you in Austin. I had six armed men chasing me down, but I got away. I know how to handle this. I've dealt with IEDs, snipers and all sorts of nasty things."

"Maybe, but you don't know how to cook." She winks.

"Well, you should be happy for that because there's much less likelihood of me killing either one of us, then."

"I guess that's a good thing." Her palm massages my cheek. "I think I have some clothes I need to try on."

"Model them for me?"

"Okay."

She hops off and digs through the bag. Then she grimaces. "I think Jill bought these for Gertrude or Ethel." She holds up some jeans with an elasticized waistband that look like something my grandmother might wear.

"Fuck. She's trying to pull a number on you. Well, she just

nailed her own coffin. I'm not only moving her to a different department, I may be moving her out of the company. What else is in there?"

Everything she pulls out is ridiculous.

"Tell you what. Trust me?"

"Well, yeah. Why?"

"Because I'm taking this shit back and buying you some different things. The stores don't open for another hour so that give us some time for, oh, I don't know ..."

Her giggle delivers the response I'd hoped for.

MY PHONE RINGS as I'm walking out the door. It's Huff, calling to let me know Gemini's phony IDs are ready to go.

"Excellent. Can you call Brady and let him know he can call in her prescriptions? And tell him to use that pharmacy DWInvestigations uses. Have them call me when they're ready. And can you get Dr. Davis in to implant a chip? I want to make sure if anything happens to her, we can find her. Thanks, Huff."

"We're getting you back in business, babe," I call out. She's got the TV on so I have to shout.

"What?"

I walk into the living area and let her know the good news. "I should be back soon and then we'll grab some lunch on the way to the office."

"See you in a bit."

It only takes a few minutes to get to the shopping area in town. I head straight to the main department store where we maintain a personal shopper. She's expecting me, and I've given her a heads-up of what I need. By the time I arrive, the shopper has jeans, a few tops, a dress, and shoes for each outfit. She's also picked out some lingerie. I hand over the bag filled with items that need to be returned and I'm back out the door.

When I get home, Gemini is on the computer.

"What are you doing?"

She jumps up and her hand flies to her chest. "Shit, Drex, you scared me."

"Sorry. You're not checking your email are you?"

"No, I thought about it but then I figured someone would be spying on it or whatever you call it."

"Damn. It's a good thing you didn't. They're probably tracking the IP address. Mine is untraceable, but once they saw your account had been hit, they'd know it was from you."

"I was looking up Panama City, thinking about how weird it was that we went there all the time. Out of all the places to go, why there? There has to be some connection with that, don't you think?"

She may have something. "The storage unit in Austin may open that clue for us."

"When can we go?"

"I think we need to wait a few more days."

"No! We need that information."

"Come here." I walk her into the living area and sit. "Austin is filled with people we need to avoid. I want to throw them off. If we run back there, they're going to know that we know something. That's the last thing we want."

"But everything we need is there."

"Not true. I still want you to focus on things your mom did, things she said. Anything you can think of. It can be the tiniest thing. I also want you to start the meds Brady prescribed. I want to kick those migraines in the ass."

"But I haven't had one all day."

"And that's great. But Gemini, let's do this my way. And before you say anything else, all I want to do is help you. Got that? I have no ulterior motives." She rubs her hands together and I know something's not sitting well with her. "Talk to me, babe."

"It's just that I want this to be over. I'm afraid you're going to get hurt. Or someone else will."

"That makes us even then, 'cuz it scares the hell out of me that you're going to get hurt ... that you won't listen to me and you'll do something impulsive, like maybe go to Austin on your own." When her eyes widen, I know I've hit on something. "And if that were to happen, that would be the worst thing ever. Do you wanna know why?"

She looks at me, those wide black orbs, and nods.

I take her hands in mine. "You won't like what you hear, but I've been trained to kill, Gemini. To take out the enemy. I'm the expert here, not you. I was trained by the best. I'm not your everyday, run-of-the-mill agent or street cop. I'm specialized in mixed martial arts. I'm a trained sniper. I can tell by the dilation of someone's pupils if they're lying. I know how to read people, interrogate them. You should've figured that out when I had you handcuffed to the bed back in Austin. My expertise is well beyond yours, so don't even think of doing this on your own. You have to put your faith and trust in me.

"Let me tell you a story. It's about a former client of mine. His girlfriend was abducted by her ex and he was a crazy fucker. Used to beat the shit out of her. We didn't know where he took her because he left no clues. We didn't even know the asswipe's name. My guys tracked him down and Shan, my client and I went in after Riviera. We got to her in time. But it was because we used the proper methods. Shan wanted to drop and go, but I wouldn't let him. I forced him to follow my rules. Put your trust in me, Gemini, and my team will get this solved."

She launches herself at me and says against my neck, "Okay. I will. But I'm still scared for you, for me, and for everyone else involved. Because these guys are bad. And if they're like the terrorists I've read about, they don't use guns. They use bombs,

Drex. Suicide bombs, even. And then no one will be safe around them."

My arms wind around her and I hold her tight, but I don't dare confirm her fears. The truth is, she's hit closer to home than I want to let on. What she doesn't know is that I'm already monitoring this place and the office for that kind of activity. I don't take anything for granted.

I kiss her head. "Do you want to try on your new clothes? I thought we were going to lunch? And I know you haven't had a headache, but don't forget to keep up with your Lortabs."

"Yeah, sorry. I got sidetracked. And I did take a pill already."

She rummages through the bag and pulls out the clothes. "Damn, you really know how to pick things out!"

I laugh at her. "I didn't do it. Heather, the personal shopper, did. If it doesn't work, her card is in the bag. You can take it all back and she'll help you."

"Hey, what's the dress for?"

"Our dinner date."

"When's that?" She smiles.

"This weekend."

The look of pure joy on her face almost brings me to my knees. If she asked me there and then to give her the world, I'd find a way to do it. No questions asked.

"You're a sneak," she says. But she's happy with my plans because her grin isn't going anywhere.

She holds up the dress, a deep blue that looks stunning next to her dark hair. God, can she be any more gorgeous? "We also need to get you to a salon to have your hair evened out."

"Oh, I forgot." She bunches her hair and twists it into a bun.

"Okay, start trying on."

She pulls out the jeans first and they fit just right.

"Too tight?" she asks.

"They were made for you." I swallow and lick my suddenly

dry lips. The next pair fits perfectly too.

"Are you sure these aren't too tight?"

"No, they fit you like they should." Her ass couldn't possibly look any better. It's all I can do not to grab her and strip them off and fuck the hell out of her.

She flashes another huge smile. "Okay, I'm ready, then."

GEMINI IS IN my office, working on a laptop, trying to tie Panama City and Austin together. I've had a chat with Jill and dismissed her. She was none too pleased and we had quite the verbal battle. It got ugly by the time I had her escorted out of the building. Human resources is now searching for a Gertrude or an Ethel as a replacement. In the meantime, Ellie has the position. She's efficient and knows the company fairly well. I'm hoping she can handle the workload because I can't afford to train someone right now.

"I'm sending Huff and Blake to Austin."

Gemini looks up from the computer and doesn't say anything. She doesn't have to. Her scowl speaks loudly enough.

"You're not going, so don't even think about it. Too risky."

"But what if they don't find what they're looking for?"

"Then they'll come back here and we start over," I say.

She looks at the documents spread out on the coffee table. She's been trying to dissect each one, the same way I did at Jeff's. We're interrupted by a knock on the door.

"It's open."

Ellie sticks her head in and whispers, "Ms. Sheridan, there's a delivery out here for you. From the pharmacy." Then she looks at me. "And Mr. Wolfe, Dr. Davis is here."

"Thank you," Gemini says as she gets up.

"Send Dr. Davis in," I tell Ellie. Gemini shoots me a questioning look "Wait." I intercept her before she can get to the door. "Don't forget, you're Mindy Simmons. And I'll explain about Dr. Davis in a minute."

"Got it."

She signs for the delivery and immediately opens up the new medications. "Wow, that seems like a lot of pills."

"As long as you're headache-free, it's worth it."

"Right. It's so nice not waking up with the axe man in the morning."

"Who?"

"The axe man. You know, the head-splitter."

I hate to be reminded of Gemini's medical ordeal. If I hadn't witnessed her suffering, I doubt I would've ever believed that headaches could be so severe.

Ellie ushers Dr. Davis in and I know I have a battle ahead.

"Gemini, this is Dr. Davis. He's here to implant a microchip in you."

"A what?" She looks like she wants to punch me. "Were we going to discuss this?"

"The idea didn't occur to me until this morning. But listen to me."

Dr. Davis interrupts. "Do you need some privacy?"

Our conflicting shouts piggyback one another.

"Yes!"

"No!" I groan and my hand flies to the back of my neck. I should've anticipated her reaction. "Dr. Davis, stay put. Gemini, listen to me." I'm using my authoritative voice, and I know she won't be pleased, but I don't give a damn. She needs to understand the importance of this. "If something happens, if they find you, take you, this tiny microchip will lead us to you. I don't really care what you think about this—it's for your safety. I have one. Huff has one. Blake has one. All of my field agents have one. And you'll have one too, even if I have to tie you down while Davis puts it in you. Are we clear?"

She's about as pissed off as a human being can be. "And where do you want this invasive thing to go?"

She exasperates the hell out of me. "Do you not get this? This is for your own goddamn safety."

"Yes, Drex, I get it. But a discussion would've been nice. Now, Dr. Davis, where is this thing going to be placed in *my body*?"

Dr. Davis looks at me and I nod. "They usually are placed under the arm, in the triceps area."

"That won't do," I say. "They'd find it. It needs to go somewhere else."

"Where else did you have in mind?" she sneers.

Two can play this game. "I would normally recommend placement in an area on the body where there is hair, but since you have a full Brazilian without so much as a landing strip, I'm at a loss."

Her quick intake of breath tells me I've hit my mark. Instead of feeling a sense of satisfaction, I feel quite the opposite, like the biggest ass in the world.

Dr. Davis saves the day. "Why don't we put it next to her hipbone? The bone will help camouflage it."

"Great idea."

"Ms. Sheridan, I'll need you to slip your jeans down your hips a bit."

She looks at me and isn't at all happy, but she does what the good doctor requests.

It only takes a few moments for him to complete the procedure. The flat microchip slips right beneath the skin, so it's undetectable. Then he glues her together and applies a small bandage.

"Keep it dry for the rest of the day, but you can get it wet tomorrow. The incision is so tiny that you won't even notice it. In a few days, the glue will disappear and you'll be fine," Dr. Davis says.

"That's it?"

"That's it."

He packs up his kit and I thank him as he leaves.

"Thank you for being so forthcoming," she says, voice dripping with sarcasm.

"Gemini, I'm sorry." And I am. "But the idea hit me and I knew it needed to be done ASAP. Before anything happened to you. I didn't have the opportunity to discuss it. I would have if the time had presented itself. I told Huff to get Davis here when I spoke to him this morning, on my way to pick up your clothes. I'm sorry. Please forgive me."

She nods. I give her a hug. "Thank you. And I'm sorry for being an ass, but I'm not sorry for getting this chip into you. Your safety is that important to me."

"You didn't have to be such a crass-hole in front of the doctor." She punches me in the arm. "That bit you said about my ... my ... was that really necessary?"

"No. You're right. I am a crass-hole. And I apologize. But if I have to be a crass-hole again to keep you safe, you can bet I will."

"DREX, TAKE A look at this."

It's Friday, late afternoon, and we're in my office. Gemini has spent the last few days working on Panama City. She's relentless, as good as anyone I have here in the company. I need her to come to work for me.

She's sitting on the couch, her feet curled under her, working on the laptop. I take a seat next to her.

"A hospital—address is 615. And another storage facility on Sixth Street. A bank with an address of 615. All within a mile radius of each other. And there are all sorts of military bases around the Panama City area. Coincidence? Or part of the answer?"

"Damn, you're good."

"I think that whatever is in Austin is only the beginning."

"Or do you think Austin is just a decoy?"

"Why'd you have to say that? Now I'm confused again." She wrinkles her brow.

"You have to look at every angle. You mom was smart. Like a fox. But Gemini, I don't think her death was an accident."

"What?" Her head whips toward me.

"I know. Listen, for all the precautions your mom took, I can't think she would've gotten into a car accident. I had Huff pull her accident report and I've gone over the details. It doesn't add up. The report says there were more than three sets of tire tracks, but only one witness who claims she lost control of the car. I think someone forced her off the road. Maybe more than one other car. Forced her into that embankment. She was too aware of everything to take her focus off the road like that. So I'm saying that you shouldn't look for the obvious—she wants us to think Austin, but there's way more to it than that. And I agree with your Panama City theory. In fact, I'm wondering if this key opens something there, and that Austin is the decoy. Or maybe Panama City will lead us back to Austin. We have to keep our minds open to everything."

She's silent for a few minutes. "So now what?"

I smile. "We take a team to Panama City. But we don't fly directly there. We fly somewhere else and then split up into three to throw them off."

Now she's smiling. "When?"

"Next week. I want everything to be arranged down to the last letter."

We are all disappointed in Huff and Blake's trip to Austin when they return with nothing. The storage unit had no rental in the name of Michelle Sheridan, Rachel Miller or Gemini. We go back to the drawing board on that one. Simply put, there has to be a connection between Panama City and Austin.

SATURDAY MORNING I wake and reach out for Gemini, but she's not in bed. She's been working like a demon is chasing her, so I assume she's back on the computer, but I hear a faint sound coming from the opposite side of the bed. I find her on the floor, curled in a ball, her arms hugging her head.

"Shit." I hit the bathroom in search of medicine and water, and hurry back to her. "Here. I have you." Taking one of her hands, I give her a Maxalt and a Lortab. I hold the water so she can drink. The blinds aren't completely closed, so I hit the button and the room darkens. Then I run to the freezer to make her an ice bag. My first inclination is to move her back into bed, but I know any motion sends waves of pain and nausea rolling through her.

What the hell brought this on? She started on Brady's prescribed regimen. And then it hits me. She was on the computer all day yesterday and when we got home last night, she went back to work. We were both so tired, we ended up crashing. It was the first time since ... well, since *then* that we didn't have sex. Does this really mean that a day without sex for her turns into one of those fucking migraines?

She's still on the floor, so I curl behind her and pull her against me. Then I kiss her neck and tell her what I've just discovered. Her hand squeezes mine, letting me knows she hears me. Then she moves my hand between her legs, giving me my answer. She wants me to make love to her, even though I question if she can get into it. My hesitation tells her my concerns.

She turns in my arms and says, "Drex, you have to help me." Her face is wet. Her eyes beg me to help her. She hurts so much, I know I can't resist.

"You're sure?"

"Make it go away. Now. I know you can." Her words are ragged whispers, but they resonate in my head. It's easy to remove her scant clothing. An orgasm is what she needs most, so that's what she'll get. There won't be any teasing or taunting this time. I go straight to her sex with my mouth. My tongue is on her clit and I know exactly what she likes, so that's what I do. Her fingers wrap in my hair and pull me closer while my tongue brings her to that place she so desperately seeks. As soon as she finishes, she pulls me to her mouth and greedily kisses me.

Kissing her is pure pleasure, but I need to know how she feels. "Tell me, Gemini. Better?"

"Yeah. But I need you, Drex. I need more. Now. Inside me."

She pulls my boxers off and reaches for me.

"Wait, babe. I need to get a condom." I find what I need, put the damn thing on, and haul her ass into the bed. I'm all for a good lay, but not on the floor. When she's spread out on the bed, I lean back on my knees and look at her for a minute.

"What a lovely sight you are."

"You just gonna stare at me, or are you gonna please your girlfriend?"

"Put your legs on my shoulders."

She does and I thrust into her. "This good for you?"

"Ah, yeah." She moans and so do I. We go at it like we've never had sex before. I brush my thumbs across her hardened nipples and she demands I fuck her harder. It's all I can do not to lose it when she tells me how much she loves the way my cock makes her feel. My hands move over every part of her that I can touch. Every time we're together, I walk away with a stronger need to be with her. My fingers burn with the memory of her skin.

"Like this?" I ask.

"Yes!" she says as her fingers sink into the muscles of my

hips.

We're a pair, I think, as I watch her. She likes it hard and fast. Rough and gritty, just like I do. Not always, but she'll tell me when she wants it that way.

"Damn, you're so tight on me." I lift one of her legs and put it on my other shoulder, so both of her legs are together. Then I roll her slightly on her side and continue to slide in. "Do you like this?"

"Ah ... ah ... yeah."

"Babe, I love to hear you when I slide in and out of you. Your voice turns me on even more."

"This is so good, Drex."

"Do you want me to make you come again?"

"Yes."

"Tell me or I'll stop."

"No."

"No what?" I stop for a second and she grabs me.

"Please."

"Please what?"

"Make me come, Drex."

"That's what I'm going to do." Her body is so beautiful as she moves with my rhythm and I bring my hand to her clit because I want to set her off. Her back arches as the muscles on her inner thighs tighten and contract, indicating she's so close.

"Look at me so I can watch as your body works my dick. Then I want you to watch me come." I can tell she's right there. She gives off signals. The way her fingers grasp me, the sound of her voice, the clenching of all her muscles. And then there it is. When she calls out my name, I know I can let loose.

We're both dripping with sweat afterward. I love the way she brushes my hair off my forehead as I lean over her to nuzzle her neck.

"Unlike any other."

"What?" she asks.

"You. You're unlike any other. Your taste, smell, the way you feel."

"I don't quite know what to say to that, Drex."

"Hmm, no witty comeback?"

She looks at me and then touches my cheek. I suppose this is one of those tender moments that two lovers share. I can't really say, because I've not had any like this before. I've always been a fuck and go kind of guy. But not with her. Never could I do that with her. It's impossible to refrain from kissing her. How the hell could I get up and walk away from this? She's so alluring as she lies there, gazing at me. She has my head and guts tied up in knots like they've never been. I dip down to her mouth and trail my tongue across her lips. Knowing I can't just remain silent, I break it with, "I take it your headache is gone?"

She nods, still staring at me.

I grin at her. "You know, you're going to have to say something, sooner or later. My preference is sooner rather than later."

She grins.

"You sure know how to make your girlfriend think."

"Think? My intentions were to make you come and to get rid of your migraine." I think my comment went way too deep. Why did I speak my mind?

"You certainly did that. Did you really mean it?"

"Mean what?"

"Don't play dumb on me here, Drex. You know damn well what I mean."

"Yeah, I meant it. I wouldn't have said it if I hadn't."

"This scares me. I don't want it to be my lifeline. I used to be this girl who had no fears. My dreams were to take on the world, like anyone feels when they get out of school. From the first time I rode a mountain bike, I was hooked. That's when I knew I wanted to turn it into a career. My knowledge of the sport could put me ahead of the competition in marketing. I would dream about it. But then that dang crash stole everything from me. And now all this about my mom. I'm worried I'm latching onto you because you offer me an out ... a safety net."

Her voice trembles with her words. "I don't care, babe. If you want to latch on, do it. I'll worry about that later. Right now I want you like I've wanted nothing else before. If this thing between us fizzles, then it fizzles. But let's ride this wave while it's here. Stop overthinking it."

"Have you been with a lot of women?"

Her question derails me. "What?"

She doesn't look away. "Women? Have you been with many?"

"Damn, Gemini. Why would you want to know *that*? Especially now, while I'm still deep inside you?"

"I don't know. I just do. Because I'm curious. And because I haven't."

"You haven't been with many women?"

"Funny. No, I haven't been with many men."

"That's nice of you to share, but you want to know the truth?" My fingers trace the outline of her brows.

"Yeah."

"I don't care about any of that, because I would feel the same about you if you'd been with a hundred men."

"You really would?" Doubt echoes in her voice.

"Yes. Because it wouldn't change what's here." I point to her head. "Or here." I lay my hand over her heart. "Do our mistakes define us? And should we pay for them forever?"

"I don't follow," she says.

"Let's say you slept with a hundred guys. You were trying to figure yourself out. Or you were lonely. Whatever the reason. Should you hate yourself for that and pay for those mistakes forever? I don't think so. Because they wouldn't define the true you."

"I think I see what you mean. You really are a good man, Drexel Wolfe." She kisses my cheek.

"Maybe, maybe not. And, yes, I have."

"Huh?"

"I've been with a lot of women."

"A lot?"

"'Fraid so. But I won't apologize for my behavior. I never made false promises to any of them. And I'll never make any to you, either."

She nods and I see her swallow. "Fair enough. I don't want you to. I want complete honesty between us, always. And if I get in the way of things, just let me know. Got it?"

"Oh, Onyx, you getting in the way isn't what I'm concerned about. It's my past that's the issue."

"What do you mean?"

"It's complicated."

She laughs. "Oh, and my past isn't?"

"You're right. Yours is as bad as mine, although mine is all my doing. You didn't have a choice in yours."

I move to get up.

"Where are you going?"

"Condom." I point down. After I take care of business, I crawl back in bed and pull her next to me. She's got that just-fucked look, and I tell her so.

She laughs. "What do you expect? You just thoroughly fucked me." Then she tilts her head. "Is that water I hear?"

"Yep. We're going for a swim."

"Huh?"

"Come on." I take her hand and pull her behind me. The tub is half full by now so I tell her to add the bubbles. "I'm not a bubble kind of guy."

"I never took you for one. I'm surprised you even have

bubbles on hand."

"I just got them. For you. Since I've never used this damn thing, I thought you and I would christen it. And it wouldn't be proper without bubbles, now, would it?"

She giggles. "I haven't had a bubble bath since I was a kid."

"Then this will be a blast."

She pours in the bubble bath and we get in as the water continues to rise.

I spin her around, pulling her back against my chest. Brushing her hair to the side, I lick her neck. Next, I move to her shoulder and my fingers tease her nipples.

"I want to kiss you," she says.

I release her arms and she turns in my lap. Her hands grip the sides of my face and her mouth is on mine, hungry and wet. My dick has turned to stone as it stands firm between us, and I don't want to get out of the tub for another condom. When she takes my bottom lip between her teeth and bites down, I almost lose it. My groan makes her release it.

"How're we gonna do this?"

"You play dirty, Gemini. Look at me."

"I am looking at you."

"No! I mean here." I take her hand and put it on me. "This is what your mouth does to me."

"Well, what are you gonna do about it?"

"Well, smarty-pants, the condoms are on the counter."

"Um, I can't be smarty-pants because I'm not wearing any pants."

My hand spreads across her chest and I gently push her aside. Then I stand and shake the water off. Her eyes are glued to my erection.

"Is this what you want?"

She nods.

I step out of the tub and head for the condoms.

Chapter 14

GEMINI
Unraveling

WHEN DREX STANDS up, I want to put my hand around him. He's magnificent. His body is all muscle and smooth skin. But mostly raw sexuality. He's utterly beautiful. It's impossible not to suck in my breath; I know he hears me when the corner of his mouth lifts.

Water sloshes as he gets out of the massive tub. His ass is unreal. Droplets glisten as rivulets roll down his backside. I'm mesmerized by the sight of all that glory, packaged in one hot man. I can almost feel the drool dripping off my chin.

"How long before those pills take effect?" he asks.

"Huh?"

"Your birth control pills?"

"I'm not sure. I think one full cycle, but I need to check."

"Good. Then we won't have to worry about these things. Are you okay?" he asks as he notices I still haven't blinked.

"Oh, yeah. Just enjoying the view."

"Stand up."

"What?"

"You heard me."

I rise to my feet. He leans against the side of the tub and stares at me. I move to cross my arms.

"Don't do that." He stares for a moment, then says, "Turn around."

"Why?"

"Because I asked you to."

"No, you didn't. You told me to."

"Will you turn around, Gemini? I would like to enjoy the view, too."

I do, and my body heats even though I can't see him.

"Bend over and lean on your hands against the side of the tub." I do as he says, because I'm anxious to see where this is going. "Damn, you have a pretty ass." Then I feel his fingers. They slide along me and then penetrate deep. If he keeps this up, I won't last very long and I tell him.

"Is that a bad thing, Onyx?"

"No, ahh, but I want you."

He chuckles. "And you'll have me ... soon."

Holy hell, his fingers are magic as they swirl and circle inside and out. When he stops, I want to scream.

"Don't move. I want you just like that."

I look over my shoulder when I hear water splashing. He stands and puts on the condom. Soon I feel him pushing inside me, and I'm so full, so stretched. It's almost too much like this. And then he starts to move hard and fast. Rough. His hands are on my hips and he's moving in and out, but he's making those groans that spur me on.

I cry out ... loud.

He stops and asks, "Too much?"

"No! Don't stop." He picks up where he left off. Forceful, aggressive. His hips slap into my ass and then his hand reaches around and finds my sex, but it isn't necessary. I'm in orgasm land anyway. I squirm something fierce. And his fingers work me in unison with the motion of his body. I want him to stop. I need him to stop because I'm overly sensitive now, but he doesn't. He's on a different track altogether. And he holds me so tight I can't move away.

"Come on, babe, again. Do it for me again."

What the hell is he talking about?

He pounds into me and I'm imprisoned by his arm and hand. I'm almost screaming, locked between pleasure and pain. Right when I think it's more than I can bear, another climax rips into me. He follows, calling my name. I'm oblivious to all else. My legs can barely hold me up, but his arms have me. He pulls me back in the water onto his lap, holding me against his chest.

"Are you trying to fuck me to death?" I pant.

His chest rumbles with laughter.

"I was just getting you back."

"For what?"

"For working that mouth of yours on me like you did."

"It was just a kiss. And I still think you're trying to kill me."

His hand grabs my chin and turns my head so he can look at me. His eyes smolder. "Gemini, there's no such thing as just a kiss with you. You unravel me."

He's earnest and my core tightens. "I'll keep that in mind the next time."

"See that you do. I would hate for that to happen at an inopportune time."

What does he mean by that? He doesn't give me time to think about it because he starts washing me from top to bottom. He's turned on the jets so the bubbles multiply. I can't stop the giggles.

Before we know it, bubbles are threatening to overtake us. "I think we may have used too much bubble bath," he says.

"Whatever gave you that idea?" I'm dying with laughter. Bubbles everywhere. "Think you need to shut the jets off?"

He hits the off button and then stands. "Let's get in the shower."

"The shower?"

"How else are we gonna get all these suds off?"

We're covered about three inches deep. You can't see any skin.

"Next time, buy bath salts. They don't make suds."

"I'll keep that in mind."

NOW THAT WE'RE squeaky clean, we wait for the hair stylist to arrive that Drex has arranged to come to his place.

"I'm going to tell her my boyfriend wanted to try his hand at hairstyling."

He smirks and grabs my hand. "I think you should have them change the color."

"You don't like my color?"

"I love your color and would keep it like that forever. But I'm thinking about your safety. And don't let them cut it. This way you can still pin it up. Besides, I love it like this too much."

"Wouldn't it be better to get wigs?"

He's quiet for a brief moment. "Yeah, and I should probably have a couple different IDs made up for you too. After we get the wigs, we can do that."

The doorbell rings and he lets Stacy in.

Ninety minutes later, I'm newly coiffed and ready for the big reveal. Drex stands as he sees me walk toward him. He appraises me without uttering a word. He wears that brooding look that he sometimes gets and I wonder if my cut displeases him. I don't have time to ponder it because he grabs a wad of cash, stuffs it in Stacy's hand and practically shoves her out the door.

"Whoa. I take it you don't like it," I say.

He doesn't say anything but tromps toward me. When he reaches me, he leans over and says against my mouth, "Don't you ever think of cutting your hair. Ever." Then his mouth is on mine ... possessive and insistent. It ends as abruptly as it began. He straightens, gives me one more look, and says, "You look perfect."

"GET OUT OF here," I say.

"No. I've seen you naked. I don't know why this is such a big deal."

I cross my arms. "It just is. Now scram."

Since this is our first official date, I want to surprise him. This is so new to me that I want to look special. That's why I'm kicking him out of the room.

He groans as he moves to leave.

"You're forgetting something."

"Oh yeah? What?" he says.

"Your clothes."

He nods, heads for the huge closet, and pulls out what he's going to wear. My eyes are closed because I want to be surprised too.

Even though we had the bubble bath and shower earlier, I hit the shower again. My legs need a quick shave and I have to make sure I'm smooth as silk for my date. Next, it's makeup. Running on some eyeliner and then brushing on blush, I look to make sure I'm presentable.

Now it's dress time. Pulling the garment out of the bag, I smile at how pretty it is. I slip into my lacy undergarments, or what little bits of them there are, and smile. Drex loves those tiny lacy things, as proven by the second delivery from the personal shopper. I step into the dress, a side zip so I don't have trouble fastening up. And last, the shoes. The man must love sky-high heels. Too bad he doesn't have to wear them—maybe he'd change his mind. On second thought, no, he wouldn't. As I look at myself in the mirror, I know exactly why he chose these shoes. And dress. They're perfect.

When I walk into the den, I look around and I'm surprised to see the place is lit by dozens of candles. Drex is waiting for me on the sofa, holding a glass of amber liquor. Upon seeing me, his lips part and he slowly licks them. He sets his glass down and stands. When he gets about a foot away, he reaches out and brushes the hair off my shoulder.

"You're the most beautiful thing I've ever seen," he says, moving his lips to my neck. When he straightens, he asks me to turn around. He says, "Perfect."

"Thank you. And thank you for the dress. And the shoes, too." My heart bangs so loudly I'm positive he can hear it. I move to kiss him, but he stops me.

"Don't. If you do that, I'll start something I can't finish." He smiles to soften his rejection. I still want to kiss him so I tug him to me and kiss his cheek instead.

The ring of the doorbell interrupts us, signaling the arrival of the caterer. We've decided it would be safer for us to eat at home. Drex lets him in and we wait while he sets up our dinner. Fifteen minutes later, it's just the two of us.

WE'RE SEATED AT the candlelit dining room table, sipping a glass of wine and eating our appetizers.

"You know, this is my first official dinner date," I confess.

He cocks his head. "You're joking."

"Nope. That's why I wanted to get dressed without you in the room."

"But what about Nick? Didn't he take you out?"

My face falls. I think back to Nick and his death.

Drex's hand is on mine. "I'm sorry. I wasn't thinking."

"No, it's okay. I still can't believe he's dead. All because of me. And Drex, I didn't love him like that. I mean, I think I loved him more as a friend, you know? The thing about Nick and me—he was very sweet and all, but there was never any spark. When things went south, they went south fast. There wasn't any substance to us. As for dating, we didn't have any money. Or at least he didn't. I never told him I had money. I thought that if my mom felt it was important enough to hide from me, then I'd better not let anyone know about it, either.

"So I continued to live the way I'd always lived. I worked in a mountain bike shop and earned money that way. And that was my only extravagance too ... mountain bikes and all the accessories. Nick never took me out like this, and I didn't care."

"You're so different."

"Different? From what?"

"Just different. And let's leave it at that."

"Okay." I'm not sure what to say. "I hope that's a good thing?"

Drexel laughs. "Oh, it's a very good thing."

A grin spreads across my face. "That's nice to know."

"And you speak your mind."

"Yep, that's me," I say, scrunching my face.

"But that's what I like about you. I don't have to guess at what you're thinking. You usually tell it like it is. I love that you don't give a shit about things most women do. You're not materialistic."

I shrug. "That's probably because I was raised without the fluff, and then I never had any friends so I didn't know what it was like to have it."

"It's nice. Really nice, Gemini."

"It's not something I'm even aware of."

"That's what's so great about it. I wanted to ask you earlier ...

your headaches seem to be doing better."

I can't help but beam. "Yes. I'm not sure if it's the medication or the ... " My cheeks heat. "Or maybe it's a combination of both."

"Honey, I don't care what it is, as long as you're not hurting." He smiles and I turn into a puddle.

"So Drexel Wolfe, tell me something about you. I don't know much about you at all."

A mask slips into place and suddenly he's a different person. "What do you want to know?" His voice has an edge to it. He's not the Drex who was relaxed and smiling just seconds ago.

"Everything. Your favorite foods, places to eat, vacation destinations, what you to do relax. I want to know Drex. What he loves to do." I place my other hand on top of his.

He suddenly stands and busies himself with removing our appetizer plates and bringing our salads. I mull over what could be going through Drex's mind.

He interrupts my thoughts. "It's not what you think," he says as he sits back down.

My eyes meet his and I try to read him, but he's so good at covering things, I come up empty.

"What I think is that whatever it is must be bad enough to make the fun-loving man who just sat here a minute ago vanish like that." I snap my fingers.

"There is so much shit, Gemini."

"Like there isn't with me?"

"Yeah, but it was out of your control."

"You know, I know this guy who made a great point earlier. He told me that people make all sorts of mistakes and they shouldn't have to pay for them forever. I happen to agree with him."

"The mistakes were pretty fucking bad."

"Were they all your fault and done intentionally?"

"No."

"So move on."

He laughs. Not a carefree laugh but a sinister one. "I wish it were that easy."

I need to inject humor into this situation. "Okay International PI of Mystery, whenever you're ready to talk, you know where to come. I'll be right here with open arms and willing ears. And if you need a shoulder to lean on, I've got you covered there too."

He looks away and I can see his throat working as he swallows. Then he nails me with a dark look and he says, "You got it. And just so you know, one day I may need those arms, ears, shoulders, and the rest of that body of yours to ease my pain."

It's one of those moments that implants in my memory and I know I'll remember this day forever. I push my chair back and quickly move to his side. Then I'm crouching next to him as I take his face in my hands. "I've got you on this, Drex. Whatever it is. I've got your back. You understand me?"

He pulls me onto his lap and hugs me tightly. "Yeah, I understand." We stay like this for a bit and when he finally releases me, he smiles. "You have a way of bringing my walls down, Gemini."

As I brush my hand through his hair, I say, "I don't really mean to. I only want to know you, Drex."

"You already know me better than most. You just don't realize it. Now let me grab our main course before it gets cold." He moves to stand but I stop him.

"Let me get this," I say, as I retrieve the rest of our meal.

Throughout dinner, I watch him for clues, subtle hints at who he is, but he gives nothing away. Conversation is about me, my issue at hand, about the food or what our next steps are on Tuesday. He's reticent to talk about himself. It makes me wonder why I never noticed this before. He never talks about growing up, his family, where he went to school. It's as if he didn't exist before me. Was I so immersed in my own problems that I didn't see it, or is it that he is so good at dodging questions?

When we're finished and the plates are cleared, he turns on soft music and pulls me against him. I think he's going to kiss me, but instead he says, "I've wanted to do this since the first night I saw you."

"What's that?"

"Dance with you."

"I didn't take you for a dancing kind of guy."

"I'm not, but I want to move to the music with you in my arms, feeling your body against mine."

It feels so nice. He guides me around the room, his muscles beneath my fingers tensing and relaxing as his body sways to the tempo.

"Gemini."

"Hmm?"

"When I'm with you, you're all I can focus on. And it worries me."

"I don't know what to say to that, Drex. Do you want us to be apart from each other? I can get my own place."

"No! Then I would have to put a team of guards on you, and frankly, I don't trust anyone to watch over you as well as I can."

I smirk. "Is it because you have an ulterior motive?"

His expression turns dark and I'm surprised by it. "No. I worry about your life, Gemini. I'm concerned someone will kill you. You need to take this threat seriously."

"I do take this seriously. My God, what do you think I've been doing?" I stiffen and pull away from him, out of his arms. "Do you think I've been poring over all that information on the Internet for kicks and giggles? I'm scared out of my wits. I'm scared someone's going to hurt you or your men too. Fuck, Drex."

He scrubs his face and sighs. "I'm sorry. I don't know why I'm acting like an ass other than the fact that I'm uneasy. Those men have to realize you're with me and I'm afraid they'll show up here one day. So we need to be more aware of things ... be more on guard and such."

"What do you want me to do? How can I help?"

He rolls his shoulders and says, "I don't want you to go anywhere without a bodyguard."

"Okay."

"But right now, I want you to kiss me."

Wow. Rapid change of gears. I slowly approach, trying to read his expression. His hands are fisted and I don't know if it's because he's frustrated with me, the case, or with himself. I place my hands on his shoulders and lean in to touch my lips to his.

"No, Onyx, kiss me like you mean it. Like the world's gonna end and this is your last chance."

"Why are you talking like this? You're scaring me."

"Because I want your passion. I want your aggression. I want to feel you, Gemini. All over. I want to know that I've gotten into your blood as much as you've gotten into mine."

"Drex, how can you even doubt that?"

"Show me," he demands.

I do and when we come together, it's with everything we both have burning within us. All the fire and lust we feel explodes. What is it about us? Every time we come together, it's as if a fuse ignites and sets off an eruption of sexual energy that we can't control or get enough of. And it's always different. He's demanding, rough, and gentle, all at the same time as he lifts and carries me to the bedroom. Our mouths are greedy for each other and I think how strange it is because it's almost as if we've been apart for months.

Right before I fall asleep, I hear him say, "It will always be this way between us, Gemini. I'll never get enough of you."

Chapter 15

DREXEL
Out. Of. Control.

AND WHAT I told her is true. There will never be enough of Gemini to satisfy me. She's completely invested in and mindful of me. She's deep in my blood, on my mind, everywhere, and that's what has me the most troubled. My shrewdness is gone. The clarity has disappeared and I'm not thinking the way I need to be. My dick has taken over and things need to change.

But I don't want them to. Gemini hasn't the slightest idea of what she does to me. I'm a fucked-up mess over her. When I move her away from me, she moans in protest and it makes my dick jerk. I groan in response. I always give in to my needs, and to hers. But who am I kidding? It's impossible not to. If I had a mind to, I could take her again, right here, right now. And I know she'd be all over me, just as much as I would be her. But I'll wait. We need sleep.

I pull her against me. We fit, like puzzle pieces. As I drift off, I try to count the things about her that turn me on, but there are just too damn many of them. I shut my mind off and let sleep claim my body.

In the middle of the night, something fires up my senses. At first, as I lie there, I'm not sure what it is. Gemini breathes softly next to me, snuggled into my side. A brief scan of the room doesn't reveal anything in particular, so I tune in my hearing. There's not anything I can pinpoint, but I learned long ago not to ignore these feelings. I gently move Gemini, trying not to disturb her slumber, and ease out of bed. I walk to the door and glance down the hall to see if anything's amiss. All looks good, so I head back to the window to check outside. That's when I see it. There's an SUV parked right beneath my window, and it's not one of mine.

"Shit! Gemini, get up. Now!" I yell.

She sits up, confused.

I'm already pulling on my discarded pants.

"What's going on?"

Tossing her my button-down shirt, I yell, "Hurry! Now! Get dressed. We gotta get outta here!" My urgency lets her know I mean business. "Back door. When we hit the alley, go right and run like hell!"

"I don't have shoes," she yells.

"Neither do I. Let's go!"

Then I say, "Security, code red. Activate alarm," as we run down the hallway.

We bust through the back door and hit the alley. By the time we're halfway to the corner, the warehouse erupts in a fireball and knocks us about fifteen feet down the street. The noise is deafening. Pushing myself to my hands and knees, I look to see if Gemini is all right.

"Are you okay?" Gemini cocks her head and looks at me like she doesn't understand me. "Gemini, are you okay?"

She nods. Her hands rub her head and I can see her hands are scraped, but we don't have time for this. I pull her to her feet.

"Come on. We gotta move." She gets up but I can tell she's dizzy when she stumbles and falls.

"My head!" she yells.

I carry her to the corner, where I deem it's safer, to wait for someone to help us. My legs fold beneath me as I collapse and we end up on the curb, my arms coiled around Gemini as she rests in my lap. I pull the shirt together and try to button it. She's naked underneath and didn't have time to do the buttons. My head tells me we need to run, but my legs won't move. I try to stand, but fall back on my ass.

Her hands frame my face and when I look at her, tears streak her cheeks.

"Hey, babe, it's okay. You're fine. We got out and everything's good," I lie.

"No! Drex, this is not good. You almost died because of me. Your house is in ruins because of me. You're covered in blood." Then her mouth is on mine and her hands are in my hair. She stops and her hands are everywhere, on my chest and my abs, and then I get it—she's looking for wounds.

"Hey, Gemini, nothing major other than cuts and bruises. I promise, I'm good." I point to myself so she can see I'm fine.

When she's satisfied I'm not mortally wounded, she breaks down. She speaks but I can't understand what she's saying because she's sobbing too hard. She's in shock, and I recognize that she needs medical attention, but right now, I can only try to soothe her.

Police cars and fire engines swarm the area, along with an ambulance. Huff isn't far behind. Two police officers approach us and immediately start to question us. It's apparent Gemini is in no condition to answer them and I act like I'm bewildered by everything. The cops are the last people I want involved so I let Huff handle them. He knows what to do because we've worked with them before. He'll make them think it could be someone we've been investigating.

The paramedics push everyone aside and try to take Gemini away from me, but she screams and won't release me.

"Sir, she needs to let us examine her," one of them says.

"You can examine her right here."

"No, sir, we need to get her inside the vehicle, where our equipment is."

The truth is, I can't move right now—I'm pretty positive I'm in shock too. The thought of her dying shoots ripples of fear through me like I've never known before.

"Help me to my feet. I'll carry her there."

Two of them assist me and I walk her to the waiting ambulance on trembling legs. I sit on the gurney that awaits us and they put us both inside.

"This is not what we normally do, sir."

"I don't give a damn what you normally do!"

He doesn't say another word but slides the bed into the ambulance and takes our vital signs. He gets all our information and then tells me that Gemini is in shock. I want to scream by this point because I already know that, but I try to remain calm. I tell him about her post-concussion syndrome and that she was complaining about her head. I also tell him her name is Mindy Simmons. Her arms are still latched onto me like a vise, so I whisper that everything is going to be fine.

"Hey, babe, can you hear me?"

She lifts her head and looks at me. "Yeah, but don't let me go."

"I won't, Mindy." I want to make sure she understands I've used her alias. She nods.

The paramedic asks questions and she answers, but her voice is muffled because her head is buried in my neck.

"Mr. Wolfe, is there any way you can get her to release you?"

"I doubt it. We need a blanket. I'm sure she's cold." They cover her up.

"We need to start an IV on her and check you too."

"You're gonna have to work around us," I tell him.

"Can you lie down, sir?"

I tell Gemini, "Babe, you have to lie down. Okay?" She nods, so I lay her back onto the narrow bed while she continues to hold me.

"Babe, you're gonna have to let me go. The medics are getting pissed off at us."

"I don't care. I'm not letting you go."

"What are you gonna do when we get to the hospital? Look at me—you're safe. You know that, right?"

"I'm not concerned about me. It's you I'm worried about." Then she starts sobbing again. I swing my legs onto the bed and roll on my right side, pulling her next to me to make as much room as I can. I catch the eye of the medic so he can give her something to calm her down.

Once her IV is started, they put something in it to sedate her. There's a knock on the ambulance door and a police officer sticks his head inside, wanting to ask questions again. I tell him he's going to have to do it at the hospital. Then Huff is there and I tell him to meet us at the hospital too. The medic shuts the doors and we're on the way.

"Mr. Wolfe, I need to check you out."

"I'm fine. It can wait." Right now, Gemini is my main concern. I want her to be cared for first.

"No, sir, it can't. You need to let us examine you. Ms. Simmons is resting now."

I give in to their pestering and a few moments later, they examine me.

"Sir, you're bleeding. We need to determine the location of your injury."

They explain that I have glass and metal in my arm and back. Funny, I hadn't even noticed. I'm glad Gemini didn't see it during her inspection. She would've been even more freaked out. I glance at her, glad that she's drifted off.

"How bad is it?" I ask.

"All of them are superficial, except for one. We're going to leave it alone and let the doctor in the emergency department handle it. You'll need to be X-rayed to determine the depth."

"Okay."

I hear him on the radio telling the triage nurse at the hospital that he's coming in with a patient with a possible internal injury.

A team awaits as we're wheeled inside. I'm sent to one room, Gemini to another. They bring in a portable X-ray machine and quickly get that taken care of. I'm still wondering why I'm in no pain. A few minutes later, the doctor tells me I need surgery to have the shrapnel removed, as it's quite deep and they're afraid it may have caused some damage to my left lung.

"Why doesn't it hurt?"

"You're most likely compensating."

"I need to see my girlfriend before."

"That's not advisable. We're prepping the OR right now."

"Then send in my friend, Huff. He should be right outside."

"I'll look for him, but Mr. Wolfe, if he's not here, we need to move. This is quite urgent."

A few seconds later, Huff shows up. "I've gotta get this thing taken out. Make sure you keep her calm. Don't let her know how severe this is. She'll fucking freak."

"Drex. I'm sorry, man."

"Just take care of her for me. Lie if you have to. And you know how to handle the police."

"Don't worry about her or the other. She'll be fine. I'll make sure of that."

"Thanks."

The nurse says, "We have to go now, Mr. Wolfe."

And then I'm being wheeled into the OR, bright lights fading as I fall under.

WHEN I WAKE, it seems like I've only slept for two minutes. Anesthesia sure is weird. The nurse checks on me but I want to know how it went. She says the doctor will be in right away.

I'm so damn sleepy, I can't stay awake.

"Mr. Wolfe? I'm Dr. Wilson. The surgery went great. Just a minor tear to your lung, but you're all patched up now and should be good to go."

"I can go home?" My mouth feels like cotton. My throat is scratchy.

"Um, that would be a big no. You had quite an injury. The repair was simple, but nevertheless, you have to heal. You're on IV antibiotics, you have a chest tube in to prevent your lung from collapsing and to remove the blood from the area surrounding the injury. You'll need to stay here for a while because of that."

He's telling me these things and I feel like I'm watching a movie.

"You're kidding, right?"

"No, Mr. Wolfe, I'm not. You're a very lucky man. Just rest for now and let that anesthesia wear off."

"When can I see my girlfriend?"

"As soon as you're awake and we move you out of recovery."

"Can you let her know I'm fine? But just tell her it was a scratch and you had to stitch me up. She's gonna freak."

He chuckles and says, "Okay, I'll let her know."

THE NEXT TIME I wake up, I'm in a room. It's dark and Huff is sitting in the chair beside the bed.

"How do you feel?"

"I was better before the surgery." My chest, back, and arm

scream at me.

"Hit that little button," Huff says.

"What button?"

"Here." He picks up a little gizmo attached to my IV pole. A line running through it goes into my arm.

"What's that?"

"Morphine. For pain. Just push this button when you need it."

"Oh. Nice." I hit the button and in seconds, I feel the effect. "That's cool. Better already. So, the doctor told you?"

"Yeah. You'll be here a while. Until they remove the chest tube."

"What tube?"

"Fuck. You don't remember anything? They took out a huge piece of shrapnel."

"Yeah, I know."

"Well, it tore into your lung. So now you have to keep a chest tube in until you're out of danger of your lung collapsing. And you have to be on IV antibiotics to prevent infection."

"Really?"

"Yeah. And Mindy—"

"Who's Mindy?"

"Damn, Drex. Mindy. Your girlfriend."

"Oh, yeah. Mindy." I give him an exaggerated wink. He rolls his eyes and I chuckle. "Shit, Huff. Don't make me laugh. It hurts."

"Holy fuck, what am I gonna do with you like this?"

"Like what?"

A knock on the door is followed by it opening. A soft voice asks, "Is it okay if I come in?"

I can't see who it is because it's so dark, but with a voice like that, it has to be an angel.

Huff says, "Come in if you can stand it."

And there, standing before me is the most gorgeous thing I've ever seen. Gemini is wearing hospital scrubs and a hospital gown.

"Jesus Christ, you're beautiful. I've never seen anything so goddamn good-looking in my whole fucking life. Oh my God. Just look at you. Huff, have you ever seen anything so fucking hot? Look at her amazing eyes. You know I call her Onyx? Can you please come closer so I can touch you? I want to feel your hair. Shit, Gemini, can you take off those fucking clothes so I can see that body of yours?"

"Drex!"

"What? Come on, babe. You know how much I love it when you strip for me."

"Whoa, buddy, you got company, remember?"

"What? Oh, sorry." I forgot that Huff was in the room. My head swings to Gemini and she's giggling. I try to smile but I think it's a bit lopsided.

"Get over here. I need some loving."

Huff says, "That's it. I can't take any more of this shit. I'm out of here. Mindy, you know where to find me, if you need me. And just a warning, he's high as hell on morphine."

"Yeah, I figured as much," she says.

When Huff leaves, I look at Gemini standing beside me. Every now and again, she turns a little fuzzy.

"Oh, my gorgeous Onyx, come here. Oh God, I can't tell you how much I want to touch you. Can't you just maybe lift up that little dress you're wearing and let me see what's underneath? I didn't know anyone could make hospital clothes look so fucking sexy."

She's on me like a magnet on a refrigerator. "Drexel Wolfe, don't you ever get hurt on me again. I'll kick your ass all the way to China and back if you do."

"I'd rather you dig your nails in and scratch the hell out of it while I'm fucking you. Kiss me, babe."

"Drex! You're all sorts of horny, aren't you?"

"Come here." I hook my finger and pull it toward me, motioning for her to lean closer. When she does, I whisper, "I need to tell you a secret."

"A secret? What kind of secret?"

"A really good one." I smile. Then my back hurts a little. "Hey, where's that little button I'm supposed to push when I hurt?"

"Let me look."

She bends over the bed and her hair brushes against my face.

"Oh God, babe," I groan. "You smell so good. I love your hair. You have the best hair in the whole wide world. I've never ever seen hair like yours before. I love your hair when it hangs over my face, when we're fucking and you're on top."

"Drex!"

"What? It's true. Sweet, sweet Onyx, I can't help it. Did you find my button? If you can't find it, don't worry."

"I found it, honey. Here."

She hands me my button and I press it.

"Thank you." I reach out to touch her face and smile. "God sure knew what the hell He was doing when He made you, babe. Now will you do me a big favor?"

"What's that?"

"Will you take off those pants so I can play with your beautiful little button?"

"Jeez, Drex! You have to stop this!"

"I do? Why? Don't you like me?"

"I *do* like you. You're my guy. But it's inappropriate."

"It is? But you're so beautiful. You look like the most perfect angel sent from heaven. And you're all mine. You *are* mine, aren't you?"

"Yes, I'm yours."

"Then let's fuck. Right now."

"Drex! Honestly, I don't know what's gotten into you!"

"You, babe. No, I have that backwards. I'm the one that's

gotten into you! Get it?" I find that so funny, I start laughing and can't stop.

"You certainly have. But I'm afraid you're not going to do it here."

"No? Why not?"

"Drex, we're in the hospital. It's inappropriate."

"It is? But no one's here."

"Yes, there is. Now stop!"

Oh no. She's angry with me. I must behave, but I don't want to. "I'm sorry. Please don't be mad at me. You're too pretty to be mad. Get in bed and hold me."

"I'm afraid I'll hurt you. You have tubes and things."

"You can't ever hurt me. Now kiss me or I'm gonna make a scene."

She does and damn, she feels good.

Then I get an amazing idea. "Hey. My lip hurts really bad, babe. Right here." I point to the far corner of my mouth. "Will you kiss it and make it better?"

She gives me a funny look. "I know what you're up to, Drex."

"What do you mean? My lip really hurts. It needs medical attention."

"I'll call the nurse, then."

"You want *her* to kiss it for me?"

She laughs and leans over me as she brushes my hair off my forehead. "What am I going to do with you? This morphine has turned you into a jacked-up horny freak."

"Is that a bad thing?"

"Yes! You have to behave!"

"I don't want to behave. I want to get naked and be bad with you. I want you to lay that luscious body of yours on top of mine and lick me all over."

"Oh, Drex. You're just out of surgery. And you have that chest tube and all sorts of other things hooked up to you."

"But baby ..."

"I'll make you a promise."

"You will? I love promises. Can you make me a chocolate cake too?"

She laughs. "Yes, I'll make you a chocolate cake."

"Can I eat it off your tummy? Or maybe your hoo-hah?"

"Oh hell. Can you stop thinking about sex for a little bit?"

"Nope. See, here's the thing about you. You fucking blow me away. Every time we're together, I think this is it. It's as good as it's ever gonna get. But I'm wrong. I'm always wrong, babe, 'cuz the next time blows me away even more. It's like my fingertips have memorized every inch of you and they need to touch you. And my mouth ... my mouth waters at the thought of kissing you, of tasting your lips. And then the way you like to play rough and dirty with me. Oh God, Gem, I can't think straight when it comes to you because we fit ... like that perfect pair of shoes you've had forever. So, I can't. And I won't ever stop thinking about sex with you because I love everything about you. You know how you do that little thing with your tongue when you're sucking me off ..."

"Drexel Wolfe! You have to stop this now!"

Oh boy. I'm in big trouble. "Are you gonna ground me?"

"Yes. If you don't stop this sex talk. Right now. Got it?"

She's very stern. So I nod. Then a thought pops into my fuzzy brain. Maybe she's still hurt. She looks okay, but she might be hurt somewhere. "So are *you* okay, babe? You're not hurt, are you?"

"No, I was shaken up, but I'm okay. Just banged up."

"Thank God. I was so worried. Will you sleep with me tonight? I can't stand to sleep without you. Tell me you will. Please?"

"I doubt they'll let me, but I'll try. I had to beg the nurse just to visit you. I'll be discharged tomorrow, so I'll move in here then."

"No, I want you to go back to the big house and get some real sleep."

"The big house?"

"You know, the office."

"Right. I won't sleep knowing you're here."

"I still have a secret to tell you."

"Oh, yeah, what is it?"

"I'm not gonna tell you."

"You're not? Then why'd you say that?"

"I don't know. I thought I wanted to tell you, but now I don't know if I should let you know that I was so afraid when I thought you were hurt. Because I love you so much and I didn't want anything to happen to you."

She gasps and says, "Oh!"

Her mouth forms a huge O and her face turns fuzzy. Did I just tell her that I love her? I can't really remember. I scoot over and she slides under the sheet. When she curls up next to me, I put her hands in mine, bring them to my heart, and say, "So beautiful," right before I drift away.

IT WAS A rough week, but I'm finally getting released. Gemini won't stop teasing me about my stupid comments while under the influence of morphine. Apparently, they were quite lewd and I had no filter whatsoever. It didn't matter who was in the room, I said whatever I pleased. She's vowed to get me back, but I don't see how. I keep having visions of me telling her that I love her too. I pray it's a damn dream because I can't possibly be in love with her. I barely know her. Yeah, we've spent an assload of time together the last few weeks, not to mention that horrendous explosion we experienced. And yes, I'm as close, if not closer, to her than I've been to any woman in my life. But love?

We'll be staying at corporate headquarters for now. I've

always kept an executive apartment there, so I'll take advantage of it now. Gemini's things, or what she's picked up since the bombing, are already there. Huff has given her the rundown and she has a team of bodyguards at all times. She's not allowed to go anywhere unaccompanied. In fact, we both have a full detail. No way am I taking any chances, especially where she's concerned.

On the way home, Huff briefs me on what's been happening. "The bomb was C-4 loaded into the SUV right outside your window, set off from a remote detonator. We think it was a warning. Either to leave everything be or give them what they want if they contact Gemini."

"Why do you say that?" I ask. Since I'm still on pain meds, my mind isn't as clear as it should be.

"If they'd wanted you both dead, they would've used a timer and not a remote detonator. They were watching your place. They knew exactly when you exited the building. They were sending you a message."

This doesn't sit well for several reasons. First, they know where we are. Second, they've been watching us, so Gemini's been in danger for a while. And third, what the hell do they want from her?

"Huff, we leave in a week. I'd go tomorrow, but I know I'll get flack from you if I try. We have to find that file. We'll go through everything again. And then once we have our plans set, we leave for Panama City. I want two teams on the G-550. The plane will land in Jacksonville. One team will deplane and drive to Panama City. Then the plane will head to Tallahassee where the second team will get off. They'll also drive to Panama City. The plane will stay the night in Tallahassee and at daylight, it'll fly to Panama City and wait on us. Gemini and I will fly commercial to Pensacola. We'll rent a car and drive to meet up with the teams. Each will have their assignments as decoys. We'll not communicate except on safe phones. I want this to be a very confusing journey for anyone to track. The jet stays in Panama City to take us all home. We'll fine-tune things this week. But as soon as we get back, I want you and our top ten guys working on everything in that box. Understand? I also want another thorough search of what that key can open in Austin."

"Got it, boss."

The more I think about this whole thing, the more I realize that the CIA as a whole can't be involved. My connections with them are too strong. They would be beating down my door by now to get Gemini. If my suspicions are correct, it must be some covert group operating within the CIA—perhaps even without the CIA's knowledge. This is even a more frightening thought because those guys won't play by any rules at all. They could be as bad or worse than the terrorists.

Chapter 16

GEMINI
Mom! What In The Hell Were You Thinking?

THIS WHOLE BOMB thing has brought me to my knees, literally and figuratively. My heart is in my gut most of the time, and when it's not there, it's usually hanging around somewhere near my feet. And the last thing I want is to let Drex know how damned worried I am.

He was so adorable and funny when he came out of surgery. Of course, he was on a decent dose of morphine, but the things he said were too cute for such a tough guy. Even now when I think about it, my heart flips and I feel gooey inside. I have to wonder if he really feels like that about me or if it was all drunk speak. He acted like I was the greatest thing in the world—and that bit about being in love with me ... I'm not quite sure about that. It's entirely too soon, but it was sweet to hear him say it.

We're at the big house, as he calls it. This is where we'll be living, with a full team of bodyguards. The fact that I'm putting Drex and his men in danger doesn't escape me. I'd like to slip away to take that danger away, but I know he would never let me go. If I leave, he'll follow, with his team of men, and then we'll be out in the open. It's safer this way, which is why I'm staying. Or at least that's what I keep telling myself.

We walk through the executive level of DWInvestigations, past the offices, and head to the conference room. When everyone is assembled, Drex tells them that Huff will remain in charge for the day and will relay the plans for the trip to Panama City and the continued search in Austin. He also increases the already tight security here. Then he looks at me. "Let's get out of here."

He confuses me. For everything we've been through, I think he would want to stay and have his finger on the game. When we leave the room, he grabs me by the elbow and steers me toward the apartment.

As soon as we get inside, he shuts the door and turns the lock. "We need to talk." He never wastes time with flowery conversation. I actually like that about him.

"Are you all right?"

"Physically. Well, I've been better in that regard too. What about you? Are you okay? Physically and mentally? That was rough … going through a bombing. PTSD can set in and I want to make sure if that happens, we handle it appropriately. And your headaches. What's going on with them?" He rattles off questions like he's checking them off a list.

"Wow. Can we start with a hug instead?"

"Huh?"

He's confusing me. He's a different person now. He's the Drex I first met in Austin. Brusque and in charge. Our eyes meet and there's something different in his. It worries me.

My voice is low when I speak. "Drex … what's going on?"

He scrapes his teeth over his lower lip but doesn't look away from me. This will have to be my move because I need his arms around me, holding me close. I don't want this weird behavior.

We just experienced something very traumatic and I need to be reassured, not drilled ... soothed and kissed, not treated like an employee.

I move toward him and when I'm in front of him, I say, "I'm fine. Except for one thing."

"What's that?"

"This." And I kiss him. Like I did the night of the bombing. Like there are no tomorrows. I need to show him that I'm here and we'll get through this. My heart plummets and my stomach twists when he doesn't respond. I start to pull away but then his arms reach around me, jerking my body hard against his. He groans in my mouth and his hands move to my T-shirt's hem. I feel him lifting it up and suddenly it whooshes over my head. Then his fingers are unbuttoning my jeans.

"Off. Clothes." That's all he says.

Two can play at this game. "You too."

I eye him as he strips. He moves without his usual fluidity, indicating he's in pain.

"Do you hurt?" I whisper.

"Not enough to stop me from doing this."

When we're both naked, we stand and stare at each other. But then I have to see for myself the damage inflicted upon him.

"Turn around."

"No."

"Yes. Now."

His half-open eyes tell me he's not pleased, but I don't care. He stands, unmoving, refusing to do what I ask, so I walk around him to see for myself. I'm shocked by the large bandage still covering his left side. As I move my hand over it, I whisper, "You could be dead right now."

"Stop it, Gemini," he says gruffly, and he turns to face me. I'm in his arms and he's kissing me again. "I'm alive and here and I'm fine."

This is the first time we've kissed when we haven't closed our eyes. It seems that neither one of us is willing to look away from the other. And oh God, the emotion pouring out of his is so impassioned, I can't stop looking at them.

"In the hospital, you told me I was the most beautiful thing you'd ever seen."

"I said that?" His hands gently cradle my face.

"Yeah. You told me that God knew what He was doing when He made me."

"I'm glad to know I wasn't drunk out of my head after all, then. I was right. He created perfection in you."

"I'm not perfect."

"You are to me. You're so damned beautiful that sometimes when I look at you, I forget to breathe. That's pretty fucking perfect in my book."

His hands seize my hair, winding strands around his fingers. "What else did I tell you in the hospital?"

His gaze is so compelling, I find myself talking before I'm aware of it. "You told me that you were so afraid when you thought I was hurt." I swallow and place my hands on his cheeks. "And that you love me and you didn't want anything to happen to me."

His mouth imprisons mine and there is no more conversation after that. He backs me into the closest wall and we're manic as our hands find each other. When he discovers that I'm soaked for him, he slides into me and I moan at the fierceness of him. He's rough and dominating. This is about his need for control; I recognize that. And it's about the power. It's about the fact that we both survived and he wants to assure himself that he's as strong as ever. And I *need* for him to be. I *want* him to be like this.

Suddenly, he stops and I cry out in protest. But he spins me around until I'm facing the wall and he raises my right arm. And then he's back inside me, filling me so deep, touching me and making me want to scream. I don't think I can take it like this, but I'm so needful of him. His fingers lace with mine and it's weirdly intimate, this soft gesture, as he roughly thrusts into me.

Then his cheek rubs mine and his voice is gruff in my ear. "I can feel you're so close. Let it go, babe. I need to feel you come on me." His left hand slips around me and finds the place that will set me off. Within moments, my orgasm crashes into me and then he pulls out and cries, "Oh, my sweet Gemini." He leans against my back as he climaxes and I feel his come running down my butt. His breath is hot as it fans across my shoulder and I flutter back to reality like a soft snowflake falling to Earth.

"Drexel?"

"Yeah."

"You didn't need to pull out."

"No?"

"I called Brady and he said that the pill starts to work right away if taken every day."

"Oh. That's good." His lips leave a trail on my neck. "And you need to know that I'm safe. I've been checked. I'm healthy."

Is it bad of me that I never even gave that a thought? He has my mind and body in so many twists and tangles, his sexual health never occurred to me.

"Drex?"

"Hmm?"

I turn around and wrap him in my arms. "I need your mouth on mine, but first, I never thanked you."

"For what?"

"You saved my life. Our lives."

"Not according to Huff."

"Whatever. You were there for me when I needed you. You held me and didn't let me go when I was so scared. So yeah, you saved my life." Then I kiss him. When I stop, I say, "Let's go lie down."

"Good idea. My girlfriend's worn me out."

I hook my arm through his and walk the short distance to the bedroom. As we move, he asks, "Are you finding the apartment comfortable?"

"Not until now." He gives me a bewildered look. "You weren't here, so I was out of sorts."

"Ah, I see. Well, I'll try to change that," he says.

"Oh, I have faith that you will."

I pull the covers back. He moves gingerly, which tells me he's in pain.

"When was your last pain pill?"

"I'm in need of one now. And can you bring me a damp cloth?"

I retrieve water, the pills, and a cloth. Upon my return, he's waiting for me, propped up on the pillows, a smirk on his face. "What's that smile for?"

"I wish you'd been my naked nurse in the hospital."

"Oh, you tried. Believe me. You were the horniest patient on record, I'm sure. You said the naughtiest things to me."

"Well, sweet thing, they were all true." He swallows his pill and thanks me. "Turn around."

"Huh?"

"Turn around. I need to clean you up a bit."

"Oh!" My face is on fire.

He laughs. "Why does this embarrass you?"

"Because!"

"Come on, Onyx, turn around."

I do as he asks and he cleans me up. "There, my mess is all gone now." He's all smiles. "You have the prettiest ass." He pats the bed next to him. "Get in here. I want you next to me. I'm tired."

"So am I. I don't think I've slept since this whole thing

happened."

"Me neither, babe. It was hard sleeping without you."

"Are you comfy?" I need to know this. I don't want him to hurt.

"Yeah. So tell me about your headaches."

I smile when I tell him that I have only had a couple and they've been minor. Nothing that I couldn't handle and the Maxalt took them away.

"That's awesome. Now lay on your back, so I can see your gorgeous face."

"Oh, Drex."

"No words, babe. Just let me look."

But he's the gorgeous one. His blue-grays watch me intently, as if he's afraid I'll disappear. He's playing with my hair, wrapping it around his fingers and holding it against his face. He lets my hair go to hold my hand and brings it to his mouth to kiss. It's hard to lie next to him and not touch him. I want to run my hands all over him, feel every bit of him as much as he wants to feel me.

"You wanna know something?" I ask.

"Maybe. It depends on what you're gonna tell me."

Smiling, I say, "God got it right with you too." Then I press a kiss to the little hollow at his throat.

He runs his hand down my chest until he hits my pearled nipple. Taking it between his finger and thumb, he squeezes and rolls it until I groan. Then he does the same to my other one. I arch into him, wanting more. His hand travels across my body, setting my blood on fire. My nerves tingle and I cry out for him.

When his hand slips between my thighs, I melt. He slides a finger into me. "I love the way you feel inside, all warm and slick."

I can't help but pull his mouth to mine. "More, Drex. I want all of you."

"On top. Now."

He leans back on his elbows while I straddle his hips and when he slides into me, he's in so deep, it's almost too much. But then he starts thrusting and the friction is so exact, he hits me just right. I know when I explode, it will be exquisite.

"Ah, fuck, Gemini, kiss me, babe."

I put my lips against his and his tongue plays with mine. My hair falls forward and curtains our faces. He whispers in my mouth, "I love it when your hair does that."

Then he surprises me by sitting up. "Touch yourself, babe. Lean back a bit and touch yourself. I want to watch."

Whoa. He's never asked me to do this. This is a little weird.

"Don't be shy. I've fantasized about watching you do this. Please indulge me."

"You've fantasized about this?"

"Oh yeah. A lot. Do it for me."

"Where?"

"Wherever it pleases you the most."

If I do it, I'll come right away and maybe he'd rather this lasted a bit longer. So I start elsewhere.

"Like this?" My hands slide across my breasts and then I imitate what he does to my nipples.

"That's nice."

I let my hands move south until they get to where we're joined. First I touch him. "Mmm, this feels good."

"Yes, it does. But I don't want you to touch me."

My fingers massage my clit. I feel awkward, almost clumsy at first, but only for a few moments. Then I'm into it so much I forget. He starts moving again and I can hear he's close. I'm right there with him. It hits me hard and I open my eyes to see his on me. Right as I do, I watch his orgasm nail him, and dear God, he looks amazing. I can't stop my hand from touching his face. When he calms, he takes my fingers and sucks on them, one at a time.

"You're a fucking sex princess. The things you do to me, Gemini. I should be incapacitated, but you ... you make me want to fuck you all day long." He moves his hand to where we're still joined. "You're always so warm and wet and luscious. Every damn time. So tight around me. And when you come, it's ..." His voice trails off as he shakes his head.

"Sex princess, huh?"

"Yeah. That's exactly what you are. Now get your ass over here so we can sleep." I kiss him and pull the covers over us.

I put my arm around him as he lies on his side and I look at him for a little while. He's asleep quickly, and I wish I could hop into his mind. What exactly is going on between us? Part of me wants to push him away, but I know that isn't possible. One look from him and all my big talk dissipates, and it's just mushy old Gemini. And what's going on with him? He seems so desperate right now. As I watch him, my lids get too heavy to fight sleep anymore.

STRANGE SOUNDS SURROUND me and I'm disoriented, but I can't see because I'm blindfolded. Then I feel hands on my arms and someone's carrying me. Someone ties me up and I cry out for help, but no one comes. My blindfold is removed and I'm under bright lights. I'm blindsided by a fist to my face and stars burst in my head. Then the pain hits. When I try to examine the damage, I can't because my hands are bound behind me. I know I'm whimpering, but they strike me again and again. My eyes swell and I can't open them. Why are these people beating me? They won't speak to me. I beg them to stop, but the punches keep coming. When they stop, I crumple to the floor.

One of them speaks, but I don't know which, because I can't see. "You think we are finished? You are mistaken."

Footsteps approach. Then I hear a deep growl. Someone pulls my eyelids up so I can see.

"Now, you will give us what want, or your friend here dies."

What I see is beyond horrific. They have Drex and he's bloody. They've beaten him and two men are holding him up because he can't stand on his own. A third stands behind and has his hand in his hair, holding Drex's head up. The man's other arm is around Drex's neck, a large knife in his hand. I know if I don't tell them what they want to know, they will slit his throat. He will die right before me.

I can't give them what they want because I don't have anything. I scream, "I don't have anything, I swear! Don't hurt him. Please."

"Baby, wake up! Gemini, babe! Wake up!"

Drex is shaking me when I'm dragged out of my sleep. My whole body quivers and my face is soaked with tears. "Shit!" I say, swiping my cheeks. He grabs my hands in his.

"What was that about?"

"A nightmare." Even my voice is trembling.

"Tell me."

That's the last thing I want to do after the way he's been acting. "No. I'd rather not."

"I'd rather you did. I've not seen you this upset since I first found you and you were in the midst of one of your head-splitters. Talk. Now."

The ever-commanding Drex is back and in a way, it comforts me.

"Some men had me and were going to kill you if I didn't give them the file. Of course I couldn't because I don't have a fucking thing." As I speak, panic pushes my voice to the point of shouting.

"It's okay. Calm down."

"No. You calm down. You didn't see what I saw. You were ..." I cover my face and try to stop the horrors from flashing through my mind.

His arms encircle me. "It's gonna be all right."

"No! It's not, Drex. These guys aren't going to give up until they get what they want and I would gladly give it to them if I only had it! I think Huff is wrong. I think that bombing was a message to *me*. They're telling me if I don't give them what they seek, they're going to kill *you*! And I can't live with that."

"Oh and you think I can? You think *I* can live with something happening to *you*? They came to my house, invaded my space, and tried to hurt *you*. And you think I don't mind that?"

"No! That's not what I mean at all."

"Gemini, I have the best guys on this. We'll get this solved. I promise you. And my word is good, if nothing else. One other thing. You're safer here than any other place. Our security is tighter than anywhere else. I'll protect you with everything I've got."

"Why? Why are you doing this, Drex?"

He doesn't say anything, but his blue-grays pierce me. They pin me down and paralyze me.

His voice is deep with emotion when he asks, "Why do you think, Gemini?"

I'm afraid to answer him. That question has been poking around in my mind for the last week and it honestly scares me as much as those crazy people who want to kill me. His lids finally drift down, cutting me off from the intensity and emotion of his gaze. I sigh—this is clearly a topic I'm not prepared to address.

My dream has me so worked up and sweaty. I need a shower. Before I can get in, I sense his presence behind me.

"You can only go so far before I come and find you, you know."

"What's that supposed to mean?"

"Don't run from me."

"I'm not going anywhere."

"I don't mean in the physical sense, Gemini."

This is ridiculous, him talking to the back of my head. I turn off the shower.

"There are so many things whirling through my mind right now, I don't know what to say, Drex."

Damn his eyes! They have a way of digging into mine, and searching for the truth. He won't let up until he's satisfied. "That nightmare shook me up."

He nods but is silent.

"I can't tear apart my feelings right now, so please don't ask me to."

"Fair enough. I only ask one thing. Honesty between us."

I nod. "Okay. I can do that."

Then he leans in and lightly touches his lips to mine.

"You wanna shower with me?" I ask.

"Yeah, but I can't. I still have to be careful with this incision. It's better I don't. I was threatened by my surgeon."

He leaves me standing there alone, and I suddenly miss him. I'm a screwed-up heap of emotions. In the shower I think about how badly I want to know what my mom hid. For everything I knew about her, it's so hard for me to believe what I've learned. At least I know she wasn't involved in terrorist activities. Her letter assured me of that. But what file could she have taken that put us in such danger? What did you do, Mom?

IT'S LATE AFTERNOON when we make our way to the conference room. Ten men are already working, and Drex jumps right in like he hasn't been gone for several days. The whole thing confuses me because they're using unfamiliar terms, doing things on their computers I can't follow. A wall of monitors shows maps of Panama City, Austin, Las Vegas and the Grand Canyon. They also have all sorts of dates and timelines up for Aali Imaam. It all looks like absolute chaos to me. It must work for them, though, because they all function cohesively and keep adding notes on their computers as I see them pop up on the monitors. I decide to take a seat and observe until they need me for something.

"Gemini, I need you over here please," Drex says. When I move to his side, he takes my hands and says, "Hear me out a second. We think your mom stole a file that either tracked the patterns of Khalid Ahmad, the head of Aali Imaan, or the location of some kind of nuclear warhead."

"Holy crapballs! If that file contains information on the whereabouts of a nuclear warhead, we need to find that thing fast." *Oh my God, Mom! What in the hell were you thinking?*

"Stay calm here, babe. The other thing is just as important. Khalid Ahmad is invisible. No one, and I mean no one knows where this guy hangs. If this file has that kind of information, it could help us take him out."

What is he saying here? "You mean like kill him?"

"Yes! This is geo-terrorism we're talking about Gem. This guy is responsible for so many deaths, it's incomprehensible. So either way, we're looking at something epic."

"Shit! This is crazy. Why aren't they trying to kidnap me or something?"

"It's only a matter of time, in my estimation. That's why we have the bodyguards now. I need you to focus. Try to search your memory for every single relevant thing. Think about church, school, things your mom said, did, places she mentioned, people she knew, phrases, anything at all that sticks out in your mind. And I mean anything. It may seem minor to you, but it may be exactly what we need."

He's so animated, it's almost like he's on speed.

"Hey, are you all right?" I ask.

"Yeah, I'm fine. The guys pieced all this together and I'm psyched."

"Have you had a lot of coffee?"

He really laughs this time. "Not a drop. Come on. Think, Gem. I need your brain engaged here."

"Okay." I sit and let my mind wander to when I was growing up.

"Relax if you can. Close your eyes. Picture your mom. Go back and remember the way things were with the two of you."

Nodding, I smile. Her face comes into focus. She's so pretty. I used to love watching her put on her lipstick. She would let me brush her long hair and I would tell her I wanted to be as pretty as she was when I grew up.

"Why, darling, you're prettier than I'll ever be."

"No, I'm not, Mommy. I want my eyes to look just like the sky. The same way yours do."

"Well, I want mine to look like dark chocolate. That's what yours remind me of. What could be better than chocolate?"

"I know. Chocolate on vanilla ice cream."

And she laughs. She has such a lovely laugh, it makes me laugh too.

"So, what do you want to do today?"

"Let's go to the lake. I want to go swimming."

"How about we go to the pool instead?" she says.

"Yay! The pool. Then can we go and get an ICEE afterward?"

"We sure can."

"Mommy, can we go on vacation this summer?"

"Maybe. Where would you like to go, missy?"

"Disneyland to see Cinderella."

"Ah, you would, huh?"

"Yup. Can we go?"

"I don't think so honey. Maybe we can go somewhere else."

"Okaaaaay."

"Maybe we'll go there another time."

"Really?"

"Yeah."

My brain switches to another time when we had a huge argument over when I wanted to go on a school trip.

"But Mom, it's a school trip, for crying out loud."

"They don't have enough supervision."

"Then go with us and be a chaperone. Everyone else is going."

"Gemini, we've had this discussion before. I don't care what everyone else does. I only care about you."

"Then come with us."

"There is no us because you're not going."

"Mom, please. I never get to go anywhere. Don't you see? I have no friends. Everyone thinks I'm weird because I can't ever go anywhere or have anybody over. Please, just this one time."

"I wish I could say yes, but I can't."

"Why can't you? I don't understand."

"I know you don't, sweetie, and I wish I could explain. I just worry about you. It's not a safe world anymore. There are people out there who would hurt you."

"Oh, Mom. You're so dramatic."

"I know you think that. But it's not drama, Gemini. It's fact."

I stomped out of the room.

We had so many arguments like this, but she would never give in.

My mind spins. We chatted about so many things but there is nothing that stands out. Something nags at the back of my mind and I can't bring it forward.

"Think, Gemini, think," I say out loud to myself. The only times we ever left town together were for vacations. We went to Austin, San Antonio, or Panama City. That's it. But then it smashes into me. We were playing trivia one night. And we started discussing things we always wanted to do. I was in high school, maybe a junior. I told her Disneyland was still high on my list of places to go. And that I wanted to see the Pacific Ocean and big mountains so I could learn how to mountain bike. She nearly died and told me under no circumstances should I ever try such a dangerous sport. I laughed and then asked her where she would like to go. She said the Grand Canyon and the Hoover Dam. And then she told me if anything ever happened to her that I should go there as a memorial to her. I thought she was just being weird but now I'm not so sure.

"The Grand Canyon or the Hoover Dam!" I holler as I jump to my feet. "Try the Grand Canyon or the Hoover Dam." I share the memory with Drex, as best as I can remember.

"It points to what the guys are thinking too. Look at this." He shows me what they've been working on. All the documents from the box are posted up on boards. They've highlighted all the things we missed the first time around. There are addresses that point to Nevada and Arizona.

"How did we miss that?"

"It's not like it was obvious. It's just a mention of both states in one document."

"But still. Now what?" I ask.

"We decide after we get back from Panama City. Our hopes are that we'll find more clues there. They've come up with another possibility in Austin too. There's another storage facility at 1991 W. 15th Street. So we'll try there next."

"Sounds reasonable."

"I'm glad you agree." He pivots on his heel and winces.

"Hey," I say, "when was your last pain pill?"

"This morning."

"We're both due. We also need to eat."

"Hang on. I'll go with you." He tells Huff, "You guys need to break for the night. We're leaving to eat too. Why don't we reconvene at nine?"

"Nine? Why so late?" Huff asks.

"Because I recently got out of the hospital and I thought you'd give me shit if I said any earlier."

"Oh. Okay, yeah. Nine's good. See you then."

"If you decide to keep at it, check out the Nevada-Las Vegas link and see what you come up with. I'd go with the Vegas suburbs, maybe on the side of town that's closest to the Hoover Dam. My gut is singing to me on this. And thanks guys, for everything. I appreciate all your hard work and efforts here. Call if you need me."

We wave to the guys as we leave.

Chapter 17

DREXEL
Black Ops

IT'S DIFFICULT TO stem my anxiety. In order to ensure we're not being followed, Gemini and I catch a cab downtown. After some quick moves through a couple of cafes, Ellie picks us up and drives us to the airport.

The other teams should be in the air. We sent two look-alikes in our place, just in case. The plan is to meet late this evening in our hotel rooms. If all goes as planned, we should be on the Gulfstream 550 by tomorrow afternoon, heading home. I only hope we find the file to solve this damn thing.

Gemini and I enter the airport and go our separate ways. I think it's best this way, but I'm keeping a close watch on her. I'm not comfortable at all with this situation because I can't carry a weapon, but there's no alternative. We're flying first class, but we'll be sitting across the aisle from each other in the last row.

As we wait for our flight to board, I check out the other passengers. Everything appears normal. There's a young woman flying with two toddlers and an infant. I feel sorry for her because she has her hands full. Gemini sits next to her and plays with the baby. I overhear her tell Gemini her husband is in the military and she's moving to Panama City. When it's time to board, I walk over to assist her. She looks at me in gratitude as I offer to take her infant carrier and other bags aboard, freeing her to handle the kids. Gemini smiles at me and I nod.

The flight is uneventful. Once we reach Panama City, we grab our rental and drive to our hotel. The warm air feels nice after the chill in Denver, and the orange glow of the setting sun over the deep blue ocean is appealing. I wish we could relax on the white sandy beach instead of jumping into work, but we're not here for a vacation. We settle into our hotel and grab a quick dinner through room service. My mind churned the entire flight, so I have a lot of questions for Gemini.

"Hey. I have to ask you some things. And don't think this is for anything other than this case."

"Okay."

"How long did you know Nick?"

The question throws her, as I knew it would. Her mouth works around a bit and then says, "A few years. I met him not too long after my mom died. Why?"

"And he was with you until after your accident?"

"Um, yeah. I told you what happened with that. Drex, I really hate talking about this. I feel so terrible about what happened to him."

"I know you do. But, tell me exactly how you met again."

"I was sitting in the campus union where everyone hangs out, drinking coffee, looking over lecture notes, and he asked to sit with me. I thought he was kinda cute so I said yeah. And then we started seeing each other. Hanging out at first and then we were together. It was pretty fast, now that I look back." She looks at me and says, "Kind of like us."

"Do you doubt me?"

She's silent for a long minute. So am I.

"Why all this about Nick?"

"I have reasons. So, you started seeing each other and then you're together. Like that?"

"Yeah. Like that."

"Okay. What did he study?"

"Engineering. He was a senior. I was a freshman."

"What did he do after he graduated?"

"He went to work for a small local company. He said he wanted to be close to me."

"And what did you think about that?"

"Drex, I was eighteen and thought I was in love. I was thrilled. What would you think?"

"Then what?"

"He got his job and I moved in with him. I was alone, no family. I didn't have anyone to guide me. He was a nice, sweet guy. He never did anything mean or bad to me. Looking back, I realize I wasn't in love with him. He just happened upon me at the right time. I was vulnerable. I had no one and he fit at the time."

"Gem, it wasn't a coincidence."

"What are you saying?"

"He was sent. To watch you. To track you. To get information from you. And I think he was killed because he messed up somehow."

"No. Not Nick. He was always ..."

"I know. Sweet. Kind. Almost nerdy, right?"

"Yeah. Precisely."

"The perfect tracker and a trained assassin. One you would never suspect. Even-tempered. Did everything for you or anything you wanted. Was always there for you. He was working for them. But here's what doesn't make sense. Why would he post the missing person's report? He had to have known it would bring everyone down on you."

Gemini's head swings like a pendulum as she listens to my preposterous story. I can see the wheels spinning, her thoughts almost screaming to me.

"Nick? An assassin? You're crazy. Not possible. I would've known if he were a bad person."

"Would you? Think about it. Did you know about your mom? I'm not trying to destroy your faith in everyone ..."

"Well, you're doing a damn good job of it!" She glares at me.

"Gemini, listen."

"No! I think I've heard enough for now." She moves toward the door.

"Please don't walk out there. It's not safe." My voice has an edge to it. I'm frightened I've scared her to the point that she's going to run.

My words must penetrate because she stops. My hopes are that she sees I'm right, that it would be stupid to leave.

"I know this hurts you."

It's obvious I've pissed her off. "Yeah. How would you feel?" she asks.

"Destroyed. Crushed. Exactly what you're feeling."

"I feel like I've been played my entire life. Like everything's been a sham and I don't know anything anymore. What's real and what isn't. I'm not hurt, Drex. I'm pissed. At my mom, mostly. I mean, come on! And then the first person I get close to allegedly used me? Now I'm wondering ..."

"About me."

"Yes. Do you blame me?"

"No. After everything you've learned, it would make perfect sense for me to fall in line with the rest of them."

"That's exactly what I'm thinking. But then I ask myself why would you put yourself in danger? Why would you risk your life? Logic tells me that you can't be like the others. Please, Drex, tell me you aren't. Right now, and right here. Look into my eyes and tell me what I need to hear, because I need to know the truth ... to hear something that grounds me."

I grab her hands and hold them tightly. Then I look at her. "I'm not playing you, Gem. I'm telling you the truth. Think about it. Why would I go through the trouble of having my home blown up? If I were working with them, all I'd have to do is put us out in the open and let them find us. Or when they had you, I could've left you there. Or when we were at your house in San Angelo, I could've stayed and let them get us. I'm not with them. I'm with *you*. And only you. And I'm true to you. I swear it!"

Her eyes search mine. She simply stares at me and finally, finally she gives me a slight nod. When I see that, I don't waste time wrapping my arms around her. "I'm sorry I had to bring this up, but it was a necessary evil. I promise you this. I'll always have your back. You got that?"

"Yeah." Her voice is muffled, her face buried in my chest.

When I move to pull away from her, she stops me. "Thanks, Drex. You're the first person who's ever been honest with me." She stands on her toes and kisses my cheek.

"We'll figure this out, babe. Come here." I take her to the small sofa. "Sit. We still need to talk about Nick. You okay with this?"

"Yeah, I guess. It's hard to believe because he always seemed so meek. I can't believe he could be an assassin."

"Maybe he wasn't, but he fits the profile. You have to think outside the box. When someone is trained to do a job, there are all sorts of things they do. Maybe Nick wasn't really meek and mild. Maybe it was all a put-on for your benefit."

"How could I have been so duped? I lived with him for three years!"

"Babe, he was a professional. If I wanted to, I could do the same. I was trained to do the same things. I'm not telling you this to dispel your trust in me ... when you've just given it back. But you need to understand this. He was recruited for his ability to perform."

"Were you? How do you know all this?"

She's hit on something I'm not prepared to discuss with her. And yet I can't avoid it or this tenuous trust will be destroyed.

"Have you ever heard of the Black Ops?"

"Yeah, but I don't know specifics."

"Black Ops are hand-selected from the Special Forces. They're an elite group of soldiers who go in and perform top-secret missions. If they get caught, the US government denies any knowledge of their existence. In other words, it's plausible deniability. But they operate within a strict code of ethics, some of which are to tell no one about each other, share no information about each mission or take it to your death, and leave no man behind, alive or dead. Gemini, I was Black Ops. I'm violating more than one code by telling you this. The sworn oath isn't just for the time spent in the military, it's for life."

"What does this mean?"

"It means that I understand a lot more about covert operations and how these people function. If Nick was undercover and trained as such, he would've had no problem fooling you. I could do the same thing. As bad as it sounds, it would be easy as hell. I'm not. I swear to you I'm not. But I could. You have to understand this, Gem."

"Was this something you wanted?"

"That's a tough question. In the beginning, yeah."

"And then?"

My body freezes.

"What is it, Drex? What happened?"

Abruptly, I stand. This is something I *never* talk about. I'm fighting with myself about what to tell her. My fists clench, anger streaming through me. When I feel her hands on my shoulders, I flinch. Then they begin to squeeze and my muscles relax.

"It must be terrible to elicit this type of response."

If I tell her, I'm not sure I can look at her when I do. Her hands move and I know she's walking around to face me. Shit, what am I going to do?

My eyes are so tightly clenched, the muscles in my face ache.

"You can tell me. I won't judge you."

I open and look at the pure innocence reflected in her face—I know in my heart what she said isn't true. When she hears what I've done and what's been done to me, everything she believes about me will change.

"Oh, Gemini, if only that were true."

"Drex, let me help. You've proven yourself to me. At least let me do the same."

My breath rushes out of me with such force I think it shocks her. She leaves me with no choice and I know this will be a game changer for us.

I motion for her to take a seat. "When you're first pulled in, they put you through strict, severe testing to see if you're a true candidate. When they confirm you are, then your training begins. It's physically and mentally rigorous. They push you until you break. And then they build you back up. It's all about endurance and going beyond the mental and physical pain."

"What does that mean?"

"Beyond what you can imagine."

"Spell it out for me, Drex."

"Torture. Mental and physical."

"Oh my God."

"They have to, Gem. How do they know you'll perform when you need to if they don't put you through it to see? Then they teach you to push past the pain so it doesn't break you. That's probably why I wasn't even aware I was wounded in the bombing. My adrenaline takes over and I go beyond it."

She frowns, but says nothing.

"So it happened in Iraq. We were sent in to infiltrate this official's home. Take him out because we had intel that he was tied in with Aali Imaam. It was covert, of course. No one ever knows where we are, except for the ones on the mission, the officer in charge, and maybe two government officials."

"So what happened?"

"All of our intel had this dude at home and in bed. His schedule was pristine. He never deviated from it. We watched him for weeks. We went in and the thing about these guys is they pretty much revere their male kids. Especially their firstborn, so they always keep them safe. That night my job was to take out the Iraqi official."

"As in kill him?"

"Yeah. It's what I was trained to do. I know it sounds abhorrent, but these guys are evil, Gemini. They don't think twice about killing thousands of innocent people.

"I go into his bedroom and do what I'm trained to do. But we always require confirmation of our kills—photos and DNA. When I pull off the covers and roll him over, it's a kid in there with a bunch of pillows stacked around him to make him look like an adult. He's maybe ten years old. It was his son. The guy put his son in his bed to protect himself. My guys on the outside kept calling me on my headset, telling me to get the hell out, but I froze. I couldn't believe I took out a kid. And it cost me. Big. My radio kept buzzing with the guys, screaming at me to move because the house was coming to life, but I was paralyzed by then, and subsequently caught by the enemy. They put me in a box for weeks and did their usual torture routine. I'm not even sure how long I was there. The government does its song and dance of saying they have no knowledge of this activity. I'm the fuck-up. I should've ID'd the figure in the bed before I fired the shot and I didn't. That was my fatal error. My training allows me to retreat into my mind and eventually my men come and get me the hell out of there. They did it without the knowledge of our commanding officer. They found out where I was and busted me out. Ended up killing an assload of people too … and not just guilty ones. Innocent people lost their lives because of my negligence. I made a grave error and I'll never forget that.

"When I get back to base, I'm a total wreck. And then I was court-martialed and dishonorably discharged from the Special Forces. Of course, I was given strict instructions not to ever speak of this incident. You're the first person I've ever told. My family all but disowned me because my dad is ex-military and the story that was publicly told made me look like I went on an AWOL killing spree. The select people who knew the truth were the ones who helped me with the business. I'm sworn to uphold this secrecy indefinitely. I knew that's how it all worked going into it, so I have no legal recourse."

"So what I don't get is why are you so hard on yourself?"

Oh, she's so innocent, she doesn't even realize.

"Because in everything I did before that day, I did it with the knowledge that it was for the good of the cause … for the fight against terrorism. To get the bad guys. To stop all this shit. But I fucked up. I didn't do my job. I didn't follow procedure. I left out one important detail. I didn't look at who I was supposed to kill and I killed a kid, Gemini. And then, because of that negligence, many other innocent people died in my rescue. I can never change that. And those men who helped me, they're paying the price now too. Many lost their status with the military, like I did. All because they stuck by my side. That's a tough thing to live with."

"It must be." By some miracle, I feel her tenderness through her eyes. But the moment is shattered by my ringing phone. The last thing I want to do is answer it.

My hand shakes as I push the button. "Wolfe."

"Hey, boss. You ready for us?" It's Huff and I want to tell him to go away and come back in the morning, but I force the necessary words past my lips. "Yeah. Room 324."

"We're on the way."

I want to hurl my phone across the room and watch it break apart. Gemini stands and puts her hand on my arm.

"It's okay, Drex."

"This is anything *but* okay. Promise me something, Gem. Promise me you'll act like you don't know anything. Okay? My men can't know *anything* about this."

"I won't say a word. You have my promise."

"Thank you. They'll ask if I've talked with you about Nick. You can say what you want on that. One other thing—we ran a search on Nick's identity and it came up fairly blank. Like yours did when we checked it, right after we first found you. There really wasn't anything there. He never belonged to any clubs in high school, there was no information on his family, no church affiliations, not a damn thing. So either he had a false identity, was working undercover, or he was also in the witness protection program. We quickly threw out the third one and I have my doubts about the second. So that leaves us with the first."

She stares at me and nods.

"Please believe me when I tell you I'm looking out for you, Gemini. If nothing else, believe that. No matter what."

"I do, Drex. I trust you."

Her comment eases me a bit, but I'm still worried that her suspicions will flare at some point. A knock on the door stems any further discussion. I give her one final glance and she nods as I move to open the door.

After the men file into the room, we make our final arrangements for the morning. Our departure time from the hotel will be at 9 a.m. The storage facility office doesn't open until then. While Gemini, Huff, and I go there, the other two teams will go to two different storage facilities as decoys. Once we check out the facility where we think Michelle Sheridan may have hidden the file, we'll get out of here. The pilot will be on standby for wheels up all day long. Once we have everything set for tomorrow, the men depart and we're finally alone again.

"How are you feeling?" Gemini asks.

"Shouldn't I be the one asking you that question?"

"No, because I'm not the one who had a huge piece of metal removed from my chest."

Oh. I wasn't even thinking about my physical condition. Funny how you forget these things.

"I'm fine. Just a bit sore. What about you?"

"Um, is this you trying to avoid me, Drex?"

"No, this is Drex asking a legitimate question. How's your head feeling?"

"Really good. I'm taking fewer pills. I know what the doctor said, but now I feel like I don't need it as much. I'm not quitting cold turkey and I haven't had those awful withdrawals like I did that one time."

"Shit, Gemini. Why didn't you tell me?"

"I didn't want to bother you with it. I've been doing it for the last five days."

"And you're down to how many a day?"

"I break them in half now, so I take a half four times a day."

"And you're good?"

"Yeah." She beams. Literally.

"That other medication he put you on must be working."

"Yeah, I think so. I'm up to my maintenance dose. Drex, I'm so excited about it all. You know, we were in the middle of a very important conversation when the guys interrupted us. Are you planning on walking away from that?"

"Can we get ready for bed and talk about it then?"

"As long as you promise not to avoid the subject," she says.

That's exactly what I want to do, but now I know she won't let me.

"I promise."

As we ready for bed, I watch her strip off her clothes. "You didn't bring any pajamas?" I ask.

"Um, I suppose I could wear a T-shirt." She looks at me uneasily. We've always slept naked so I know I've surprised her.

"That would be best."

"Okay. What's wrong, Drex? Are we suddenly strangers, because if we are, I need to get my own room."

Shit! What am I doing? "Do you want your own room?"

"No, damn it. What's going on with you?"

"I don't know. This whole thing ... how you know about me now. I wasn't sure. I didn't want you to feel you had to stay if ..."

Her fingers are on my cheeks. "Hush. You told me the truth about yourself. You're human, Drex. You made a mistake. Human error. Was it bad? Yes. It was. I won't sugarcoat that. Did it ruin people's lives? Yes. It was a costly error. But are you going to torture yourself forever because of it? You have to forgive yourself."

"Gemini, you can't mend my broken soul."

"Who said I was trying to? I can't mend anything on you. Just as you can't mend anything on me. When someone is broken, they have to find the means within themselves to get fixed. Either by their own hand or by getting outside help. And part of that fix for you is forgiveness. You need to find a way to forgive yourself."

She seems so wise for someone so young. "I'm sorry for acting strange. Part of this is guilt for telling you. This oath I took ... you're the only one I've ever told what really happened. And I didn't even tell you all the details. For the past few years, I've pushed it back in my mind and haven't really faced the truth of it all. The bad part is, as far as my family is concerned, I'm trash. And I want to tell my dad it's not true. That the awful stuff he heard about me isn't what happened. And the sorrow in my mom's eyes … Jesus, they nearly bled it was that rough. Bringing it all up made me remember that day and I keep thinking you'll feel like they did."

"I don't. And I won't. I don't want you to tell me the rest. I've heard enough and I have my opinions. Do you want to hear them?"

"Yeah. I do. Because I know you'll be honest."

"Here's what I think. You were under pressure to kill this guy. So you sneak in and you're alone in his house. You have to rely on the intelligence you've received to make a split-second decision. You can't ask your buddy next to you to help confirm if this is the right guy, because there isn't anyone there. So you take the shot. Then, your heart's pounding and you finally realize it's a kid. That's why you froze, right? If you were some dude who didn't give a shit, you would've been able to bolt without a second glance. But you *did* care. In fact, you cared *so* much you got caught. *That* was the worst error, because it caused problems for the people who helped you. But it was an honest reaction. So, you end up getting fucked by the government and this thing you call plausible deniability. And it's killed you and I'm terribly sorry, Drex.

"But you have to forgive yourself. And as far as your parents go, tell them. They're strong. They can keep your secret. Enough time has passed now, so tell them. Tell them they can't breathe a word of it to anyone or you'll be killed. Make something up, but make your point strong enough that they believe you. But Drex, they have a right to know their son is a good man. And not the fucked-up piece of shit that they've been led to believe he is."

Then her arms are around me. "This is just me hugging you. I'm not trying to fix you. Understand?"

"You really are something, you know?"

"Yeah. I do." I know she's smirking.

"So what about you?" I ask. We're still hugging. I don't want to let her go. "Are you okay for tomorrow?"

"As good as I'll ever be."

I lean away a bit so I can look at her. "You sure? This could be the big day. We could find that file and our crazy chase could be over."

"Nah, it's too easy. I think she's leaving breadcrumbs. And now with this info about Nick, I really don't know what to think anymore. If there weren't people trying to kill me, I think I'd give it up."

"Oh babe, there's no giving up on this now. If the guys are right, there's entirely too much at stake here to give up. This could mean a possible change in the war on terrorism. Come on, let's get some sleep. We're wiped and morning will be here soon."

As we climb into bed, she scoots close to me and says, "Thank you for everything, Drex. You've gone way beyond by doing this and I'm sorry I doubted you, even for a minute. And I'm sorry for what happened to you. If you ever need to talk, you know I'm here."

"Thanks." I hold her hand and fall asleep fast, thoughts of opening up to my parents swirling in my head.

Chapter 18

GEMINI
Complexities

DREX CRASHES HARD. When he falls asleep, there's no preamble. It's awake, then out. This night was so strange with his confession. My heart aches for him and I want to soothe his anguish, but it's not possible and I realize that. The release must come from within. He has to forgive himself. I pray he does, or it has the potential to destroy him.

As I drink in the sight of him, it's a fight not to brush the hair off his forehead and massage away the lines that have formed between his eyes. He's achingly beautiful to watch. His chest moves with each breath and his slightly parted lips form a tiny triangle where they come together. Just looking at him makes my desire spark.

This is the first time since we've been together that he sleeps in a T-shirt. He robs me of my magnificent view of his body and my teeth grind in frustration. This craving for him makes sleep elusive. I slip my hand in my panties and discover exactly how soaked I am for him. How can he do this to me?

To hell with it. Sexual frustration be damned. I pull the covers off and I think he'll stir, but he doesn't. So I slide down and stroke him. Then I take him in my mouth and move my head up and down, licking and sucking, swirling my tongue around the crown of his dick. I hear him groan as his hands bury themselves in my hair.

"Gemini, oh babe, what are you doing?"

I stop and look at him. "What does it look like?"

"You never wake me up like this, you naughty girl."

Hmm, naughty girl. I like that. "I couldn't sleep."

"Stop. As much as I love to fuck your mouth, I'd much rather have you."

Since I don't want to disappoint, I crawl up next to him. "Take off that damn shirt."

I love to watch his muscles tighten and flex when he moves. It's such a lovely treat.

"Now you." I'd forgotten I had on a shirt myself. I rip it off.

"Panties?" I follow his eyes as they move downward.

"Gone," I say as I discard them. And then the man lunges, but it's followed by a wince.

"Fuck. This damn incision."

"Lay back. Let me do the pleasuring tonight."

He sits back and I straddle him. My lips are on his and his tongue takes me apart, bit by bit, until I'm a panting, quivering heap.

"How do you do that with just a kiss?" I ask.

His eyes search mine and I feel like I'm collapsing beneath their stare. "Gemini, we never *just* kiss. We share ourselves with our mouths. Haven't you figured that out yet? You could make me sign all my financial assets over to you because of that sweet mouth of yours." And his hands wind up in my hair and he's kissing me again. His erection is beneath me, hitting me right *there*, and I feel as though a nuclear blast rockets through me. My hips automatically find that rhythm that will add what I need, but he stills me.

"Not yet. Slow, babe."

"I don't want slow. I want now."

"You always want now."

He slides down the bed, carefully, and then tells me to slide up until I hover over his mouth. Oh yes, I like this. But not as much as his cock inside me.

He teases and I fidget, but his grip on my hips tightens. The scruff of his chin rubs me just so and I moan. Then he blows on me and I moan again. He's not going to make me come; he's only torturing me.

"Please, Drex. I need you."

He holds me against him, unrelenting, and his tongue teases me more. Then his teeth nibble on me, and his lips suck my clit until I'm not sure how much more I can take.

"Drex, I ... I ..."

He blows again and in between them, he asks, "What do you want, Gem? Tell me."

"You."

"My hand, my tongue, what?"

"No! Your dick."

He pushes me back and then says, "Get on your hands and knees." I waste no time in complying. The bed moves as he gets up and then he's behind me. I can feel him spreading me and his tip enters me ever so slowly. I want to scream in frustration.

"God, can you go any slower?" I finally say.

"Yeah. Or I can always stop," he teases, as he incrementally moves into me.

I'm so full of need for him, I don't find him humorous. "If you stop, I'm going to hurt you."

"Hmm. Then how's this?"

And he slams into me and quickens the pace to exactly what I need. He fills me to the breaking point, then retreats. I want to scream once again, but now with that pleasure-pain I love so damn much.

"Oh, Drex. Yes, that's so good. Right there."

"Here?"

"Yes! There." He hits that perfect spot over and over until I'm in Eden-gasm.

"Ah, Gem, that's so damn good," he cries out as he climaxes.

When our heart rates have normalized, he says, "So my little sex princess, you're absolutely not fond of slow, are you?"

"Depends. I was in bad shape and you teased me until I was about to go up in flames. You can't be funny at a time like that."

"I'm sorry, hon, but I couldn't resist. You were very demanding."

"Damn straight I was."

"So what precipitated all this?"

"You. It's all your fault."

"Me? What did I do?"

"You fell asleep and I was watching you look all kinds of sexy. Then I wanted to brush your hair off your face, like this," and I reach over and do just that. "But I didn't because I didn't want to disturb you." I watch him as his lips vibrate with laughter.

"So you decided that instead of brushing my hair off my face, you'd suck my dick? Because I certainly would never wake up to that."

"Exactly. But I got pissed because tonight was the first time since we've been sleeping together that you wore a stupid T-shirt to bed and you stole something from me."

"What did I steal from you?"

"This perfectly gorgeous view."

My hand travels from his neck, down to his chest where I briefly stop to brush my fingers across his nipples and then on down to his abs. I watch him as my hand moves south, tripping lightly along the happy trail, and then landing on my final goal at last.

His hand locks onto my wrist and pulls it back to his mouth, where he places a chaste kiss on the back of it. "Hmm. Well, if I had known my girlfriend was so deprived, I never would've done such a terrible thing."

"Don't you ever do something so cruel again."

"That and I won't ever fuck you slowly again, either, or you might hurt me."

"Yep, that too!"

"Come over here." He motions with his finger. "I'm more than glad you woke me up and please do that more often. And if fast and hard is what you want, that's what you'll get, babe. I can do fast and hard."

"Good. And thanks for relieving me. The land of Orgasmia was very enjoyable."

NINE O'CLOCK ARRIVES and Huff, Drex, and I head to Storage and More on Sixth Avenue in Panama City. This is a lovely town and it hits me now why my mom liked it so much. The views of the water are amazing as we cross the bridge and head into town. The clear water of the Florida Gulf coast sparkles with the morning sun. Panama City isn't huge, but it's large enough to offer everything from nice restaurants and fancy hotels to casual beachfront dining. The other teams are off on their own ventures. We'll be in touch as soon as we find something.

The storage office reeks of cigarette smoke. The guy behind the desk looks up as the little bell over the door tinkles; his face registers surprise as he takes in the intimidating sight of Drex and Huff. The placard on the desk reads John Stuben. Mid- to late thirties, mousy-brown, long greasy hair. His teeth look like they haven't seen a toothbrush in ages. He also reeks of body odor.

Between him and the cigarette smoke, I want to gag.

"Um, are you Mr. Stuben?" I ask.

"That's me. Just like the sign says." He barely looks at me. He's focused on Huff and Drex who have taken up positions behind me. If he didn't stink so badly, I might feel sorry for him.

"My name is Gemini Sheridan. I believe my mother, Michelle Sheridan, may have had a unit rented in this facility. She died in a car accident several years ago and I'm trying to close out all her accounts. Can you check for me?"

"Um, yeah. Hang on." He stabs at his computer's keyboard. "Yeah, we have a unit rented to a Ms. Sheridan." Then he gets up and goes to a file cabinet and pulls out a lease. His back is facing us as he thumbs through the file. "According to this file, only Ms. Sheridan is to have access to this unit."

"Yes, I suppose that would be correct, but she was killed in 2009. I have a copy of her death certificate here if you would like to see it. I am her only living relative—everything in her possession was willed to me. I also have a copy of her Last Will and Testament where that is stated." Of course, I don't really, but Drex had some fake ones procured that look real enough.

"Yeah, I'm gonna have to check those out."

I quickly look at Drex and he gives me a slight nod. I rifle through my backpack for the papers and hand them to Mr. StinkGrease.

He looks at them and then at me. "Have any ID?"

"Oh yeah. Sorry." I pull out my driver's license, making sure to give him the one that says I'm Gemini Sheridan.

"Thanks," he says as he grabs it. He checks things out and says, "This is pretty unusual. I need to call my supervisor on this."

Now Drex steps in. I've never seen him in action like this, other than when he pulled me out of my apartment. He gently shifts me to the side as he leans over Mr. Stuben's desk and gets right in his face.

"Okay, let's cut the bullshit here, *John*. You're going to give Ms. Sheridan access to everything she asks for right now, without delay, or you're going to have all kinds of issues on your hands."

Stuben screws up his face and says, "Who do you think you are, coming in here and demanding things like this?"

"What you need to worry about is what you're gonna do when cops swarm all over this place because of the phone call I make over your little drug operation you've got going on here. You know, Stuben, your little meth lab? So I suggest you give Ms. Sheridan the code to get into that fucking unit so she can remove her deceased mother's belongings and we'll be out of your greasy hair. If not, this whole place will be crumbling on your head in a matter of minutes. Now, what's it gonna be?"

Stuben snatches a piece of paper, scribbles on it, and hands it to me, his hand shaking. "Here. The first code is for the gate. The second will get you into the building her unit is in. I hope you have a key to the lock. It's the second building on the right."

Drex grabs the paper before I have a chance to and ushers me out. But then he stops. "By the way, I imagine Ms. Sheridan will be owed a refund for the months she won't be needing this unit, since I'm sure her mother has paid for it well in advance."

"Um, yes. She's paid up until 2016."

"Good. Make that check out to Gemini Sheridan. We'll pick it up on the way out."

When we get in the car, I ask, "How did you know?"

Drex shrugs and says, "I didn't. It was a hunch."

"Damn, you're good."

"Oh God," Huff moans from the back seat. "Why'd you have to go and say that, Gemini? Now he's gonna be prancing around like a fucking peacock."

Drex swivels his head to look at Huff. "Since when have I ever pranced?" Huff groans as Drex parks next to the building containing my mom's unit. I feel anxious.

"What if there's nothing inside?" I ask as I grip Drex's hand.

He gives me a firm squeeze back. "Then we keep going forward until we do find something."

We get inside and sitting on the floor in the middle of the unit is another metal box, just like the one we found at my house. As I examine the box, I notice a fine arrow that has been crudely gouged into it. If you didn't look closely, you'd miss it altogether.

"Hey, check this out," I say.

"Interesting," Drex says.

"This is weird." I walk to the wall and stand there, hoping something will jump out.

Drex is on one side of me and Huff is on the other. "Huff, what do you think the layout of this building is?" Drex asks.

"More units on the back of this one. Why?"

"My thoughts too. You think maybe she has the unit behind this one in a different name?"

"I'll go check."

Huff leaves and Drex starts tapping on the wall. "This sounds hollow but the walls in these places are ultra thin."

My head tilts as I follow the wall to the ceiling, opened to metal rafters. "Hey, how's your back feel?"

"Still sore. Why?"

"I want to look up there, but let's wait until Huff gets back."

"I can do it."

"No. That's unnecessary stress. Besides, I'd rather you save your strength for other things."

He barks out a laugh. "Oh, you would, would you?"

"Mmm, yeah."

Then he gives me a burning look and desire uncoils within me as I feel myself become damp with it.

"Stop it now."

"Stop what?" He feigns innocence.

"You know damn well what."

"If we're fast ..."

"No! And we're never fast. Jeez, Drex."

"Okay. So should we open the box?"

"We don't have a key here." Now it's difficult for me to concentrate. I'm too sexed up.

Thankfully, Huff walks back in then and says, "The unit behind this one has been vacant for almost a year."

"Huff, put me on your shoulders."

"Huh?"

"We think there may be something hidden up there. I don't want Drex to do it with his healing injury."

Huff bends down. Drex watches us with narrowed eyes. Jealous much?

Once I'm up there, I see only the aluminum ceiling rafters and tons of dust.

"I don't think there's anything up here."

"Babe, don't look for the obvious. Run your hand along those rafters. Remember, your mom was clever. She wouldn't want anything to jump out at you."

I move my hands as far as I can. "Can you walk over a little to the right?"

We move in a pattern, covering the back wall. I'm sure if she put anything up there, that's where it'll be since the arrow was pointing there. Just as I'm about to give up, my finger hits something. "Here. I feel something taped here." I loosen the tape with my fingernails and find another key. When I free it, I hand it to Drex. Now I'm more frustrated than ever.

Huff puts me down. "Now what? What the hell do we do with this? Why did she have to be so damn secretive?"

Drex grabs my hand. "We've been here too long. Let's go."

Huff grabs the box. We jump in the car and on the way out, I ask Drex about the check.

"You don't want a check from them. That was just to scare that dude. If you cash it, they'll be all over this place. Once we don't pick it up, he'll destroy it and be on pins and needles for a few days, waiting to see if we call the cops. When we don't, his lips will be sealed."

"Nice plan," I say.

"You don't need that money anyway."

"I guess not. I don't have access to any money right now as it is."

"And that's fine." Drex has told me that before. Many times. But it doesn't make me feel good. I want to repay him.

"I'll pay you back. For all this. I'm good for it."

"It's cool, Gem."

He calls the other teams and tells them to head to the airport. Then he lets the pilot know we're on the way. Now I'm eager to see what's inside the box. Twenty-five minutes later, we pull onto the tarmac and the pilot is waiting for us. Another man greets us and tells us he's there to return our car. A couple of minutes after that, the other guys show up. We board the Gulfstream 550 and in no time, we're in the air.

"You okay?" Drex asks.

"Yeah," I say as I pull my hand out of his and rub it on my jeans. "Sorry for the clammy palm. I want to get back and see what's in the box."

His look morphs instantly from concerned to heated. "Kiss me, Gem."

Whoa. What brought this on? And who am I to ignore this request? Leaning in, I touch my lips to his. He pulls the lower one in his mouth and sucks on it. His way of playing with me unleashes a sexual need I can't ignore.

"You're one big, bad tease, you know."

"Yep."

"I'll get you back when you least expect it."

He shocks me when he says, "I hated watching you on Huff's shoulders." His eyes turn dark again.

"It wasn't anything. I needed to get up there."

"Logic tells me that. But I don't want anyone other than me touching you."

"Possessive much?"

He hits me with those blue-grays again. "Never before you."

Now I'm speechless. Why does he throw these comments out so nonchalantly? When we're in a place where they can't be addressed? Then I get it. That's exactly why he does it. Because he doesn't want to address them. I glance around the plane and check to see what the others are doing, either reading or listening to music. That makes this fair game.

"So, you think by tossing out a comment like that, I'm going to what? Ignore it?"

"Uh ..."

"And you think because of where we are that I'm not going to respond?"

"I don't know what I think."

"Um, yeah, you do. You're telling me these things because you think I won't say or do anything since we're not alone. Not this time, Drex."

"What does that mean?"

"I want to know what's in that head of yours. Now. And don't distract me."

"Are you going to tell me what's in *your* head first?"

I want to smack him. But I have a better idea. The back of this plane has sleeping quarters that will afford us privacy, so I unbuckle my belt and stand. Then I grab his hand and say, "Let's go. We have to talk."

He's so tall that he can't stand to full height but he follows me. When I close the door behind us, I don't take time to marvel at the luxury. I simply turn to him and say, “Sit down.” I sit next to him on the large bed.

“What happened to you? I’m not trying to be accusatory here, but ever since the bombing, you’re different. More reticent. And sometimes I’m uncomfortable around you. You run hot and cold with me. I feel like you want to push me out one minute and then suffocate me the next. I’m in Yo-Yo-Ville with you right now and you won’t talk to me, other than to drop little comments and innuendos every now and then. I’m tired of being confused, Drex.”

He blows out his breath with a groan. I don’t break the silence but give him time to collect his thoughts. “I’m confused too, Gem.” Then he’s silent again.

“My mom used to call me that all the time. Gem. Her little Gem. ‘Precious as a diamond,’ she’d say.”

“I can see why she’d say that. But to me, you’re my precious Onyx.”

“See, there you go again. Saying things like that and then ... nothing.”

“I don’t mean to do that. It’s just ... I think we’re on the cusp of something here. I need to stay away from you because my head’s not in the game as it should be when I’m around you. You fuck with my head, Gemini. I know you don’t mean to. And I don’t blame you. It’s just that you’ve gotten to me and I can’t pull myself away. And I’m fucking scared as hell that I’m going to blow it, like I did in Iraq. If I do that, and something happens to you, I won’t be able to live with that. But the other side of me doesn’t trust anyone else to take care of you like I can. Like today when Huff had you on his shoulders, I wanted to knock the shit out of him. I’m an ass. I’m sorry.”

“Drex. Let’s just quit this whole thing. I’m to blame for all of this and I don’t want you to feel that way. I’m the one who’s sorry. You didn’t sign up for this. This isn’t your problem. It’s mine."

"Stop being obtuse. Do you think I can let you walk away now? That's a fucking joke. Why do you think I'm a mess? I'm so wrapped up in *you*, I can't think straight. And you don't have a choice. You're in danger with or without me. And I'd rather be part of it, crazy as it may sound. So enough of that talk."

"Then can we at least agree on some things here?"

"Go on."

"Before you start weirding out on me, will you at least talk to me first?"

He gives me a soul-digging stare. "That's a pretty tall order. Sometimes I react before I think, you know. I assess situations quickly and sometimes the status of them makes me overthink things. I always … always have that shitstorm experience hanging over me. I'll try to discuss them, but I make judgment calls fast, and as I see fit, Gem."

"No, I get that part. What I'm talking about is how you withdraw from me. And then go all alpha and I never know what you're thinking. And like last night. You went to bed with your shirt on. We never sleep with clothes on and while it may seem like a small thing to you, it wasn't to me. It was like you put up a barrier between us." The corners of his mouth slowly turn up, but then his mouth breaks into a huge grin.

"Well, damn, babe, if I'd have known you were gonna get so upset by a little bit of cotton, I would never have done such a rude thing to you."

"It wasn't just a little piece of cotton, and you know it. And you're making fun of me."

"Yeah, I am."

He picks up my hand and turns it around so my palm is facing up. Then he traces the creases with his index finger.

I want to pull it out of his grasp, but I don't. "Now you're deflecting."

"I suppose I am. Maybe this topic is just a difficult one for me because I don't understand my feelings yet for you. I know I don't want to lose you. Not having you in my life is a thought I can't stand. And the thing is, I don't just want you. I want to own you ... all of you, every single bit. I want you as mine. I don't want anyone else to look at or touch you. And quite frankly, I'm not sure how to deal with that. We haven't known each other long enough for all of this. I suppose the fact that we've spent almost every waking hour together changes things. And then that damn bombing. When I thought we might not get out of there, I can't even tell you how that made me feel. It pushed my feelings for you up several thousand notches. I think what would've taken months actually was hastened by that incident. But I don't even know where you stand. When I told you about Nick, and my thoughts about him, the way you reacted made my confidence in us bottom out."

Whoa. He really is opening up. Much more than I expected.

"Okay, forget about Nick. He shouldn't even enter this conversation. But you want to *own* me? You don't want anyone else to *look* at or *touch* me?"

His head swings back and forth. That's a big no, Gemini. And there is no humor in him. The man is serious. Oh fuck.

"You asked. I'm telling."

I take a cleansing breath and try to clear my thoughts. "Wow. Just wow."

"You said you wanted honesty between us, so here I am, laying myself open to you."

After a few moments of quiet, I ask, "You told me you loved me when you were in the hospital. Are you in love with me?"

He snorts. "Now that's the million-dollar question, isn't it?" He drops his head and rubs it with his free hand. My hand is still cocooned in his other one. "My brain wants to say no, but my heart disagrees. How's that for a concrete answer?"

"It's about the same way I feel. In a way, I'm glad. At least we're both on the same plane, no pun intended."

He moves so fast I'm stunned when his mouth crashes into mine. His urgency leaves me breathless as his arms clutch me tightly to his chest. I get the feeling that he wants to invade every part of me. My lips are bruised and his tongue isn't playing at all. It's demanding, possessing, branding me. His mouth is marking me and I know this is exactly what he wants ... what he needs. It's what I need too. When our mouths break apart, my fingers touch his lips and I see a drop of blood.

"You're bleeding."

He doesn't speak, but his mouth moves down my neck, teasing me with his teeth. When he gets to my breast, he tugs my bra down just enough so his mouth has access. Then he nips and sucks me. The way he's going at me, I know he'll leave a mark, but I couldn't care less. I want him to do that. I want him to brand me, because the truth of it is I've been his all along. Whether this is love or lust, I don't give a damn. I only know that he's in my blood, and he's in it so thick, I don't ever want him to leave.

"You're mine, Gemini, and only mine. Do you understand me? No one else's, only mine."

"Yes, Drex. I understand. And I hope you know this goes both ways."

"That's a given for me. Now kiss me again, babe. I can't get enough of your sexy mouth."

We're like two teenagers making out on the bed until I feel my ears popping. "We're descending."

"Yeah, I felt that too. Here ..." He offers me his hand and pulls me into a seated position. Then he runs his fingers through my hair, taming it back into some semblance of what it looked like before.

"Do I have bed head?"

"Hell yeah, and it's hot as fuck."

"Drex! I don't want to go out there with sexed-up hair."

"Hang on." He opens a drawer and pulls out a brush. "Allow me." He brushes my hair. It feels so nice.

"I love this. It reminds me of how my mom used to brush my hair. I always loved it."

"Hmm. I'll have to do this more often, then. There. All nice and tidy."

Turning, I give him a quick kiss on his cheek and we go back to our seats. No one even notices us return because they're all asleep.

We hold hands as the plane makes it final descent. What an odd turn of events my life has taken. My thoughts are filled with this man who sits next to me and how much he's done for me in the brief time I've known him. He's changed my life, and whether anything permanent happens with us, who's to say, but for right now, I'm happy to take things one day at a time.

Chapter 19

Drex
Superman

FOR ONCE IN a very long time, I feel at peace. Gemini knows the truth about my past and she hasn't condemned me. She's even aware of how deep my feelings are for her. Fuck, I act like such a damn troglodyte around her. How is it possible that I feel this way? I need to stop overthinking this and push past it because the why isn't what's important. It just *is* and I need to be satisfied with that. The best thing about it is that I didn't scare the hell out of her and she's still sitting next to me, holding my hand.

But then again, where the hell is she going to go? It's not like she can bail out of the plane. Even so, as I rifle through my memories, I can't remember feeling this relieved before. The ache in my heart has dissipated. Maybe Gem is right. Maybe I do need to tell my parents. To hell with that oath I took. When I think about how they've been torn to pieces, thinking the worst of me, the ache returns with a vengeance, but this time, the anger deepens.

"What is it?" Gemini asks.

"What do you mean?"

"You're squeezing the crap out of my hand."

Immediately, I raise it to my lips and kiss it. "Aw, fuck. I'm sorry, babe. I was thinking about what you said. You know, with regard to telling my parents."

"Hey, Drex, look at me."

She puts her hands on my cheeks and I know I'm going to turn to mush. When she looks at me that way, Christ, I would jump out of this plane if she asked.

"They need to know what kind of a man their son is. That he's honorable, loyal, courageous, and trustworthy, that he defended his country to the best of his ability. They also need to know that he is human, but that he would go to the ends of the earth for his true friends and fellow soldiers. If you don't want to tell them, I can do it for you.

"You saved my life, more than once, and you did it not because you had to, not because you were paid to, but because it was the right thing to do. And you put yourself in danger doing it. So, your parents are very deserving of hearing about what a fine son they have. Please tell them, Drex."

It takes several swallows to rid my throat of the lump. "You make me forget about the bad."

"I only say what's true."

The plane rolls to a stop and the guys get up and stretch. I stuff my emotions in my back pocket for now and stand up with the rest of the team.

"After you." Gemini leads the way, but Huff is in front as we deplane. There are two company SUVs waiting to take us back to headquarters. "Let's go to work," I say.

Huff drives us back to the office taking the back roads to avoid traffic. He's tailing the first SUV. I'm in the back seat while Gemini is in the front. The other guys are in the lead car. We're talking about what we'll do when we get back when the vehicle violently lurches and I'm jerked into my seat as the seatbelt catches. The sound of crunching metal and breaking glass echoes in my head and I hear Gemini scream as the SUV is pushed sideways for several hundred feet. It comes to a stop against a big black van, pinning us in. Shaking my head to clear it, it's then I realize we've just been T-boned. My head is bleeding and so is my arm. Other than that, I appear to be fine.

My hand automatically reaches for my weapon and I yell, "Is everyone okay? Gemini? Huff?"

"I think I am," Gemini yells back. "Just scratched up."

"Huff?"

No answer.

"Gemini, what's going on up there?"

I scan the exterior. My window is blocked by the black van and all the windows on the other side of the car are shattered. I'm fucked.

"He's knocked out. His head is bleeding, Drex." Panic etches her voice.

I'm already dialing the other guys. "Code red here." There's no answer so I don't know if they're alive or dead.

"Gemini, can you see the other SUV?"

"No! I can't see through the windshield. It's all cracked."

"Goddammit!" We're on a deserted road so there'll be no help for us out here.

Then Gemini's door opens, followed by the rear door. An accented voice demands, "Get out of the car."

Gemini looks at me and I nod. "Do as he says." We have no other choice right now. And I need to see what's going on. It was stupid of me to put myself in the back seat. Just another damn example of my lack of focus.

We get out and are greeted by six armed men, two wearing traditional Middle Eastern attire while others look like your average American.

"Hello, Mr. Wolfe. My, haven't you been an elusive one?"

I've seen this face before but I can't recall where. Maybe when I was in Iraq or Afghanistan. I'm positive he's one of the top men with Aali Imaam.

"Please forgive me. You seem to have me at a slight disadvantage. Have we met?"

His laugh is sinister. "No, not exactly. But you have been in my family's home. At least once. The night you put a bullet in my nephew's head."

My mind reels. These people are definitely Aali Imaam and we were right that night. That Iraqi official *is* tied to this group. But where's the connection with Gemini?

"You can put that blame back on your brother. What kind of man sets up his own child like that?"

"Quiet!"

"What do you want?"

"Oh, come now, Wolfe. You didn't acquire that name by accident. You know exactly what we want."

"Fair enough. Why do you want her?"

"You know damn well why. The same reason why you're guarding her so closely."

Hmm. Interesting. He thinks I know.

He looks at Gemini and says, "Come. I'm taking you home now."

There's one thing I've learned about Gemini, and that's when she makes up her mind about something, you're not going to change it. And she's decided she does *not* like this man. Her glare is chewing him up and spitting him out like nothing I've ever seen before.

"I *am* home and the *only* way I'm going anywhere with you is if you kill me."

Aw, fuck, now why'd she have to go and say that?

I expect him to slap her, but he doesn't. He only nods once and then digs his phone out of the inner pocket of his suit coat and taps a button. As he's doing this, he walks out of hearing distance. I catch Gem's eye and try to signal to her not to say anything else, but I'm not sure if she gets me.

Soon the suit is back with us and he looks at Gemini. He walks a circle around her very slowly, and then stops when he's in front of her again. "It's really a shame."

I'm hoping she doesn't take his bait, but it's too much for her.

"What's that?" she asks.

"That you've been lied to by the infidels all these years."

"I haven't been lied to."

"Oh? So you know the truth then?"

"All of it," Gem yells.

She starts to walk toward me when a hand on her shoulder stops her. I force myself not to break that man's arm in two for touching her.

"Don't move. You were not given permission to move!" the owner of said hand yells.

"Don't touch her!" Now it's my turn to yell.

"Shut up, Wolfe. You have no say in this." I now have two guns aimed at me—one at my head, one at my heart.

"Stop it! Now!" Gemini cries.

"Let's all calm down here." My hands are raised so they know I'm no threat.

The suit finally nods and looks back at Gemini. "Come, Amira, I'm taking you home." He moves to take her arm and it's all I can do not to launch myself at him.

"My name is Gemini and I *am* home," she grits out.

"Of course, that's what they want you to think. But your homeland isn't here. You are the daughter of Allah and I am taking you back where you belong."

"I *am* where I belong and it's right here."

He looks at one of his guards and says, "Drug her."

The guard approaches Gemini and she tries to move toward me. They grab her and she yells, "No! I won't go! I don't know anything. Leave me alone!"

"She doesn't know a thing! She's telling you the truth. Whatever information you think you can get out of her, she doesn't have. Her mother never told her anything before she died," I say.

The suit stops and stares at me. "If what you say is true, then why did you kill the traitor whore?"

Why the hell would he think that *I* killed Gemini's mother?

"*I* didn't kill her. Why would you think that?"

For a split second, his face registers surprise. I need to strike now. "Someone else killed her. That's what we're trying to figure out. So you weren't involved in that?"

He doesn't answer but stares first at Gemini, then me. "Does she know the truth about you, Wolfe?"

Oh, shit. Where is he going with this?

"Yes, I know everything about him," she answers for me.

"You do? I don't think so. You only think you do."

"That's not true," she insists.

"Is it not? Has he told you he murdered an innocent child?"

"Yes! And he explained the circumstances."

"I see." The suit paces a bit and then stops in front of Gemini. He bends down a bit so his face is inches from her. "Has he told you his real name? It isn't Wolfe, you know. Are you aware he is a CIA operative?"

Fuck! Goddammit! How the hell did he dig up that information? I look at Gemini's face and she's as white as a sheet. Her eyes are pleading for the truth, and I know it's going to kill her when I give it to her.

The suit sneers. "I can tell he hasn't. You don't know the truth, then. Just as I suspected."

Then the suit turns to me and says, "You expect me to believe you when you say you didn't kill the whore, and you haven't even told her daughter the truth? The truth that you were sent to find her?"

"No! That's not true!" Where is he getting this information? This is the first time I'm hearing it.

In the distance, I hear the faint hum of an engine and I'm hoping that reinforcements are arriving. The suit's head snaps around but he's comfortable when he doesn't notice anything out of the ordinary. I reassess the situation, trying to see if there's a way out of this. I detect movement out of the corner of my eye, but pretend not to notice. The best thing I can do now is to keep him distracted.

"I was never sent to find her. I found her by accident, working on a different case. It was you and your men who were in Austin, wasn't it?" I ask.

He tips his head. "Let's just say those were my associates and you have quite a knack for eluding us. Do you expect me to believe you knew nothing about her?"

"Yes, because it's the truth."

"The CIA needs to start training their men better. They are also on your tail, because we've been tracking both of you for weeks now. And if you didn't know her, how did you find her, when my stupid men had her in her apartment?"

"Easy! I knew her address by then. Anyone could've found her there. So who killed her mother? And why did you kill Nick Lowry, one of your own recruits?"

"Lowry wasn't ours. We didn't even know about him until he posted the missing persons' report on Amira. He led us to her. After the whore disappeared all those years ago, we searched for Amira. It was only her picture on the news that led us to her."

So who's the third party in this clusterfuck? Could it actually be the CIA? And why would they be doing this?

Suddenly, the sound of suppressed gunfire erupts and two of the men surrounding the suit drop like flies. One man grabs Gemini from behind and uses her as a shield. My heart stops when I see he has a gun to her head.

"Cease fire," I shout.

The suit is still standing and I say, "Walk away and leave the girl. We can end here, but you need to leave the girl. You're surrounded. My snipers will take you both down before he even has a chance to squeeze that trigger."

"You're going to regret this. We *will* take her one day and she will come to understand the true traitor that you are." Then he turns to the one holding Gemini and orders him in Farsi to release her. The man obeys and forcefully shoves her to the ground. They back away, collect their casualties, climb into the van, and drive off.

"Gemini!" I shout as I run to her. She's on her hands and knees, shaking. She lifts her head, and the hurt and anger that spill forth skewer me. I know she wants the truth.

"The answer is yes, but it's not what you think."

"Then you better explain now." She's still on the ground, unmoving.

"I can't. Not here."

"Drex."

"Please. You have to understand."

"No! You have to understand. A fucking CIA operative? And all this time you've led me to believe that you abhor the government?"

"Not here. Not now." This has just blown everything for me and I'm now fucked every which way to Sunday. I have to get her to shut up.

"Then when?"

I get down on the ground and grab her shoulders. "Please," I whisper, "please trust me and give me a chance. But not here.

When we're alone. Please, Gem."

The desperation in my voice must have gotten through to her. My arms go around her because I'm overjoyed she's safe, but she mistakes this for something else entirely.

"Let me go, Drex." Her words like razors slice me open and extract my heart. I thought I was wrecked after the incident in Iraq and then the court-martial. But this … this has slaughtered me. I never knew how a few words from the woman I love could gut me so brutally. And there I have my answer. I love her. I am in love with her. Deeply, thoroughly. And leave it to me to fuck it up so badly and discover it when it's too late.

MY MEN ARE charged with getting the scene cleaned up. The only thing they leave behind is the van, which the terrorists used to pin our SUV. The ride back to headquarters is silent, but I will have to offer her some kind of explanation when we get back. I'm not sure what to say, but I guess it doesn't matter, because I've been compromised now. Fuck! How did this happen? Glancing at Gemini, she stares straight ahead, her expression stony. My gut tightens when I think about the thoughts running through her mind. I want to hold her hand right now, pick it up and unclench her fist, to ease her discomfort. But I don't.

The SUV heads directly to the underground garage and then we're in the elevator, riding in uncomfortable silence. As soon as the doors open, there's a flurry of activity surrounding us.

Blake is there and I tell him to handle the debriefing. Huff was taken to the emergency room, but word is he has a concussion and a laceration that will need stitching. He'll spend the night for observation and most likely be released tomorrow. Everyone else is fine.

My hand is on Gemini's arm and I escort her to the apartment. Before I can close the door, she takes a swing at me.

Her left fist connects with my right deltoid and she follows it up with an uppercut to my jaw. It's a good thing I see it coming and block her with my open palm.

"Goddammit, what the fuck are you playing at here?" Her chest heaves and her lips are thinned into a straight line.

There's no use wasting time with a preamble, so I jump right in.

"The guy in the suit compromised everything and put us all in danger. How he found out about me is a head scratcher. Yes, I work for the CIA and Homeland Security and sometimes the FBI. I don't do any international stuff, only domestic. No, you couldn't know. No one knows about my work with the CIA. Not Huff, not Blake, not anyone. I didn't tell you because I couldn't. That's the whole meaning of undercover. I don't work for them full-time. They came to me after the whole incident in Iraq. After my court-martial. They offered me a deal and I grabbed it. They wanted me for my inside knowledge of the terror cells and how they operate. My fluency in their languages is also a huge bonus. That's why everything is so easy for me to get ... fake IDs, passports, you name it. My connections with them. They also drive business my way. Yeah, they piss me off because sometimes they have a tendency to think they own me, but they don't. I apologize for you finding out the way you did, but Gemini, I can't apologize for not telling you. This is a case of national security. You have to understand this. The other things he said were all lies. I was *not* involved in your mother's death. I knew *nothing* about you until that night in Austin. You have to believe me. Everything I've told you about me, other than the CIA, is the truth. I swear to God."

She's quiet for a minute. Finally, she says, "I'm so fucking tired of feeling confused. Every time I think I have things figured out, someone drops a bomb. Literally." She rubs her head.

"I know, babe, and I'm sorry. This is a fucking mess, right?"

She snorts. "Um, a mess? That's a nice way to put it." She glares at me and says, "I don't know if I can believe you anymore, Drex. And I'm sick of feeling like I'm living in a fucking cage."

I nod. "I don't blame you. I'd feel the same way. But all I can do is swear to you that what I'm saying is the truth."

"Who was that guy?"

"Can we sit and talk about this without me worrying that you're gonna take another swing at me?"

The look she gives me is anything but loving. It's full of distrust and anger. But she nods, so I have to be satisfied with that. She sits and I continue, "I think he was the brother of the Iraqi official I was supposed to take out that night. Or maybe his brother-in-law. He said I killed his nephew."

"So how am I connected to him? Was my father Iraqi?"

"Don't know that, either. We know he was Middle Eastern. Want to see what's in the box?"

"You know something? I don't know if I want to find out anymore."

"Oh, babe, don't say that. You have to know. At least to protect yourself." I crouch in front of her. "Are you okay? Physically? You weren't injured, were you?"

"No, just shaken up ... again."

Her hands are fisted so I pry them apart. "I'm so sorry. I want to protect you, Gem. I'll do my best, but I made a huge mistake by allowing you to sit in the front seat. I keep making stupid errors with you."

"So who are you, Drex? I mean, really? He said Drexel Wolfe isn't your real name. And you never talk about yourself. Like where you're from, where you grew up. You're a huge mystery, which makes me even more suspicious of you."

She's spot on. It's time to come clean.

"My birth name is James Baxter Drexel. When I joined the Black Ops, they called me Lone Wolf, so it seemed appropriate to change my name after my discharge. The stigma associated with what I did was pretty damn large, so large that I wanted to start over. So that's what I did. I ceased being James Drexel and that's when Drexel Wolfe came to be.

"I was born in Annapolis, Maryland. My mom was a schoolteacher and a taskmaster at that. My dad was a general in the Marine Corp. I graduated from high school at sixteen and obtained an appointment to West Point. My folks were so proud. You see where this is going, right? We moved around a lot, but I was pushed in the path of my dad. And it was okay because it's all I ever wanted to do. And everything came easy to me. I completed all my coursework for graduation from West Point in three years. But I couldn't receive a commission because I was too young. So I had to join the Marines as an enlisted man and then wait until I was twenty-one for my commission. I was put in the Special Forces and then after I received my commission, it was only a matter of time before I was singled out for Black Ops. I was already fluent in Farsi, Pashto, and Arabic so I was the perfect fit. And you know the rest of the story."

She stares at me for a long time and gives nothing away. I'm at a loss.

She drops her head and then says, "You're like fucking Superman."

"No, just your average guy, Gem."

"Drex, you're anything *but* average. So what happens now?"

"We check the box and see what it tells us. You ready?"

"No, but it doesn't matter now, does it?"

Chapter 20

GEMINI
Against The Wind

THE CONTENTS OF the box are spread out on the huge table when we walk in the room. My thoughts are a cluttered mass of confusion and I just want to go and lie down and forget about this whole thing for a day. No, make that a month. Just go somewhere where I don't have to worry about someone trying to kill me.

And then there's Drex. His story confuses me even more. He's an amazing person. Wickedly smart, driven, and talented, I look at him and realize he could do anything in the world and succeed. But on the other hand, I'm angry. His explanation makes perfect sense, but I'm still not sure if I trust him. He has kept me safe. But what happens when I find what I'm looking for? Is that when he will turn me over to the CIA and I'll be hauled off, hidden away for the rest of my life? I don't know what to think anymore. He talks about how I cloud his judgment. Well, he ought to take a peek inside *my* head. Talk about whiplash! I'm all over the place with him. One minute I want to punch his lights out and the next I want him to fuck me silly. What kind of damn crazy train am I on? And how long will I be able to keep this up?

My throat tightens, and I massage it, but the air in the room feels too hot and thick to breathe. Sweat beads on my forehead and my hands grow damp. As I scan the room, everyone has their heads bent over whatever it is they're working on and they're not paying me any attention. I have an urgent desire to flee, to escape this prison. The noise is just too much. Turning around, I dash out of the room and toward Drex's office. Ellie stares as I fly by.

I close the door behind me, unable to breathe. The toe of my shoe catches on the edge of one of the Persian rugs and I end up on my hands and knees, fighting for air. My vision clouds with black dots, and my face tingles. What the hell is going on? The harder I try to get oxygen into my lungs, the tighter my throat gets. After all I've been through in the last month, am I going to die by some strange reaction to something?

"Gemini? What's going on?"

He's here but I can't respond because my throat is too tight to speak.

He grabs me from behind and pulls me into his lap. "Breathe, nice and slow. You're having a panic attack."

A panic attack? I want to answer him but I can't. I've never had a panic attack in my life. His voice whispers in my ear, soft and gentle, "Keep breathing, babe. Easy does it. You're fine here. I've got you."

My hands clutch his arms to me, my nails biting into his flesh, but he acts like he doesn't notice. I'm vaguely aware that the dots in my vision have disappeared, along with the buzzing in my ears. "Focus on your breathing. In and out. Nice and slow." His chest behind me is a balm to my nerves, as the vibrations from his voice calm me. The band around my throat eases then disappears and I inhale deeply.

"Good girl." He stays put and holds me to him. I loosen my grip and when I do, so does he. But this whole thing has unhinged me. Nothing is the same. My entire life has been rewritten. I'm a character in a novel and I'm not sure how this story is going to end. Even Drex, who I thought was the most solid thing I've ever known, has been dissected right before me. It frightens me to death.

Before I can think about what I'm doing, I spin in his arms. He starts to speak, but I stop him. My words gush out of me. "I'm not sure what just happened, but I've never had a panic attack before and it freaks me. I need to get out of here, Drex. I need to get away from all this. Everything I've ever known is false. Me, my name, my mother, my origins, my father, Nick, and now you. I'm a caged bird with broken wings. I know they'll never heal, but I have to find a way to try." He starts to speak again, but I stop him, my palm in the air. "I know what you're going to say. That they'll kill me or take me away or whatever. But I don't care anymore. They can have what fucked-up parts of me that are left. And they'll find out soon enough that I'm not worth anything to them anyway. And as for my mom. You can have all that stuff in there. Maybe it's worth something to someone. The woman who raised me isn't the one who left all these clues and boxes behind. I'd rather cherish the memories I have left of her and go on with those. I'm tired of all this."

"You can't leave, Gemini. Please, listen to me. Don't go. It's dangerous for you." There was something in his voice I hadn't heard before.

"I don't care. I can't stay locked away like this forever. I'll get a wig and move to some remote place where they won't think to look for me."

When I try to slide away, he pulls me to him and kisses me hard. "I can't let you leave like this. At least sleep on it. Aali Imaam will find you within a day and take you to the Middle

East. You heard what they said. They think you have that file. If you think you're caged here, it won't be anything compared to how you'll live over there. Please, I'm imploring you to listen to me."

He's right and I know it. I agree to stay but my plans are firm. It will only be for the night.

"Okay, but I'm not going back in there. I don't want to know what you find."

He nods and we stand. Then he leaves and I'm alone. As I look out his office windows, I can see the mountains in the distance, soon to be covered in snow. My longing for a bike ride smashes into me and I close my eyes, thinking back about the pleasure of feeling the wind sting my cheeks as I push through the forest. I imagine myself on my bike, the one that was destroyed, still lost on the side of a mountain somewhere, pedaling up a steep grade as my lungs burn. My fingers grip the handles as I shift gears, accommodating for the grade to pick up speed. When I crest the hill, the views are so splendid, I have to stop for a minute, just so I can let them sink in. These are the things I want to experience again, the ones my body cries for. Soon, I'm pedaling through rocks and roots again, bunny-hopping the larger trees and stumps, winding my way up and around the obstacles. I'm sweaty from my efforts. Riding through creeks, over rocks small and large, I emerge as muddy as a kid stomping through puddles. But I don't notice. It's not until my ride is over that I even see how much mud I've accumulated. It represents the ultimate freedom but when I open my eyes, I'm weighed down with such sadness that I slide down the wall and fold up in the corner.

First it was my mom who wouldn't allow me to enjoy the simple things most kids do. I was raised in a cage under a disguise called love. Then it was the accident that stole my newfound freedom. It even stole the future I had envisioned ... a career in marketing. Now, this. Drex has bound me again, and though it's not his fault, I feel like a prisoner. My heart is attached to his, yet it's not enough for me. I need freedom. The simple pleasure of being able to walk around and not be afraid. And of being myself again. Independent and without all these mysteries.

That night, as we prepare for bed, Drex studies me and I know he suspects something.

"You don't want to know anything at all?"

Shaking my head, I say, "No. I told you already. I don't care. My parents shit on me. Why would I care about what's in there? They've ruined my life."

"But they ..."

"Stop, Drex. I don't want to know."

He shrugs and leaves me alone in the bathroom.

When I walk out, he's sitting up in bed, his back against the headboard. "Gem, what can I do?"

"Nothing. There's not a thing in the world."

"I feel so helpless."

"That makes two of us."

"Will you at least let me hold you?"

If I do that, I'm worried I won't be able to do what needs to be done. But when I look at his face, his beautiful face, I know I'm breaking his heart. So I get into bed and as I curl up next to him, I say, "You can always hold me, Drex. I love you."

"God, Gem, I love you too. More than anything. And I don't know how to help you here. I'm losing you. It's written, on your face, in the way you move. Please stay."

Every word pulls me apart, bit by bit, but I know I can't give in to him. Staying will only make things more toxic between us. But I know he won't let me leave, either. Knowing Drex the way I do, he'll stop at nothing to guarantee my safety, even if it means locking me up.

"Yes, I'll stay." I dare not look at him; he'll see the lies written all over my face. Even I can hear them in my voice. He doesn't say anything but I'm sure he hears them too. He slides down and holds me close. My head rests on his chest, my arm around him. I wish I could kiss him, but it would be my greatest mistake. He would taste the salt from the tears lining my cheeks, and there's nothing I can do to stop them.

Our brief time together zips through my mind, and I know I'll always ache for Drex. There will be nothing about him that I won't miss. I'm not sure how much time passes, but I feel the soft rise and fall of his chest. It's time now so I ease away, careful not to disturb him. My backpack holds everything I'll be taking, which isn't much. I grab a small knife from the kitchen and bring it back to the bathroom where I've got the alcohol and bandages out. I press around with my fingers, hunting for the tiny lump of the microchip. Then I scrub my hip and fingers with the alcohol and do the same to the knife. I grit my teeth and make a tiny incision. It stings but I keep going. Using the knife tip, I gouge out the chip and pour more alcohol on the wound. It burns like fire, but I apply pressure to stop the bleeding, pad it with gauze, and tape it.

Once dressed, I grab the pack and go to the small room that Drex uses as an office. I find his wallet and take out a wad of cash. Right before I walk out the door, I leave an envelope on the kitchen counter for him.

Since this place has as much security as the Pentagon, I realize that he'll know in about five minutes that I've gone. I hit the service elevator and take it to the first floor. When I hit the open air, I get away from DWInvestigations as fast as I can. There's an all-night club called The Open Container about two blocks away, so I hurry inside to the restroom.

As soon as I'm inside, I head to a stall. It's pretty gross, but I don't care. I pull off my black sweater and toss it aside. Inside my pack is a long blond wig. I put it on along with a pale blue hoodie, black leggings, and a black skirt. My jeans go back in the pack and I put on a ton of lipstick. After I check myself out in the mirror, I'm out the door. On a security camera, I won't look like me. Up close is another thing.

I walk around the huge bar, hunting for a rear exit. When I find it, I move. At the last minute, I change my mind. I know there'll be cameras everywhere so I reroute to the front. Less conspicuous that way. Easier to catch a cab too.

I tell the cabbie to take me to any rental car service at Denver International Airport. I need a car because I'm going to Boulder. I don't dare breathe until I get my car and am on the highway.

Forty-five minutes later, I'm in Boulder. It's close to dawn and I drive by the store where I used to work. As the sun rises, I can feel my body humming with energy like I haven't felt in ages. The store doesn't open until nine, so I head over to a breakfast joint and find a place to plant for a couple of hours. As I sip my coffee, my excitement nearly bursts out of me for what's ahead. I need to buy just about everything—a bike, suit, socks, shoes. And a helmet.

Minutes tick by and when it's five until nine, I'm parked in front of the store. My blond wig is gone and it's just the old Gemini getting ready to waltz inside. When I spy a hand flip the "Closed" sign over, I'm almost running for the door.

The electronic buzzer dings when I walk in. Jason is working today. He's one of the owners—it'll be great to see him.

"Hey, just let me know if I can help you with anything," he shouts.

"Aren't you at least going to say hi?"

He peeks over the counter and stares for a moment before breaking into a laugh. "Oh my God ... it's a blast from the not-so-distant past. How the hell are you, girl?"

"Okay, I guess. You?"

He scoots around and picks me up for a huge hug. "So, what

brings you back this way? I suppose you heard about Nick …"

"Yeah, it's awful."

"Do you know what happened?"

"Not really. I just happened upon it by accident. I only heard he was shot."

"Fuck. How does shit like that happen?"

This is so not what I want to talk about. "I don't know. Crazy people, I guess. But I'm here because I'm dying to ride. I need a bike, Jason. And some gear."

"So is this the first time since …?"

"Yeah. So I have nothing. I'm starting from scratch."

"Well, you've come to the right place."

"Which is exactly why I chose your store. What do you recommend these days?"

He looks thoughtful and says, "I have just the thing. It's a bike designed for Enduro racing. It's ultralight with dual shocks."

"Stop. You know how I love a hardtail."

"Yeah, but you'll love the rear shocks on this one. They're super smooth and not squirrelly at all. You won't feel like it's too squishy, or like the tail is sliding out behind you. It's just a softer ride. I swear you'll love it when you catch some air. It'll make your landings so amazing and you'll have that control you like with a hardtail. The front fork has awesome suspension and your wrists, elbows, and shoulders are going to love it too. Take it out for a demo. But I have to tell you … you damage it, you own it, and it ain't cheap, Gemini. With your skills, you're gonna love this baby."

"Okay, let me take a look at her."

He walks me to the back and I'm instantly smitten. She's red and black with an X-wing-shaped frame. Love at first sight.

"Jason, if she rides half as good as she looks, I'll be a happy trailer."

"Oh, just wait until you're pedaling. And the gear-changing is the damn smoothest you'll get. Now what else you need?"

"I want a full suit. A racing helmet, gloves, shoes, get me an extra inner tube, and some tools, and an Allen wrench set. Set me up with the whole package."

"Damn, girl, you just made my day." He's grinning like he won the lottery. I suppose he should be. I'm getting ready to drop over ten grand in here today.

"Jason, I need a CamelBak too. One with a good-sized bladder. Oh, and some grub."

"Sure thing. I'll pull this stuff together, so go try on some shoes. You know where they are. While I'm putting your cleats in, you can try on some riding suits."

"Cool." I head to the back where all the shoes are and find my size. I'm quick to pick out my style. It's easy—mountain-biking shoe with a rugged sole, black, and I'm happy. I hand Jason the box and head to the clothing. I find the onesie I want and try it on. Next I hunt down the helmet and I choose one that covers my entire face. I'm all set. I also pick out some liners for my top and bottom and put everything on for my ride.

Jason has everything ready for me and when he goes to ring it up, I ask, "Can you do me a big favor and not run this card until the end of the day? I'll even leave my card with you. I swear I'm good for it. And one other thing. When I'm done riding, can I store my stuff here? I'm only here for a little while and until I can figure out a place to keep this, would it be okay?"

"Yeah, that won't be a problem. Where are you living these days?"

"Denver for now. I was in Austin for a while, but I miss this too much."

"Okay. Go on now and have a muddy day."

"You can count on it."

IN LESS THAN a half hour, I'm at the trailhead and pulling my bike out of the back seat. This car is going to be a muddy mess when I return it to the rental place. I don't give a damn. The only thing I want right now is to ride. My CamelBak is filled with water and snacks, and it's strapped and tightened on my back. My gloves and helmet are on.

I get on the bike, clip my shoes into the pedals, and I'm off. I play with the gears a bit before I actually get on the trail. I want to be comfortable with how they feel when they switch. I'm jumping the bike in place and I realize Jason was right about the rear shocks. They feel firm like a hardtail but much more comfortable. Once I'm content with the feel of the bike, I shoot off toward the trail.

Considering how out of shape I am, my adrenaline has me pushing the limits. I'm huffing as I pedal, climbing a steep grade and moving around the obstacles as if I'd last ridden yesterday. The very thought of being here and doing what I love fills me with such joy that I shout it for the world to hear. A few months ago, when my migraines controlled my life, I never thought I'd be able to do this again. Now that I'm nearly free of them, this ride makes me doubly happy.

My quads and hamstrings burn every bit as much as my lungs, but I don't give a shit. I'm golden because I'm doing what I love best. Oh, how I've missed this. The air rushes around me and my eyes water. I didn't put the shield on my helmet down, so I flip it into place and continue my ride.

This is heaven. Everything about it has me in a state of bliss. My body is long overdue for this workout, and though I'm sorely out of shape, I love the burn. Branches tear at me since I'm on a single-track trail, and I even love that. My trepidation passes after my first couple of spills, knowing that I can still do this without busting my head.

When I get to my first stream crossing, I laugh as I skirt the rocks and water splashes everywhere, sending mud flying. Some lands on my face shield and I wipe it off with my hand, still laughing. At the crest of the next ridge, I stop for a water break and a snack. The view is unreal and I'd forgotten how amazing the mountains were in late summer, when the tips of the leaves were dabbed in reds, oranges, and yellows. I gasp as I gaze across the vista and a peace seeps into my bones that's been absent for months.

When I feel a chill hit my body, I check my watch and am surprised to see it's almost three. Time has gotten away from me and I'm astounded at how happy I feel. It only lasts for a moment, though. I have to get back down the mountain and figure out what I'm going to do next. Time's running short and I'm against the wind.

The plans I made were only for today. What should I do? Go back to Drex? As much as I love him, the thought of living as a captive again fills me with panic. On the other hand, I know I'm risking myself, even being out here. My comfort lies in these woods because I know my way around the trails. They could blindfold me and spin me around until dizzy, and I could still find my way out of here.

Pushing the pressure of making that decision out of my head, I fly down the trail as if I were being chased by the devil himself. My bike catches air over and over again, and I'm thankful for the excellent shocks. I remind myself to thank Jason when I get back to the store. I'm hauling ass, pushing to my limits, chewing up rocks and mud, wanting to see how far and fast my body can take me. When I round the final curve of the descent, I laugh, because I'm happy with the outcome. Not bad for someone who hasn't ridden in close to a year.

After another couple hundred yards, I bust out of the trees and I'm back in the parking lot. When I see him leaning against my car, his arms folded across his chest, I squeeze my front brakes so hard, I almost fly over the front wheel. Why am I surprised to see him here? I should've known he'd find me.

Chapter 21

Drex
Playing For Keeps

When I wake, I know right away something's wrong. My hand reaches for Gemini and the bed's cold. She's gone. I don't have to get up to figure it out. I already know. I lie there for a few minutes and then move through the apartment. When I walk into the bathroom, I see the bloody knife and the microchip on the counter. She doesn't want me to follow her. Fuck. That.

After a quick shower, I head to the kitchen to make coffee. That's when I see the envelope. I rip into it like a mad man.

Drex,

I hated lying to you last night, but there was no other way for me to do this. After that panic attack, I knew I had to leave. I think you know how I feel about you and if you don't, then I'll spell it out. I love you … I'm in love with you. But for now, it's not enough. I'm so confused by everything and I feel caged in to the point I can't breathe or think straight anymore. Yes, it's dangerous out there, but I don't see any other way right now. I'm sorry for all the pain

I've put you and your men through. All of this is my fault and I should've walked away a lot sooner than this. That was most selfish of me and I hope you can find some way to forgive me.

Please don't come and find me. I need this time to sort things through ... clear my head and get my joy back. You always said I clouded your judgment. I wish like hell you could get inside my head because it's so damn foggy in here, I don't think it'll ever clear up.

Thank you for everything, for caring so deeply, for showing me love, for loving me so deeply and for being so kind when I needed you the most. Take care of yourself.

Always yours,

Gem

Ten minutes later I'm in my office with Huff and we go over security tapes as we see her leave the building. I'm a bit surprised nobody woke me when she left. But then again, I never gave anyone instructions to do so. They were only instructed to report to me where she went as they followed her. And building security was only to report unusual entries into the building, not exits. It doesn't take me long to figure out where she's gone. The trail she leaves is as obvious as the nose on her face, but for once I feel giddy because of it.

As I get ready to head out, Huff says, "You'll find her, Drex, and she'll be fine." I hope to hell he's right.

When I get to the bike shop, the owner provides me with the information about the trails she'll be riding. He also tells me about her purchases and I write him a check, to avoid the credit card alert on her. Then I head to the trail, park and wait for her. By the time she shows up, I'm not at all surprised to see how muddy she is. Before she even emerges from the woods, I can hear her laughing. That sound can bring me to my knees on most days, but today, it does something even more. It wedges its way into my soul. I'm ecstatic she's okay, I'm pissed that she left, I'm overjoyed that she's had fun, but most of all, I want her in my arms to convince myself she's here and everything's going to be fine.

She stops in front of me and I've got to say, she looks hot as hell all suited up in her gear.

"Have a nice ride?" I ask. My voice is deceptively smooth. I'm seething but doing a damn good job of keeping it contained.

"Yeah."

My head motions toward her bike. "I like your new wheels."

"Thanks. Just bought her today."

"Yeah. Your friend Jason told me. You look damn good in that suit."

"Thanks. Um, did you get my letter?"

"Yep."

She looks at me and finally flicks her shield up so I can see her face.

"Got a little muddy, did ya?"

"Yeah. It was great." She grins and looks so damned happy, I could cry.

"Feel better now?"

"Uh-huh."

"Good. Take off the helmet."

She dips her head for a second, like she's going to argue, but then she does as I say.

"Now get off that bike."

One of her feet is still attached to the pedal so she unclips and swings her leg over the bike. She lays the bike gently on the ground, like it's something precious she doesn't want to hurt. When she stands back up, I say, "Now come here."

"I don't ..."

My voice is gruff. "I'm not asking. I'm telling. Come. Here. Now."

Her shoes make a clicking noise as she takes the few steps to reach me and when she's within arm's length, my fingers hook into the neckline of her suit and I jerk her in the rest of the way. My mouth is on hers before the gasp can make it past her lips. I kiss her hard and without mercy, bruising her. When she has no air left and I know she needs to breathe, I release her.

"What part about when I told you that you are mine did you not understand? I play for keeps, Gemini. When I told you I wanted to own you, I didn't mean for an hour, a day, or a week. I meant forever. You don't get up and walk out of my life in the middle of the night. Do I make myself clear?"

Her lips press together into a thin line, but she shakes her head up and down.

"Good. Now, do you love me? Yes or no."

"Yes, damn it! My letter ..."

I cut her off. "Good. Get in the car."

Her nostrils flare as she starts to head for her damn rental car.

"Not that car. *My* car."

"But ..."

"One of my men is on the way to pick that one up."

"My bike? I'm not leaving it here."

"I'll get it. Just. Get. In. The. Fucking. Car. *Now.*" My jaws are clenched.

She stomps over to the passenger door and I fetch her bike. When it's nestled in the back, I get behind the wheel.

"Won't he need these?" Her voice is as snarky as I've ever heard it.

She holds up the keys to the rental car. I snatch them out of her hand and toss them out the window. They land by the trunk of the rental and I keep driving. There's no mistaking I'm pissed as hell, but she's not exactly smiling either.

My mouth is clamped shut for a few more minutes because I

can't say anything for fear of exploding. When I finally cool down, I say, "If you wanted to go on a fucking bike ride, why didn't you just say so? I have a shit ton of employees who come up here all the time. I could've arranged it for you."

"It was more than a fucking bike ride. It was saving my sanity." She slams her fist against her palm.

"Then talk to me, goddammit. Don't leave me a letter and sneak out in the middle of the night after gouging a microchip out of your body. What the fuck is wrong with you?"

"I needed to get away from you. From everything. I needed a break. Even from you."

"Why didn't you just say so?"

"I tried but every time I mentioned it, you'd tell me how dangerous it was."

"It *is* dangerous. When are you going to get that?"

"I *do* get it but I can't live like that."

"I'm setting you up in your own place. You'll have bodyguards. Apparently you don't want to be around me, so you'll get your wish. But you can't go traipsing off like this. You will die if you keep this up. And I can't live with you dead."

"Fine." She crosses her arms.

That's it. She's silent for the rest of the drive and I don't speak, either. We pull up in front of a high-rise, close to the office. It has underground secure parking. I park and then enter the codes to open the elevator. She's so quiet, I can hear her breathing. We get off on the third floor. What she doesn't know is that I own every unit on this floor. My men are outside and step aside as we arrive. We walk inside and I close the door behind us.

Before she says anything, I tell her, "Get out of that suit now, unless you want me to tear it off you."

She gives me a hard look and then slowly unzips. Before she can get it off, I'm on her, tugging the top of it down until it traps her arms to her sides. I pull her bra up and over her breasts and my head dives to her pearled nipples. Her skin is salty from sweat, but it drives me mad with want. I don't know what's come over me but I have to possess her … all of her. I want to hear her scream my name. I want to pleasure and punish her at the same time.

I trap her against the wall and my mouth and tongue are nearly cruel as they suck and bite her nipples. She wants more, I know, but I want her to feel my pain too. As my mouth works my torture on her, my hands unzip her suit the rest of the way and tug it lower, right to the point where it hits her panty line. The sight of that bandage makes me shudder, but I push those thoughts aside and turn them back to her sex. Then my fingers find her and my cock jolts as I feel how drenched she is. I plunge inside of her, punishing, teasing, but I won't let her come. She's begging me, but I won't relent. When I'm just as tormented as she is, I pull her to the sofa and rip the suit and her panties off. I bend her over the back of it and slam into her.

"Don't you ever think of leaving me again, because if you do, you'll *never* have this. You'll *never* feel this again. And you love this every bit as much as I do. Tell me, Gemini. Tell me now."

"Yes!"

"Yes what?"

"I love this."

"What do you love?"

"I love it when you fuck me like this. Ah, Drex. Harder."

"What else do you love, Gem?"

"You. I love you!"

"Damn it all, you're so fucking amazing. Don't ever leave me. Promise me or I'll stop right now."

"I promise."

Then I need to kiss her so badly, I pull out.

"What are you doing?" she cries.

"This." Spinning her around, I pull her back up and my mouth covers hers in a heated, possessive kiss. "This mouth is mine, Onyx. Only mine." I'm not surprised one iota when I feel her teeth sink into my lip and I taste blood.

"You think you own me, Drex. But I own you too." Then she bites the other side of my lip before she invades my mouth with her tongue. Fire pours through me as her lips and tongue match my moves, play for play. I walk her around to the other side of the couch and push her back. She plops down and I fall to my knees in front of her. I lift and bend her legs, spreading them wide, exposing all of her. "Look at this," I tell her as I enter her, ever so slowly. I'm teasing her now. I know this drives her wild, which is why I'm doing it. "You're so perfect here. Everywhere."

"Ahh, Drex. Yesss." She pulls my face to hers and we kiss again. My hands grip her ass, fingers sinking into the soft flesh of her cheeks as I thrust in and out. I pick up a bit of speed and she catches my rhythm, matching my every thrust. Her hands are on my hips and I love it when her nails dig into me.

"I love to fuck you, Gem. Your body was made for me. Don't you ever think about leaving me again."

"No. Never."

My thumb moves to her clit and I press on it, as we continue to move against one another.

"Yesss, right there, Drex. That's perfect."

"Look at me when you come, babe." I can tell she's about to have her due. She nods and then it happens. Every time I watch her, it catapults me over the edge too. My hands are braced on the back of the sofa and I lean in to kiss her.

My voice is gruff with emotion. "When two people love each other, they share their hopes and dreams along with their fears. They don't run, Gem. Please don't ever run from me again. I've loved you from the start. I felt it from the first moment I saw you. You didn't, but it didn't take long for you to figure it out. We've never just liked each other. We didn't fall in love. We plummeted. It's been hard and fast for us since the first time we slept together. After that, I knew my life was going to change and that you would be the reason. Only I didn't know how much or that I would go to any lengths to make sure you were safe. I kept asking myself why I was doing all these things for you. But deep in my heart I knew. I knew all along."

She starts to weep and says, "I'm so afraid something terrible will happen to you."

My arms wind around her and I pull her into me. "Don't cry, babe. We'll watch over each other, but it's way too dangerous to be out there alone. Then you put me in more danger, because you know I'm going to come after you... that I won't leave you out there. Stay close to me. Let me protect you. If you don't love me, that's one thing. But if you do, let me do my job for the one I love the most."

"Oh, Drex. You know I love you ... so damn much. And that's what freaks me out."

My hands run through her hair. "I'll handle it. Just stay with me. Okay?"

"Do I have to stay here?"

"Not unless you want to."

"I want to be with you."

"Then let's go home."

"I can't go back to the way things were. You have to give me some room. Room to be involved. No secrets from each other. You can't control me. I know you want to protect me but I need to know that I have independence too. And you have to promise me."

"But it's dangerous. You know Aali Imaam will try to take you again."

"Then use your men to protect me. But I can't be caged anymore. I'm willing to take that chance."

"I guess you leave me with no choice, don't you?"

"Not if you want me with you."

ON THE WAY home, I tease her about how she looked coming out of the woods. "You're the only woman I know who looks sexy as fuck in hospital attire or when you're muddy and sweaty as hell too. Tell me about your ride."

"It was so much fun. I'd forgotten how much I love biking. Did you really mean what you said?"

"About what?"

"Getting someone to ride with me?"

"Of course I did."

"I would love that."

"Then consider it done. Do you like your new wheels?"

"For an off-the-floor model, it's great, though I would prefer custom made. I really screwed up by using my credit cards, didn't I?"

"Well, I paid for all of your things at the bike shop, so the only charge was the rental car. Fact is, it might just throw them off a bit. They might think we're up to something."

"Really?" Her face lights up.

"Yeah. So, when I did my research on you a while back, I learned that you're quite the pro with that bike."

Her skin flushes and she drops her head. "I'm fair."

"Fair? Gem, the articles referred to you as 'unbeatable,' and '*the* one to beat.' Why so shy about this?"

"Because it's not a big deal. I just happen to love to ride. I raced for the fun."

"I want to go out there with you sometime." I want to watch her. I want to see her handle her bike, watch her maneuver through the obstacles of the forest and hear her laughter.

"You ride?"

"Yeah, but I'm a novice. You'd have to slow down."

"I would definitely slow down for you. Oh, let's go. I want to go right now!"

It's hard not to catch her enthusiasm. "I'd love to babe, but we can't today. It's late and we have work to do. We need to get another chip implanted in you ASAP. I can't believe you dug that thing out of yourself." I glance at her and catch her squirming.

"I didn't want you to find me."

"Gem, I can find you if you leave on your own. That chip is to protect you if Aali Imaam takes you. Please, this is Drex here—you know, that guy that loves the hell out of you—asking you not to remove the next one."

"I won't, I promise." She reaches for my hand and grasps it.

"I'll get Dr. Davis in as soon as we get back to implant another. But tomorrow evening, I want to take you out to dinner. A special evening for just the two of us."

"Bodyguards?"

"Oh, there will be a full detail of them. We'll be surrounded."

I see a blur of dark hair fly at me and then I'm being kissed all over. "Thank you, Drex. That sounds amazing."

"Hey, take it easy on me. I'm trying to drive here!" If I'd known a dinner date would've elicited this kind of response, I would've done it sooner. As soon as we get back, Dr. Davis is there, waiting on us and this time, Gemini greets him with a smile.

***

The next day I get Ellie to pick up some clothes for Gemini and me. Heather, the personal shopper, has some items ready for her to bring back. We were both in need of the clothing as our wardrobes were thinned in the bombing.

When Ellie gets back, a contingency of men carry garment and shopping bags inside. Gemini tries to make a big fuss over all the things that were purchased, but I put a stop to it.

"Now, want to know what we figured out about your mom's clues?"

For a brief moment, I think she's going to tell me to go to hell. "Okay. You really want me to know this, don't you?"

My hand reaches for hers. "One of the things I'd hate to see you have to deal with is regret. I want you to know as much about your mom as you can. My heart is telling me that there's a good reason for everything she did, and while you may believe the worst, I don't happen to think that. I think she went to great lengths to protect you."

Her hand grips mine in turn. "Then tell me. What do you know?"

"It's not the Grand Canyon. It's Las Vegas. The intersection of Las Vegas Boulevard or Highway 91 and Interstate 15. Clever, isn't she?"

Gemini snorts. "Er, yeah, date and year, this time. What's there? Another storage unit?"

"Yep."

"When in the hell did she go there?"

"That I can't answer."

"So now what?"

I realize my girl is trembling. It claws at my heart and my tough exterior crumbles as I bring her into my embrace. She grabs my shirt and buries her face against my neck and I feel her breath, fast and furious, as it fans across me.

"Tell me, sweetheart, what is it?" Without waiting for her to speak, I pick her up and carry her to the sofa and settle her on my lap. I cup my hand against her head and hold her close in the cage of my arms.

"When she died, I was away at school. They called me to let me know she'd been killed. I've never felt so alone. It was right before I met Nick. I never talk about this because it's not a time I care to remember. In fact, I don't remember a whole lot about it.

I think I block it out. I didn't even have a funeral for her because it was just the two of us. That's it. No family or friends. No one to pat me on the back and offer condolences. Then I went back to college and acted like nothing happened. My roommates never knew my mom had been killed in a car wreck. I never told them. How fucked up is that? They all just thought I was that weird girl from Texas who cried all the time."

"Jesus, Gem." I didn't know how terribly my heart could break for someone until this moment. I want to help her ... to take the giant ache away, but I don't know how. I don't have the right words, but I have my arms to protect her, my hands to touch and hopefully soothe her. And my lips to whisper words, sweet words in her ear. Words that let her know I'm here for her and that I love her.

"Gem, you're not alone anymore. I'll help you get through this. You have me now and I'll do anything for you."

"You've already done more than I could ever have hoped for."

Chapter 22

Gemini
Quite A Speech

When I think about the life my mom led, it saddens me. "She sacrificed everything she had. And she did it all for me," I say to Drex.

"Maybe so. But like I said before, you would do the same. You wouldn't want a terrorist to go free and you wouldn't want hundreds to die because of one. "

"Oh, but Drex, I don't know if I would have the strength or courage to turn you in." When I think about it, I truly don't know how my mom did it, loving my father the way she did.

"Yeah, I see your point. I know I sure as hell couldn't do it to you. I'd run away and hide you somewhere. I love you too much to live without you." He kisses me on the top of my head. "Go shower. All this thinking will drive you crazy. I want you to take your time getting ready because we're going out for a nice dinner tonight. Remember?"

Smiling, I lean in and kiss his lips. "Thanks. What about you?"

"I have a couple things to do in the office and I'll shower

there. Can you be ready in an hour and a half?"

"Yep."

THE WAY HE licks his lower lip and stares at me ravenously when I walk into the living room tells me everything I need to know.

"Well, fuck. Yeah, just fuck. You look like sex on wheels. My perfect Gem." Drex ogles my deep V neckline of the black lacy dress I wear. It's form fitting and shows my curves. The way he stares at me already has me filled with need for him.

"Er, thanks, I think."

"What? Not good enough?"

"How about, 'Gemini, you look pretty in that dress'?"

"I can say that but it doesn't do you justice. Sex on wheels is way better. Come, my sex princess."

"Drex, really."

"Hmm. I can't think of a more appropriate name, so I'm keeping it."

We walk out of the apartment where our team of bodyguards awaits. Drex gives them instructions and we head out. We're in one car with three other men. There's a car ahead of us and one behind.

"Um, isn't this a little overkill? We'll be surrounded at the restaurant. I feel like the President." I say.

"Not overkill at all. I'm taking zero chances." He's in work mode right now so I'm not going to distract him. He reaches for my hand and fastens his fingers with mine. He watches everything around us and I watch him. I love the way he looks in a suit. Dark and seductive, but he's not so fixed that he looks like an uptight businessman. Everything he's wearing is navy blue, except for his crisp white shirt. His tie is perfectly knotted. His face has a bit of scruff and his hair looks like he just rolled out of bed. Every time I look at him and his hair is like this, I want to sink my hands into it.

The drive to the restaurant doesn't take long. Drex chose an inconspicuous one, located on a quiet side street so we wouldn't draw too much attention to us. The men let us out at the front door. Escorted by our team, we're seated at a back corner table, which affords Drex a view of the whole place. Ever watchful, we have a very romantic dinner. Even though I know he constantly scans the place, he never makes me feel like I'm not the most important thing in the room.

"Drex, what happens to us when this is all over?"

"What do you want to happen?"

My heart pounds. Why did I ask him that? I don't really know what I want. "I want you to stop answering my questions with questions."

He laughs, a look on his face that screams, "I'm a cool son of a bitch."

"Is that what I do?" he says.

My brows shoot up. "You're the mastermind behind this huge corporation and you ask me that?"

His look is so playful, I laugh. "God, I'm such a sucker for you, Drex."

"No more than I am for you."

We're silent for a moment.

"Why does this make you nervous?" he asks in a soft voice.

"Because it's so important to me."

He leans toward me and takes my hand. "Sometimes when I look at you, like now, it takes every ounce of my self-control not to walk around this table and pick you up out of that chair and do all sorts of unspeakable things to you. I want to hear you beg for more, to tell me not to stop and to say how great I make you feel. But most of all, I want to hear you tell me you'll love me until your heart stops beating and the sun doesn't rise anymore, because that's how I feel about you. So if you want to know what

I want to do after this, I think you have my answer. I want to be with you, Gemini, in whatever way you choose. You name it and we'll do it your way."

My breath seizes in my throat and my lungs will not fill, no matter what my head tells them to do. I stare at him, trying to soak in every word he's just said. Finally, I push myself away from the table and go to him. He leans back in his chair and I sit on his lap.

"For such a controlling badass, you can deliver quite a speech." My mouth is on his and my hands are in his hair. I don't hold back as I kiss him and then I move my lips to his ear and say, "I want so much more than just this, and I don't ever want us to stop because you make me feel so much better than my insignificant words can describe. But know this, Drex—I do love you, and I will always love you until there are no more beats left in my heart, or breaths left in my lungs and until the sun dies and the earth ceases to exist. What we decide to do after all this ends will be a joint decision. And wherever you are is where I want to be." I kiss him again and am satisfied to hear him groan into my mouth.

"Jesus, babe, you make me want to forget about dinner and just take you back home."

Desire and want are written all over his face as he licks his lips. "You wouldn't want me to starve, would you?"

He grabs my hand and bites the tip of my index finger. "I could feed you in other ways."

"Hmm, I'm sure you could."

The waitress chooses that moment to approach us. "Can I bring you something to drink?"

Drex orders a bottle of wine, ice water, and an appetizer. She starts to hand over menus, but he stops her and asks for the lobster tails and baked potatoes. I don't pay close attention because I'm fascinated with his raw male sensuality.

I return to my seat just in time for the waitress to deliver our wine. Drex barely notices her because he's looking at me with his half-closed, sexy-as-hell blue-grays. His hand holds mine and every so often he kisses it.

Dinner is delicious, but I'm so excited about what's going to happen when we get home, I don't even care about it after a certain point. I don't care that he asks me what my dreams were before all of this. And I don't care that I tell him how I wanted to be a marketing specialist for a mountain bike manufacturer before the crash. I care about nothing but him and how he makes me feel. When we're finished, Drex takes my hand and leads me to the door. We walk outside, again surrounded by our team, to where our car is waiting. As we round the corner, we hear odd popping sounds and Drex pushes me to the ground. I'm blindsided and don't know what's going on.

Then I'm dragged away from Drex, something stinging at my neck. My vision blurs and everything fades away.

Chapter 23

Drex
Panic

Dawn is breaking as I regain consciousness—I've been out for six or seven hours. I'm in some alley on a filthy mattress. My shirt is unbuttoned, my tie undone, and I'm leaning against a brick wall. My hands move to my throbbing head.

Gemini! Where the hell is she? Upon looking around, I find my team of six men here too, but no Gemini. Fuck!

"Wake up!" I yell. My hands reach into my pocket for my phone—it's gone. That's no surprise.

It takes a couple of attempts but I finally stand.

"Hey," I nudge the other guys. "Wake up! We gotta get out of here." My heart races as I think about Gemini and where she could be. The guys groan as they begin to stir.

"What happened?" one of them asks.

"We were hit and drugged. They took Gemini. Does anyone have a cell phone?"

Only one guy still has his phone, stashed in his boot. Damn, I'll have to remember that. I call Huff. Reinforcements arrive within twenty minutes.

"What the fuck happened?" Huff asks. "We've been calling everyone but no answer. We've been combing the area. I was just about to run a chip search."

"We were ambushed coming out of the restaurant. They used silencers. They drugged us. They must've thrown us in the back of a van or something. They took everyone's phone but Jason's." I explain.

"I don't know why Jason's phone didn't pop up on the GPS locator," Huff responds. "It must be malfunctioning.

Turns out we're in an alley on the other side of Denver, in a part of town that is relatively deserted.

I'm so angry I want to scream but my head is splitting open. Huff, Blake, and a few other guys who weren't with us last night look around for evidence but come up empty.

"The restaurant!" I yell.

We pile into the cars and head there. The guys check everything out but don't find a thing. Luckily, all the bodyguards were wearing Kevlar vests, so no one took a bullet.

"Fucking shit! Where is she?"

"We'll find her. I'll contact the restaurant and see if they have security cameras," Huff says.

We get back to headquarters and I'm physically ill. My head swims from whatever drug they used. The men who were drugged are also in bad shape. Huff calls in Dr. Davis and he gives us anti-nausea medication. It helps.

"Fuck, I can't believe this happened with all the protection we had," Huff says.

"They have her, Huff. We have to find her. If they kill her, I don't know what I'll do."

"Okay, okay, just try to stay calm."

Mania takes over and my voice booms. "I can't stay calm! Aali Imaam has her and so help me God if they do anything to her, I'll fucking take them all out. I want you to call The Company. Now."

"Drex, are you sure?"

"Do it. Tell them I want to meet with Alex Michaels. Alone. Do it, Huff. Now!"

"Okay. But why alone?"

"Because I said so, that's why. In the meantime, track her chip. And see what you can come up with from the restaurant."

"Got it, boss."

Light speed can't come close to how fast my thoughts churn. It's so ridiculous, even I can't keep up. Sitting won't work and neither does standing. Pacing doesn't suffice. I want to hit something or someone, namely the fucking asshole who took her. Thinking straight is impossible. This is the craziest my mind has ever been and I feel so fucked because I need clarity and I'm in a murky pond with zero visibility. The fact that I'm this knee deep in shit makes it even worse for Gemini. *Pull it together, Drex. She needs you, goddammit!*

Before I know what I'm doing, my hand is through the wall. Huff comes running and he calls Dr. Davis back to my office.

"Can you move your fingers?"

"Yeah." I know it's not broken. "It's just bruised." I flex my fingers for the doctor and he seems satisfied. They hurt but not too bad. The skin on my knuckles is torn off. Whatever. I need to get my mind right because I'm worthless like this.

Blake runs in and tells me they have a location on Gemini—she's in Denver. Not too far from where we picked you up.

"Why would they keep her in Denver?"

"Can't answer that," he says. "I can only tell you the location of the chip."

Huff is on his heels with some information about the restaurant. "The owner says he'll meet us in thirty minutes. But Drex, you need to stay here. Alex Michaels is supposed to call you."

"Fuck that. I'll forward my number to my cell, which I'll need another one by the way. I need to see that scene again. Maybe it'll come back to me."

"Drex. You won't remember, not if it was rohypnol," Dr. Davis says.

"Yeah, well, I have to take that chance. What if it was a different drug?"

I know I'm a pressure cooker and at any time, my lid's going to blow. Forcing myself to use controlled breathing techniques, I feel much more stable by the time we get to the restaurant. Upon looking around, I don't remember being here at all. Nothing about the evening rings a bell. We review the tapes and I see Gemini and I walking out, and then we're surrounded. There's gunfire, and then I'm pushing Gemini out of the way. I don't see who takes her. Someone lays one right in my kisser and then drugs me, but I can't see his face. He's wearing a *keffiyeh*, a Middle Eastern headdress, but that's about it. I seethe, not only with anger but with a need so strong to find her and get her to safety.

My phone rings but I don't hear it.

"Drex, your phone," Huff nudges me.

"Fuck." I shake my head and tap the screen. "Wolfe."

"Wolfe. Michaels here. You wanted to speak?"

"Yeah. My office. One hour."

"No. That won't work. We meet on neutral ground. You come alone."

"When and where?" I ask.

"One hour at your house."

"You mean my place that was bombed?"

"The same."

The fucking bastard. What is he up to?

"See you there."

"And Wolfe. No wires or cameras. You come alone or no deal.

Got it?"

"Sure do."

I rejoin the crowd.

"Well?" Huff asks.

"I'm going to meet him in an hour."

"Who's going with you?"

"No one. Just me."

"Drex ..."

"I'll be fine. I need to go back to the office and get some gear." Huff isn't at all happy and none of the other guys will be, either, but they can't come with me. They don't know about my covert activity with the CIA. It's classified. End of story.

When we get back to the office, I arm myself to the teeth. Shoulder and leg holsters, back belt holster, knife, extra magazines for my guns. I hope to hell he gives me what I want and need because I don't know what I'll do if he doesn't.

"You ready?" Blake asks.

"As ready as I'll ever be. Listen, I want you to send two teams out. One goes to the storage unit in Austin and the other hits Vegas. I want them to bring back whatever Gemini's mother left for her in either location. Use threats, break in at night, do whatever you need to. Just bring back what's there. If the file is there, it's most likely on an old floppy disc."

"We'll get it, Drex. And you need to take it easy." Blake looks at me. "I mean it. If you get hurt, who will she rely on?"

"I got you, Blake. And thanks. Find out everything you can about where she's being held."

Huff says, "Drex, man, let me go with you."

"You can't. No time for explanations. Find my girl and let me know how I can get her. As soon as I'm done with Michaels, I'm going after her."

"Drex, you're gonna need more than three guns and a couple of knives."

"You're wrong, Huff. I'll only need my bare hands."

MICHAELS IS WAITING for me in the parking lot across the street from my demolished warehouse that I used to call home. Just looking at it pisses me off. But when I see him, the top of my head wants to blow.

My feet hit the ground and I walk with a purpose. The thing is, I want to punch his lights out, but I can't. I need him. I need his information. But after I get it, then I'll punch his lights out.

"What do you have for me?"

Michaels gives me an eat-shit grin and asks, "What do you have for *me*?"

"Are you fucking with me, because right now, I'm about to come unglued. First of all, the goddamn terror cell knows I'm CIA and now I find out that somehow your man was involved with Gemini. Tell me how this all worked out for you, Michaels. And how did Nick Lowry end up dead? How did you guys manage to fuck this up so badly?"

"Who told you about Lowry?"

"Are you guys that stupid or do you just have your heads so far up your asses you don't know what the fuck is going on out here? Is Leo aware of this?"

When his face turns a tad paler, I can tell I've hit on something big. "What is it, Alex? You sneaking around behind the boss's back? Is that it? Leo doesn't even know you're here, does he? He doesn't know anything about you and your involvement in the Sheridan case, does he? So who's paying you off and who did you pay to try and implicate me in all this mess?"

"Wait a minute!"

"No, *you* wait a goddamn minute. Whatever you're doing smells rotten. I see sellout and double-crossing all over this shit. And I can call in the big guys right now if you don't start talking.

It looks to me that you've gotten pretty fucking cozy with Aali Imaam. How else would they know about Gemini and her mom? How else would they have gotten information about me? Only a few select people even know I work for the CIA. Hell, the fucking CIA doesn't even know I work for them. And Aali Imaam knows? So you tell me and tell me something fast, or I'm making that goddamn phone call and you're gonna have all sorts of shit crawling up your ass. Tell me what the fuck you know."

He's even whiter than he was before and I know I have him cornered.

"Lowry was recruited to keep an eye on her right after her mother was killed. But when she had the damn accident, she got so schizo on him, he went haywire on us. I'm not sure what happened with him. He was way too involved with her because he went fucking nuts. Started making all kinds of threats so we had to take him out."

What the fuck! They took out one of their own. "You guys are unbelievable. You don't even think about helping people anymore. Your answer is a bullet to the head. End of story. Is that what you did to Michelle Sheridan too?"

"No. We wanted her alive. She has something that ..." His mouth clamps shut so hard, I hear his teeth click.

"Go on," I urge.

"Nothing. There's nothing."

"What the fuck turnip truck do you think I fell off? With the smarts I'm dealing with out here, I'm surprised every single one of our government secrets hasn't been given away yet. You guys are incredible."

His fingers hook into his collar and he pulls it away from his neck, trying to loosen it a bit. Then his head jerks around, avoiding my glance.

"You really can't stand to look at me, can you?"

"That's not it. I just have nothing to say about that."

A laugh escapes me. "Well, I suggest you come up with something fast because time's running out. Tell me everything you know, dickhead."

"What exactly do you know?"

"No, no, no, Michaels! That's not how this works. I'm asking the questions now. So if you don't want my fist in your face, you'd better get talking, and fast."

He looks at me, hard. "The Sheridan case goes back to 1993. The Company approached Rachel Miller, aka Michelle Sheridan, to get information about her lover, Hakeem Assaf. The dossier reads that she didn't have a clue who or what he was. She only knew he had money. They were most definitely in love, because from all accounts, she was broken after she turned him in. Although she didn't really turn him in. She gave us the means to capture him. And when we did, he asked us how we found out. According to the story, he crumbled and cried like a baby when he found out it all came from his beloved mistress and mother of his daughter. He begged and begged them to let him see Amira and Rachel one more time, but The Company refused. They were already placed in the program and had new identities. Her death had been set up and the day it appeared in the news, the account of his reaction says he had to be sedated. He thought she took her own life. Of course, it looked perfect for us, but he obsessed over Amira. They assured him she would be okay, but every day, his condition worsened until they were forced to put him in the psych unit. When he finally recovered, he supplied them with everything they asked in return for a life in solitude within the confines of our prison system. He lost the desire to live and he knew he could never return to the Middle East. They would hunt and kill him, but he didn't care. He didn't want them to find his daughter. So we changed his name but he died a few years later of cancer."

He's telling me the truth because most of it coincides with

what Gemini's mom wrote.

"Okay, Michaels, if what you're saying is true, what kind of info did you glean from Rachel Miller and why are you still after her daughter?"

He's back to being that twitchy guy he was a couple minutes ago.

"Okay, first off, it wasn't me. It was a group of people before my time."

"Whatever. You're involved in this and from what I can see, you're in deep. Start talking."

"She turned over all of his connections. Financial docs of where he sent his money. Lists of who it went to. Remember, this was in '93, well before the encryption that we have today on personal computers. They taught her how to tap into this stuff and then send it to one of The Company's computers. From there, they hooked into other records and got everything they needed."

"So what happened? What aren't you telling me?"

"She found a shitload of info on how the US was involved in supplying arms to the Afghans during their war with the Soviets. And how a lot of those arms ended up in the hands of terrorists. But she also ended up with a file that we didn't know about. And we need that file."

"Why didn't you just ask her for it?"

Now he tugs on his shirt collar. This is bad. He paces.

"We didn't know until recently that she had it." He looks me in the eye and now I'm beginning to understand.

"How recently?" I know when I ask this I'm not going to like the answer.

"About the same time they did."

"They, as in Aali Imaam?"

"Yes."

"Michaels, they claim they didn't kill her. Did you guys?"

He scrubs his face. "It was an accident. We were trying to get her to stop so we could talk to her, but she wouldn't. It all happened so fast. That's when we put Nick on the daughter. Then when the daughter went missing, we thought they found her. We went round and round with Nick on going to the authorities. We didn't want him to do it, but he went against us. He was really worried about her. And that was our biggest mistake because he fell in love with her."

"Fuck. So what did Rachel take?"

"I can't ..."

"Goddammit, Michaels! I don't have time to fuck around with you! They have Gemini and will kill her if I don't get to her."

"They won't kill her, Wolfe. At least not yet. They need her to get what they want."

I'm on him like a fucking pit bull. My hand wraps around his neck, my thumb against his trachea. It wouldn't take much for me to kill him and he knows it.

"You better fucking tell me something fast because I'm at the end of my rope with you."

He struggles for air and ekes out, "They need her. And I'll tell you if you release me."

My hand eases up, just enough so he can speak. "Rachel Miller stole a file that contained locations of plutonium-238, cesium-137, and polonium-210. There's enough of those substances to create dirty bombs for massive destruction that would make 9/11 look like a walk in the park. No one in Aali Imaam knew where that stuff is stored other than Hakeem Assaf, and then Rachel Miller. Our friends think Gemini has the file, or at least knows where it is. That's why they want her. Nick was there to protect her. And you, you fuckhead, we've been trying to get you to call us but your assface wouldn't return any of those calls. Not even after your fucking house was destroyed. Only a select group of people in the CIA knows about this."

"There's still one question that remains unanswered. How the fuck did Aali Imaam know I work for the CIA when almost *no one* in the CIA knows?"

"I don't know!"

"You're gonna have to do better than that."

"Wolfe, you're gonna have to search that one out for yourself 'cuz I can't answer that."

Goddammit. Who the hell would know all this shit? It would have to be someone from inside. My hand releases and Michaels rubs his neck.

My phone is in my hand.

"What's up?" Huff answers.

"I want every goddamn security code in our system changed. Right now. Drop everything you're doing and get that done. We have a breach."

"You know who?"

"Not a clue, but I aim to find out and when I do, I'm going to nail his or her ass. Any word from the teams in the field?"

"Our jet is en route to Vegas and we should hear something in a couple of hours. The other team has their jet chartered and wheels should be up any minute."

"Good. Any news on Gemini?" I need to get my ass back to the office.

"Drex, no word or demands yet."

"I'm on my way back."

Michaels looks at me and says, "Let me help with this, Wolfe."

I flash him a withering look. "You guys have fucked this up so badly—what makes you think I want you along? So you can destroy this country?"

"You have every right to think that, but maybe I can help. I don't know."

"No. I don't want you anywhere near Gemini when we find her. Your hands are dirty enough. You killed your own operative.

I don't want you getting anywhere close to her."

He has that look about him, one that tells me something's up. "What now, Michaels?"

"They want her dead."

"I know that."

"Not Aali Imaam. The CIA."

He's stopped me dead in my tracks. "What did you just say?"

"She knows way too much now and this whole operation has been compromised."

"That operation has been dead in the water for years."

"But it's not, Wolfe. That's why I'm involved. There's a group of us that need that file. So we can shut this thing down."

"Oh, no. It doesn't work like that. Not anymore. I'll get that file. But I'm gonna do it my way. To ensure Gemini's safety." I watch his hand and there is it. "Goddamn you, Michaels." He should've known I'd be the faster of the two of us.

When he's lying there with a bullet in his head, I realize that now *I'm* on someone's hit list. I immediately pull on a pair of latex gloves and rifle through his pockets for his cell phone. Then I send the contacts list to my email and destroy his SIM card. After I wipe the phone clean of any prints, I slip it back into his pocket and pick up the pieces of the card. Holding his hand, I squeeze off one round from his gun. I scan for the bullet casing from my gun and stick it in my pocket.

Next, I roll Michaels over, checking his wound to see if the bullet is still in him. We were at such close range, I'm hoping it was a through shot. When I find that it is, I now need to find the damn bullet that killed him. When I finally find it, I wash it off, pocket it, and head back to the office.

It's been a couple of years since I've had to kill anyone. My head is back to the night I shot that little kid. I can't let this incident screw me up right now. I need to focus on getting Gemini back safely. Why did that fucker have to pull a gun? Who the hell is compromising me? And who are the moles in the CIA?

As I storm in, everyone knows there's something wrong. Huff pulls me into my office and closes the door.

"Well?"

"Sit. There's a lot you don't know and this stays between the two of us. I need that oath from you. Do I have it?"

"Jesus, Drex. What the fuck is going on?"

"The oath. Do I have it?"

"Yes!"

"I just killed Michaels because he was going to kill me. We need to get rid of these." I pull out the bullet and casing. "This needs to be burned. I'm CIA. Not full-time, and only a select few in The Company know." I explain how they recruited me after I left the military and I end with what happened with Michaels.

"Damn! Nothing is ever easy with you, is it?"

"No, not a goddamn thing. Now if you want your walking papers, I'll understand. But if you're going to stay, there are some key things you need to know about what went on with Michelle Sheridan."

Huff looks at me. "Do you think a little thing like this is gonna scare me off? You take me for some kind of pussy?"

That actually makes me laugh. Hard.

"No, not a pussy. Definitely not a pussy."

"Good. Glad we got that straight. So, the CIA, huh."

"Yeah. And not just them. Homeland Security and the FBI. Domestic shit, basically. Sorry I couldn't say anything. Now that the fucking Aali Imaam cell and half the population in Denver seem to know about it, I suppose it's not so top secret anymore. There's a group in the CIA that's dirty. They killed Lowry and Gemini's mom."

"Our suspicions were true. So what's next?"

"As soon as we find out if the file is in Vegas or Austin, I go get Gemini."

"Not before?"

"It's killing me not to because all I can think of is what they're doing to her, but they need her. At least that's what Michaels said. I hope to fuck he wasn't feeding me a line. If we have that file in hand, that's her life insurance."

"Want me to go in and take a look?"

My leg bounces. It can't sit still. "Think you can get a camera in there?"

"I don't know about that. I can take a look, though. Wish we had a drone to do a flyby."

A thought plows into me. "Hang on a sec. My CIA pseudo-boss might be our Obi-wan Kenobi." Grabbing my phone, I tap in some numbers and hear a familiar voice. I hit the speakerphone so Huff can hear this.

"Leo Stanton. Drexel Wolfe here."

"Drexel Wolfe. What can I do for you?"

"What do you know about Project Gemini?"

"Doesn't ring a bell."

"You sure about that?"

"Yeah, why?"

"Because your man, Alex Michaels, sure did and he just tried to kill me. You can find his body across from my house. You know, the one that Aali Imaam blew up a few weeks ago."

"What the fuck are you talking about?"

Huff mouths to me, "He doesn't know."

I nod in response.

"Look, Leo, you and I need to have a serious chat. How soon can you be at my office?"

"I'm in Colorado Springs."

"Have one of those flyboys get you up here. One of my guys will pick you up at the municipal airport. We have a lot to discuss."

"I'll call you when I have an ETA."

Ten minutes later Leo calls and says he'll be here in forty-five minutes.

"Huff, send one of the guys to meet him. He has the clout to get us a drone to scope out where Gem is being held and with the shit that's at stake here, I think we can make this happen. But we have to play our cards right. Our guys in the air need to know what's going on. No calls on any unsecured lines and in front of Leo. The radioactive shit will be our leverage to find Gemini."

Huff nods. "What will he do when he finds out he's been played?"

Snorting, I ask, "Right now I don't give a damn. But in then end, if we get that file, then he'll come out smelling like a rose."

"Right. I'll call the guys."

AN HOUR LATER I present Leo with all this information and he's pissed. He's mad because he's been played too.

"Someone inside is dirty. All this stuff is news to me, but I'm going to break it wide open."

"We need a drone," I say.

"Oh, and you think I can pull one out of my ass? A drone? Come on, Drex. I'm not the Secretary of Defense."

"No, but we have a shitload of polonium, plutonium, and cesium somewhere in the US that Aali Imaam wants and *will* find. And Leo, if they do, we may be looking at doomsday here. Now get me a fucking drone so I can find Gemini. I have an idea where she is, but if I go in there, guns blazing, she might get hurt and the whole mission could be ruined. We need intel on what's inside so they don't kill her and we lose our opportunity at stopping them. You can give the order to have it launched from Peterson AFB. You were just there at Homeland in Colorado Springs. I know you have the connections to get it done, and I suggest you do it."

He rubs his chin for a moment and then nods. "How secure are your phones?"

"I have two secure lines. Follow me." I take him into the conference room.

He takes one look around and says, "What the fuck, Wolfe. You have as much shit in here as we have."

I point to the phone and he makes the call. When he's done, he says, "We're in business. In an hour, we'll be getting a live stream. They'll need your IP addy so they can link up a secure feed."

"Tell them not to worry about that. My shit is so damn tight here, no one could bust in. Tell them I want their addy."

"Come on, Wolfe. We're talking the US military here. They're not going to give that to you. Don't be a dickhead."

He's right. I write down a series of numbers and dots and he sends it on over. I'll get our IT guys to change everything after this is over. A few minutes later, the screen lights up when they activate it from their side. My comfort level is pretty fucking low, even though I know they can't access anything, but just the fact that the US government is in my system makes my skin crawl.

Now we sit and wait. It takes what feels like a year but the damn thing is launched and then another year passes before it's over the warehouse where Gemini is. My heart is in my damn throat.

"Okay, we're live. No activity on the outside," Leo says.

"No surprise there. I want to see if we can have a look on anything inside."

"That will take a few minutes."

"Right." He's acting like I'm in kindergarten.

"Huff, you getting all this?"

"Yeah, boss. Windows all over the fucking place, which surprises me."

"Me too," I say.

Leo asks the moronic question, "Why does that surprise you?"

Neither of us answers him.

"Huff, what do you think about the roof? Weight bearing?" The building is so old it looks like the roof may be unsafe. I would hate to have one of the guys drop on it and then crash straight through and get hurt or killed in the process.

"Hard to tell. Let's check it out on the next pass and Leo, see if we can get a closer view of that glass section." A part of the roof has a very small section a bit of glass on the peak. Huff thinks maybe the drone can get a view of what's inside.

Since we're linked to the guys at Peterson on audio, Leo asks, "Did you guys copy that?"

"Roger that."

Eventually, the screen changes again and we're getting close to our target. We all stand and focus on the infrared images. This time we can see bodies moving inside, but it's not possible to identify them. The glass is a plus as it allows the drone to glimpse what's inside from above. It looks like at least ten warm bodies from this angle.

"Huff, aren't those steel girders supporting the roof?"

"Yeah, I think so. I think we can put a few guys up there. They can bust the glass as a diversion and then others can swarm in through the other windows. But—what if they're rigged?"

"Yeah, I was thinking that too. Can you see any wires on these?"

Huff shakes his head. "No way. The images aren't clear enough. We'll have to check for that before we go in."

Leo is looking at us both. "What do you think?"

"We're going in," I answer.

"When?"

My eyes find Huff's because I want to wait until we hear from my guys. "The middle of the night." My phone startles me when it rings. It's my guy in Vegas. "What do you have?"

"I've got an old-time floppy disc, boss."

Smiling, I say, "Bring it and the team home. Nice work!"

After I move away from Leo, I tell my guy, "Listen to me. This is a matter of national security. Do *not* let that disc out of your possession. You understand me? I cannot stress to you the importance of that thing. As soon as you're on the G-550, I want you to copy it onto a flash drive. Download it and send it to our secure line. Not the main line we usually use, but the one we have set up for special cases. Got that? You brought that old floppy disc drive, right?"

"Yeah, boss. I'll get it taken care of."

"Once it's done, put both the disc and the flash drive in the safe."

"Yes, sir."

"No stops between there and the plane. If you have to piss, you go in your pants. Call me as soon as you're on board."

"Will do."

"It's coming around again," I hear Leo say from the other side of the room.

"Huff, get a log on every window in the place. Then cross-ref it with every satellite pic you can get. I want to see every vantage point we have. I also want to see any back entrances, cars around the building, and so on."

My brain buzzes and won't rest until my guys are home safe with that damn disc. Two minutes later my phone rings—my team in Austin. I leave the conference room to talk. They've found an old floppy disc too. I give them the same instructions I gave the Vegas team. I'm not sure if Rachel Miller split the info and put it on two discs or created a dummy disc. Either way, I'm not taking any chances. My concern with the Austin team is they don't have a secure line, other than the computer and floppy disc drive they're carrying, to transfer it. I won't breathe easy until they're back here. If anything happens to any of those men, I'll hold myself responsible.

When I walk back in the conference room, I tell Leo that we have enough to get Gemini out.

"What do you mean? Have you confirmed she's in there?"

"Yeah, I have. I knew she was in there before the drone did its flyover. She's wearing a microchip."

"So, how many agents do you need?"

I laugh. "Zero."

"What?"

"You heard me. I'll handle this on my own."

"No, you won't. The Company will be there."

"Leo, if the CIA shows up, this operation is sure to fail. You have a gigantic leak in your organization. Your agents have become grossly incompetent, to the point of ridiculous. I don't know if it's the bureaucratic bullshit you have to deal with or what, but you guys FUBARed this one. I refuse to allow you on this op."

"Wolfe," he threatens. "It is fucked up beyond all recognition. But this can come back to fuck *you*."

"I think you guys did that to me a while back when someone leaked my name to Aali Imaam. Yeah, they know I'm one of you guys. That's how good your agents are. But hey, thanks for getting the drone. That was awful nice of you. If this works out the way I think it will, I'll have something for you in the very near future. Make yourself comfortable here while we go to work."

The expression on his face is priceless. I leave one man in the conference room with him to ensure he doesn't go anywhere.

A FEW HOURS later, we have everything we need. We're going to get two guys on the roof, and the rest coming through the windows. The big disturbance will take place through the glass windows on the roof. We'll set C-4 explosives and let the damn thing blow like a nice little Fourth of July for our buddies inside. While they're distracted, we'll flow in from the windows. I usually like stealth, but in this case a blast of surprise will work better for us.

All the guys have returned and I breathe easier. We have both the discs along with the copies, and the data is entered into our system. She was smart, Rachel Miller. Both discs contained partial information. One was necessary for the other. Neither disc could give whoever found it the appropriate information so one would've been useless without the other. The worst part about it all is all that radioactive material is buried in the desert in Nevada. We have no idea if it's even leaked out of the containers it's in or whether the area around it has been contaminated. I have to wonder if Rachel even knew the magnitude of what she held in her possession all these years and that by taking that information, she perhaps prevented the largest catastrophic event this world could ever imagine.

I check my watch and see we have about three hours until we need to get ready to go. Huff comes in and asks if I need anything to eat.

"I suppose I should, huh?"

"Yeah, and it's an order." The sandwich tastes like sawdust thrown on top of a churning sea called my stomach. I force it down and chase it with some Gatorade.

"Drex, you'll get her back. I know you will."

"I hope so, Huff."

"You really love her, don't you? I know it's not my business, but you're different around her. Gentler. Affectionate. It's a nice change."

"I don't know what I'll do if anything happens to her."

"It won't. You said yourself they want her alive. Our plan is solid. Believe in yourself, Drex. You're the best."

My insecurities slither all over me as the next couple of hours creep by. As we're suiting up, it's clear everyone knows their role and our mission: get in, get out. Bring Gemini home alive. So I ram my way past every doubt I own and put on my game face. This is how I need to be and how I will be for my men. And for Gem.

"Guys, listen up here. These dudes don't play by our rules. They don't give a shit about their lives. They will sacrifice themselves in the name of Allah. Don't underestimate them. When we get inside, make sure you can see their hands at all times. IEDs are commonplace. We want to be positive that all doors and windows are free from wires before we even attempt to open them. And that goes for Gemini too. She may be wired so that if we move her, everything blows. Where's Juan?"

"Right here."

"You have everything you need?" Juan is our explosives expert. If it's a bomb, he knows which wire to cut.

"Yes, boss. And as long as I have enough time, we'll be good."

"Okay, we go on night vision—we're gonna cut power to the warehouse before we go in. All on board here?"

"Yes, sir," everyone answers. This is it. When we come back, I come back with Gemini, or I don't come back at all.

Chapter 24

Drex
Plan B

We're in place. The single patrol in the parking lot is taken out with a quick chokehold. Now he's bound, gagged and immobilized. We wait for the guys on the roof to set the explosives and bust up the party. We want the surprise to have the maximum effect and not give them any chance of regrouping. Getting away will be a problem for the terrorists because my men have flattened every one of their tires. One thing I know for certain is that under pressure, these guys convert to anarchy and then their plans usually crumble. My problem is I don't want them setting anything off that could harm Gemini.

The back window gives me the best view of what's going on inside and when I get my first solid look, everything in me seizes. I am momentarily frozen as I stare at Gemini.

"Fuck."

Blake's hand clamps down on my arm so hard, it brings me back into focus. Then I hear his voice in my headset. "Command to Team Two. Break off. Do you copy?"

"Team Two leader copies. What's the sitch?"

"Target is wearing a vest."

"Fuck," I hear Team Two leader respond. "Team Two is in place and will wait for alternate orders."

My brain buzzes with so much shit, I can't think straight. Blake looks at me, covers up his mike, and asks, "Can you lead this op?"

Shaking my head, I ask, "What are our options?"

"Create an outside diversion and take them out one by one, or make some firepower out here to bring them outside. You said yourself that Gemini was a bargaining chip and you doubted they would kill her. So what's it gonna be?"

"Do you think they'll fall for the diversion ... taking them out one by one?"

"Drex, you know them better than I do. You tell me."

"Get Huff over here."

A couple minutes later, Huff shows and we run everything by him.

"Drex, they'll try to bluff you. Do you think you can hold out? Emotionally?" Huff asks.

"I'm just gonna have to, won't I?"

"Outside diversion then, one by one. If that doesn't work, we move to firepower," Huff decides.

"Let all teams know," I tell them. "And pull the guys off the roof. We need them down here."

Half an hour and a stomach ulcer later, we're all set. We decide to begin with tripping a car alarm. It works and brings one man out. Pop. He's taken care of.

The next one is easy. We bust a car window. When the first guy doesn't return, two others come outside to see where he is. Wam-bam. Three down, seven to go. My eyes are glued to Gemini and the dudes inside aren't paying any attention to her. Five guys are arguing now and gesturing toward the back door. This time, they send out two armed guys. I wonder why they didn't do that the last time. We're not worried, though, because they can't see once they get out here and they go down without a fight.

We're down to five and we cut their power. Sweat pours off me and they've finally figured out what's going on. Gemini starts screaming and they begin to yell.

"Move now! Use the rear entrance since we know it's not rigged. No windows. I repeat, no windows! Juan, get to Gemini, STAT!"

It's dark as pitch inside and we hear yelling and things crashing. My heart is jammed in my throat and I pray they're not doing anything to her. I'm listening to everything they're saying and they're freaking out, yelling at each other, blaming each other for the screw-up. This is exactly what I expected from them. They're terrible at teamwork unless their real leader is around. This can either work for or against us. If they get trigger happy, we're fucked. That vest on Gemini can take out this entire building, so I hope they don't set anything off.

We get inside and when I see Gem, I almost go into cardiac arrest. A man has his arm around her throat, a gun to her head. Another man is next to them and he's holding a cell phone in his hand. I can only assume it's a detonator. They know we're inside and can see them, so I waste no time.

"Let's stay calm." I speak to them in Pashto. In the darkness with my night-vision goggles, I can see the surprise on their faces. "You know you don't want to kill her or me, because if you do, your boss will never get the information he's looking for. And if he doesn't get it, the head of Aali Imaam, Khalid Ahmad, will shame you and the members of your family. Now, put your weapon down, along with the detonator, and we'll have a civilized discussion. Or if you choose not to, my snipers will take you out in the next five seconds. What will it be?"

The man with the gun drops his weapon, but the man holding

the detonator doesn't. He starts praying to Allah, and then I interrupt him.

"Allah will forsake you because there is so much more at stake here than just us. What Khalid Ahmad wants from this girl is so huge, even you can't imagine. And if you destroy us, then Allah will never allow you to enter Jannah. Is that what you really want? You will bring shame upon your name, your family's name, upon the name of your children."

"How do I know you speak the truth?"

"Because I have what Ahmad wants. But you won't know that until you drop that detonator."

He drops it and then smirks. "No matter. It's set to go off in thirty minutes." Then he drops to his knees and puts his hands behind his head.

"Juan! Get on this now!" I yell. I run to Gemini and pull the tape from her wrists.

"Are you okay, baby?"

"This is going to explode! You need to get out of here!"

"No, Juan is going to disarm it."

The lights come on and I lift my goggles off. Gemini's face is a mess. Bruised and cut, they've knocked her around quite a bit. Juan kneels in front of her and we cut the cable ties that bind her ankles.

"Jesus, boss, this one's a mess."

"I don't care, just get the fucker off her."

There are so many damn wires, I don't know how he can tell which one does what. I'm holding the cell phone—a timer—and it's counting down.

"Can you lift your arms?" Juan asks her.

"I'll do it for her." Juan is making me nervous—he's sweating.

"How you doing there, Juan?"

He looks up at me but doesn't say anything. What the fuck is that all about? There is enough C-4 in this vest that I'm not sure how they stuffed it all in here. I bend my head down and kiss the top of Gemini's head.

"More light. I need more light." Is there an edge of panic to Juan's voice?

"We need a flashlight here!" I yell. Several men come running and shine lights on the exposed wires.

"Huff! Get over here!" Huff runs over and I tell him, "I want you to interrogate those bastards and find out who the hell they were getting their information from inside DWInvestigations or The Company. I want to know who the leaky pipe is. And get everyone outside now. Far enough away from here so no one gets hurt if this thing blows. Got it?"

"Got it, Drex."

"Juan? Any closer?"

"Working on it, boss."

"Drex?" Gemini asks. "If he's not close at five minutes, I want you to run. You hear me?"

I move to her side and crouch so we can look at each other. I put her hands on my shoulders, "Are you kidding me? There's not a thing in this world that would make me run from you. And if I can't have you in my life, well, then, we leave this world together, babe, hand in hand. Got that?" I kiss her cheek. "Don't cry. We'll be fine." I glance at the timer and we're down to fifteen minutes.

"Juan?"

"I know, boss, but this looks like the biggest pile of shit I've ever seen. It's like they crammed all this crap in here and hope it works. I'm not even sure this thing will go off."

"Yeah, well, we're not gonna test your theory, are we?"

"No, sir. I was just sayin'."

"Good. Stop sayin' and start prayin' 'cuz this is a Gem right here, Juan. So get her the fuck out of this."

"Got it, sir."

I hold my breath as he snips one and then another wire. The timer on the floor stops at eleven minutes. We smile at each other. As I reach to take the vest off Gemini, Juan says, "Whoa, not so fast, sir. Sometimes they put trigger wires on these, so hang on." He tells Gemini to scoot forward in the chair and he looks underneath the vest and sure enough, there's a tiny wire attached to the vest and then her dress. If the vest is pulled off, the bomb will detonate.

"Okay, let me check this out," Juan says.

"Can you cut it?" I ask.

"Not unless I know where it leads. Sometimes cutting these things will make them detonate too. Just hang tight, ma'am." Juan looks around the room a second and spies a table. "I need her to lie down on that table so I can see where that wire leads."

Gemini looks up at me and I give her my hand. She stands but her legs are wobbly. "I'm shaky."

"I got you, babe."

"Sir, don't let her fall and don't grab her around that area."

We get to the table and she lies down. Juan takes a utility knife and carefully cuts into the vest, exposing the wires in the back. We see where the wire leads and he finds the terminals so he can cut them. When it's completely disarmed, we help Gemini stand and remove the vest.

"Juan, get all the C-4 out of that thing." Then I turn to Gemini and pull her into my arms. "You okay, babe?"

"Now I am. You're sweating."

"Uh, yeah. My girl was just laced into a shit ton of C-4." I kiss her. "God, Gem, are you hurt? Did those bastards hurt you? I was so damn worried and we had to wait to get in here. Shit."

"I'm okay, now that you're here."

I run my hands over her, to let myself know she's good. Then it hits me. The red haze of rage. "Just hang here a sec. I'll be right back."

Fury washes over me so quickly. My feet carry me outside to where Huff and Blake have the scumbags lined up. I locate their so-called leader and before I can comprehend what I'm doing, my fists slam into him like a machine on repeat. Over and over I pound his face, body, anywhere I can make contact.

"How dare you strap a fucking piece of shit bomb to her!" My men are yelling but I don't really hear them. My engines are running but there's no comprehension in me other than revenge. When he's nothing but a bloody mass, I move to the next man and then the next until somewhere her voice busts through my layers of madness.

"Drexel, stop! Please, you have to stop this! They're not worth it. And you're so much more than this."

I turn my head and her face comes into focus. Regret hammers me. My emotions fly all over the board. I want to kill those men. I want to weep with relief and I want to protect her from anything that could ever hurt her again. Tears burn trails down her cheeks and I want to wipe them away, but I can't because my hands are stained in blood. I wrap her in my arms and kiss the tears away instead.

"I'm sorry. I'm so sorry."

"For what?"

"For this. For you seeing me do this. For not doing a better job of protecting you. For failing you. For you having to go through this. Oh God, Gem, I wanted them all dead."

"Failing me? You've never failed me. You've saved me when I didn't know I needed saving and pulled me out of the worst place I've ever been when everyone told me there was no help for me. And here you come again, risking your life for me. How can you possibly think that you failed me? I'd be dead without you. Can we go home now?"

"I don't want to touch you like this."

"Like what?"

"I'm all bloody."

"I don't give a damn." She grabs me and kisses me. "Thank you for finding me."

I laugh. "The microchip. But we had to wait until we had everything we needed before we came in here guns blazing."

"What aren't you telling me?"

"Oh, babe, you won't believe it. It's a long story. But I've got to make a dreaded phone call first."

I reach in my pocket for my phone and call my guy watching Leo. Then I have him put Leo on the phone. It's not long before this place is swarming with government agents. After questioning both of us, they finally release us.

"Take me home," Gemini says. "You need a shower. You're a mess and I could use one too."

Chapter 25

GEMINI
The Mole

THE HOT WATER pounds my skin and it feels heavenly. The relief to be in Drexel's arms is so profound that I don't ever want him to let me go.

"Babe, are you okay? Physically? Did they hurt you, other than your face?" His voice drips worry.

My face is pressed against his chest when I speak. "No. I'm fine. Oh God, Drex. When I saw you and heard your voice, I knew they were going to blow us all up. How did you know they wouldn't?"

"I know how they think. But I almost died when I saw that vest on you. They wanted the locations of the radioactive compounds badly enough. In their minds, they would've been heroes forever if they'd released dirty bombs. Of course, it would've been horrible. Massive loss of life. You mom was so smart, Gem. The way she hid that information. She knew what she stumbled upon was so grave that she had to do it the way she did. She trusted no one."

My heart aches for her and I move to bury my head in the crook of his neck.

"What is it?"

"I'm so sad for her. She was all alone with this huge secret. What a burden. I can't imagine. No wonder she lived in such fear."

"True. She was strong, though. And your father ... he died of cancer. They said he was so heartbroken after all of it went down. He had to be admitted to a psych ward and he never quite recovered. He really loved you both."

"Too bad he supported all this evil." Reaching for Drex's hand, I examine it closely. It's quite a mess.

"The other one is just as bad. Something came over me. I couldn't help it."

"You scared me. I was worried I wouldn't get you back."

"It all crashed into me ... what they did to you. They hit you. Then put you in that suicide vest. I snapped. Revenge was the only thing on my mind."

"None of them were worth one second of your energy. Or this pain you'll suffer because of it." I kiss one hand and then the other. "Drex, did you really mean what you said in there?"

"What?"

"That you felt like you failed me?"

"I did fail you."

"Don't ever say that again. Ever. You've brought me back to life. So I don't ever want to hear those words come out of your mouth again."

"Gem, you're the one who's breathed life into me. You know how I said that my thoughts got all messed up because of you and that I couldn't think clearly anymore? Well, I was wrong. You've made me think the way I'm supposed to think. You make me look at things in a different way. I used to approach things one-dimensionally. And that's not life. I used to look at things simply from the physical standpoint.

"But after I met you, things shifted. That's when I didn't think I had clarity anymore. But I was wrong. It was then that I got the total picture—when things became clearer. Life isn't one-dimensional. Gem, it's three. It's physical, spiritual, and emotional. I didn't simply fall in love with you. I fell *into you* and you breathed your life *into me*. You opened my heart and mind to the other two—the spiritual and emotional. You changed everything for me. It started sinking in at our first dinner, but after the bombing, I knew I was different. Then when you freaked out and left, I thought I died inside."

There's something so primal about his declaration that I want to love and comfort him, but I also want to show him how much I love him in return. His words touch a place deep in my heart, I stop breathing for a moment.

"Drex." My hands frame his face and I kiss him, but this time, there is no burning urgency. I take my time and slowly explore every part of his lips and mouth, teasing and nipping at him. When his hands try to find that part of me that he knows I love, I stop him and I know how surprised he is. Instead, I lower myself to my knees and take him in my mouth. I want this to be about him. His sighs tell me he's into it, so I keep going, but when he taps me on the head, he wants me to stop. I will give him what he wants, but not in the shower. Standing, I reach around him and turn off the water.

The look on his face is priceless, but I only smile in return.

"What are you doing?" he asks.

"We're going to dry off and then make love."

"Okay."

When we're dry, I take his hand and pull him toward the bed. He tries to kiss me and I shake my head.

"We're going to do this nice and slow."

His brows arch. This is so not what I normally do, but today is special and I want to make this last and last. I splay my hand across his chest and push him back. He sits on the bed and grins. Gah, he looks so damn delicious, I could lick him all over.

"What's it gonna be, sex princess?"

His lap looks ideal so I straddle it and lock my hands around his neck. Then I lean in for a kiss. His fingers find me and he starts to play with me. While we kiss, he has me on fire in no time.

"You feel so fucking sweet inside. I can't wait to have you all around me, babe."

I move up and he guides himself inside. I slide down and I'm in heaven, just like that. As much as I want to move fast, the appeal of slow is in my blood, so that's what I do. And I focus on his face as we're locked in each other's stares, unable to look away. And why would I ever want to? He is so damn beautiful, and I love the way he looks at me. His scruff is the perfect length and when I brush my hand across it, he leans his cheek into my palm. My head dips down for a moment and I note how his muscles flex with each movement. His body is perfect. I'll never get enough of him.

Suddenly, he repositions me and I'm now lying on my side facing Drex. He brings my leg over his hip and moves close to me so that our noses are all but touching.

"You're so fucking perfect, Gem. So damn beautiful." And he thrusts in and out in an agonizingly drawn-out manner.

"How does this feel?"

"Unreal," I answer.

"Tell me if you need more."

"I love you, Drex."

"Oh, babe, I'm gonna come. You know when you say that, it makes me come." Then he stops moving.

"Don't stop. I want you to come."

"No. Not before you. I want to watch you climax first."

He pulls out and slides down so he can go down on me. "Shit, Drex." My hands tangle in his hair as his mouth works magic on my clit. I was so close to an orgasm before, but now, hell. "Stop, Drex. I want to come with you inside me."

He grins as he moves back up and slides back in.

"Yes, that's it. I was worried I'd come with you down there."

"Ah, Gem."

He's thrusting in and out, while working my clit with his thumb, and that does it. As soon as he feels me let go, he calls out my name and is right behind me.

Then his mouth is on mine and he kisses me softly at first. But it grows much deeper and more meaningful than our usual kisses. He's still deep inside me and my heart stirs with intense emotion.

"I need you so much, Gem. I never knew what this need could be until you. I love you with my all, babe."

"Drex, I hope you understand just how much I love you too."

He brushes my hair back from my face and kisses me again. "I do. We own each other, Gem. You're in everything I do. My thoughts, my senses. I can feel your touch on me every single minute of the day. I can taste you on my lips and tongue, even when you're away from me. You're such a part of me that I can't separate myself from you anymore. And the best part of all is I don't have to because you're mine." When he speaks those words, I melt.

"You make my heart so happy when you tell me these things. And you must know that I couldn't possibly love you any more than I do right now." I touch my lips to his.

"I need to ask you something."

"What is it?"

"Will you go with me to my parents'? I want to explain to them what happened and I'd like for you to be there."

"You know I will."

"Thanks."

"Drex, you know, when two people love each other, they share their hopes and dreams, along with their biggest fears. Someone I love more than anything said that to me once. You know I'll be by your side because I know how it worries you. I'll be with you every step of the way, holding your hand, doing whatever it is you want or need for me to do."

"This is one of the reasons I love you so much."

I laugh. "Hell, those were your words of wisdom, not mine." I kiss the tip of his nose. "So, when do you want to see your parents? And where do they live?"

"My dad retired a few years ago and they moved to Beaufort, South Carolina. We used to live there when he was stationed at Parris Island. I was young, so I don't remember it much."

My mind spins with ideas about a possible vacation. It would be nice to get away for a few days and when we do, we could go see his parents. "How about we turn this into a little vacation?"

"I have to tie up some loose ends here," he says, "but yeah, that sounds awesome. Where would you like to go?"

This is way out of my league. He needs to decide since we'll be taking his plane.

"I can handle that." He has a sneaky smile on his face.

"What?"

"Not a thing. I'll work something out and make the arrangements. We'll go see my parents first and get that out of the way, and then we'll spend a few days somewhere relaxing."

"Sounds perfect."

WE STAND IN the conference room as Leo and several other men from the CIA join us. They offer their condolences over the death of my mother and Nick. I don't say what I'd really like to because what would that accomplish? It's over and even though the CIA was responsible, these particular men didn't have anything to do with it. They discuss the capture and subsequent dealings of the men who allegedly were responsible for my mom and Nick's death, and who were involved with Project Gemini. It seems this was a side mission that wasn't sanctioned by the CIA. At the time, the government was also trying to hush the fact that the US had supplied arms to the Afghans to help fight the Soviets. This group sought out links to terrorists but got out of hand and took it upon themselves to become their own authority. That's why Leo didn't know anything about it.

Drex hands over the briefcase that contains all the information with the locations of the radioactive substances. He also gives them his demands for my safety and security. They assure him, in writing, that I will be assigned a team of men to protect me for an undetermined length of time. This team will be approved by Drex. I smile because Drexel Wolfe has just finagled himself another paid job. But I do feel safer because of it.

Our little meeting ends and I breathe easier. I haven't been comfortable knowing Drex had that information in his possession and I've been eager for him to get rid of it. Too many people have died because of it. When they're gone, I hug him.

"Happy now?" he asks.

"Oh yeah."

MY HAND TREMBLES slightly as it reaches for the doorbell. Taking a deep breath, I push it and hear the ring on the other side of the door that separates me from the two people who have the ability to change the future of the man I so desperately love. When the door opens, I'm face to face with a very attractive woman in her mid-fifties, and I find myself looking into the same eyes I've fallen in love with.

"Hi, Mrs. Drexel, my name is Gemini Sheridan and I'd like to speak to you, if I may, about someone I love more than anything in this world. Your son, James."

Her eyes widen and then her face turns red and angry. "I have nothing to say to you."

"I know, but I have a ton of things to say to you. Things that probably should've been said long ago, but Drex didn't because he took an oath. Mrs. Drexel, you understand those oaths, don't you? You've been married to a military general for how many years? You know how secretive they can be. I want to clear Drex's name, not for the world, but for you and his father. Your son is a good man. The very best. He saved my life I don't know how many times. Please listen to me. And after I tell you the truth of what happened to him that day in Iraq, you can choose to believe what you will. As his mother, you deserve to know the truth. Can I please come in?"

She glares at me for a second and then says, "My husband isn't home right now."

"I can come back this afternoon."

"No, come in now. And then maybe I can talk to him. Or you can come back too."

An hour later, a teary-eyed Linda Drexel holds my hand as we both shed tears. "Mrs. Drexel, would you like to see your son?"

"W-what?"

"He's outside. In the car. I can call him inside if you'd like."

"After everything we said to him, he still wants to see us?"

"Why don't you ask him yourself?"

She nods. I send Drex a text and then go to the front door. He's walking up the steps when I open it. When he sees my watery smile, he uses both thumbs to wipe my tears away. "She's in the kitchen." I remain in the den. It's a moment mother and son should share alone.

After some time passes, I hear their footsteps and I stand as they both enter the room. Linda thanks me for bringing her son back to her.

"It was his idea, to come here, Mrs. Drexel. He wanted to."

We hear the back door open and close, which tells us that Drex's father is home.

"Honey, come in here. Someone's here to see us," Linda calls out.

When Drex's father walks in, I can see where Drex gets his looks. And I also have a good idea of what he'll look like in another thirty years. I smile.

"Hi, Dad."

"What are you doing here?"

Linda runs interference and explains everything before any other words between father and son can be exchanged. The pain in James Sr.'s eyes is so raw, it breaks my heart.

"Why didn't they tell me? I had clearance for this kind of thing. Those goddamn assholes let me believe all these years that you were a ..." He collapses in a chair and hangs his head in despair.

"Dad, stop. It's okay. We're all okay here."

"No, it's not okay, son. They hung you out there. They would've let you rot in an Iraqi prison and if you didn't have such a great team of men behind you, you'd still be there."

"But I'm not. I'm here. I'm the CEO of my own company because of it and I don't need them anymore. It's all good. We have to put it all behind us. And you have to promise me something. You can't breathe a word of this to anyone. I don't trust anyone in the government anymore. Tell me you understand this."

James looks at Drex and nods. "I do. I know exactly what you're saying here. And son, I'm so sorry for all those terrible things I said to you."

The two men hug for a long time. I can't stop the tears.

Then Drex looks at me and says, "We have to leave. Everyone

thinks that we don't have a relationship anymore. It wouldn't surprise me if we're being watched. There's still a lot of stuff you don't know, but I'd like for you to visit us in Denver. I want you to see my company."

"I think we can arrange that," James says.

"Good. Now we have to get out of here. But I'll be in touch soon." We hug and say goodbye.

Drex and I drive to the airport in Hilton Head where his jet is waiting. When we board, I ask, "Where to next?"

"Just a short hop over to Kiawah Island. We're going to the Sanctuary for a few days for some R&R."

"Sounds great." I've always heard great things about the Sanctuary. "Are you okay?"

He gives me an incredibly sexy look and raises my hand to his lips, kissing it. "I don't think I could possibly be any better. Thank you. For everything. I'm not sure how I ever functioned without you. And thank you for being the icebreaker with my mom. That was much more than I could've ever hoped for."

"WHOA!" THAT'S THE only thing I can say when I get my first sighting of the Sanctuary. Kiawah Island is beautiful but this resort is something else. "I'm not sure I belong here. This is fancy, Drex."

"Get used to it, Gem." A valet opens my door and before he can help me out of the car, our bodyguards are right there, pushing him out of the way.

After we're checked in and escorted to our suite, I'm a kid with a giant lollipop. I'm hopping all over the place, checking everything out. A fully stocked refrigerator offers a grand selection of wines and beers and food. The bathroom is amazing, a huge soaker tub sprawled in the corner.

"Hey, babe, how 'bout we put that tub to use?" he says.

"Only if you let me add the bubbles. I promise I won't add so many this time."

"I wasn't complaining, if you recall."

"No, you weren't."

"And, as I remember, you were pretty damn clean afterward."

"Yep, squeaky clean."

"All slippery inside and out," he teases.

His lips are on mine and that's it for me. I'm all his and he knows it.

"You like me slippery."

"Oh, yeah, that I do."

WE RETURN TO Denver rested and refreshed, though Drex is preoccupied on the flight back. My attempts at pulling him back to me fail, and I can't figure out what has him like this. He's keeping something from me, but refuses to admit it.

After an hour of this, I finally pull him out of his seat. "In the back, now."

When were in the sleeping quarters, I see the creases between his eyes. My fingers move to massage them away.

"Don't shut me out like this. It only makes me suspicious. You made a promise about this type of thing."

He grabs my hand and kisses it. "I'm sorry. I'm thinking. There's a leak in the company and I'm running through all the possibilities in my head. I'm usually dead-on with this shit, but I've been through it over and over a dozen or more times and come up empty."

"A leak? Tell me."

"I'm trying to find out how Aali Imaam knew I was CIA. There's no way they could've found that out unless someone spoonfed them that info. So who was it? Alex Michaels said he didn't do it. Leo says he knows nothing about it. All my stuff here is encrypted so even if they tapped into the system, they couldn't figure it out. It had to come from within my organization. But who? I've had Huff working on it and he can't figure it out."

He's not going to like this suggestion but I throw it out anyway. "Could it be Huff?"

"No. I've already discounted him, Blake, and everyone close to me."

"It's Jill. Or one of the girls. You think that info was released to Aali Imaam when?"

"Most likely right after your accident."

"When was Jill hired?"

"Right before ..." He looks at me and says, "Aw, fuck. Why didn't I put two and two together?"

"Because she used that flirty shit to throw you off. And then she did that stuff with me to make it look like she was jealous. She had access to everything as your admin. She probably tapped your office too. Or maybe just got into your computer."

"Fuck!"

He calls Huff right away and tells him to have his office swept for bugs.

"If I ever get my hands on that bitch ..."

"What? You gonna kill her? Forget about her. Besides, who cares? Aali Imaam knows you work for the CIA. Big deal. You hate the CIA anyway. You don't care what they think of you. You play by your own rules and do things the right way. Maybe now, those guys know you mean business."

"Yeah, but I can't fly under the radar anymore."

I snort. "Drex, since when have you ever flown under the radar?"

"What's that supposed to mean?"

"Look at you. I mean, really. No one ever forgets you once they see you. How can they? Women drool all over you. Men envy the hell out of you." I laugh. "I can't imagine how you ever thought you could fly under the radar. Even that time you wore the blond wig and those perfectly nasty brown teeth, you had such a damn presence about you. You can't hide that kind of thing. You're completely unforgettable. When I first saw you and didn't know your name, I dubbed you tall, dark, and mysterious. And even when I had my worst migraine, I fell in love with your sexy-as-hell eyes. You know something? The Special Forces needs women to handpick forgettable men, because if they keep picking ones like you, this country is fucked."

He laughs. "Maybe I should pass this advice on to them."

"Naw, knowing them, they wouldn't listen." I wink at him.

"Babe, I've been so remiss. How are your migraines?"

"I'm so much better, all because of you."

He laughs. "It's not all me. The drugs are partially responsible."

"But Drex, you led me to Dr. Griffith. So it really is you. Sex and drugs." I giggle. He looks at me with the funniest expression on his face.

TWO DAYS LATER, Huff lets us know that Drex's desk, and computer were bugged. No wonder everyone and their brother knew about his supposedly covert activities with the CIA.

He's so disgusted with himself. "Come on, Drex, it could've happened to anyone. Even Huff and Blake missed it."

"Even so, I told Huff I want her apartment under surveillance ... audio and video. I want to know who her connection is and why she's doing it."

It bothers me that he would go to such lengths to uncover this information, especially at this point in the game. "Why? Why go to all this trouble?"

His eyes laser into mine. "Gem, your mom died because of this shit. Jill is a national security risk. We *have* to know who her connection is and she has to go to prison. This isn't a vendetta. This is fucking *war* we're fighting, babe."

When stated like that, I realize it isn't just me—countless lives are at stake in this mess and he's absolutely right. "Go get her, Drex. Take the bitch down."

THINGS HAVE SETTLED down and Drex and I have begun a search for a new place to live. We're still staying at the corporate apartment, but we've decided it's time to move on. Drex has tied up all the loose ends to my mom's case and we are moving around town a bit more freely. We still use our large contingency of bodyguards, but now that I've gotten used to them, I don't mind.

It's mid-morning and we're at work, looking at a new case, when Huff barges into Drex's office unannounced.

"What is it, man?"

"Jill. She's neck deep into Aali Imaam. She was sent here as a toddler with her aunt and uncle to become Americanized and to do exactly what she did. What we still haven't connected yet is how she found you," Huff says.

Drex rubs his chin thoughtfully. "Probably my high-profile cases."

It's time for me to pipe up. "Nope. That's not it. Aali Imaam isn't dumb. They were tracking you, Drex, ever since ... well, you know. And when you came back to the States, they kept tracking you because they knew you'd end up working in this capacity somehow."

"Why do you say that?" he asks.

Since Huff is in the room, I don't want to go into too much depth about his service with the Black Ops, but he gets my drift. "They knew how committed you were to your country. It was no secret ... your dad, West Point, your commission, the Special

Forces, and then you get here and start DWInvestigations and immediately pick up military contracts. It wouldn't take a genius to figure out your connections if they were tracking you."

Drex looks at Huff. "Do you have enough to take her down?"

"More than enough."

"I'll call Leo and let him know. We can take her out today. Nice work, Huff. Tell the guys to take some time off."

"Thanks, Drex. I'll let you know how it goes. Oh, and one other thing. I thought you'd want to know this. They caught those guys that were abducting the women in Austin."

Drex's head immediately snaps up. "Go on."

"Your friend was right. It was human trafficking. They were sending them to Thailand. They're trying to work with the government over there to get the missing girls back. Colt said it was the two guys that you suspected."

My stomach flips because that could've been me. "Oh my gosh!"

Huff says, "You were lucky that night, Gemini."

I nod because I can't speak.

Drex says, "I wish I had done some damage to those fuckers that night."

"Well, they're going to prison now. They have enough evidence on them to keep them there for the rest of their lives," Huff says. "Our men are on their way home."

"Thanks for letting us know. I'll give Colt a call later today," Drex says.

When Huff is gone, Drex gives me an intense look. "You okay?"

I nod and say, "Yeah. I'm just thinking about how close I came to that."

He picks up my hand and gives it a squeeze. Then he says, "I want you here."

"I am here. Helloooo!"

"No. I mean I want you with us. At DWInvestigations. I know your dream job is to work as a marketing specialist for a mountain bike manufacturer, but I want you to work with us, Gem. You have a great head for this stuff. I love the way your mind works and you're tenacious as all hell. I'll make you a really great offer." He gives me a sexy grin.

Whoa. This hits me out of nowhere. My wheels spin for a second and then I think, why not? It makes sense. I'm with him at the office all the time. I may as well be on the payroll. And what chance do I really have now of getting hired in marketing? I've been away from the biking scene for a year now.

"That sounds reasonable. On one condition. I swear to God, if you ever order me around, I'll cut your balls off so fast you won't know what hit you."

"You got it. I value my balls greatly. No ordering you around. So it's a deal, then?"

I stick out my hand to shake on it, but he grabs it and yanks me so hard, I fly into his arms.

"We're way past shaking hands. I think a kiss and a fuck are more like it. And if you think you're going to HR over this, you can forget about it. I'm putting this into your employment contract."

"I'm cool with that. But shut up. You're wasting time."

And that's one thing my guy doesn't ever do ... waste time. He knows exactly what I like and how I like it and he demonstrates that to me today, again and again. Yeah, I think I'm going to love working at DWInvestigations. And I know the pay will be right. Oh yeah, will it ever be!

Epilogue

2 months later

GEMINI
Home

THE TEXAS AIR is hot and still as we walk through the cemetery. When we reach her grave, I stare at the words on the headstone. Michelle Sheridan. How strange. That small chunk of granite should shout to the world what a courageous woman my mother was. That she was a true patriot and gave up her freedom and eventually her life to save this country. She risked everything she had because she believed in freedom and because the lives of so many meant more to her than her love for one man.

As I think about this, I turn and look at the man who stands next to me and wonder if I would have the backbone to give him up so easily.

He knows me so well. His arm tightens around my waist and he hugs me to his side, giving me the strength I need for this visit. This is something I've thought about for a while but haven't had the courage to do. After my mom died, I left here and haven't returned. It was simply too painful. But with Drex by my side, I know he'll help me get through this.

"You ready?" he asks.

"Yeah." I bend down and place the small flag into the ground next to her headstone. I want the world to know that she was the bravest woman I've ever known and that she died for something meaningful; she died for her country.

"I love you, Mom. Thanks for being the best mom you could possibly be. Thank you for doing what you did. Because if you hadn't, so many people would've died. Because of you, they didn't. You're a true hero, Mom. And I miss you more than anything."

When I finish, tears rush freely down my cheeks as I blow her a kiss. Drex holds me close as we walk back to our car.

"You know, this information will only be kept secret for so long. Then they have to reveal it. The world will know the truth one day."

"It won't matter because it can't bring her back."

"No, but she deserves the honor, Gem."

"She wouldn't care a thing about that. She only ever cared about doing what was right."

He stops and turns to face me. "I understand. You're just like her, you know. In everything you do. You always think about what the right thing to do is."

Then his lips find mine.

"Thanks for bringing me," I tell him.

His hand wraps around mine. "You ready to go home?"

"I'm always home when I'm with you."

The End

About the Author

A.M. Hargrove lives in South Carolina with her husband and family. After spending years in the corporate world, she now enjoys writing fiction while she is fully caffeinated. She also thinks coffee and chocolate should be added to the USDA food groups. Oh, and ice cream too!

Other books by A.M Hargrove include *Tragically Flawed, Exquisite Betrayal, Edge of Disaster, Shattered Edge, Kissing Fire,* The *GUARDIANS OF VESTURON* Series (*Survival, Resurrection, Determinant, Beginnings* and *reEMERGENT*) and *Dark Waltz* (A Praestani Novel).

Follow A.M Hargrove:
www.amhargrove.com
www.twitter.com/amhargrove1
www.facebook.com/AMHargroveAuthor
www.facebook.com/anne.m.hargrove
www.goodreads.com/amhargrove1
www.pinterest/amhargrove1
annie@amhargrove.com

If you enjoyed this book, please consider leaving a review wherever you purchased it. Thank you!

A note from the author:

Post-Concussion Syndrome has gained a great deal of exposure in the news recently, particularly with regard to professional athletes. Though I'm not a professional athlete, I've had the misfortune of having to deal with this syndrome myself. After a skiing accident two years ago (and yes, I was wearing a helmet), I suffered a severe concussion, which subsequently developed into post-concussion syndrome. The migraines were initially severe enough to send me to the hospital with complete loss of memory. Multiple tests were run, (the same that were written for Gemini) but the headaches were absolutely debilitating. Fortunately, I was sent to a wonderful neurologist who set me on the right track to recovery. Two years later, however, I still experience migraines, though they are with much less frequency. If you or your children engage in any activities where a head injury could take place, please take care to protect yourselves. Don't take a concussion lightly. They can have unpleasant and even dangerous long-term effects.

Acknowledgements

Thank you, Henry, for being second to my MacBook during the writing of Tragic Desires. It was a crazy train, I know, but the ride is over ... well maybe. *wink*

This book would not be anything close to what it is without the diligence of my editor, Jennifer Sommersby Young. All I can say is what would I do without you? (Don't answer that please!)

Thank you Beta Readers! You came through for me on the spur of the moment, even during the busy holiday season. I love you ladies to Venus and back! Megan Bracken-Bagley, Heather Carver, Kathryn Grimes, Alana Rock, Andrea Stafford, Terri Thomas and Kristie Wittenberg.

I'd love to acknowledge my street team here, not only for all their help in shouting out my stuff, but for all the fun times we have on FB! You ladies totally ROCK! XOXO

So many people have entered my life since I began this thing called writing, but the thing that touches me the most are the relationships and friends I've made in the past two years. It would be impossible to name everyone here so I will just say thank you to everyone. I'm amazed every day at what meaningful friendships I've made over this and I can only hope that one day I get to meet each one of you in person.

I have to thank my dear, sweet friends from the blogosphere. Gosh, what an AMAZING group of people and I count my blessings every day. From the blurbs, and shares I get from you all to the amazing graphics that Hetty Rasmussen at Bestsellers and Beststellars creates for me, I am WOWED by this hardworking group of people that do this thing for the love of the written word. So I'd like to thank in alphabetical order: Mandy Anderson, Megan Bracken-Bagley, Nancy Byers, Heather Carver, Kathryn Grimes, Courtney and Ellie Lovenbooks, Delphina Miyares, Hetty Rasmussen, Alana Rock, Jen D. Smith,

Simone Smith, Andrea Stafford, Terri Thomas and Kristie Wittenberg. There are so many more of you but it would take pages so please know that I appreciate everything you do.

My last thank you goes out to Ellie at Love N. Books for helping me nail down the juicy cover photo.

Cover Design by Sarah Hansen at Okay Creations
Photo by Scott Hoover Photography
Cover Model Emmanuel Delcour
Formatting by Inkstain Interior Book Designing

AND A VERY SPECIAL THANKS TO KATHRYN GRIMES AND KRISTIE WITTENBERG WHO HELPED ME NAIL THE PLAYLIST!

Tragic Desires Playlist

Pearl Jam – Sirens
Skillet – Hero
Metallica – Fade To Black
Red – The Moment We Come Alive
Red – Breathe Into Me - Remix Acústica
The Fray – Love Don't Die
The Neighbourhood – Afraid
Fall Out Boy – Alone Together
Boys Like Girls – Be Your Everything
Labrinth – Beneath Your Beautiful
Luke Bryan – Crash My Party
New Politics – Give Me Hope
Mayday Parade – Hold onto Me
The Cranberries – Dreams
Alt-J – Dissolve Me
Thirty Seconds To Mars – Do Or Die
Chevelle – Send the Pain Below
10 Years – One More Day
Flyleaf – All Around Me
Bob Seger & The Silver Bullet Band – Against The Wind

Made in the USA
Las Vegas, NV
17 August 2021

28347053R00188